# THE LOST TRIBES

WITHDRAWN

C. TAYLOR-BUTLER

◆ ◆ ◆

MOVE BOOKS

To my Ken, Alexis, Olivia and my extended family.
To my editor, Eileen Robinson
for her faith, friendship and vision.
• *C. Taylor-Butler*

◆ ◆ ◆

For Mina
• *Patrick Arrasmith*

NOTE FROM THE PUBLISHER:
*For Readers Everywhere*

Text copyright © 2015 by C. Taylor-Butler
Illustration copyright © by Patrick Arrasmith
Book design by Virginia Pope

Library of Congress Control Number: 2014960256

10 9 8 7 6 5 4 3 2 1      11 12 13 14 15 16
Printed in the U.S.A.
First edition, March 2015

MOVING BOYS TO READ

P.O. Box 183
Beacon Falls, Connecticut, 06403

# Contents

◆　　　　　　◆　◆　　　　　　◆　◆　◆

# Jemadari

"They (the Dogon) have no business knowing this."

• *Kenneth Brecher, MIT professor, Sirius Enigma, 1979*

## Hell's Gate • 90 kms NW of Nairobi, Kenya.
## Friday, October 24 – 5:00 a.m. EAT

Crouched at the entrance of a gorge, a hunter studied fissures in the obsidian rock. Steam spit and hissed through the cracks as his companions, two men and one woman, gathered samples of the smooth black rock and placed them in a cloth pouch.

"When?"

"The damage was discovered two days ago." The guide gestured toward a towering black cloud overhead. "How long before . . ."

"Eight days," the hunter answered, his voice barely above a whisper. Something had changed. Some variable. The timetable had been reduced from four years to —

— *eight days.*

"Let's get to work," the hunter said, sprinting towards a predator stirring in the tall dry grass. He raised a hollow tube to his lips and blew a dart fifty feet across the plain. The lion was down in an instant.

"How are you able to do such a thing from this distance?" asked the guide, struggling to keep up with the hunter's long strides.

The hunter shrugged as he slowed to inspect his prize. The lion growled and swiped his meaty paw, slicing the hunter's leg. Expressionless, the hunter pulled another dart from his pack, bit off the cap, and stabbed it into the rear flank of the beast. The lion fell silent.

"I'll need thirty more. My team will supply the needed materials."

"That is impossible!" the guide protested. "The authorities will have my head if I am caught!"

The woman opened a silk-lined box filled with uncut gems. The hunter selected the largest — a twenty-carat diamond — paused and then placed the entire box in the guide's hand. "More will be sent if you complete the transaction."

"You are bleeding," said the guide. "We have medical supplies in the Jeep."

Limping, the hunter waved him off. "No time. I'm overdue for dinner."

"Dinner?" asked the guide. "It is barely dawn."

The hunter glanced at his watch and frowned. "Not in California."

## Bandiagara Escarpment. Mopti region. Mali, East Africa, Friday, October 24 — 5:00 a.m. EAT

Three thousand miles northwest, a mysterious man surveyed a village from the edge of a cliff. More than a thousand feet below, members of the cult of Awa danced to control the forces that had caused the Earth to shift out of balance. *The time for dancing has passed,* he thought. *"Ancient rituals will not solve the problem."*

"Welcome back, Jemadari," said the Dogon priest. "How goes your search for serpents?"

"They are elusive."

The visitor shook his head but said nothing. He pulled a strand of beads from his belt and wrapped them around his fingers. In the distance, a towering black cloud flashed intermittently. Its shadow crept along the ground, devouring the light.

"The skies are angry," said the priest.

"Indeed," the visitor replied. "The earth is angry." His beads clicked as he stroked them with his thumb. One bead shimmered and glowed red in the darkness.

The priest nodded. "There has been no rain for some time."

"And yet the storm clouds appear."

"To mock us," said the priest. "But we are not worried. We received a sign from the Nommos." He pointed. "A new light appears in the night sky. Near Po Tolo."

The visitor didn't bother to look up. "Not a star," he said, his cloak whipping in the wind.

The priest frowned and wrapped his own robe tightly around his body. "I know."

"Will you abandon the village," asked the visitor, "if the spirits remain restless?"

"No, Jemadari. This is home now."

"But you will die."

"Perhaps," said the priest. "But I have faith that it will not come to that."

The two men studied the vast rolling plains in silence, watching as animals hunted and were hunted. The thundercloud flashed once more then moved west.

The visitor narrowed his eyes, pulled a device from his pocket, and studied streaming images of a boy crawling among small shrubs. He frowned and put the device away.

"The diviner read your future in the sand drawings. He has proclaimed a difficult path ahead." The priest held out a mud cloth satchel. "For your shrine."

The visitor bowed but declined to touch it. "I will send someone for it within the week."

The priest eyed him curiously. "How will I know this messenger? Will it be one of the Nommos?"

"No. He will look like me — " The visitor ran his fingers across his bald head, then reached beneath his cloak and produced a flawless blue diamond. " — and he will have this with him."

# PART I

# The Challenge

◆

# CHAPTER ONE

# Ben

"When my cats aren't happy, I'm not happy.
Not because I care about their mood but because I know
they're just sitting there thinking up ways to get even.

• *Percy Bysshe Shelley*

## Paradise Circle, Sunnyslope, CA, USA,
## Thursday, October 23 – 6 p.m. PST

• *"Here, kitty, kitty!"*

Ben tracked a shadow as it crept along the far wall of the greenhouse. Ten times larger than normal, the silhouette made it easy to pinpoint the target hiding among the plants.

Somewhere on the other side of the world, his father was on another glorious expedition, hunting for ancient artifacts. He'd flown to Nazca, Petra, and Bamiyan — wherever that was — and now a safari in Kenya. Ben had begged to tag along but the answer was always the same, *"No"* . . . *"Too dangerous"* . . . *"When you're older"* . . . *"When your grades are better."* That last comment was as good as saying, "never."

He tightened his grip on the empty collar. The war escalated after Ben tossed the cat into the whirlpool tub — with all fifteen jets running. In return, Aris dumped dead animals on Ben's bed, each one bigger and more disgusting than the day before. A dead opossum, a squirrel, and a rat — at least Ben thought it was a rat. Today's "gift" was covered with tire tracks so Ben knew Aris had not killed it. Still, finding a raccoon with its insides hanging out was the last straw. A night leashed to a tree would teach the cat some manners.

*You're toast, Aris!*

Ben crouched behind a terra cotta pot. The label read, "*Osmanthus Fragrans. Himalaya - BC 4030.*" He blinked. The date had to be a typo. The peach fragrance, however, made Ben's stomach growl. He panicked, held his breath and sank lower to the ground.

The cat's shadow paused, then continued on its way. Ben studied a wind chime hanging to the left of a mutant avocado plant — *Amorphophallus Titanum, Sumatra, A.C.E. 2014.* The chimes were twenty feet away but would mask his approach if he could hit them.

A few months ago he couldn't hit the side of the garage let alone the chimes. But with his father's frequent trips away, he'd been shooting hoops three hours each day hoping for a spot on the basketball team. Now he rarely missed a shot. So how hard could hitting the chimes be?

He found a rock and aimed. Ripples of sound filtered throughout the garden as the rock hit dead center. The shadow stopped, lowered to the ground, then headed toward the disturbance. Ben wondered how a cat so small could cast a shadow the size of a Volkswagen.

Ben rolled under a potting table, slipped past a mass of ferns and emerged behind his quarry, collar open and at the ready.

The shadow remained, but the cat was gone.

Startled, Ben sucked in his breath and scanned the green-house for movement.

Something stirred to his right.

*Got ya!*

He pounced only to find a broken pot, a puddle of muddy water and tiny paw prints.

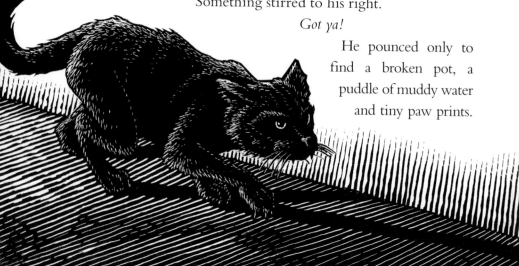

He narrowly missed a hole where Aris had left a new gift for him —
one meant for a litter box.

*Okay, cat! It's on!*

Rustling leaves signaled the enemy's position overhead. Horrified,
Ben spun around to find orange eyes glowing at him from a ledge.
Then it dawned on him. While he was stalking the cat . . .

. . . the cat was stalking him.

Aris, cat from hell, hissed, lowered his front legs and assumed an
attack position.

Ben's muscles tensed.

Aris's tail twitched.

Their eyes narrowed.

Payback time!

Growling, Aris leapt into the air, claws extended. Suddenly, he froze
mid-strike, reversed direction and escaped through a small opening in
the wall. But not before whipping the collar out of Ben's hands with
his tail.

Perplexed and alarmed, Ben turned to see what had spooked the cat
and smiled.

◆

"Welcome back, Dad! How was Kenya?"

"Same old, same old." Jeremiah Webster stepped through the
doorway and wrapped Ben in a bear hug. "How's school?"

Ben grinned. "Same old, same old."

"Too bad. I was hoping for a miracle while I was away." His father
laughed and released Ben from his grip. "Where is everyone?"

"April's at Serise's house getting her nails done." Ben grimaced for
effect. "Mom's at the lab. She said she'd be home soon to start dinner."

A brief look of horror registered on his father's face. He rolled a
black pouch in his hands before tossing it on the potting table.

"What's that?" Ben said, reaching for the
pouch.

His father snatched the pouch out of reach. Something fell out and bounced underneath the table. "Rock samples for your mother."

"Rocks? That's it? Where's the good stuff?" Ben ran into the garage, peered through the tinted windows of the SUV. "What else did you bring back?"

"Nothing." His father winced. "You cut your hair?"

"Took you long enough to notice!" Ben pivoted so his father could see the initials he'd carved above his ear. He wasn't bald, but his hair was as close as he could get without risking banishment from the house. "What do you think?"

His father walked around him in a slow arc. "What'd your mother say? You know she has a rule about you cutting your hair."

"I know, I know. Ancient history. Samson. Losing my strength. She hasn't seen it yet. Just did it today. Think she'll go ballistic?"

"Ballistic?" his father chuckled grimly. "Try nuclear. I'd rather take my chances with a pride of hungry lions until it grows back."

Ben grinned. "Sounds like a good excuse to skip dinner. Can I go with you?"

"When your grades — "

"I know, I know. Don't say it." Ben considered telling his father about the basketball tryouts, but decided it could wait. For now, he had something better in mind like annihilating an unsuspecting opponent. "Until Mom gets home and grounds me, you up for a game of H.O.R.S.E?"

"Sure," his father said. "In Spanish. Might help you bring up that grade. Last time I looked, C did not stand for 'comprende'!"

"C is still passing and that should equal safari!"

"Nice try but the answer is still no."

"Fine. Be that way." Ben pulled a ball from the deck box. "I can spell 'caballo.' Can you spell 'defeat'? You don't have a prayer of beating me."

"I don't need a prayer. Last time we played I had to hoist you up to the basket and you still missed." His father pulled his hair into a ponytail.

"Last time we played you couldn't find the basket with a GPS and Google Maps!" Ben said.

"Let's see what you've got." His father dropped into an exaggerated bow. "Court's all yours, Sir Brags-A-Lot."

Ben aimed from the equivalent of a free-throw line. The ball swooped effortlessly through the hoop.

A look of surprise crossed his father's face. He took the ball, moved to the same position and aimed. The ball hit the roof, rolled to the gutter then dropped onto the rim of the basket where it spun like a top before falling onto the driveway.

"C! The loser gets the letter. That — " Ben said through a series of coughs, "would be you."

"Uh-oh! Someone's got an attitude. The afternoon's still young!"

"And so am I, old man. Try this. Left handed hook shot." Ben ran toward the basket, extended his arm and released the ball.

*Whoosh!* Nothing but net!

His father stared at the basket, mouth gaped open in shock. "Someone's been practicing."

"Obviously." Ben grinned and tossed the ball to his father, who dropped it. *Pitiful.* His father's arms were as long as the wings of a jumbo jet but there wasn't a single basketball-playing gene in his DNA. "Don't try so hard, Dad. Just run up to it and flick your wrist."

His father winked, lunged toward the garage and released the ball. It completed four revolutions on the inside of the rim before falling backwards in the wrong direction.

Ben tried to erase the sarcasm in his voice. "Sorry, Dad. I'm afraid that's an 'A' for you. Would you like to pick a longer word?"

His father stretched in the sunlight. "You wish you were as good as me. Know anyone else who can do tricks like that?"

"No one who'd admit it!" Ben paused. His father was favoring his left leg. "You okay? You're limping."

"Just a cat scratch." His father did a little dance to mock him. "I'm just warming up."

"Better hop in a microwave," Ben said. "It would be faster."

His father retrieved the ball from the middle of a peony bush. "Just play, will ya!"

Ben tried a shot he thought his father could handle. He swung the ball between his legs and tossed it in a slow easy arc. As planned, the ball swished through the net. He rebounded and lobbed it at his father. "Heads up, Dad."

The ball hit his father's shoulder, bounced on the driveway and rolled to a stop on the grass.

*All that height going to waste.*

"Dad? What's up?"

His father cocked his head to the side, brow furrowed. "Looks like a storm's brewing. Been raining much while I was away?"

"A couple of times, but it's not raining now so quit stalling! What's the matter? Scared of a challenge?"

"Challenge?" his father asked, his voice low. "Hardly."

To the west, fluffy white clouds punctuated a sunlit sky. But something about their movement struck Ben as odd. The clouds elongated into tentacles of mist. Ben swiveled his head in the opposite direction. An enormous black cloud approached rapidly from the east, light flashing from inside.

Ben dribbled while he counted; *one Mississippi, two Mississippi . . .* He reached twelve before he heard a distant crack of thunder. There was still time to get into the house before the storm arrived.

A fierce gust of wind blew chairs off the deck. The temperature grew uncomfortably hot and yet goosebumps erupted on Ben's arms as if the storm was an omen. All the while, his father stared at the sky.

Searching.

Watching.

*Searching for what?*

The clouds flowed east as if the storm was sucking them in. That didn't make sense. The clouds should have been moving in the same direction as the storm. Ben's eyes followed a flock of birds fleeing to the west.

"Dad? What's wrong?"

His father tensed and scanned the yard as if he expected someone or something to appear out of thin air. His eyes narrowed into tight slits as his prayer beads swayed and clicked in the wind. He glanced at the beads, then blew out a lungful of air. "Cumulonimbus, Jeremiah. Just a thunderhead."

Now Ben was confused. His father was the ultimate Zen master. Not much bothered him. He braced against the wind and tapped his father on the shoulder. "Dad? We should go in before the storm gets here. We can play later."

His father frowned. "Go get your sister. Your uncle's going to be joining us for dinner."

Ben groaned. The incoming storm *was* an omen. His father was home, but he'd brought trouble home with him.

# CHAPTER TWO

# The Nature of Things to Come

"Human history becomes more and more a race
between education and catastrophe."

• *H. G. Wells*

• "Theory of Evolution? Natural selection?" Uncle Henry's booming voice filled every square inch of the dining room and he wasn't even yelling — yet. He snared a piece of steak and eyed it as if it were prey.

Ben grimaced. *Smooth move, Webster, bringing up Darwin in front of a world-class archeologist with a galaxy-class ego. When he asked about your school project, you could have said crystal growth or recycling. Heck, you should have just said you were making weapons of mass destruction.* Ben tried to explain the class assignment, but his uncle kept on barking.

"Centuries of contributions and we're not even a footnote! I suspect it would suit the world if we disappeared off the face of the planet." Uncle Henry stabbed his steak as if trying to kill the animal one more time.

Ben tuned out. His uncle's rants were as predictable as a morning sunrise. *Next up on Henry Webster's greatest hits:*

1. *Know your ancestors* — easy, all dead.
2. *Know where you came from* — the shady side of Sunnyslope.
3. *Cradle of life* — covered. Ben wondered if he should tell his
   uncle he'd caught up on the "Cradle" by watching Tomb
   Raider at a classmate's house. Nope. That would be suicide.
4. *Never settle for second place* — Ben was still working on that one.

"Well?" asked Uncle Henry.

Ben blinked and wondered how much of the lecture he'd missed. "Huh?"

"You were explaining what passes for a seventh grade education these days. By all means, continue to enlighten me with your evolutionary theories."

"Pick a new tune, Henry." Ben's father frowned then shoved raw spinach in his mouth.

Massive as a redwood, Henry Webster rested the elbows of his silk shirt on the table and looked incredulous. Ben's father stared back, his slender frame dwarfed by an oversized blue sweatshirt that read, "Sunnyslope University". Ben found it hard to believe they were brothers. Ben's mother called them "Yin" and "Yang." Polar opposites — but a perfect balance.

"Wait until you hear the best part!" April blurted out. "Ben's teacher said humans evolved from some people called Cro-Magnons!"

"April," Ben's father spoke gently, but his narrowed eyes meant business. "Drop it!"

"Well I think it's a stupid theory," she continued.

"Oh? And why is that?" asked Uncle Henry, one eyebrow raised beyond the normal limits of facial expression.

"Because Ben's a mutant alien." April shot a sly smile at Ben.

Ben fumed and fantasized whether his sister would fit through a basketball net.

"Wouldn't that make you a mutant as well?" asked Uncle Henry.

Ben's mother shot an ice-cold glare across the table, clutched her amulet and thrust her right hand forward. "Henry, it appears you have neglected daily meditation. May I be of assistance?"

She smiled the kind of half-smile that always warned Ben he should seek asylum in a foreign country.

Uncle Henry abruptly moved his hands into his lap. "Fine. Have it your way. What new tofu recipe did you synthesize this time, Medie? I'd swear this was steak."

"It's real, Henry. One hundred percent, open-range, grass-fed beef from Argentina. Compliments of Frank Lopez."

"Frank Lopez? Did you check it for arsenic?" Uncle Henry poked at a chunk and inspected every inch before popping it into his mouth. Eyes closed, he shuddered in delight as juices dripped down his fork and formed a red puddle on his plate.

For Ben, the revelation was a welcome relief. His mother's vegetarian cooking could be considered a lethal weapon in most of the fifty states — especially her bioorganic tofu steaks. The next-door neighbors, on the other hand, were the world's biggest carnivores. Real steak. Ben snagged a small filet and took a bite. Seasoned with garlic, onions and spices, the meat melted on his tongue.

His mother frowned and snatched the remaining portions out of his reach. Ben groaned, popped soybeans out of a pod and sloshed them in meat juice to make them more edible.

"Henry, it would be appropriate to say a prayer of thanks to the animal that was sacrificed for this meal," his mother said.

"If the circumstances were reversed, do you think it would pray over us?" Uncle Henry asked.

Ben stifled a laugh. But his mother leaned forward as if she were searching for weaknesses in his uncle's defenses. Ben's father glanced back and forth between them as if watching the ball in a tennis match.

Uncle Henry finally growled and bowed his head. "Thank you, anonymous steer, whose spirit now nourishes the cosmos and whose flesh will now nourish me." He shoved a super-sized chunk of beef in his mouth.

April giggled but Ben and his father ducked as if World War III were about to break out.

Instead, Ben's mother offered a withering glare. "Now, change the subject. No more philosophy, no more anthropology, no more doom and gloom. Don't utter another word unless it's something happy. Do I make myself clear?"

Uncle Henry pursed his lips. "I know something that would make me happy. Why don't you let Ben come along on the next expedition?"

Ben nearly choked on a piece of tofu. "Dad says I have to wait until I'm older."

"Indeed? And why is that, Jeremiah?" his uncle asked, sarcasm dripping from the words.

"Drop it," Ben's father said quietly.

Uncle Henry seemed amused. "I just thought you might want to clarify your position."

Ben's father glowered and kept eating.

"In many cultures, boys Ben's age are already hunting with their fathers." Ben's uncle leaned back in his chair and folded his muscular arms against his chest.

"Give it a rest, Henry." Ben's father said, his voice a low growl.

"A rite of passage to prove their manhood," Uncle Henry continued, unfazed. "The next mission starts in eight days." He paused. "The last mission."

Ben's heart sank as he realized his safari dreams were about to slip away. "Last?"

"Afraid so." Uncle Henry glanced at Ben's mother then sighed as he shoved soybeans in his mouth, pods and all. "It's time to move on."

"Dad?" Ben pleaded.

"I said, no."

"I think the children should explore their roots," Uncle Henry mumbled through a mouthful of vegetables.

Jeremiah Webster's eyes grew dark. "Henry, I'm warning you."

"Oh! We're learning all about history in fifth grade." April waved her hands with excitement. "All sorts of stuff like in fourteen hundred and ninety two, Columbus sailed the ocean blue and . . ."

*Activate full body shields now!*

Uncle Henry shifted in his chair. Veins pulsed on top of his bald head. "See what I mean? Even the Dogon have known about — "

"HENRY!" Ben's father slammed his fists on the table and rose from his chair.

April gasped. Ben held his breath until his lungs hurt. His father NEVER raised his voice.

"Welcome, Jeremiah. I knew a spark of fire still burned inside of you." Ben's uncle speared a chunk of meat with his fork and tossed it across the table. "Have some steak to celebrate your reawakening."

"Forgive me, Henry," said Ben's mother, a hard edge creeping into her voice. "I now see that your bad mood is caused by constipation."

Ben looked in horror as she tossed tofu casserole onto his uncle's plate.

Jeremiah Webster pointed an index finger at his brother. "Ease up, Henry. Do you understand me? Ease up!"

The arctic chill that settled in the room was enough to send penguins scrambling for shelter. Even April remained frozen in her chair, her mouth gaping and her fork hovering midway to its destination.

Searching for a way to defuse the argument, Ben reached into his pocket, smoothed the wrinkles from a letter and held it up. "I have some news! I'm trying out for the basketball team. Just wait. In a few years I'm going to be famous — like Jackson Carter!"

"Basketball? Now there's a useful skill," said his uncle. "Years from now, what will history remember of Mr. Carter? If the world were to end tomorrow will his sky hook have made a difference?" He rested his chin on the top of his clasped hands. Three African masks hanging above the buffet flanked him like bodyguards.

*Score zero for the home team.* Thirteen years of trying to impress his uncle, thirteen years of failing even with a home court advantage.

Aris leapt on the buffet and joined the opposing team.

Ben bared his teeth. Aris arched his back to up the ante.

"Aris!" Ben's mother hissed.

The cat relaxed his posture but stayed put on the buffet.

"Henry, we encourage the children to choose their own path," Ben's father said, his voice calmer but firm.

"So it appears. And how does one decide on a path without the relevant facts?"

"My children are doing just fine." Ben's father snatched the permission slip and scribbled his signature on the bottom. He winked and gave Ben a thumbs up. "Ben has many years to decide what he wants to do with his life."

"Perhaps," Uncle Henry said. "Perhaps not." He tilted his head as if seeing Ben in a different light. "I see you cut your hair."

"I thought it would make me more aerodynamic . . ."

"I know," Uncle Henry interrupted. "For basketball." His eyes bored through Ben as if he were analyzing every strand of his DNA. "The initials over your ear are crooked."

*Personal foul. Game over.*

Ben caught a glint in his uncle's eyes. He braced for another lecture on history, ancient empires and civic responsibility. Instead, his uncle stood and left the room. He returned with an elaborate leather saddlebag.

"That new?" asked April. "It's cool!"

"It serves its purpose," Uncle Henry said, unlatching the carved silver clasp. He reached inside a pocket and produced an emerald green disk.

"What's that?" Ben's father asked, his eyes narrowing.

"A game for Ben to try," Uncle Henry said. It isn't as exciting as a real safari — " he paused. "or basketball. However, Ben should find the challenge sufficiently stimulating."

Ecstatic, Ben reached for the disk. His parents glared, but remained silent.

"It's a new level of interactive gaming," Uncle Henry continued. "It will run on any computer but there are special effects if you use your own. Perhaps you could beta test it with your friends and tell me if it's any good."

"You programmed this yourself?" asked Ben.

Uncle Henry nodded. "With help from some business associates."

"I thought you were an archeologist."

Uncle Henry's sly smile grew a centimeter. "I am many things."

Ben swallowed hard. There was no label on the disk, only an etched star shaped like his uncle's earring. "What's the catch?"

"No catch," Uncle Henry said. "Think of it as a mini-adventure to whet your appetite."

"Awwww man! How come Ben always gets all the good stuff?" April whined.

Ben grinned at his sister. "Okay, I'm in. What's it called?"

"The Lost Tribes of Xenobia," Uncle Henry said.

The color drained from Ben's parent's faces.

His mother snatched the disk from his hand. "It's a school night and Ben's got homework."

"Mom! It's just a game! What's the big deal?" Ben pleaded.

Uncle Henry clucked his tongue. "It's harmless, Medie. A bit of mindless fun with a few educational things thrown in so not to be a total waste of time."

Ben's excitement deflated like a spent balloon. His uncle's gift was really a top-secret way to get Ben's grades up.

"You'll have fun with this," his uncle said. "But don't be fooled. It *will* challenge you."

"Bet it won't. Grace and I solved a safe cracker game in two days." Grace Choedon had been his buddy since kindergarten. It came in handy that she lived across the street. "What do I have to do?"

"Search for lost treasure around the planet. If you solve all the puzzles, there's a surprise ending."

"What's the surprise?" asked his father. The words spilled out as more of a threat than a question.

"Now, if I told him, it wouldn't *BE* a surprise, would it, Jeremiah?" Uncle Henry's eyes sparkled. He tugged the disk away from Ben's mother and gave it back to Ben. "You'll have to have your wits about you to get through this. No asking your parents for help." He winked. "Solve it and I'll persuade them to let you tag along next week."

Ben's jaw dropped wide enough to drive a truck through. Basketball *and* an expedition? How could life get any better? "But they already said no."

Uncle Henry leaned across the table, his voice dropping to a conspiratorial whisper. "I'm pretty sure I can get them to change their minds. Trust me on that one."

Ben didn't know how his uncle was going to accomplish that miracle and he didn't care. "Seriously?"

"I always keep my end of a bargain," Uncle Henry said. " But you've only got a week. Think you can handle the challenge?"

"Are you kidding? It's a slam dunk!"

Ben shot up from the table. His father pointed a single index finger in his direction. In both human and dog language it meant *"sit, stay and shut up."*

Ben slumped back into his chair.

"What about me?" April asked, batting her eyes at twice the speed of light.

Ben's uncle slid a red case across the table. "You can link your programs and play as a team."

"Not a chance! I'm going to beat Ben and get the safari all for myself." April grinned and twirled the disk in her hands.

"Dream on, bird brain!" Mimicking his mother, Ben attempted to freeze April into a block of ice with an arctic stare. It didn't work.

"Remember," Uncle Henry said. "The clock is ticking. You've got one week. After that, the game is over."

"Deal!" Ben felt a surge of adrenaline and clutched the DVD as if it were a treasure in itself.

His parents, however, looked as though they were plotting his uncle's funeral.

# CHAPTER THREE

# Secrets and Lies

"If you reveal your secrets to the wind,
you should not blame the wind
for revealing them to the trees."

• *Kahlil Gibran*

♦ Ben raced up the staircase just as angry voices erupted from the dining room. He was torn between starting the game and sneaking back downstairs. The decision was easy — Ultimate Fighting match now. Game later.

"What were you thinking?"

" . . . been over this before."

" . . . you had no right!"

Ben strained to hear. His father and uncle sounded so much alike he couldn't tell which voice belonged to which person. The voices were garbled and fragmented, like a radio tuned between stations.

" . . . isn't a request!"

" . . . made our decision . . . all of us!"

After a few frustrating minutes, Ben ran to his room and pulled a voice-activated recorder from his desk drawer. He fastened a leather belt around it then returned to the landing and slid his makeshift surveillance equipment down the staircase.

" . . . seen the signs."

" . . . been there for years."

". . . calling the teams in."

" . . . won't make a difference . . ."

" . . . cover's blown!"

The voices came into focus, but the strain gave Ben a headache.

"We can't stop it . . . might be able to outrun it." Uncle Henry shouted.

"We have time!" Ben's father said.

"Time's up!" snapped Uncle Henry. "It's time to introduce the children to the family business!"

A door slammed.

Ben rushed to a hallway window in time to see his uncle cut across the lawn, trampling two rose bushes in the process. He stormed toward the main road, passing in and out of the pools of light cast by street lamps.

Ben lifted the window sash and leaned out. In the darkness, a tiny flash of red light hovered above the ground then winked out.

Ben allowed his eyes to adjust to the low light. A car entered the cul-de-sac. The Choedon's headlights focused on the area where Ben last saw his uncle.

Uncle Henry had vanished.

# CHAPTER FOUR

# The Game's Afoot

"From the first, I made my learning,

what little it was,

useful every way I could."

• *Mary McLeod Bethune*

---

◆ Shaken, Ben retrieved his recorder, returned to his room and pressed "play".

No sound played back.

He adjusted the volume control.

Silence.

"Testing. One, two, three, testing."

*"Testing. One, two, three, testing,"* the recorder repeated.

Ben tossed the useless device into the drawer then sank into his chair. "Jackson! Log on!"

While the computer — which he'd named after his favorite NBA player — booted up, Ben's mind replayed the conversation.

*"Seen the signs . . . calling the teams in . . . Times up!"*

And what was that comment about the *family business*? Archeology? Anthropology? Ben wanted to go on an adventure. That didn't mean he wanted to follow in their footsteps. Whatever "Save the Planet" crusade they were on, it didn't concern him.

He slid the disk into his computer and watched as eddies of sand swirled across the monitor.

The graphics looked so real he could almost feel the wind on the back of his neck. Then he remembered he'd left his window open. He clicked on a gold handle peeking out from beneath the sand.

"Please type password," a computerized woman's voice asked.

Ben's heart sank. He squinted, unable to make out the faint carvings below the handle. The symbols zoomed larger as the cursor slid over them.

"Please type password," the computer repeated.

"I heard you!" Ben groaned. He should have known the game was a set-up. He'd been blowing off his Social Studies module on Egypt and his teacher had probably ratted him out.

"Got it!" April yelled from her bedroom.

"Got what?" Ben yelled back.

"The password. Want some help?"

"No! I'm already *WAY* past the first level."

Ben stared at the eight symbols with no clue how to start.

"How many symbols did you have?" he yelled.

"Five!" April yelled back.

That figured. April's disk was a different color. Probably had the junior version of the game. Ben pulled a Scrabble game from the bookshelf, dumped the tiles on his desk. E was a common letter and at the end of a lot of words. He rearranged the letters until he came up with his first guess. *Creature? From the Black Lagoon? Like his sister?*

C R E A T U R E

Nope. Not that simple. The R's didn't fit. How about something more logical? What would be behind a trap door? Secret passageways, dangers and . . . *hidden treasure! Of course!*

## TREASURE

Drats! Same problem. Knowing his uncle, the password wasn't going to be obvious. He thought about his uncle's personality — evil drill sergeant archeologist. What do commanders do to people they don't like?

*"There is a mission starting in eight days."*

Goosebumps erupted on Ben's arms. Deceased? It was like being a red shirt on old Star Trek reruns. If you were sent on a mission, you weren't coming back. That would fit Uncle Henry's twisted sense of humor.

## DECEASED

Nope. He sighed, partly in relief that he was still "alive."

"How's it going?" yelled April. "Bet I'm going to beat you!"

"Fat chance!" he yelled back.

Seething, Ben pulled a dictionary from the shelf and ripped off the shrink wrap. The book groaned and popped as he cracked the spine for the first time. Acerbate? A synonym for April. It meant, "irritating."

Failure.

"Arggh!"

April poked her head inside the door, her voice a mocking lilt. "Something wrong?"

Ben plastered on his game face and waved her away. "I took a wrong turn and plunged to my death. I have to start over."

"Really? Can I see?" She put a fluffy pink slipper over the threshold.

"No! Stay out of my room!"

"Fine! Knew you couldn't beat me!" April stomped off to the bathroom.

Frustrated, Ben scoured the dictionary. What if the E's were in the wrong place? Ben breezed through the puzzle magazines his mother brought home from the grocery store. Although sometimes he cheated and peeked at the back of the book. No hints this time. He pushed the Scrabble tiles around without success.

Aris pounced on the desk and stared at the screen, his orange eyes glowing in the monitor's reflection. Ben could swear the cat was grinning as he stretched a paw toward the keyboard.

"Don't even think about it!" Ben snapped.

Aris growled and swatted at Ben before jumping down from the desk. The weight of his paw on the delete key erased Ben's worthless attempt at a solution. Aris sauntered into the hallway with a hiss and evil flick of his tail.

"Stupid cat! I was going to do that anyway!"

Ben returned his attention to the newly blank spaces. Dr. Lopez had talked him out of wasting his money on the MegaMax lottery by teaching him how to calculate the number of combinations. Eighty million to be exact. That pretty much canceled his plans for an easy boost to his allowance. The principle was the same, though.

He whipped out his calculator and a pencil. Eight symbols — two were the same so he could eliminate one of them. There were twenty-six letters in the alphabet. Each time he picked a letter, he'd have one less option for the next slot. All that was left was to multiply the options together.

$$\underline{26}\ \underline{25}\ \underline{24}\ \underline{23}\ \underline{22}\ \underline{21}\ \underline{20}\ \underline{1}$$

Ben's heart sank as he felt the expedition slip away. There were thirty-three billion combinations including nonsense words. The Earth would be sucked into a black hole before he solved this problem.

To torture himself, he did the calculation for April's password: less than eight million. But it didn't matter how many options she did or didn't have — she'd cracked the first puzzle and would be gloating about it in the morning.

Ben shoved the Scrabble pieces aside and slumped in his chair. He was going to have to ask Grace for help. Her parents were fluent in most

Asian and Romance languages plus hundreds of ancient languages like Egyptian and Latin. He could barely get through Spanish. He didn't understand how you could learn that many languages and keep them all straight. It was too late to call. He sent a text message instead.

Grace answered right away. *"Stuck on a game? It's late. Figure it out tomorrow."*

*"I need help now! It's driving me crazy."*

*"Any clues?"*

*"No. Just eight blank spaces. The third and last symbols are the same."*

*"Can you send me the program?"*

*"Yeah. Try this."* Ben compressed the file and attached it to an email.

*"Okay, give me a minute."*

Ben looked at the clock: 10:45 pm. He waited for what seemed like hours. The clock read *"10:49 pm"* when Grace logged back on.

*"Got it! Cool graphics. Can I keep this copy to play?"*

*"That fast? Does it have something to do with girls?"*

*"Nope. It's pretty obvious if you ask me. As plain as that big nose on your face."*

*"What? WHAT?"*

*"It's sooooooo easy I'm not going to tell you. If you still don't get it by morning, wear a code. White rose if you figured it out. Red rose if you didn't. Trust me you'll kick yourself for not getting it right away. Next time give me a real challenge instead of this easy stuff!"*

Ben knew her weak spot. *"I've got one for you now!"*

*"Take your best shot. I dare you."*

Ben typed:

> *"What is greater than God?*
> *More evil than the Devil?*
> *The poor have it.*
> *The rich need it.*
> *And if you eat it you will die?"*

*"Huh? What? I hate riddles. Can you give me a hint?"*

*"Nope. Remember what rose to wear. Sayonara! :-)"*

*"It's Kali shu! I'm from Tibet not Japan you moron!"*

*"Yeah, whatever. See ya in the a.m."*

Ben laughed, logged off and flopped on the bed. Grace and April had figured out the passwords in record time, so how hard could it be? His father said the mind was like a cross between a super computer and old library stacks. Just plug in the question and let the "little men" run around the archives until they find the data. While Ben was waiting for that miracle to happen, Grace could stew on his riddle.

He stared at his posters of the Los Angeles Lakers and the Chicago Bulls, both digitally altered to show his face on the rosters. He crumbled notebook paper and lobbed it at a basketball hoop hung on his wall. The wads fell into the trashcan sitting below it. He tossed them with his right hand, then his left. He even stuck a wad of paper between his toes and flung it across the room. No matter how creative he got, he never missed the basket.

His mother knocked on the door and slipped in, as she did every night. She stared at the hieroglyphics on the computer screen, picked up a single tile from the Scrabble pile and studied it for several seconds. She sighed, placed the tile on the top of the monitor, then stepped over the pile of dirty clothes at the foot of the bed.

"I know what you're thinking. I'll do my laundry tomorrow, I swear," Ben said.

"Actually, I was thinking that a few more months in this room and you'll be immune to all known diseases. It's your room, do what you want, but I'd prefer a promise to a swear." Something in her voice seemed sad.

"Everything okay, Mom?"

"Why do you ask?"

"Just wondering."

His mother pursed her lips and placed a candle on the nightstand. When he was little, she told him it kept the monsters away.

"I don't need that. I'm not a kid anymore."

"I know. But you'll always be my little prince." She sighed and lit the wick.

Ben frowned. "Does that mean I have to slay evil dragons and stuff?"

"If us grownups do our jobs, maybe you won't have to."

"Fine. But no lavender, okay? It makes me smell like a girl."

"I remembered," she whispered. Tonight's candle smelled like his mother — jasmine. He'd humor her in preparation for future battles over the car keys.

His mother glanced at the computer again. "Try to get some sleep. You've got a big test tomorrow. The game can wait." She rubbed his hands, hummed an old lullaby, then kissed him on the forehead. "There are more important things to think about right now. Trying to impress your uncle isn't one of them."

Then, as quietly as she arrived, she slipped out again.

Ben relaxed as hieroglyphics marched past his closed eyelids. Birds, praying priests and odd squiggles appeared and disappeared beneath the sand as he drifted to sleep.

He woke with a start, jumped out of bed and ran to the computer. The answer was so obvious, so simple. His reflection blinked back at him from the darkened screen.

"Jackson, wake up!"

The clock read 3:00 am.

*This had better work!*

He typed eight letters and hit enter.

"Welcome," said the female voice as the channels deepened to reveal a trapdoor.

"Yes!" Ben struck high fives with invisible teammates.

He clicked and dragged the handle to the left. The sound of stone sliding on stone filled the computer speakers. The door opened to reveal a long, dark passageway and more hieroglyphics.

Ben collapsed on his bed, excited and exhausted. He'd suffered a temporary setback, but he was on a roll now. He'd have this mystery solved before the end of the week.

Across the room, the password dissolved into its original hieroglyphic form. Soon, very little of the solution remained . . .

B E N J A M I N

# CHAPTER FIVE

# Morning Rituals

"The sun, with all those planets revolving around it,
can still ripen a bunch of grapes
as if it had nothing else in the universe to do."

• *Galileo Galilei*

◆ Ben jumped out of bed, hit the space bar and roused the computer from sleep mode. He had thirty minutes to shower, grab something to eat, and be out the door for school. Fifteen if he peeked at the game.

He paused at the bathroom window. As usual, April was practicing Tai Chi with his parents. Bathed in sunlight, they flowed through a synchronized routine, crouching and swaying in their bare feet. The sun's glow always seemed more intense on his mother. Nearby, the garden bloomed brighter than the day before. When it was over, his mother smiled until April was back inside the house, then yanked an iron Shepherd's hook out of the ground and swung the sharp end toward his father. Surprised, Jeremiah Webster deflected the blow with his arm, then rolled out of the way. Ben's heart stopped.

Twirling the rod over and under her arm like a baton, his mother jabbed without holding back. Ben sucked air through his teeth. Still favoring his left leg, his father dodged left and then right to avoid the attack. He somersaulted over the edge of the deck, pulled a garden stake from the ground then stumbled as she swept his injured leg. He winced in pain, fell to the ground and raised his hand to stop the match. His face flushed red as Ben's mother helped him to his feet and examined the wound.

"*Definitely not Tai Chi.*" Ben glanced at the clock and groaned. Uncle Henry's lost tribes would have to wait to be discovered.

◆

"Here you go!"

Ben's mother planted a kiss on his cheek before shoving a pill and a juice glass into his hands. It signaled the daily ritual of a multivitamin so large it could choke a dinosaur and a slimy blue-green drink so vile it probably lead to their extinction. The juice he called "green glob" sparkled and moved as if it were an alien life form.

"I'm trying something new," his mother said, beaming. "What do you think?"

Ben closed his eyes and drew a tiny sip across his lips. He forced his grimace into a smile. "Tastes like pomegranate."

Her eyes arched in surprise. "Pomegranate? Good idea! Full of antioxidants. I'll add some tomorrow!" She placed a second glass on the granite countertop and filled it with the remaining glob, using a spatula to force the last tenuous drops out of the blender. "Finish up."

Tongue tingling in a way that didn't seem natural, Ben stared into his glass while slipping the pill into his pocket. This morning, all his friends were sitting down to a breakfast where pancakes, bacon and clearly identifiable fruit juices were on the menu. He was stuck with a botanical concoction his mother brewed — probably in a cauldron.

"You sure this stuff's good for me?"

"It will counteract the effects of all the junk food you eat when you think I'm not looking. So will that pill in your pocket."

*Busted!* He closed his eyes, put the pill in his mouth and took another sip of the drink. The glob had the consistency of partially formed Jell-O.

"I saw you and Dad doing a new weapons kata this morning," Ben said.

His mother froze a few seconds too long, then smiled again. "Did you?"

"Yeah! You looked fierce! What style was that?"

"Capoeira," she said, turning to rinse the dishes.

Ben paused. *That wasn't Caporeira.*

"How far did you get on the game?" asked April strolling into the kitchen with Aris. "I found a key and an iron gate. There's a jungle on the other side."

Ben had guessed right. April was playing a junior version of the game. He wondered if he could sabotage her computer to slow her down. "My password leads into a pyramid or maybe a tomb."

"Sweet!" April said. "I bet it's got hidden chambers and booby traps. Evil curses and mummies and stuff."

"Ah hmm!" His mother held out a glass of glob.

"Uh, uh. No! Nada! Nyet! I'm not drinking any more of that awful stuff!" April made a dash for the door.

"Come on, Tiger. We all have to get a healthy start in the morning." Blocking April's escape, Ben's father stared at the glass, clearly trying to mask his alarm.

April scowled. "How come you don't drink it?"

"I'm not a growing child." He ducked as Ben's mother cast him a backwards glance.

"And if I drink it I won't be one either," April sniffed the glass. "Smells awful. And . . . eeeew! Did a bug fall in the glass? Something's moving!"

"Well, then eat one of these." Ben's mother held out a homemade granola bar.

April recoiled in horror.

"So what's in this new juice?" Ben asked.

"Trust me," his father said. "You don't want to know."

Ben's mother threw a dish towel at him. "Bio-organic tofu, seaweed, kelp, soy beans, mango, kiwi, banana," she said proudly, "and a few secret ingredients from my garden."

Ben grimaced. He'd seen the weird stuff growing in her garden.

"I told you not to ask," said his father. "Let's go, we're late as usual and I promised to give Grace a ride. I've got to run next door first. I'll be back in five minutes."

"I call shotgun!" April yelled, racing out the door.

Ben rolled his eyes and tossed his drink on a rose bush just outside the door. He stopped, cut a single stem with his pocketknife and shoved it through a loop on his backpack. His father sprinted into the garage, grabbed a box from the trunk of the SUV, then jogged toward the Lopez's house.

If something had been wrong with his leg this morning, it seemed fine now.

# CHAPTER SIX

# Amazing Grace

Tell me your friends,
and I'll tell you who you are.

• *Assyrian Proverb*

◆ "Your mom has the weirdest plants on the planet." Grace stepped inside the greenhouse and pointed at the avocado plant. It had tripled in size overnight. A plump fleshy stalk rose from the center. "Looks like it has a body inside of it."

Ben shrugged. "Mom planted it a few days ago."

"Kind of creepy." Grace studied the plant from all angles but kept her distance. "I thought avocado plants were supposed to look like trees, not mutant flowers from outer space."

Ben wondered if he should tell Grace that there was more to it. A chemist by training but health nut by practice, his mother was always inventing some weird all-natural food. He'd take a bite then dump the rest on the plants. The avocado plant was his latest victim. His mother had the most spectacular gardens in Sunnyslope. She assumed it was because she mixed coffee grounds into the soil. Ben knew it was the macrobiotic tofu granola bars with green glob chasers.

"Where's your rose?" he asked.

"What?"

"Your rose? Did you figure out the riddle?"

"Oh! That rose. "Grace pushed her hair behind her ears. "I won't give you the satisfaction."

Ben was beside himself. Could it be? Had he finally stumped the amazing Grace? "Don't know the answer do you?"

She wagged an index finger at him. "Do you?"

Ben smiled. "Got it. After I logged off."

"So I guess you know what the white crystal does."

Ben crossed his fingers behind his back. "It was awesome."

"Liar! There wasn't any crystal! Do you even KNOW the password, Pinocchio?" Grace wrinkled her nose and gave him a triumphant grin.

"Xenobia?" Ben touched his own nose to see if it was growing.

"No! Admit it. You're stuck!"

"Hmmm . . . Sunnyslope?"

Grace burst out laughing. "Hah! I gave you a hint and you still didn't get it!" She offered high fives to her own invisible audience. "Yes, ladies and gentlemen! Grace is still the password champ!"

Ben reached over to his backpack, and produced a white rosebud. He grinned as wide as his face would allow. "Could it be . . . Benjamin?"

Grace's mouth gaped open in disbelief. Ben was delighted. It wasn't often that he won a game of one-upmanship with her.

"Grace!" Mei-Ling Choedon rushed across the lawn and held out a silver Bugs Bunny eyeglass case. She scowled and muttered something in Chinese.

"What'd she say?" asked Ben.

"She wasn't talking to me," Grace said, taking the case, then pointing to her own ear. "Wireless headphones. You can't see them. They're tiny — sort of like a hearing aid."

"What ya listening to, Dr. Choedon?" Ben asked.

"Trade negotiations with China," she whispered, covering the microphone with her hand. She adjusted Grace's wire-rimmed glasses, straightened the pleats in her skirt, then hurried back to her house.

Ben's father honked the horn. "Let's go people. I've got papers to grade and you've got knowledge to absorb."

"I know what took them so long," April said, as Ben and Grace climbed into the car. "Look! Ben gave Grace a rose. I think he likes her."

"Eeeew!" gasped Ben and Grace in unison. They slid apart as if pulled by electromagnets. Grace's cheeks blushed bright red as she dropped the flower. It bounced and landed on the floor.

Ben shot imaginary death rays at the back of April's head. He heard no satisfying sizzle of flesh, no cries of pain. It worked for one of the X-Men, but as luck would have it, he was stuck with ordinary DNA.

On the other hand, his father's driving might take care of the problem permanently. He accelerated like he was trying to break the sound barrier. Ben pulled his seat belt tighter as the Mercedes sped toward Sunnyslope Preparatory Academy, which students called "Sinking Ship," when teachers were out of earshot. He hoped that they would make it to school in one piece — or go out in a blaze of glory thereby ending his fraternal and academic misery simultaneously. Grace conducted a silent chant of her own as they whizzed by cars on the highway.

"So how far did you get?" Ben whispered once they were safely on city streets and his father was forced to drive at the posted speed.

Grace folded her arms and stared out the window. A few minutes later, her eyebrows relaxed. Ben saw this as an opening.

"On the game? How far did you get? Come on. Fess up."

Grace frowned and let out a long, slow sigh. "I got to the end of the secret passage. There's an old book and an ancient door."

"And?"

"And I'm stuck, okay? There's a bunch of weird riddles and a gross booby trap."

Ben stifled a laugh. Gross? Booby traps? He couldn't wait to dig in. "Want to work together? You're the smartest person I know." Ben held out his hand in friendship. "We work better as a team."

There was a long pause while Grace considered the offer. "Yeah?"

Ben nodded.

Grace smiled and gave his hand a quick squeeze. "That would be fun."

"Okay," whispered Ben. "Call you tonight after school."

April swiveled around to face them. "What ya whispering about?"

Ben pressed himself as close to the door as possible. "Nothing."

◆

That evening, Ben called shotgun as he climbed into the car. The air conditioner was blasting, but the black leather seats were still hot.

"Grace forgot her flower." April tossed it into the front seat. "Admit it. You've got a secret crush."

Ben ignored her as he twirled the rose between his fingers. His mother's cooking was dreadful but she had a magic touch with plants. The soft white petals formed a pinwheel pattern. Pollen-covered filaments sprang from the center like a fireworks display.

He froze. The rosebud had lain on the floor of the car all day — in the unshaded university parking lot. The petals should have wilted.

Instead, the rose was blooming.

# CHAPTER SEVEN

# The Legend

Luck that lasts is always suspect.

• *Tibetan Proverb*

◆ "So what do you think?" Grace said, in the tiny webcam window.

"Hang on. I need to look around." Ben said, brushing a pile of homework aside.

His monitor displayed panoramic views of drab gray walls shrouded in shadows. Although it was a computer simulation, Ben couldn't shake a feeling of claustrophobia as he proceeded down the hallway. Along the walls, hieroglyphic symbols were arranged in horizontal bands, each with scenes of daily life or violent battles. Those near the ceiling showed birds that looked like people soaring through the air. Those near the floor showed whales, fish, squid and jellyfish swimming in and out of coral reefs that resembled futuristic towns.

"These pictures might mean the tribes evolved from the sea and became birds. Or, maybe they evolved from birds and became amphibians." He thought about April's braids, how they hung from her head like tentacles. "If that's true, then April's a mutant jellyfish!"

"Stay focused," said Grace. "We've got homework so find a clue already!"

Ben sighed and "walked" into the light where an ancient book rested on a wooden pedestal. The front cover was embossed with a pyramid surrounded by eight hieroglyphs. Dust flew into the air as the book slammed open, its yellowed pages old and crumbling.

"Much better!" Ben said.

"What? Do you have it?" Grace pressed her face into the webcam until it looked like a distorted image in a funhouse mirror.

"No. Just happy the pages are in English. Now bring on the mutant monsters!"

"This would go so much faster if you read something besides X-Men comic books."

Ben stuck out his tongue. "Okay. I found a pyramid with a light ray coming out of the top."

"I can see that for myself," Grace said. "Now tell me something I don't know."

Ben grinned. "I see a riddle. But then I guess you know that too."

"You're killing me with your amazing powers of deduction," Grace groaned.

If you seek to unlock this mystery
Search throughout Earth for eight ancient keys
These keys were not forged by human hands.
But bring forth gifts I alone understand.

"Huh?"

"That's what I said," Grace said. "What kind of keys aren't made by human hands?"

"Keys made by monster hands, of course!" Ben read the introduction again. "There isn't any place for a password. Even if we come up with an answer, where would we put it?" He clicked the mouse. The paper crackled as it turned, coming to rest on a medallion surrounded by twelve circles.

Treasures await
For those who honor their fate.
The key to your future lies beyond the door.
Choose wisely.

"Did you turn the page, Grace?"

She threw her hands up in frustration. "Duhhh! But what's the answer?"

"I don't think there is one."

"Then what are we supposed to choose?"

"Beat's me. The rest of the pages are blank. Maybe they'll fill in when we collect clues." He spotted a wooden door with hinges bolted on both sides. Ben tried the left bolts. They shook and rattled, but refused to budge. He clicked on the right. The bolts slid out of place and the door opened with a creak and a groan.

"I wouldn't go through there," Grace said, dryly.

"What's the worst thing that could happen?" Ben "stepped" across the threshold and was greeted by a ghostly skull hovering in front of him. Skeletal hands reached out, dragged him inside and shut him inside a sarcophagus.

You did not choose wisely
Not all answers in life are obvious
Game over

"Aww man!"

The skeleton laughed in a deep, throaty voice reminiscent of Uncle Henry.

"If you press 'Try Again' the game lets you start where you left off right before you died," Grace said. "Kind of like a bookmark. At least your uncle has a heart."

"You're the only one on the planet who thinks so." Ben followed Grace's instructions and found himself outside the old door again. "This shortcut will come in handy when we're farther into the game."

"What's down that dark hallway?" asked Grace. "To the right. There's a red door. I'm going in."

There was silence followed by nervous giggling. "That was gross."

"What happened?"

"See for yourself," she said.

Ben found the door and clicked, his heart pausing a brief second while he waited for his fate. This time he fell through a trap door. Before the lights extinguished, the screen was "covered" in thousands of crawling, chittering black bugs.

You don't appear to be getting any wiser
— or any closer to a solution
Game over

He grinned. The bugs were pretty funny. Now what? He explored endless corridors, finding nothing but dead-ends or routes that returned him his starting place. The chamber was a giant labyrinth. He drew a map, keeping track of each step.

"Any luck?" he asked.

"Obviously not," Grace said. "This is irritating. Whatever we find better be worth it."

On his way back to the book, Ben stumbled upon a corridor hidden in the shadows. After a few minutes of searching, he saw it — shining like a beacon of hope.

"Grace! I found the door!"

Using his map as a reference, Ben guided Grace to a gold door embossed with a sun and rays of light streaming toward the Earth.

"You're the man!" Grace yelped. "This has to be it!"

"Okay. On a count of three we'll open the door together. One . . . two . . . three!"

Ben found himself back in the desert, buried up to his neck in sand with thousands of snakes and scorpions headed in his direction.

The definition of true insanity
is doing the same thing over and over again
and expecting a different outcome.
Game over.

Ben unleashed a loud belly laugh. Uncle Henry's sarcastic monotone delivery, the booby traps were hilarious in a sick kind of way. Still, something nagged at him. There had to be a way out of the chamber besides death. Then it hit him.

"Grace! Remember? In class, Mrs. Hooks said there was always a false door built for the escape of the dead Pharaohs. It wouldn't look like a real door."

"Why didn't I think of that? Search the walls! Some tombs had instructions for the dead."

"Can you read ancient pyramid texts?" asked Ben.

"Do you have a better idea?" Grace's eyebrows arched up to the edge of her bangs. Grace made a goofy face at him.

Ben stuck out his tongue again, but had to admit that she had a point. There weren't any other options. He moved in and out of the shadows, focusing first on the massive columns that flanked the entrance to the chamber. Then every stone and every star-engraved map on the walls.

Nothing.

He studied a carving of a king running beside a bull. This legend he remembered from class. The king ran a marked route to show his fitness to rule. Ben had just explored enough musty corridors to claim the "kingdom". So where was the stupid door for it?

"Find anything new yet?"

"No," Ben sighed. "This is going to take a while and I've got to finish the math homework that was due today."

"Good thing Mr. Bundy was sick. I wasn't looking forward to the math midterm."

"I wasn't looking forward to explaining another 'Incomplete' to my mom." Ben aimlessly clicked the screen. "I was going to fake the flu, but Mom catches on every time."

"I don't bother. It would be disrespectful," Grace said.

"When I was six, I pretended to have the measles," Ben continued. "I put dots all over my face with a red marker and put a hot water bottle on my forehead to raise my temperature." Ben inspected objects strewn about the floor: pieces of broken pottery, an empty box, and a torn cloth below a damaged cartouche of Osiris.

"So what happened?" Grace asked.

"I haven't found anything yet," Ben said.

"No, I mean with your fake measles."

"Oh! I got caught. Mom took one look at me and wiped the marks off with a soapy washcloth. She's scary that way."

"Yeah, mine too. They must trade notes or have a secret parent manual." Grace furrowed her eyebrows. "Hey, speaking of scary, what was up with your father today? He drove like he was trying to outrun Air Force One. We got to school in ten minutes."

"No way! It takes twenty-five minutes even when he's speeding."

"I checked my watch. We left at 7:30. We got there at 7:40."

"That's impossible. It's fifteen miles. Your watch must be broken." He glanced at the vase to the right of his monitor. "Hey, Grace! Remember that flower I gave you?"

Grace sighed. "You win. I still don't know the answer to the riddle. Go ahead and gloat! You know you want to."

Ben shook his head. "That's not why I asked. It's been sitting in the car all day but it still looks like it's fresh from the garden."

Grace sighed and rolled her eyes.

"No, really. Take a look." Ben held the vase in front of the webcam.

"After I got home I tried an experiment. I cut a rose from the greenhouse. Then I cut one from the garden in Carlos's yard. That one is shriveled up. But Mom's roses don't wilt even though there's no water in the vase."

"Are they real? Maybe she plants silk flowers when no one's looking."

"Actually, it's where I've been dumping the glob."

Grace gasped. "On those poor defenseless plants? That's attempted murder!"

"It was them or me. And there's something else."

"Hello! Could we get back to the game?"

"Yeah, in a minute. I've got another question." Ben heard Grace clicking in the background.

"Go ahead as long as it isn't another stupid riddle."

"You ever remember being sick?"

"Huh?"

"Chicken pox, measles, sprained ankle, stomach ache? Ever have to go to the doctor?"

Grace furrowed her brow as if searching her brain's entire thirteen-year database for an answer. "No. Just check-ups with Dr. Danine."

"Me too. You don't suppose it's the green glob do you?"

"I don't drink that awful stuff so that wouldn't explain it. There's nothing sinister going on here. Your mom's just got a green thumb." She paused. "Hey! That's it! She does say you're growing like a weed. She's turning you into a plant!" Grace laughed hysterically.

"That's not funny," Ben grumbled. "Quit laughing or I WILL throw another riddle at you. By the way, do you want a hint?"

Grace deflated. "Huh? Oh. Umm, no. I'll figure it out. I keep sticking in logical answers and nothing works."

"It will come to you," Ben said as he stared at the flowers on his desk. "We're not going anywhere soon."

Grace suddenly yelped. "Score! Found it!"

# CHAPTER EIGHT

# The Guardian

"Success is going from failure to failure
without losing enthusiasm."

• *Winston Churchill*

• "Where?"

"Go to the original door and turn 180 degrees. There's a guy with a beard on the wall. When I put my cursor there, it changes into a hand."

"What? I looked there already." Ben wiggled the mouse back and forth, up and down. "It's not here!"

Grace rolled her eyes. "You might try slowing down. Be a tortoise, instead of a hare for a change."

Ben growled then found the spot over the damaged face of Osiris. "Okay. Found it. Thanks."

"Did that hurt you?" Grace asked. "Saying 'thanks' that is?"

Ben growled again but didn't answer.

"I'll take that as a 'yes'." Grace beamed, clearly pleased with herself. "You're welcome."

The wall suddenly dissolved. "Meet you on the other side, as the dead Pharaohs say."

In contrast to the drab grey chamber they'd left, vibrant colors jumped out from white stone walls. The reliefs showed offerings to Osiris, the sun god Ra sailing a barge through the Underworld, and people rising from Earth on the sun's rays.

Ben was unimpressed. "Where's the good stuff? The monsters?" In the center of the room stood a glass chamber containing a white marble altar. Eight symbols were carved into the circumference — duplicates of the one on the ancient book. A scale rose out of the stone. A parchment opened on the screen:

In the year 10,500 BC, a guardian of great power was placed in the East. Honed of mystical materials, her treasure now lies buried and forgotten under the sand. Open her and rewards beyond your imagination will be revealed. But you must first find the keys. Like the eight original tribes, they have been scattered across the earth.
Return them to their proper place.
Before you lies the path to your destiny.
Choose wisely.

This was promising. When Ben clicked on the scale, two enormous doors materialized at the end of the room. The polished metal surface was covered in symbols Ben didn't recognize. Half of a balance scale was carved on each side holding a feather on the left and nothing on the right. Flanking the doors stood statues of Anubis and Toth — the god in charge of the weighing and the Goddess Ammut — part crocodile, part lion, part hippopotamus. Ammut ate anyone who didn't make the cut. Above the doors crouched a woman, her wing-covered arms outstretched to either side.

"That's the symbol for Ma'at," Grace said. "This must be the entrance to the Hall of Truth."

"The place where the souls of Egypt's dead went to be judged," Ben confirmed. "Bet you didn't think I was paying attention in class."

"You weren't. You got a C- on the test. Besides, it says that right above the door."

"I got a higher grade than you did!" Ben laughed. "Burn!"

"You didn't need to go there," Grace muttered, her cheeks flushed.

The symbols translated into English as soon as Ben passed over them with his cursor.

"Enter those who have proven worthy."

A current of electricity jolted through Ben. In ancient Egypt, hearts of the dead were placed on the right side of the scale. If the scales balanced, you went on to a great reward — the afterlife. If not, you were dinner for Ammut and your death was final. If Ben solved the game, would the scale judge him to be worthy?

"Earth to Ben. Did you find something or are you daydreaming about slaying monsters with your supercharged basketball? I clicked on the doors but they don't open. Guess we have put a heart on the scale before it will let us in. Got one we can use?"

Ben snapped back to attention and sighed.

"I guess that means 'no.' "Grace chuckled. "Means we'll have to find a heart somewhere else. Mine's taken."

The Eye of Ra glowed red in the center of a large stone medallion.

Eight statues rose out of the floor and flanked the Guardian doors like royal guards — four on each side. Their arms wrapped around stone jars large enough to hold a giant. The tops were crowned with round disks embossed with ellipses and circles — like maps of a solar system. The blank obsidionfaces of the guards showed no clues as to gender, race or even species.

"I don't know about this. Is it going to be scary?" Grace frowned and squinted as if trying to block out any unexpected, horrific sights.

"Yeah!" Ben said, "If I know my uncle, this is going to be intense! What do you think is behind that big door? Zombie mummies?"

"I'm kind of hoping for something useful — like a treasure chest, a puppy, or an essay I can turn in for English."

"That would be tragic." Ben sighed. "What's up with those gigantic jars?" They look like canopic jars but without the animal heads on top."

"If those are canopic jars, then you know what's inside," Grace said.

Ben's heart kicked up a notch. "Now that's what I'm talking about! Eight jars means two monsters to defeat. Two sets of lungs, livers, stomachs and intestines. Maybe that's why those metal doors are so big. Must be hiding one huge surprise."

"Lungs and livers don't sound like treasure to me. Your uncle promised your mother no violence. Do you think he lied?"

Ben's joy evaporated. "No. Guess we're back to a history quest."

Each jar contained weird symbols and a grid pattern that looked like maps. Two parallel rods wrapped around them like serpents. Strands of gold, silver, copper, and pewter hung from the rods like fringe.

Grace frowned. "It'd be nice if we had some instructions. Did the game come with a manual?"

"Get real," Ben said. "You've met my uncle. Think he'd would make it that easy?"

After five minutes of searching Ben couldn't find anything else. No secret passages. No hidden sarcophagi. Ben would have even welcomed the evil skeleton popping up for a visit.

"Hey, Grace!" Ben said, with a sudden start. "Go back out into the hallway."

"Why? Think we missed something?"

"The book, remember?" Ben clicked "Legend" on the game panel and zoomed back to the ancient book. The blank pages were now filled with drawings. Handwritten notes appeared in the margins: star charts, colored dots, strange box shaped markings, numerical codes, and squiggles that looked like the waves of an ocean. But they didn't make any more sense than hieroglyphics. Ben passed the cursor over the new symbols. There was no way to translate.

## ⌐·⊏⊏⊔
29 59N 31 09E

## ⊔⟨□⌐·⌐⫟□⌐
29 59N 30 05E

## ⌄⟨⌐⌐⟨⌄□⊏⫟ ⊔
32 44N 117 10W

## ⌐□⫟□ ⌐⟨⫟
27 04S 109 22W . . . .

"Darn, it's a code," Grace said.

Ben groaned. "Ya think?"

"Yes, Sherlock, I do. I can breeze through cryptograms, but I have trouble with breaking codes. We need help and I know someone who loves them. Got kind of a 'Beautiful Mind' thing going on without the seeing imaginary people part."

"Who?" asked Ben. "And if you say April, I'm reporting you to Homeland Security."

"She's a really nice person if you give her a chance."

"Who, Grace? Who?"

Grace scrunched up her face as if saying the name would make her explode.

"Who?" Ben yelled.

Grace winced and ducked. "Serise."

# CHAPTER NINE

# Ode to Joy

"The Bible says make a joyful noise,
it does not say it has to be a pleasant one."

• *Author Unknown*

♦ *"You got math homework, Mister?"*

*"Yeah, but it's not due until Monday."*

*"In this house, it's due the day it was assigned! I'll expect to see it by evening — no games until you're done. Oh! Hi Grace, didn't see you."*

*"Mom!"*

*"I said now!"*

Exiled to the dining room table, Ben stared at the formulas in his math textbook. They were as bad as deciphering hieroglyphics.

A few feet away, April pounded a Steinway so big it took up half the living room. The sheet music said "Ode to Joy" but her rendition was full of variations Ben was sure the teacher had not intended. As April dipped and bobbed her head like a concert pianist, the beads on her braids began to glow.

*Motion activated beads? What dumb corporation thought of that?*

"What's that awful noise you're making?" he asked.

"Jazz," April whispered. "Mr. Windom said I could try improvisation."

"I thought you were conjuring up ancient spells to raise the dead."

"Mom! Ben's insulting me!"

"That's great," answered his mother from the kitchen.

*Huh?*

"Absolutely! Mahjong on Sunday. I hear the boys have something special planned for themselves," his mother continued.

Ben stuck his tongue out at April, clutched his throat and flung his head to the table in a mock death throe.

April ran into the kitchen. "Mom!'"

Ben laughed, happy to have peace and quiet. But he knew it wouldn't last long. The operative question was, *How to get April off that piano?*

Within minutes he crafted a solution that would benefit him and the world in general. Put April in a high security prison with her piano books and the crime rate would drop to zero.

"Ben!" His mother said, storming into the room.

"Uh oh." Ben braced for impact. "Mom! She's lying. I didn't do anything."

"I am not your personal referee. One day the two of you are going to have to learn to work out your differences without me." Her eyes flashed like Mt. Vesuvius before the volcano buried all of Pompeii. "By the way, Ben, there's no such thing as a spell to raise the dead. And April, I told Mr. Windom no jazz until you mastered Beethoven."

"Yes, Ma'am," they said in unison.

April stomped back to the piano and banged out "Für Elise." She butchered the notes over and over again, searching for the right tempo.

"A metronome would help," offered Ben. "And some talent."

"Mr. Windom called you tone deaf," April replied. "So you couldn't carry a tune even if you had a pickup truck."

At a loss for a snappy response, Ben ignored her. That did the trick. April pounded the piano keys with extra force to punctuate her frustration.

Savoring his victory, Ben returned to his homework. His math diagrams looked like a game of hangman. What was the point? His jump shot would rule the world one day. He'd just hire an accountant.

"Ben," his mother yelled from the kitchen. "If you would stop spending every waking minute thinking about basketball you would know that the hypotenuse is the side OPPOSITE the right angle. If you want to figure out the length just take the square root of the sum of the squares of the other two sides. The Pythagorean theorem is easy if you would just focus!"

*Why can't she speak English?* He powered on his calculator.

"And take your hands off that calculator! Use your brain!" she continued. "You'll need to know math so you can manage all those contracts you think will be dribbling your way."

April stuck her tongue out at him.

"April, stop making faces at your brother."

Ben grimaced. Either his mother installed secret cameras or she had X-ray eyes.

◆

He escaped to the solitude of his backyard. While Grace was stuck contacting Serise, Paradise Circle's know-it-all diva, his assignment was easy — get help deciphering the game clues from Carlos Lopez. Ben had spent endless summer nights lying on his back with all the other Paradise Circle inmates while Carlos's father, an astronomy geek, pointed out the stars. Big Dipper, Little Dipper, North Star. Who could tell the difference? To Ben space just looked like a giant piece of black construction paper with holes poked in it. Shine a super giant flashlight through it and voila . . . stars! So if anyone could figure out the star patterns it would be Dr. Lopez's son.

*Tap, bounce, bounce, bounce . . . crash!*

Carlos maneuvered his short, stocky legs toward a hoop attached to a pole in his backyard.

*Crash!*

Ben had high hopes when Carlos moved next door and doubled the cul-de-sac's population of resident boys. As luck would have it, Carlos was a nerd not a jock.

*Thud! Crash!*

Ben glanced from Carlos to the paper and back again.

"Want some company?"

"Sure, come on over," Carlos shouted without taking his eye off of the net.

*Bounce. Bounce. Crash!*

Ben climbed over the deck railing and hopped the short fence. "I need a favor."

"Can't give you the answers to the math homework. Your mom called my mom."

Ben frowned. His mother had the entire neighborhood on alert. "That's not what I need. I'm working on a puzzle. Thought I could trade you some basketball pointers if you help me decipher a code."

"Yeah, sure. Saw you practicing in the gym the other day. Dude, you crushed the competition. What happened? You used to play worse than me!"

Ben shrugged. "One day I was horsing around and everything just started to click. Know what I mean?"

"No, actually, I don't." Carlos studied the ball as if concealed the secrets to pro basketball. "Okay. What am I doing wrong?" He released the ball and clenched his fists in anticipation.

*Thud! Crash!*

Ben caught the ball as it bounced off the roof of the garage and returned to Carlos. "You're not lining up your shots."

"Isn't that the same as aiming at the basket?" Carlos asked.

"Sort of. But you have to visualize the hoop, determine the angle of trajectory, and then control the speed of release." Ben released the ball. It fell through the opening of the hoop with a whisper soft "whoosh."

"If you can explain basketball that way, then how come you can't figure out the math homework? It's kind of the same thing," Carlos said, shaking his head as he rebounded. Then he stopped cold. "Hey, you lifting weights?"

"Huh?"

"You're getting muscles. You lifting weights to get ready for the season?"

Ben pushed up the sleeves of his Laker's jersey. Sunlight glinted off bulges he hadn't noticed before. He balled up his fist, made a muscle, and poked at it. Firm like a rock. Ben was ecstatic. "Just shooting hoops. Didn't know I'd get results so fast!"

"Must be all the hours you put in this summer." Carlos held the ball in front of his face and eyed it as if it were a precious jewel. He adjusted his hands, one on the bottom, one on the top, and crouched to line the ball up with the net.

"Now imagine an arc," Ben said, still admiring the new definition in his arms and flexing his muscles over and over again. "Think smooth curve that ends in the net . . . like a rainbow. You're a nerd so think math and science formulas; parabolas, potential energy, gravity." Ben watched as the ball released into the air.

*Crash!*

The ball rolled to a stop near a blue backpack on the lawn. Carlos took it everywhere.

"Ya think you could stuff one more thing in that backpack?" Ben asked.

Carlos shrugged and took the ball from Ben. "You never know when you're going to need something."

"But you pack like you're going on an expedition," Ben said. "The only thing you're missing is a sleeping bag."

Carlos's eyes lit up.

"You don't have one in there, do you?" Ben lifted the pack and tried to use it like a dumbbell. It looked like it weighed a ton, but was surprisingly lightweight.

Carlos grinned. "One day you'll be thankful I'm so prepared. So what was that code you wanted me to look at?" He aimed, then crossed his fingers as the ball took flight.

*Crash! Thud!*

"Oh, yeah." Ben caught the ball as it bounced off the gutter and tossed it back to Carlos. "I almost forgot." He pulled the crumpled paper from his pocket and pointed to his crude drawings of the medallion and its cryptic symbols. "It's from a game my uncle gave me. Grace and I thought you would know what they were."

Carlos raised his left eyebrow. "What kind of game?"

"A digital treasure hunt. If I solve the puzzles by next week I can go on an expedition. My uncle said there would be a surprise ending. Though maybe this is just a super secret way of slipping in some math and science practice."

"Overrated," Carlos sighed, rolling the basketball in his hands.

"Math and science?" Ben asked.

"No. Expeditions. No working bathrooms. You sleep on a cot in a hot, stuffy tent while a bunch of science geeks dig stuff up one millimeter at a time. Why didn't you ask for something fun like a trip to King's Island? I heard they've got a new roller coaster. Then you could get out of town and have fun at the same time."

"I know your parents dragged you all over the planet," Ben said, "but this would be my first adventure."

"And you wouldn't mind hanging out with your uncle? He's kind of intense. I bet he could make a lemon pucker."

"He's not so bad," Ben lied. Uncle Henry was a lot of things, but he was also family and Ben wasn't going to insult him in front of Carlos. "Mom says he just needs to settle down and start a family."

"No offense but who'd be crazy enough to marry him?" Carlos traced the star patterns with his index finger.

Ben sighed. "I don't think he's the settling kind. Doesn't even have a house. Mom calls him a restless soul. Either way, this would be my chance to show him I've got what it takes."

"Did you tell him you were going out for the basketball team?"

"He wasn't impressed," Ben confessed.

"Really? I thought he'd be into all that macho sports stuff. Okay. I'll help if you let me play. Dad's in Peru digging up some petrified dead thing and Mom's in a sour mood. You'll solve it faster if we work together."

"Deal. Grace is getting help from Serise."

Carlos scowled. "Serise?"

"She's not playing. Grace is just getting help with the codes without saying what it's for."

"Then I'm in," said Carlos, giving a thumb up.

Ben laid the paper on the patio table and blocked the sun's glare with his hand. "There's an old book with star charts and weird box codes. Think they might be related?"

## ᴸ·ᴇᴄᵁ
29 59N 31 09E

## ᵁᐸᴏᴦ·ᴦᴖᴸ
29 59N 30 05E

## ᐯᐸᴸᴸᐸᴠᴼᴇᴖ ᵁ
32 44N 117 10W

## ᴦᴏᴖᴼ ᴸᐸᴖ
27 04S 109 22W . . .

"They do look like star patterns," Carlos said. "But I don't recognize them and, trust me, Dad's made me memorize them all."

"What about the numbers? Could those be another code?"

"Maybe. But it looks more like GPS data. I might be wrong, but I think they're coordinates for locations on Earth."

# CHAPTER TEN

## Queen of the Universe

If a man sought a companion who acted entirely like himself,
he would live in solitude.

• *Nigerian Proverb*

◆ "Hey Guys!"

Ben grimaced and turned toward the familiar voice walking up the driveway. Serise Hightower, self-titled Queen of the Universe, could barely move in her tight jeans and wedge-heeled shoes.

"Like my watch?" Serise thrust out her wrist. "Mom got it when she was in New Mexico. It's Sterling silver. VERY expensive."

She beamed as Grace and April took a closer look. Turquoise stones were embedded in the silver band. Serise had painted matching flowers on her nails. But the watch and nails weren't nearly as obnoxious as the maroon and purple highlights and feathers in her jet black hair.

"Sweet!" Carlos glanced at Ben and smirked.

Ben rolled his eyes and pretended to be interested. Serise's mother was Curator of the Sunnyslope Museum of Natural History. She was always off doing weird things — rock climbing in Arizona, studying crop circles in Iowa corn fields. She brought back expensive gifts for Serise who gave new meaning to the word "spoiled."

"So what do you think," asked Serise.

Ben shrugged. "What's the big deal? It doesn't have a timer or a stopwatch or a compass or . . ."

Serise yanked her arm back. "What would you know, fashion reject. Want to see something cool?"

Ben was about to say "no" when Grace elbowed him in the back.

"Yeah, sure," he said.

"Follow me." Serise pressed her fingers to her lips as she tiptoed towards her house on the south side of the cul-de-sac. "Shhh!"

The five of them crept down the driveway, across the street and around to the Hightower's backyard. A domed structure sat in the corner. Covered with blankets, canvas tarps and leather, it looked like a cross between a hut and a tent. A single opening was visible on the west side.

"What's that?" asked Carlos.

"Our new sweat lodge," Serise said. "My father's getting ready for a vision quest."

"So what's it for?" asked Ben, though he wasn't sure he wanted to know. Serise's dad was a meteorologist, but his hobby was mystic religions. He was always trying to conjure up the spirit of an ancient ancestor.

"A vision quest," Serise repeated. "He's going to cleanse himself of toxic impurities and restore his soul. He's meditating. Been fasting for a couple of days. He wants to conduct a ceremony on Sunday and get guidance for a journey."

"He does this every time he goes on a trip?" asked Ben.

"No. But after the big storm he said he was going to ask the Tribal Council for permission to conduct an Enemyway ceremony."

Ben heard an odd chanting coming from inside.

"He won't start the ritual until Sunday," Serise said.

"Just what we need," Ben said. "Ghosts of ancient ancestors moving into the neighborhood."

"I don't know," Grace said. "A sweat lodge meditation sounds cool. We're stuck with Mahjong on Sunday. I never win. I'd rather be doing this."

Serise cocked her head to the side. "You have to be naked."

Grace's jaw dropped. "Umm. Never mind. Mahjong suddenly sounds pretty good."

Serise crept toward the back of the lodge and showed them a walkie-talkie behind a large rock. While she covered it with ferns and leaves.

"Did you get what we need?" Ben whispered.

"I'm working on it," Grace said. "My parents are going out of town again and they're not happy about it. The night of that big storm they got a phone call and they've been on edge ever since."

"Mine too," Ben said. "We were shooting some hoops but Dad kept watching the clouds."

Grace shrugged. "I don't think it has anything to do with the weather. I think it's because they got stuck translating Middle East peace negotiations. I'm sleeping over at Serise's house."

Ben patted her on the back. "The CIA classifies sleepovers with Serise as torture."

Grace gave a weak smile. "She's not so bad. It's just one night. Are you playing later?"

He shook his head. "Got to work on math. Mom will ground me if I don't get some of it done. How about tomorrow morning? About 11 o'clock? Carlos gave me a clue about the numbers. He's going to help."

"Deal. Three heads are better than two," Grace said.

Serise shoved the wireless transmitter in her back pocket.

"And why do you want to do this?" asked Carlos, looking horrified.

"My father wants to hear the voice of spirits. I thought I'd help him out. One time I gave him a thrill by banging some rocks together while he was meditating."

Ben clucked his tongue in disgust."

"It's not like living on this boring cul-de-sac is a thrill. What did the builders do? Build the first house and then hit cut and paste for the rest? And what's up with all the beige? There are days when I come home and can't remember which house I live in!" Serise said.

"Your dad's a nice guy," Ben said. "I don't see what's so funny about this."

"Because you have no sense of humor!" Serise said, flipping her long hair out of her face.

"We do," countered Carlos. "You just haven't done anything that's funny."

"Fine!" she spat. "Just don't snitch. Or, Ben, I'll tell your mom what you've been dumping on her flowers."

Ben froze.

"Yeah, that's right! I saw you!" She turned on her heels, walked into the house and slammed the door shut. She returned a few minutes later. "What was I thinking? This is my yard. Get out!"

◆

That evening, Ben sat in front of the kitchen computer under his mother's watchful eye. He typed "hypotenuse" into a search engine and frowned when the computer returned the same answer over and over again.

*This site is temporarily blocked. Please enter access code.*

Foiled again by his mom's evil filters.

His father walked into the kitchen and tossed his briefcase on the table. "Hey, Ben! Exciting news! We've been invited to the Hightower's on Sunday to try out their new sweat lodge!"

Now Ben knew his forehead was painted with an invisible bullseye.

# CHAPTER ELEVEN

# The Hologram

If you don't know where you want to go,

any road will take you there.

• *Traditional proverb*

◆ Armed with the mile high deli sandwich smuggled in by Carlos, Ben logged on to his computer. "Yo, Grace. I'm back online and I've got company."

"Hola, Carlos. Welcome to the search for lost tribes, whoever they are." Grace's expression was half smile, half warning.

"What's up, Grace? You okay?"

She flicked her hair to the rear. It flopped back in place. Ben thought he saw colors in her hair — maroon and purple streaks, beads and . . . a matching feather?

"You copying Serise's hairstyle? Was that the price for getting the answers to the canopic jars? How'd you ditch her anyway?"

Grace frowned as arms appeared on each side of her shoulders.

*No! It can't be!*

"Hey, Ben!"

He stifled a groan. "Oh! Hi, Serise!"

"You really are an idiot." Carlos buried his face in a pillow, his body vibrating with laughter as he clutched his stomach.

Aris bounded into the room, jumped on the blanket and sniffed him.

"Sorry. She wouldn't help if I didn't let her play and we can go faster if we have more heads working on this." Grace shrugged in defeat. "The suspense is killing me."

Serise pushed her face close to the camera lens, puckered her lips and let loose a loud smacking sound. She winked as she pulled back. "Face it, you need me."

*Yeah. Like a hole in my head.*

Serise's bracelets clattered as she lifted her arms and flexed her fingers as if she were about to crack a safe. Grace frowned and mouthed, *"Sorry!"* She looked like a hostage and kept glancing to the right. Soon, Ben understood why.

Something shimmered behind her. . . sparkling beaded hair to be more specific. *April!* Grace's room had been invaded by the cul-de-sac's entire contingent of obnoxious girls. She WAS a hostage. Ben tried to think of ways he and Carlos could mount a rescue mission.

"Looks like it's the girls against the boys," April said, waving so hard Ben thought her arm would fall off. "Hi Carlos! This is going to be more fun then playing the game by myself. I was stuck on the part with the hidden door. Serise helped me figure it out."

Serise gave April a high-five then hugged her. "Always wanted a kid sister!"

"Sold!" Ben said under his breath.

"Huh?" Still chuckling, Carlos wiped the tears from his eyes. "There's a hidden door?"

Ben quickly brought Carlos up to speed then said, "April, I thought you were in a jungle?"

"I was lying. I couldn't figure out the password. Plus, Aris kept stepping on the keyboard and messing up my guesses so I gave up and went to bed. After I heard you tell Grace that your password was 'Benjamin,' I typed my name and it worked! But I knew you wouldn't help me with the rest, so I asked Serise."

"Fine," Ben said through gritted teeth. Realizing that anything he said or did would be transmitted to Grace's monitor, he pasted on his best fake smile. "You're right. Can't hurt to team up."

"Want to know what those boxes are?" asked Serise.

Ben bit his lip and was about to fire off a smart remark when Carlos punched him in the shoulder out of view of the camera and said in his nicest, syrupy sweet voice, "Yes! Amaze us with your brilliance, Serise."

"April," Serise continued. "Why don't you do the honors?"

"It's a pigpen code. At first I thought Serise was talking about Ben's messy room but she drew me a picture and showed me how to solve it. She figured out those hanging fringe thingies too."

Serise arched her eyebrows and grinned.

"Are you going to tell us," sighed Grace. "Or wait 'til we've died of old age?"

"I'll give you a hint. It's not fringe."

"And?" Grace glared into the camera. Ben could have sworn she was going to smack Serise. That told him a lot, since Grace was a Buddhist and a completely nonviolent person.

"Second hint. They're broken," Serise said.

"And?" asked Ben.

"They're codes."

"We know that!" shouted Ben, Carlos and Grace in unison.

"Good grief!" Grace said. "Spit it out already."

"They're people codes!" yelled April, as if keeping Serise's secret would cause her to explode. She hopped up and down in excitement.

"What?" asked Ben, totally lost at this point.

"They're genetic codes," Serise said. "If you were taking the gifted science class like I am you would have recognized them right away. The game says you have to locate eight original tribes. There are eight canopic jars. I think the fringe is DNA strands, except they're all broken."

Ben "zoomed" forward to take another look at the jars. They did look like DNA strands. Of course they also looked like the fringe on one of Serise's jackets.

"I still haven't figured out how to get the jars open, but I do know how to solve the pigpen code. May I?" Serise pointed to Grace's chair.

Grace shrugged and stood up. Serise plopped down and typed at a fanatical pace. "Hate doing stuff manually. So I worked on a program last night that will substitute the proper letters for the box codes." She stared into the camera with the expression of a well-fed alley cat. "Ready?"

"Uh. Sure!" Ben looked at Carlos and shrugged.

"Wait 'til you see this!" April hugged Serise and pushed her face so close to the webcam that the lens fogged.

Within seconds a self-extracting file appeared on Ben's desktop. There was no need to restart the computer. The file linked to the game and caused it to zoom back to the book, which opened to the medallion page. A window opened on the edge of the screen showing a game board for tic-tac-toe. The program drew a second game board but placed dots in each of the boxes. Next, the program drew two giant X's. The first was plain. The second was punctuated by dots similar to the squares sitting above it.

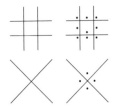

"Pretty picture," Ben said. "Now what?"

"Shut up," Grace said. "She's on to something."

The program typed letters into the empty slots generated by the program.

| a | b | c | j. | k | .l |
|---|---|---|----|---|-----|
| d | e | f | m• | n | •o |
| g | h | i | p' | q | 'r |

s     w

t    u    x • • y

v     z

*A decoder? Serise had developed a decoder overnight?*

The computer paused. *"Error. Advanced code detected. Key required. Reanalyze."* The letters of the alphabet dropped to the bottom of the screen.

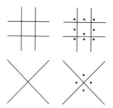

A b c d e f g h I j k l m n o p q r s t u u w x y z

"Great. Stuck again," said Ben. "We don't have any keys yet."

"Type password," the computer prompted.

"What password?" Carlos asked.

"Duhhh. Same one that let Ben log on," Serise said. "I can't do all the thinking for you."

Ben growled and typed "Benjamin." He felt Carlos's chin on his shoulder and his erratic breathing on his neck. Aris pounced on his lap, leapt to the desk and studied the monitor. The cat yawned and proceeded to groom himself as the program sprang to life, lifting the letters of Ben's name from the alphabet list, placing them sequentially in the spaces generated by the program. The remaining letters were added to the empty boxes in alphabetical order.

"Oh my gosh! She's a genius!" Carlos said.

"We could have figured this out eventually." Ben bit his lip and struggled to hide his amazement and his jealousy.

"Not the code! Did you see how fast she developed that program? Whoa, Serise! You're like . . . amazing!"

"Why yes, I am." She sat still as a rock, head raised and waited.

Grace stood behind her, mouth open wide. The computer opened a second box and began crunching data. Duplicates of the codes were copied to the blank page.

## ⌐⌐⌐⊔
29 59N 31 09E

## ⊔⟨⊓⌐⌐⌐⊐⊓⌐
29 59N 30 05E . . . .

Within minutes, Ben understood what had captured the girl's attention. A new list sprang to life on his own computer and suddenly the numerical codes made sense as well:

Home
29 59N 31 09E

Guardian
29 59N 30 05E

Sunnyslope
32 44N 117 10W

Rapa Nui
27 04S 109 22W

Xiangyang
34 22N 108 42E

Stongehenge
51 17N 1 83W

Acropolis
37 57N 23 42E

Nazca
14 42S 75 06W

Petra
30 19N 35 28E

Machu Picchu
13 06S 72 35W

Bandiagara Escarpment
14 21N 3 35W . . . .

The codes pinpointed the latitude and longitude for locations all over the world. Ben squirmed with excitement. "Now we're cooking!"

"You're welcome," Serise said. "But we still have to figure out how that translates into getting out of the room."

"I've got an idea," Carlos said. "See the dots on the medallion. Four of them are larger than the others. Could be compass points. You know North, South, East, and West."

"Hey! You're right!" Serise said. "Except, there's a problem. If we eliminate the compass points then that leaves eight buttons on the floor to push. If we have to dial a number we need access to ten digits — zero through nine."

"You've got a point. Maybe the remaining nodes serve a dual purpose," Carlos said.

"Too complicated." Serise's face was a mask of concentration.

"Okay. So then what?" Carlos asked.

Carlos and Serise took over as if on autopilot. Ben marveled. The two biggest brains on the block had found something in common. It was like Beauty and the Beast with Carlos playing the short but handsome Beauty and Serise in the role of the hideous Beast.

Left out of the technical mumbo jumbo bouncing back and forth, Ben sat on his bed and attempted to win a staring contest with the cat. He blinked, lost the contest and returned his attention to matters at hand. He waved from across the room at Grace who was relegated to the "bleachers" as well. A miniature hand waved back at him from the monitor. Meanwhile, the two newfound computer geeks chattered away about breaking codes and deciphering the meaning of the medallion as if no one else were in the room.

"Yin and Yang," Ben yelled to Grace while pointing to Carlos.

Grace nodded.

"What did you say?" asked Carlos.

"Yin and Yang. Like my father and uncle."

"That's it," Carlos yelled. "That's where the other two digits are!"

"I don't get it," Serise said. "Where?"

"Look at the border around the Eye of Ra! It's half white and half black! Binary code. On and Off. Zero and One! That would throw anyone off."

"Sweet!" Serise said. "I think we have a winner." Carlos and Serise clicked furiously.

After a few minutes, Carlos stopped and turned to Ben. "Didn't you say this thing lights up when you pass the cursor over it?"

"Yeah."

"Well, something's not working. It doesn't light up anymore. Did I miss a step?"

Ben grabbed the mouse, pushed it over the medallion and clicked. The lights glowed. "Guess I'm the only person qualified to pilot this thing." He gave Carlos a gentle nudge. "I'll take the Captain's chair back, thank you very much. Serise? You having any problems?"

"No. It lights up just fine for me."

Ben stuck his tongue out at Carlos. "Okay, here's the plan. We'll each pick a different place and see where it goes and if it comes with more instructions."

Grace leapt from her bed and cleared her throat. "Uh hmmm."

Serise rose without an argument. "Sorry, Grace. Didn't mean to hog your machine."

April frowned. "So which one do we pick? There's so many to choose from."

"Don't bother with Sunnyslope," Ben said. "We're trying to get out of this town, not see more of it. You guys take the Chinese code. We'll start with Rapa Nui. Then we can decide based on what we find. That'll make the game go faster."

"How do we know which node is north?" asked Grace.

Ben studied the medallion for a few seconds. "Use the big one that's closest to that giant door. What's the worst thing that could happen? We don't go anywhere, or we go to the wrong place. Either way, we can start over if we hit a booby trap."

Ben clicked the code for Rapa Nui. A blinding light appeared in the center of the medallion. On the right, the strands of the canopic jar closest to the Guardian clicked into place, then fell again.

"Hey, Grace. Did the jars do anything on your end?"

"Nope."

Ben clicked on the jar. Nothing else happened so he returned his attention to the column of light streaming from the portal and clicked the mouse. A golden beam shot out of the monitor like fireworks. His bedroom sparkled with stars and glitter, then transformed into a realistic, three-dimensional projection of a vast field near an ocean. Large stone heads rose out of the hillside, their wide blank eyes looking out to sea. Ben stood and walked around the virtual statues suddenly realizing he could view them from all sides. But they weren't real. His hands passed through the ghostly images when he tried to touch them.

Aris hissed and shot out of the bedroom.

"Whoa!" Carlos's mouth dropped wide open and his eyes bugged out. "Now we know what Rapa Nui means."

"What?" asked Grace. "Did you find something interesting?"

"Oh yeah! Easter Island!"

Grace seemed unimpressed.

Ben's heart went into overdrive. His computer monitor showed a digital representation of the landscape now filling his room. "Grace?"

"Yeah?"

"What do you see?"

"I'm in some kind of chamber but it's kind of dark. I need to find a light switch or a flashlight. Maybe that's part of the game. There's a little bag marked 'PC' in the corner of the screen. I think we're supposed to collect tools first. Maybe we're inside a closet."

*"It's a new level of interactive fiction,"* his uncle had said. *"It will run on any computer but there are some special effects if you use it on your own."*

Ben could feel the pulse throbbing in his neck. "How does your bedroom look?"

"Room? Like it always does? A bed, bookcase, couple of lamps, my stuffed bear Theodore, endless boring homework. What's that got to do with anything?"

Ben cut her off. "Nothing's changed?"

"No. Why?"

"Can you see what's in my room?" He panned the web cam from left to right. His hands shook violently.

"Eeew! Disgusting! Don't you ever clean up? Carlos you're going to need shots when you leave," Serise said.

"Grace, what operating system are you on?"

"My mom's old PC running at 3 gigahertz. I think it's a Wintel ultra-millennium. Mom borrowed my laptop for her trip. Just got it back and haven't set it up yet."

"Get off that thing and get on your Mac," Carlos yelled.

"Why?"

"Just do it! Do it now!" Ben and Carlos yelled in unison.

"Okay. Wait a minute." Grace logged off. Less than a minute later she was back online. "Okay, I transferred the files and I'm rebooting the game. Hmmm, that's odd."

"What's happening?" Ben asked.

"Password changed. Darn. I've got to start all over again. Unless . . ."

While Grace tapped on her keyboard, Serise and April danced behind her, lip-synching to a song.

"Hmmm," Grace said.

"What? What?" Ben yelled.

"This time the password was my name. It was 'Grace'."

"Is the corridor still there?"

"Yeah. Everything else looks the same. Hold on a minute. The game started from scratch so there's no way to zoom forward yet."

"*. . . beta test it with some of your friends and tell me if it's any good.*"

"Hurry up!" Ben nearly choked from lack of air.

"I'm hurrying, I'm hurrying! The computer's got to recompute all those codes using my name as a key. This better be good."

"Oh, it's better than good," Carlos said, his voice cracking. "It's so awesome I want Ben's uncle to adopt me. If my dad's computer games work like this, I'm playing without him."

"Remember, white is zero, black is one!" Ben shouted.

"I know! Geez! Hey! One of the jars moved. The second one on the left."

"Ignore it!" Ben yelled, trying to maintain control. "We'll figure out the jars later! Just put in your coordinates!"

"Okey dokey. I'm punching in the code."

"Now what do you see?"

Grace gasped. There was a long pause. Ben heard April squeal with delight. Serise mumbled something about a "wicked vision quest."

"Grace? You there?"

"My room," she whispered. "It's . . . oh my . . . it's filled with . . ."

Grace rose and gazed up at some unseen thing. Serise looked thunderstruck. April clamped her hands over her mouth.

"Grace! With what? Your room is filled with what?"

There was another long pause, followed by a weak reply.

". . . the Terra Cotta Army."

# CHAPTER TWELVE

# Rapa Nui

"You can't cross the sea merely by staring at the water."

• *Rabindranath Tagor*

• Ben stared up into the nostrils of a giant stone head. Hundreds more lay scattered on the ground. It was as if the stone giants were marching out to sea when they became trapped by an unseen force.

The landscape was barren — no trees to offer shelter or shade — but the breeze was warm and pleasant against his skin.

Breeze?

He could make out a faint outline of his bedroom curtains fluttering above the ocean. The breeze was real, not a computer manufactured hallucination. Even so, he could practically smell the ocean's pungent salty spray. Dry grass crunched beneath his feet as he walked.

Carlos gasped. "Whoa! What's happening?"

"Beats me. Don't think this type of technology is part of an archeology toolbox. My uncle must have had help. How can a disk do this?"

"Who cares? This is slick. If he markets this he's going to make millions!"

"You don't think . . ."

"Think what?"

"Never mind," Ben said. "Stupid thought."

"What could be more bizarre than this?" Carlos asked.

"Think he works for some new top-secret gaming company? I heard him say something about a family business. Think that's the hint? That they've got technology even the government doesn't have yet?"

"It's as good an explanation as any," Carlos said. "We won't know for sure until we solve this right? If he can invent things like this can you imagine how huge the surprise is going to be? You are going to be sooooo rich if he can pull this off."

Ben grinned. Forget his parents. He'd suck-up to Uncle Henry then hit him up for a car when he turned sixteen.

Within minutes the landscape solidified. Ben felt hard, cool stone beneath his hand.

"Whoa! Grace? Can you hear us? What's happening on your end?"

"They're real. The Terra Cotta soldiers. I can touch them. There are hundreds of them. If they weren't so dusty you'd swear they could come to life any minute."

"So what do we do now?" asked April.

"Look for treasure, I guess," Ben said, still gawking. "Or at least clues to a treasure map. Last team to collect all the keys has to drink my mother's breakfast juice for a week."

"Deal!" April said. "We've got more people. You're both going to be gagging and barfing for days!"

Ha! Not with Serise AND April on the other team. That gave Grace two handicaps. "See ya back at the Guardian."

"I had a thought," Carlos said. "You said there were booby traps."

"Yeah. They were pretty gross," Ben said.

"So these holograms kind of put a new spin on things. I mean they're solid. What happens if we mess up?"

"Right? What do we do about the booby traps?" asked Serise.

"We'll notify your next of kin!" Ben laughed and waved goodbye.

"Okay," Carlos said," I think I've got my bearings. It's been a long time since I've been here."

"You've been here before?"

Carlos nodded.

"Then why didn't you recognize the name when we dialed it?"

"Because it was a long time ago and my parents didn't call it Rapa Nui. They called it a terra something. Like terra firma? Firm land? But I do remember some stuff. Like, see that line of statues down there?"

"Yeah."

"They're called Moai. I'm guessing we're at Rano Raraku. It's a dormant volcano." He pointed toward the ocean. "Down there is Ahu Tongariki. That seems to be where these heads were headed." He cracked up over his corny joke.

Ben groaned. He was still thinking about the booby trap issue. These heads were huge. If they opened their mouths they could swallow him whole. If they climbed out of the ground, they could flatten him with one step. There would be no way to outrun or outmaneuver them.

"So where do you want to start?" asked Carlos. "Up that hill? Or down by the shore?"

Ben took another visual sweep of the landscape. "I vote for the water. Let's go see what's down there."

They trudged a half-mile down the slope as if the bedroom had no walls. Although it was just an illusion, the walk seemed hard on his calves. It was a slick trick. He'd figure out how the technology worked later.

At the shore, a line of Moai stood with their backs to the water. Ben counted fifteen in all, each a different size. Each with a different face. They were larger than the ones on the hill — in part because they weren't buried up to their necks. Their long fingers wrapped around their sides and held up their potbellies. Ben barely came up to their elbows. *How big were the others?*

The second Moai on the right was the only one wearing a hat. A round, red hat. Ben wondered if that was significant. Like the others, the bare-chested warrior wore only a loincloth and had scrollwork engraved on its backside. Something else struck Ben about the statue. It had a broad nose. The Moai on the hill all had thin, pointed noses. This one had a big wide nose that was . . . just like his.

"These don't face the water. Is that a clue? Why walk down here then turn around to face the land?" Ben asked, not expecting an answer.

"I'm not sure they're supposed to. According to my dad, a lot of them were restored by scientists who were guessing. There weren't any records except some wooden tablets called Rongorongo. The writing looks like lizard hieroglyphics."

"You're making that up."

"Am not!"

"You're kind of a walking search engine," Ben said, mostly envious.

"Just dragged everywhere as a kid," Carlos said. "I told you, expeditions are overrated. Be careful what you wish for."

"We're still kids," yelled April from the other side of the monitor.

"You're a kid," corrected Serise. "I'm thirteen, thank you very much. A few years from now I'll be driving." Her voice grew fainter as Ben and Carlos walked.

"Guys," Ben yelled. "Meet back at the computer in a half hour to compare notes. Look for treasure or some sort of marker. Might be Egyptian if it leads back to the home base."

No one answered. He hoped they heard.

"Okay, Carlos. Let's look for something unusual."

Carlos snorted. "And this isn't it?"

"Good point. Let's look for something even more unusual. A clue or a jewel or a mutant monster."

"Got hundreds to choose from," Carlos said. "Think they move?"

Ben grimaced. "I hope not. There's no 'Try Again' button out here."

They examined each of the silent sentinels. There was nothing unusual beyond the obvious. No mysterious symbols. No medallion to dial home. How would they get back?

Ben scrambled onto the chest of a statue laying nearby. "Guess this one got kicked off the team. Hey! Bud! Do you answer questions? Are you lying on the treasure? Could you roll over? Bet you snore with a big honker like that on your face! Yo! Dude!"

Carlos waved for him to stop. "What are you trying to do? Insult it so it will get up and crush us?"

Ben laughed and scrambled down. He spotted another statue off to the right — a lone figure facing out to sea. "That must be the coach!"

The "coach" bore different marks on its loincloth and buttocks. Ben touched a shallow depression in its back. The cold stone grew warm as he pushed his hand further into the space. The sound of stone sliding against stone filled the air. Ben whipped his head around in time to see the remaining statues pivoting to face the sea.

"You're the man!" Carlos gave Ben a high five as he ran toward them. The one with the red topknot advanced like a chess piece, revealing a set of dark stone steps. Hieroglyphics covered the walls.

"Booby trap?" asked Carlos, taking a step backward.

Ben just stared.

"Your game. You go first," Carlos said.

"Guests always go first," Ben said, bowing chivalrously.

Carlos frowned and shook his head vigorously. "My people come from a long line of sacrifice, and I don't mean that in a positive way. You go."

Ben considered the suggestion. If you hit a booby trap you didn't really "die" you just got returned to the altar. He could live with that. It wasn't as if he was on the real Easter Island. He peered into the darkness then stepped inside.

The dank cramped chamber filled with a low light as he entered. The rough walls were littered with crude paintings and carvings. A single set of tablets lay on the ground. Ben turned to make sure Carlos was right behind him — he was — then picked them up.

"Rongorongo. Told you," Carlos said.

"Okay, but how do we read them?" Ben said.

"I'm stumped," Carlos said, dejected.

"We need the Choedon's," Ben added, feeling like they'd hit yet another dead end. "They eat up stuff like this!"

"Or my parents," Carlos said. "They speak a bunch of weird languages. Sometimes they use one if they don't want me to know what they're talking about." He paused as if he had revealed something private. "Okay fine, I'll admit it. We need Serise's magic decoder."

Ben groaned. What was with all this decoding stuff anyway? He wished his uncle would just pick one dead language and stick with it.

This was a treasure hunt not a stupid training course for communicating with extinct civilizations.

The tablet glowed when he ran his fingers over the lizard markings. The words changed to something even more obscure. Ben kept pressing the tablet until he saw Spanish — or what looked like Spanish.

Carlos raised his arms in victory. "I can read that!" When he grabbed the tablets the letters reverted to Rongorongo. He groaned then cycled through the options until he found the Spanish translation. "Finally," he grinned. "Something we can both pilot."

"Construimos guardianes de piedra para montar guardia sobre nuestra isla y proteger a nuestro pueblo del mal."

"Gee thanks, Carlos. That clears up everything," said Ben, rolling his eyes.

Carlos laughed. "Just messin' with ya," He translated into English.

"We built guardians of stone to stand watch
over our island and protect our people from evil."

"Clearly it didn't work," Ben interjected.
Carlos continued reading.

"Something evil brought the slave traders.
Missionaries came, offering salvation
and hope — bringing with them disease,
devastation and death. We hid from both.
It was futile. The evil found us."

"Does it say what the evil was? Should we be watching out for something?" asked Ben.

"No," Carlos said. "I don't think they recognized it until it was too late."

"A treasure was lost — carried east — to Peru.
We can no longer summon the Moai.
In time the last of us shall be gone.
And the world shall cease to exist."

Ben scowled and threw up his hands. "I knew it! It IS a secret way to teach us history."

"Yeah, but who cares?" Carlos said. "This is way more fun than reading about it in a book."

"So then how do we get to Peru?" Ben pointed towards the water. "Got an inflatable boat in your backpack?"

"No, but there are dialing codes on the tablet." Carlos looked at his watch. "Uh oh. I've got to get home soon. Maybe the dialer is back by those big stone heads."

"Either that or we'll have to swim. It's a long way though — to Peru that is." Ben led the way out of the chamber and studied the fifteen Moai.

*What secrets are you hiding?*

"See anything?" Carlos asked.

"Nope."

There was nothing about the positions of the Moai on the hill to suggest a medallion.

Ben examined the Moai with the red hat. "I have this one pegged for Center."

"Center of what?" Carlos said, running his fingers across the Moai's belly as if searching for a secret button.

"Center on a basketball team," Ben said.

Carlos groaned. "Seriously? This game is like the greatest invention of all time and you're still thinking about basketball?"

"Basketball is my ticket out of Sunnyslope," Ben said, nodding enthusiastically.

Carlos shook his head. He walked in and out of the statues before returning to the Moai Ben called *The Center*. "We need to find something round. Could be up in the crater or even in this belly button." He jabbed the statue with his index finger. Moai slid backwards and descended into the ground.

Ben and Carlos gawked. The head stopped halfway down, buried up to its nostrils.

"Okay!" Ben said. "That's a clue. What kind? I don't know, but it's a clue!" He looked into the face of the Moai, half expecting it to speak to him. But it didn't. Ben studied the hat. It was the only Moai with a hat — a round hat.

A round hat!

"Could that be the dialer?" asked Ben.

"Doubt it," Carlos said. "No markings."

"Not on THIS side. What about the top?" Ben stood on his toes but it was no use. The Moai was too tall. He needed something to stand on. The only options were the exiled Moai lying on the ground yards away — too heavy — or Carlos.

"Give me a leg up!"

Carlos cocked his head to the side. "You've got to be kidding."

"You see any other way to find the dialer?"

"It wouldn't be up there. Too tall."

"Maybe, but you know we can't rule anything out."

"Awww man!" Carlos placed the Rongorongo tablets on the ground, scrunched up his face, then cupped his hands and held them out. Ben placed his oversized Sky-Jump sneaker inside Carlos's palms and pushed upward. He brushed his fingertips across the top of the hat and felt grooves — circular grooves. Grabbing the top of the hat, Ben tried to use leverage to peer over the top. But Carlos stumbled backwards sending them both tumbling to the ground.

"Sorry!" Carlos said, laying flat on his back.

Ben rubbed his sore bottom. "There's something up there. Let's try again."

"My turn," Carlos said. "Besides, you're the one with the giant muscles, Mr. Universe."

"We needed more height. I couldn't see over the top."

"So let me sit on your shoulders!"

Ben looked at Carlos as if he had lost his mind.

"Come on. We've only got a few minutes before I have to go home. Remember? Expedition in your future if we solve this. Can YOU stand to have Serise ahead of us? Or April?"

Ben gave Carlos his most evil look, then knelt so Carlos could climb on his shoulders. It was like trying to hoist a rhinoceros. "Stop wiggling," he said, as he teetered back to his feet.

"It's up here!" Carlos kicked his feet, pummeling Ben in the chest as he tried to stand on his shoulders. "You can't see it at first, but when you touch it glows. Hand me the tablets."

"No! I'll read the numbers and you dial."

Ben stooped to pick up the tablets, then struggled to his feet again. His thighs burned from the effort. Carlos wobbled then gripped the topknot and hoisted himself up.

"How do I get up there?" asked Ben.

"Maybe you don't need to. I'll hold your hand before I push the final code."

Horrified, Ben asked, "And what if only my arm goes with you?"

Carlos burst out laughing. "Then I'll bring it back! I promise!"

Ben reluctantly cycled through the options until he found the Spanish entry. Something nagged at him, so he cycled past Spanish and through several more versions. Ten entries later he found it — English. Carlos' translation was accurate. No codes to break this time, but there were new options to choose from.

Machu Picchu

13 06S 72 35W


Llactapata

13 13 S 75 49W


Pisco Islas Ballestas

13 43 S, 76 15W

"I don't see a code for Peru. I knew it was too easy."

"Hold the tablets up so I can see." Carlos scooted to the edge of the Moai on his belly. "Okay! Got it." He scooted back to the middle of the hat.

"What are you doing?"

"Dialing." Carlos grunted as he struggled to reach each of the nodes. "Llactapata is in Peru."

"How do you know that?" asked Ben. "Have you been there too?"

"No, it's where my dad went this week. With the National Geographic Team." Carlos counted "Uno, dos, tres," then reached down to grab Ben's hand as a light shot out of the top of the Moai.

# CHAPTER THIRTEEN

# Pop Goes the Weasel

"What we see depends mainly on what we look for."

• *John Lubbock*

• Eyes clamped shut, Ben maintained a tight grip on Carlos's hand and braced for whatever new weirdness the game had in store. When he finally had the courage to look he was relieved to find his entire body still intact. He released his grip on Carlos. The ground was covered with grass, ferns and purple flowers. If he lost his balance this time, there would be plenty of vegetation to cushion his fall.

Carlos completed his own personal inventory, then collapsed on the granite platform. A stone obelisk rose ten feet above him, covered in more hieroglyphics. Ruins were scattered along the side of a steep slope that was surrounded by larger, snow-covered mountains. Ben had difficulty drawing enough oxygen from the thin, cold air. His chest tightened.

"You okay?" whispered Ben, still cradling the tablet in his right arm.

"Fine," Carlos said.

"Is this it? Llactapata?" Ben asked.

Carlos put his hand up to his eyes and peered into the fog. "I don't know."

Mist shrouded the jungle and partially concealed the people working at the site. Porters darted back and forth, unloading bundles and setting up camp. Some hacked through the tangled brush with large machetes, while the scientists armed with digital cameras, picks, brushes, computers and satellite phones examined a wall forty yards away. The jungle was alive with the sound of chirping birds and insects.

Two scientists, a man and a woman, walked within ten feet of Ben and Carlos without giving them a single glance. Even so, Ben crouched low and hugged the tablets to his body. Large leafy vines kept him hidden in shadows. From the look of the overgrown plants, this part of the site had not yet been discovered. The computer generated avatars looked like the real thing.

"Did you hear what they said?" Ben whispered, unable to translate their Spanish dialect.

"They found a ceremonial chamber," Carlos said. "Something about sacrifices, drainage holes and sun worship. Sounds very gory."

"Sounds like a clue!" said Ben.

"Sacrifice. Remember?" Carlos whispered. "There might be booby traps. Do you want to be a human sacrifice even if it's a computer simulation?"

"No, but maybe we should follow them anyway." Ben shivered. In fact, he was freezing. "Hey? You cold?"

Carlos shrugged. "No. I feel fine."

Goosebumps erupted on Ben's arms. "Well, I can't breathe. There's no oxygen up here."

"We're in the Andes Mountains," Carlos said. "That would put us pretty high in the atmosphere. Air is thinner, but you'll survive because we're really in your bedroom. It's just your imagination about the air."

Ben gulped air to push oxygen into his lungs. Through the leaves, he spotted a lone scientist — dark, shoulder-length hair, neat mustache and goatee — sitting on a low wall near the excavation site. The man took a long slow drink from a flask then placed it into a bright red pouch slung across his chest. Jotting notes into a digital tablet, he pointed a device at the ruins. A laser shot out of the opening, expanded into a triangular arc of red light, then bounced back.

Ben blinked. Despite the distance and the mist, the scientist looked a lot like Carlos's father. But this was a game. It was just a coincidence that they dialed the same place where Dr. Lopez had gone. Of course his uncle would program sites into the game that were visited by the parents. That would make it easier for Ben to figure out the clues.

Another man joined the first — short black hair, slender build. He looked like Grace's father. But Dr. Choedon wasn't in Peru. He was on his way back from the United Nations headquarters in New York. The men looked so real, Ben had to keep reminding himself that this was just a simulation. He stood to get a better look. Across the valley, a storm cloud loomed, dark and menacing. It enveloped a nearby mountain, then hovered as if waiting for new prey. A warm breeze settled over Ben making it easier to breathe. He gulped air to replenish his starving lungs.

The first scientist narrowed his eyes, then pulled a pair of binoculars from a brown backpack sitting on the ground. He stood, panned the jungle and paused to examine the storm cloud. Seconds later, he continued his visual sweep of the area before stopping in Ben's direction. He gestured to the other scientist who followed his colleague's line of sight, then glanced up at the sky. The Dr. Choedon avatar looped something around his ear and spoke into a tiny wireless headphone.

"Either they see us, or they've just discovered the location of our ruins," said Ben. "I want to get closer and listen in case it's another clue."

"Huh?" Oblivious to this new set of events, Carlos continued to examine the dial. "Ben? Do you remember the code for Sunnyslope? I've got to get home before my mother has a cow."

"Yeah, in a minute. It's on the tablets. Look over at that wall on the right! Don't those guys look a lot like your dad and Dr. Choedon?"

As Ben spoke, both scientists retrieved their gear, retreated into the jungle, and disappeared into the fog. Others broke from the main site and hurried into the jungle behind them.

"Who are you talking about? Where? I don't see anyone over there."

*POP!*

The hologram disappeared.

Frowning, Ben's mother stood in the doorway of Ben's bedroom. Aris lay perched in her arms, his glowing eyes fixed on Carlos who balanced precariously on top of Ben's bookcase. The computer showed a PBS website on Easter Island. Instead of the wooden tablets, Ben found himself cradling an oversized book on the history of the National Basketball Association.

His mother took a long look at the basketball book in Ben's hands. "Uh huh." Her tone was half amused, half exasperated. "Carlos? When you're done bonding with the bookcase your mother has asked for you to come home. Your father's home early. Ben? Dinner's ready. You can eat when you can tell me how to compute a hypotenuse."

In the monitor, Ben could see Grace hiding something behind her back. Her eyes were wide, but her mouth was clamped shut.

Grace's mother peered into the camera. "Hi Medie! April's fine. We'll make sure she gets home safely."

"Thanks. See you tomorrow bright and early!" Ben's mother scanned the room one more time, then ejected the disk and waved it at Ben. "You can have this back when you pass the math exam. At the rate you're going, that will be two hundred years from now. I've got April's copy so there will be no cheating." She walked out of the bedroom.

Ben and Carlos winced, looked around the newly restored bedroom, then, in unison, mouthed the word AWESOME!

As soon as Dr. Choedon left her daughter's room, Grace brought her arms to the front and, with a triumphant grin, held out her stuffed bear, Theodore.

The camera feed suddenly went dark.

Ben and Carlos stared at each other without muttering a word. But it was clear they were thinking along the same wavelength.

A phone call shattered the silence. Ben put Grace on speaker.

"You guys okay?" asked Ben.

"What happened?" asked April. "Did someone hit an escape key by accident?"

"Don't know," Ben said. "Grace? What's up with the bear? Is it a clue?"

"I was holding something else a minute ago. A Tibetan statue with an emerald."

"Wicked vision quest," Serise said. "Kind of makes me want to do that sweat lodge thing with you guys in the morning."

"That was AWESOME!" repeated Carlos. "AWESOME! Felt like we were actually there!"

Ben was still focused on Grace's earlier comment. "You found a statue?"

"Oh! Yes!" Her trance broken, Grace became very animated. "We found clues near the emperor's tomb. The soldiers are guardians to protect him from evil. We skipped the actual tomb because it's supposed to be booby trapped, and nobody wanted to die even if it was just a computer simulation, but we found a dialer under one of the soldiers."

"It was cool," April interrupted. "It moved when I touched it. There was a hidden room."

"We found a scroll and used the clues to find the next destination," Grace explained at an increasingly rapid pace. "Serise looked at the pattern on the scroll and said it reminded her of Navajo sand paintings. But I thought it looked like Buddhist sand paintings. So we had to pick — Arizona or Tibet? We went to a Tibetan Monastery but the platform was empty. So I said we should backtrack and go to Arizona, figuring that Native Americans once traveled from Asia to North America on an ancient land bridge. But Serise reminded me that the land bridge was gone before the Terra Cotta army was built. Then we remembered that the jewel could have traveled with the Dalai Lama when he went into exile after China invaded Tibet. So we went to India and a monk gave us the statue."

Ben sighed. Grace hardly stopped to take a breath. Carlos nodded as if he had followed the whole trail of logic.

"Let me get this straight. A monk gave you something? You could talk to him?"

"He didn't say much. Just that he was expecting us and that we were on the 'path of enlightenment', whatever that means. At first, I thought we'd have to do some martial arts fighting because that seems like your uncle's style. But your uncle promised there wouldn't be any violence so we showed the monk the diagram on the scroll. He pointed to a sand painting of three girls walking toward the sun, then he took us to a secret chamber and gave us the statue. Oh! And he gave us a star chart with a triangle pointing to the letter 'S'."

*So much for being ahead.* Ben wanted to ask how they were able to accomplish so much in a such short time, but realized he was competing against Serise's instant programming skills, Grace's supercomputer brain, and April the straight-A obnoxious teacher's pet.

"But what do we do now?" April asked. "Grace's mom just took the laptop!"

"Why?" asked Ben.

"She said there was too much homework, a big math test on Monday and that Ben was a bad influence."

"Hey! I resent that!" Ben said.

Grace winced. "Can we play on your computer? We're stoked and on a roll. We need to find out what the emerald does when we get it back to the altar. We can retrace our steps."

"We don't have to," Serise said. "I linked the games when we decoded the pigpen clues. Anything done on either game should have transferred data files to the other."

"Doesn't do us any good," Carlos said. "Ben's mother took his disk."

"Why?" Grace asked.

"I still haven't figured out how to compute a hypotenuse."

"A squared plus B squared equals C squared," Serise yelled, clearly exasperated. "How basic can you get? Just add the sum of the squares of the two sides adjacent to the right angle of a triangle then take the square root of that. Easy!"

Ben groaned. "Gee thanks. I'll try that."

"We've got to get that disk back," Carlos said.

"We can use mine!" April yelled, elated.

"Sorry, but Mom has confiscated all known copies in the Webster household."

Everyone slumped. After a few minutes, Ben perked up. "Yes! We can still play!"

"How do you figure that?" asked Grace.

"Did your mother take both computers or just yours?"

"Just mine. The PC's still here."

"How does that help . . . ?" Carlos paused. Ben could tell the answer was dawning on him.

"Grace. Is the downloaded version still on that computer?"

"Yes!" Grace said, throwing her hands up with joy.

"But it doesn't do those cool 3-D graphics," April said.

Ben grinned. "Not on her PC. But if she transfers the files back to me over the Internet . . ."

"The data files from our trip are still on Ben's hard drive!" Serise said.

Grace slapped Serise's hand. "Yes! We're back in the game! The transmission's on its way." Within seconds, Grace reestablished their connection. She was beaming.

"Carlos! I'm sure I don't have to repeat myself!" yelled Ben's mother.

"Yes, Ma'am." Carlos raised his hand and extended his thumb and little finger into the sign of a phone receiver and mouthed, *Call me!* before rushing out of the bedroom. It sounded as if he cleared the staircase in three leaps.

"You're awesome," he said, once he and Grace were alone. "I can't believe how far we've gotten."

"Ben! Get off that computer. NOW!" His mother's voice boomed up the stairs. "Good night, Grace," she added sweetly.

"Want to know the answer to my riddle before I log off?" Ben whispered.

"Nope. I'll figure it out." Grace winked but her smile said everything. *Best friends forever.*

# CHAPTER FOURTEEN

# The Vision Quest

"Where there is no vision, there is no hope."

• *George Washington Carver*

• What would the Paradise Circle dads think up next? It was midmorning but the temperature was cooler than normal. Ben stood at the entrance of the sweat lodge and almost looked forward to the heat. He adjusted his makeshift toga and wondered if Serise's walkie-talkie was still hidden in the ferns. He considered checking but didn't want to get Serise in trouble. They needed her programming skills.

"I hope this doesn't take too long," Ben said after Carlos jogged across the lawn and joined him. "I spent all night thinking up game strategies. I can't wait to try the holograms again."

Carlos dragged over two lawn chairs and sat down. "I know. We've got to catch up with the girls. There were two more locations on the Rongorongo tablet. Did we go to the wrong place?"

"I don't think so." Ben sank into the other chair. Frank Lopez and Shan Choedon were deep in conversation with his father but glanced in his direction occasionally. He couldn't get over how much they looked like the computer-generated avatars in the game. Ben smiled at them, shot air balls at the lodge, then lowered his voice. "Wouldn't lost tribes be in a long-forgotten jungle?"

"That would be my guess. Machu Picchu is a bunch of ruins on the top of a mountain but it's out in the open and its filled with tourists."

Ben's jaw dropped. "You've been there too? You lucky dog!"

"Told ya, I've been dragged everywhere." Carlos scowled. "And Islas Ballestas? I looked it up on the Internet while Mom was in the shower. They're islands. The only things living there are birds and sea animals. It's completely covered with poop."

Ben grimaced. "I'm glad we didn't dial that location. Can you imagine what realistic smells and bird slime were waiting for us?"

"Getting slimed by a bird is supposed to be good luck. But from the look of that place, I doubt it." Carlos shot his own air ball at the lodge, then waved at the dads who continued whispering and nodding towards them.

"That island sounds pretty disgusting. Has to be a booby trap," Ben said.

"Or it might be where we're supposed to go. You said we couldn't rule anything out. The question is, how are we going to get back on your computer without getting caught?"

Ben frowned. "Can we play at your house if I burn a disk?"

"No can do. Our computer is in the kitchen. The one in Dad's office is strictly off limits."

"What if you come over for dinner tonight?" Ben asked.

Carlos scowled as if he had eaten something sour. "No offense but I can still taste your mother's tofu bean curd casserole from the back-to-school picnic two months ago."

"I hear ya. It's hopeless." Ben's stomach grumbled. Dr. Hightower said the sweat lodge worked better if everyone fasted first. The alternative was his mother's vitamin drink, so he was grateful that he'd been granted the stay of execution. The flower garden should be thanking him too.

A thought jolted Ben. "Hey, Carlos. You ever been sick?"

"Huh?"

"Sick. Broken leg? Sprained Ankle? Cold? Flu? Anything?"

Carlos creased his brow and shrugged. "Better knock on wood or the sweat lodge before we lose all our good luck, I guess."

"How about a doctor? Ever have to go?"

"Yeah. Kind of a weirdo but mom likes her. I do too. Dr. Danine doesn't believe in shots. Think the sweat lodge will make us sick?"

"No," Ben said, rising from his chair as the fathers gestured toward the sweat lodge. "Just wondered."

He'd seen Dr. Danine too and so had Grace. Sunnyslope had hundreds of doctors but they'd all seen the same pediatrician.

◆

"Thank you for coming," David Hightower said as he emerged from the sweat lodge. There were no traces of moisture on his body. "This experience is best shared with close friends."

He and Dr. Choedon stood on opposite sides of a sand painting at the entrance to the lodge. The detail was intricate with pictures of people, animals, and hieroglyphics — some Ben recognized, some he didn't. He wondered how they were able to put it together so fast. It wasn't there two days before. A sand "paint-by-numbers" kit was the only explanation.

"Careful not to disturb the mandala," Dr. Choedon said, "It is part of the ritual."

Once inside the lodge, Dr. Hightower smudged ash on everyone's foreheads and cheeks before directing them clockwise around a pit of steaming boulders. It seemed to Ben that Dr. Hightower slathered extra ash on him and Carlos.

"What's this stuff?" Ben asked, stifling a sneeze.

"Burnt sage," said Dr. Hightower. "Today, we will focus on the gifts of our ancestors and pray for wisdom and guidance. I should warn that if you have an illness, this is best left for another time. It is a grueling test of endurance."

That was Ben's cue to leave. Carlos blocked his way. "Mental illness doesn't count. If I have to stay, you have to stay."

Ben sat, cross-legged, on the ground and pondered his current predicament. "This is great," he whispered to Carlos. "Today's entertainment is staring at a bunch of naked men bonding in a broiling backyard sauna. Is it my imagination or have the nutty professors been working out?"

"Shhh!" Dr. Lopez said in a low hiss.

Ben knew better than to respond. Dr. Lopez could be fierce when he was upset. He was fierce when he wasn't. But the Paradise Circle dads looked like they'd been hanging out in a gym. His own father's body suddenly seemed chiseled. Flawless. When did his dad get six-pack abs? Couldn't be from those morning exercises. Ben wondered why he hadn't noticed before — or the odd tattoo on the inside of his father's shoulder. Was that new? He squinted but couldn't make out the detail.

Ben poked his own muscles. Rock hard and bigger than the day before. He pictured himself on the cover of Men's Health and smiled with satisfaction.

Serise's father hummed and chanted in his native language as he poured water over the red-hot boulders piled high inside the earthen pit. The temperature inside the lodge was the equivalent of a raging inferno. What was the heat source? Ben had not seen any charcoal. He wondered if there was a hidden extension cord connected to a heating coil. Steam rose from the rocks making the situation worse.

"I assume the rocks are heated outside and brought in afterwards. Is that right David?" Ben's father asked, his voice almost a whisper.

"Yes, can't heat them inside," Dr. Hightower said. "The carbon monoxide would kill us. The rocks retain the heat for quite a while. If it gets too hot you may go outside to refresh yourself. There are bottles of spring water in the cooler."

Outside? Ben stared at the boulders in disbelief. They had to weigh a ton. "How'd you get them inside if they were heated outside?"

"A little ingenuity," Dr. Hightower said. "Now, to continue, we must meditate on our connection to all things, and our relationship with the elements; fire, water, earth, air. As your meditation deepens and your quest begins, you may enter an altered state of mind."

"Aren't we supposed to smoke a pipe or eat some mushrooms?" Ben asked.

"Hallucinogens are an artificial path," his father said. "Get in the spirit. Feel the energy flow through you or practice some Spanish and bring your grade up. Whatever you do, show some respect!"

Ben shot his father a dirty look. He was safe. His father wouldn't see his expression in the darkened tent.

The pebble that grazed his thigh suggested otherwise.

"Hózhóogo naasháa doo," Serise's father chanted. "Shitsiji' hózhóogo naasháa doo."

Ben lay on his back, closed his eyes and waited for his vision. About now he was hoping a ghost or Uncle Henry's evil computer skeleton would appear. Something, *anything* that would break up the monotony.

"Carlos?" Ben whispered.

"What?"

"You're used to high altitudes and low levels of oxygen. If I don't suffocate first, I'm going to sweat to death. You can have my computer when I die."

"Okay," he whispered. "You've got a slick set-up. If I die first, the answers to the math homework and notes for the test are on my desk."

"Deal."

"Silence!" Ben's father said.

Carlos's father threw a handful of grass at them to make the same point.

"Shikéédéé' hózhóogo naasháa doo. T'áá altso shinaagó hózhóogo naasháa doo."

Ben rolled over to Carlos and whispered, "You don't think she is going to — "

"No, she wouldn't dare," Carlos whispered back.

"Ben!" His father growled.

Ben returned to his prone position and wiggled his feet. They were the only things on his body that weren't covered in sweat. *You put your right foot in, you put your right foot out . . .* He mentally sang "The Hokey Pokey" for a few stanzas until he ran out of things to "put in." He extended his big toe forward. *This little piggy . . .*

*"Jemadari! Askar makamu sonara!"*

A man's voice broke his concentration. His spirit guide was leading him to the brink of insanity.

Noises filled his head . . . mechanical, pulsating, pinging. The sounds were rhythmic, like a heartbeat. And then more nonsense — *"Akoosh consat!"* — a language he didn't understand. Or that someone made up.

*Someone?*

*Serise!* Ben was going to get even with her when he got out of the lodge.

A woman's voice whispered in his ear, soft and pleading, *"Don't go! The tribes are doomed. You are not."*

Startled, Ben bolted upright and looked around in the dim light. Everyone else was in deep meditation or asleep. Carlos's snoring was a dead giveaway.

*"Mission aborted . . ."*

A muffled voice answered. *"Still time . . ."*

Despite the thick, stifling heat, goose bumps broke out all over Ben's arms.

*"Okay, Serise. Give it a rest!"*

No one else seemed to be bothered by Serise's practical joke. The rest of the sweat lodge was quiet except for occasional prayers and chanting from Dr. Hightower.

"Házhó náhásdlíí. Házhó náhásdlíí"

◆

Ben didn't know how long he had been listening to strange chants and rhythmic noises but he was completely spooked. Sweat poured down his body. He opened his eyes and found no hovering ghosts, no mischievous poltergeists and no moving items. The voices stopped abruptly.

"Time to go," his father said, tapping him on the shoulder. "Let's get some cold water into you. Carlos is outside with Frank."

Dizzy and disoriented, Ben plotted his revenge against Serise. But his first priority was retreat to the comfort and safety of a cold bath.

He held his arms up and turned counterclockwise to maximize the surface area exposed to the breeze. Pulling water from the cooler he drank greedily before dousing the remainder over his head.

He jerked backward when he realized he was standing on the mandala. It had changed. The sand was fused into the ground as if exposed to an enormous heat source. What remained resembled a stained glass window but the delicate sand people were charcoal, black and outlined in red, as if they were engulfed in flames. Dr. Hightower and Dr. Choedon crouched and examined the damage, then carefully scooped samples into silver vials. When they finished, they stood and watched the remaining grains of the charcoal people scatter into the wind.

"Dad?"

"Yeah. What's up?"

"Did you hear voices while we were meditating?"

"Other than David? No." His eyes remained fixed on the sand painting, his hands curled into fists. "Did you?"

"No," Ben lied. "I guess I didn't get a spirit guide either." He watched Carlos walk away, his father's arm draped affectionately around his shoulder. Frank Lopez wore a thin terrycloth robe and leather flip-flops.

*A bathrobe. Duh!* Why didn't he think of that?

Ben's stomach lurched. Slung over Frank Lopez's shoulder was a red pouch and a drinking flask — the same red pouch and drinking flask Ben had seen the scientist carrying in the game —

*In Llactapata.*

Distracted and disoriented, Ben walked toward them to get a closer look.

"Ben?" His father held out a basketball-print bed sheet. "You might want this before you go back inside the house. Or were you planning to give the girls a show?"

# CHAPTER FIFTEEN

# Facing the East Wind

If one can only find it, there is a reason for everything.

• *Traditional proverb*

• Ben sat with his back to the obelisk, breathing the thin air and watching a team of archeology geeks clear another section of ruins.

*"Mission aborted. Tribes are doomed."*

Yeah, right! Serise would have to work harder than that to throw Ben Webster off his game.

He felt like a spy on a high-risk mission. His friends were banned from his room. His mom was in the kitchen cooking up a new form of human pesticide and he was sitting on a Peruvian mountain — or at least a cool simulation of it — hoping she wouldn't pick this moment to check on him.

Grace tried to play on her PC. The locations were the same but with no signs of human or animal life. Just a few hieroglyphics and star patterns. She did find an altar covered in blood. That pretty much ended her desire to explore Llactapata — even without the special effects.

A half-hour of searching the dense jungle — most of which involved being lost — turned up nothing but more ruins and a lot of annoying insects the size of his father's SUV. Ben found no clues, no gems, no secret passageways and, thankfully, no skeletons hovering to say he had not *"chosen wisely."*

What if he hit a booby trap? The hologram technology put a new spin on things. He picked up a sharp rock and squeezed it in his hand. It nicked his palm causing it to bleed. So he wasn't about to test the holographic booby trap with his life.

Ben returned to the obelisk to find the site abandoned. Was it a glitch in the software? Did it crash leaving him stuck in an alternate reality? The jungle fell silent, freaking him out even more. That was enough for Ben. As much as he hated to admit it, he couldn't do this alone — he needed his team.

Seconds later, Ben was back in his bedroom watching the green Tibetan emerald rotate above the altar in his computer monitor. The message was clear. He and Carlos were behind and the trail was not getting any warmer.

*Bounce. Bounce. Crash!*

Outside, the entire crew, including April, had assembled in Carlos' backyard. He raced out of his room and through the kitchen.

"Homework?" asked his mother, blocking his path to the door.

*Busted!*

"I'm almost done, Mom. Honest."

His mother sighed. "I don't suppose you'd let *me* help you?"

Ben pulled the math homework from his jeans pocket. "I thought I'd get some help from Carlos. I won't ask for the answers, just tips."

His mother gave a weak smile and waved him off. He reached for the door then paused. Her mood seemed odd — even for her.

"You okay?"

She nodded. "I've got to spend a few hours at the lab analyzing your uncle's plant samples. Try to do a few problems on your own before you lose track of time shooting hoops. Have fun." She rubbed his head affectionately then disappeared into the dining room.

*Have fun?*

Something was definitely wrong. And every trail lead back to Uncle Henry.

*Bounce. Bounce. Crash!*

Carlos seemed embarrassed when he saw Ben, and tossed the ball to him.

"What's up?" Ben rebounded and nailed a shot.

"We were hot on the trail of another gem, and found some more star charts," Serise said. "I snuck out of the house to see if Carlos knew what they meant."

Carlos shrugged. "Trust me. I know 'em all and these aren't it."

"Well, so far they haven't been important," Grace said. "There's two different star charts each with a triangle pointing to a letter."

"S and O? As in 'So what'?" Ben frowned. "Maybe it's a joke. You know, to throw us off the scent. Uncle Henry said the solutions weren't obvious. We're supposed to find eight Earth tribes. They wouldn't be in outer space or we'd be searching for the aliens." He shot another basket, then paused. "Wait a minute. You're still playing?"

April grinned. "Grace figured out a way to get into the holograms."

Ben caught the ball as it bounced to the ground and froze. "How? Did your mother give you your computer back?"

"No. She took my computer to work and left it there. So I transferred a copy from my PC to Serise's laptop."

"This whole thing is weird," April said. "Like we're all in the middle of a giant game even when we're not playing."

Ben sat and tossed the ball to Carlos who continued his tireless quest to nail a basket.

*Bounce. Crash!*

For once his sister was making sense. Getting back into the game without being caught was becoming a full-time job.

"Maybe we're all in the sweat lodge and this is a group hallucination. All we need now is for Serise to make weird noises."

Serise slapped her hands on her hips. "What are you talking about?"

"The sweat lodge yesterday. All those noises you were making on the walkie-talkie."

"Serise was with us the whole time," Grace said, "She won Mahjong."
Serise blushed. "Highest score ever!"

"Boy, was my mother upset," Grace said. "She's never been beaten. Ever. She's superstitious and said it was because Serise was facing the east wind. Serise kept drawing flowers and dragons from the wall. You should have seen her! Mom made sarcastic comments about the Hightowers and how it didn't matter what wind they were facing because they had an unfair advantage." Grace paused. "I've been meaning to ask you what that meant."

Serise shrugged. "I asked my mom. She laughed and did a victory dance but she didn't explain. Must be an inside joke."

"Getting back to the point," Ben sighed, "I saw you hide that walkie-talkie. Someone had to be making those voices."

"Like what?" asked Serise.

"Mission aborted. Ah coosh khan sat. Weird stuff like that. Is that Navajo?"

"I didn't hear anything," Carlos said.

"Because you were too busy snoring," Ben said.

Serise groaned. "No, it's not Navajo! You were just having a vision. Isn't that what was supposed to happen? Dad came out pretty loopy until he drank a quart of water and took a bath. Besides, my mother found my stuff the night before. She didn't tell my dad about it, but I'm grounded."

Now Ben was totally confused. "So it wasn't you?"

"No! I told you, it's just your imagination."

"Serise Antonia Hightower!"

"Oops! The warden calls." Serise tugged on Grace's arm. "Can you and April come over? I'm allowed visitors, just can't leave the house. She doesn't know about the game. We could play in secret."

Ben was furious. He was counting on the girls being stuck until he could even the score. He pleaded to Grace with his eyes. She just shrugged.

"Doesn't matter who wins, right? As long as we solve it, you still get your expedition! There's some cool places on the list. I looked them up. No blood. No sacrifices!" She waved then ran off to catch up with Serise and April.

"How about you, Carlos? Mom's softening," Ben said after the girls disappeared. "She said you could help with homework as long as you didn't do it for me. Want to come over?"

Carlos seemed to be debating the offer in his head, then scowled. "No can do. My parents told me to stick close to home while they were gone."

"Isn't my house close enough?"

"Apparently not. Their exact words were to stay out of your yard." Carlos frowned. "Want to shoot some hoops instead? Not that you need the practice."

Ben was stunned by this new revelation. "No thanks. I'll just coach." He didn't feel like playing basketball. He wanted to be back in the game. And now there was this new development. Serise was grounded. That was a first. She'd done worse things than hide a walkie-talkie and escaped without consequence. So why now? And Carlos, Boy Wonder, was on house arrest. Why were the parents trying to keep them apart?

*Crash!*

Ben had a brilliant idea. "My uncle said I couldn't ask my parents for clues but he didn't say you couldn't ask yours. Think your father can help us? I can make some sketches before Mom gets back from the lab."

Carlos shrugged. "Maybe. But I have to warn you, he's been edgy since his trip. Not a bad mood exactly, just different. Whenever I walk into a room he and Mom get quiet. They're NEVER quiet. So something is up and from the looks on their faces I'm not sure I want to know what it is."

"Okay," said Ben. "I'll see if I can collect more clues we can use. I'll try to find a safe location to go without a buddy. My uncle's always complaining that I don't know enough about Africa. I can go there."

"I'm jealous," Carlos said, crouching low and staring at the basket, "of the game and your basketball skills."

"Don't worry. Hitting a basket just takes practice." Ben studied Carlos's odd stance. He closed his eyes and tried to will the ball into the basket with his mind. Carlos definitely needed a win. "Visualize the basket. Visualize the ball IN the basket. Now shoot!"

Carlos sucked in a lung full of air, sprang forward and released the ball. It soared through the air before landing slightly off target.

"I'll get it." Ben wanted to be encouraging, but Carlos couldn't hit a target even if it had a bullseye painted on it and were inches away. He climbed over a retaining wall and jumped down into the wooded area behind the garage. The basketball was nowhere to be seen. He followed a trail to a clearing forty yards down the embankment.

"Hey, Carlos!" cried Ben. "Get down here! Quick!"

# CHAPTER SIXTEEN

# Searching for Superman

It is not good to look at the clouds
or your work will not progress.

• *Mayan Proverb*

♦ The satellite dish rose more than fifty feet into the air. Its stainless steel parabolic reflector was polished to a mirror-like finish and rested on steel beams that crisscrossed like an inverted geodesic dome. The basketball was stuck at the base of one of the arms.

Ben took a running leap, grabbed the bottom rung of a support arm, then pulled himself up. The dish hummed and shocked him with static electricity.

"Whoa!" Carlos said, as he came around the bend. "Never seen that before. I bet it's Dad's new satellite dish. How'd you get up there?"

"I jumped." Ben tossed the ball down to Carlos and was tempted to climb higher, but the humming vibrated through his body and tickled his eardrums.

"Jumped? Dude the first rung is at least fifteen feet off the ground."

Ben thought Carlos was exaggerating until he looked down and got dizzy. He lost his grip and slid down the dish, landing on the ground with a loud thump. "What a rush! So you think this is your dad's?"

Carlos helped him to his feet. "I don't know. He said he was getting a dish to listen to SETI signals. Who knew he'd buy one the size of Rhode Island?"

"Why doesn't he use a police scanner like everyone else?"

"Not city signals. *SETI* signals. Search for Extraterrestrial Intelligence."

Ben frowned. "Does anyone on this block have a normal hobby?"

Carlos laughed. "I know, right? He's so hooked on astronomy Mom finally gave in and told him he could get more equipment if it would stop his whining. I don't think this is what she meant. "

Ben tilted his head, a brilliant idea swirling around in his brain. "Do you think we could peek at his computer?"

Carlos eyes narrowed. "Why?"

"Well, think about it," Ben said. "What else are satellite dishes good for?"

"You tell me," said Carlos.

"Catching cool TV channels! I hear you can get stuff from all over the world. And this thing is huge. It must get awesome signals. Mom canceled our cable service last spring. Then she put a block on my browser. Grace and I broke the encryption code but it took a month to do it. Mom put a new one on. So far I can't crack it."

"So?" Carlos paused, then his eyes popped open as waved his hands wildly. "No! You aren't thinking what I think you're thinking?"

"Yeah!" Ben grinned broadly. "I never know what the other kids at school are talking about. Here's our chance to catch up on some cool shows. Your parents are gone, right?"

"They won't be back for an hour. But — "

"But what?" Ben said. "It can go back to searching for the planet Krypton when we're done."

Carlos looked skeptical. And then his eyebrow raised just a hair. "O.K. I'm in. But if we get caught you have to say you forced me into this and cop a plea at the trial."

"Deal!" said Ben.

◆

Star charts, graphs, and maps of the world covered the walls of Dr.

Lopez's office. All with stickpins protruding from them. Carlos was right. None of the charts matched the ones in the game. Ben peered into a cabinet filled with DVD's labeled "Death Rays from Space" and "Killer Mutant Attack." Even Dr. Lopez's computer looked as though it had come from outer space. The ancient iMac sat in the middle of an old pine desk, the monitor resting above a smooth white dome.

"Okay," Ben said, "turn it on."

Carlos took two steps backward. "You do it. If we get caught, I don't want my fingerprints on it."

Ben had barely touched the computer when it sprang to life and displayed a rendering of the solar system. "Whoa! That's faster than mine."

"He kept the shell but upgraded the guts," Carlos explained. "Why do parents get all the good stuff?"

"Because they have jobs and we have a tiny allowance." Ben laughed, then clicked on the wireless mouse. "Is this thing password protected? It's not responding." He placed the mouse back on the desk and tried again. No light glowed underneath.

"Maybe the batteries are dead." Carlos snatched the mouse from Ben's hand. It glowed red. While Carlos blew on it to dislodge dirt from the electric eye, the cursor followed his moves precisely.

Ben gulped. "I'd say your father has been doing more than upgrading. Look! It's wireless AND motion activated."

He snatched it back. The mouse stopped glowing. Ben shook it, tapped it, and waved it in elaborate loops through the air. The cursor did not respond.

"Must not like you." Carlos laughed and took it back. The cursor mirrored his graceful arcs. "Guess *I'm* the only one qualified to pilot this thing. Now what?"

"Click on the hard drive and see what happens," Ben said.

Carlos complied. Icons appeared and rotated on the screen.

"So what do they say?" Ben asked.

"Don't know. Dad must have coded the files knowing we'd sneak in here one day."

"You?" asked Ben. "You've never done a single dishonest thing in your life."

"Maybe it's because I live next door to *you*." Carlos snorted. "But now I'm mad they didn't trust me so I might as well live up to those expectations." He waved the mouse with the flourish of a maestro and clicked on the Earth icon.

The computer screen filled with tiny windows, each with its own navigation point. Carlos clicked on the upper right window. It rotated to the front and filled two-thirds of the monitor. A CNN reporter stood at the site of a massive mudslide in Ethiopia.

"I'll pass," Carlos said. "Let's see what else we can find."

Click.

"*. . . spewing ash and lava. The Chiliques volcano hasn't erupted in more than 10,000 years . . .*"

Click.

"*. . . Tsunami threatens Shikoku on the eastern coast of Japan. All residents are advised to evacuate.*"

Click.

"*. . . Scud missiles are pelting the Egyptian peninsula. No reports of detonations. Military officials theorize the materials used to make the bombs were old or defective.*"

"What is this?" asked Ben. "The disaster channel? Isn't there anything else on this thing?"

Carlos returned to the main menu and clicked another icon. More news, most in foreign languages. He rotated through the options until he found a live stream of NASA's control room.

"*. . . failure of the fuel system . . . cause unknown . . .*"

"*. . . launch is scrubbed . . . all rockets are affected.*"

"*. . . space station telemetry is down due to a solar flare.*"

"*Roger . . . third lens malfunction on the Hubble . . . lot of CME activity*"

"*. . . think we've solved the problem . . . new lens is reinforced with a titanium coating.*"

Ben groaned. "What else is on?"

Carlos scanned through endless streams of wars, disasters, U.N. assemblies and intelligence briefings at the White House.

"Where's the cartoons? The sports?" asked Ben. "How about some Sumo wrestling? What's the point of having a satellite dish if all you get is the same junk you can get on cable? Try the outer space channel."

Carlos navigated back to the main menu. "The what?"

"The signals from space. Maybe the aliens are broadcasting cartoons." Ben pointed to an icon that looked like the eight-pointed star on the game disk. "Click on that one."

The computer responded, *"Control — online — enter authorization code,"* then filled in the necessary information.

*"Password accepted."*

A third window displayed gray and black static on the right. A sliding scale appeared at the bottom of the monitor. It ranged from 1,000 MHz to 15,000 MHz. But when Carlos slid the mouse across the desk the bar froze at 10,000 MHz. More symbols popped up and waited for an authorization code.

"Ugh! More passwords." Carlos moved the bar back down the scale as if he were tuning an old fashioned radio. A faint rumble came from the backyard.

"That's probably the satellite dish rotating into alignment," Ben said. "Something that big would have to make a noise when it moved."

At 7,025 MHz they heard rhythmic oscillations inside the static.

"Wonder what that is," said Carlos.

"That would be E.T. phoning your satellite dish," mocked Ben.

Another mild vibration shook the house followed by a brief pulse.

"Did you feel that?" Carlos whispered.

"Earthquake?" Ben looked around to see if anything was moving.

"What else could it be?" said Carlos. "I'll try again."

At 4,357.37 MHz, the vibration reminded Ben of the sounds he heard in the sweat lodge. Like the steady pulse of a heartbeat. Seconds later it disappeared. "I'm detecting a pattern. Maybe this thing picks up seismic activity."

Carlos tried the scale again but found only static despite moving through the spectrum at an excruciatingly slow pace.

Ben threw up his hands in disgust. "So this is it?

"Dad's probably blocked it," Carlos said. "Wonder why you need a password to go above 10,000 MHz? And what's up with those symbols?"

"Don't know. Looked like some of the ones in the Guardian chamber. Think that's a clue?"

"Doubt it," Carlos said. "They're just Mayan numbers. I think it's just a coincidence." He returned to the main menu and clicked on the last remaining icon. The computer displayed star charts and real-time images from space but nothing useful or interesting.

Carlos glanced at his watch. "Mom and Dad will be back soon. We better get out of here." He tried to shut down the computer when a new window opened. It looked like an EKG printout. A second window displayed more graphs in rainbow colors, like a compressed radio frequency. Instructions appeared in an odd foreign language followed by a question mark and boxes marked "Si" and "No."

"Can you translate that?" asked Ben.

Carlos hesitated. "It isn't Spanish, but it looks like it's asking if we want to shut something down."

"Press 'Si' and see what happens," Ben said. "Isn't that universal for 'yes'?"

Carlos blew air past his lips. "Okay. But if we crash my dad's computer I'm going to have to move in with you until I graduate from college."

Instead of shutting down, the computer sprang into action. Downloads streamed across the screen at a heart-stopping rate hundreds of gigabytes per second.

A second window opened showing a massive satellite dish. A message at the bottom of the screen read, "Logging on to National Astronomy and Ionosphere — contacting Arecibo Observatory . . . enter remote access authorization . . . processing . . . password accepted." A third window appeared. "Contacting Project Phoenix — please stand by . . . password *confirmed.*" More than twenty windows opened in rapid succession, each with a similar message. The computer was accessing satellites and radio telescopes around the world, confirming passwords and then shrinking the windows to the size of a postage stamp before stacking them like file cards on the upper right hand corner of the screen.

Ben's hands flew up to his mouth in a panic. "What did we just do?"

"I don't know!" yelled Carlos, his eyes bugging out. "I don't know!"

Frantic, Ben ran his hands up and down the smooth dome base. "Can we stop it? Pull the plug? Carlos! Make it shut down!"

"I can't!" Carlos began hyperventilating as he swiveled the screen up and down and flicked the power switch on the mouse. "There's no cord. No plug. This thing is running on a self-contained power source." He shook the mouse violently but it glowed white and no longer responded to his commands.

Ben's heart hammered against his ribcage. His mouth went dry. His parents would ground him for life! As for Dr. Lopez's reaction — the thought was too horrible to imagine. He pressed and held the power button. The computer ignored his attempts. He tried moving the computer but it was stuck tight to the desk. He dropped to his knees and searched under the desk for a power source. Images of hiding in the Witness Protection Program flashed through his mind.

*"Telemetry data stream confirmed"*

A new window opened. Instructions, in English, revealed that Carlos had just activated SETI@ home software.

"Wait!" Carlos said. "This is the SETI program we were looking for! It uses volunteer's computers to analyze satellite signals. The software sends the data back to Berkeley when it finds something." Carlos drew his hand across his forehead in relief. "If it finishes before Dad gets home, we're in the clear."

The computer processed data at a rapid pace. *"Activating Casmir Array . . . standby . . ."* A world map was displayed. Red dots winked on across the globe. *"All systems on-line."*

"Okay," Ben said, still trying to calm his rapidly beating heart. "That makes sense. Your father must have a billion gigabytes of memory to handle all of this data."

"Don't be crazy," Carlos said. "No one makes a chip that big."

"Then how do you explain this?"

"I can't. Except . . . well . . . Wow! Who knew a satellite could do stuff like this."

Ben held his breath as he studied the lightning fast calculations. Pauses in the computation were accompanied by faint sounds from the Lopez's satellite dish and a ping from the Arecibo telescope. Spikes in the graph compressed into a flat line. Ben grew concerned that all was not what it seemed.

"Carlos?"

"Yeah?"

"Why does the satellite dish react when the graph shows a spike and not any other time?"

"It's scanning through a lot of data. I bet it only reports which frequency had activity." Carlos watched the monitor with rapt fascination. "This is kind of cool. Kind of like spy stuff."

The massive data stream continued. And then a message appeared.

*"Replicating CME . . . Confirming class X solar pulse . . ."*

"Solar pulse?"

"I think it's the same thing as a solar flare," Carlos said, looking worried again. "It can knock out a satellite. If it's strong enough, it can knock out power to a whole city."

Ben didn't have to wait long for confirmation. Within seconds, the windows in the left hand corner expanded and jumped to the front of the screen. Ben barely had time to read them as they flickered by:

*"Haystack Observatory — status — disabled."*

*"Hubble Space Telescope — status — disabled."*

*"VLBI Space Observatory — status — disabled."*

*"Max Planck Institute — status — disabled."*

*"Metsähovi Observatory — status — disabled."*

*"ESO Submillimetre — status — disabled."*

*"ARO Granada — status — disabled."*

*"SBV/MSX — status — disabled."*

Ben gasped. "What does this mean? Is this part of the program? The computer's shutting down systems all over the world!"

Carlos didn't answer. His hand covered his mouth. His eyes bugged out in horror.

*"Project Phoenix — status — off-line."*

*"NASA Deep Space Network — status . . . standby . . . connecting . . . "*

*" . . . confirmed — Canberra — off-line."*

*" . . . confirmed — Goldstone — off-line."*

*" . . .confirmed — Madrid — off-line."*

The list continued until the software had cycled through all remaining windows.

*"Reprogramming complete. All systems returned to active status. Elapsed time — 12.3 seconds."*

Ben looked at Carlos and hoped there was a logical explanation. The only word he could muster was a weak and pathetic, "Oops!"

The color drained from Carlos's face while the software began compiling data for upload to the SETI Institute. In a separate window, a graph showed the locations along the spectrum where activity was detected. Most of the spikes occurred above 10,000 MHz. And then, something unexpected happened. The computer deleted the data spikes below 10,000 MHz, replacing them with a flat line. Randomly generated pictures of static were inserted into the gaps in the graphics file.

Within minutes the computer signaled that its computations were complete. A final report concluded, *"No data detected,"* and was uploaded. Only the data below 10,000 MHz was sent. The computer logged off and closed the browser. Information above 10,000 MHz was saved to a password-encrypted file on the hard-drive. A blank document opened. The data translated into words, symbols, technical diagrams and complex math formulas. Ben caught a glimpse of jewels, stones, and topographic maps of Earth. He could have sworn he saw schematics for advanced weaponry. He blinked and the images were gone. It took less than five seconds for the program to finish. Once complete, the computer closed the file, stored and powered off.

After a few seconds, Ben recovered enough to risk a question. "Do you understand any of this?"

"Yes," Carlos whispered. He sank into a large tapestry chair and stared vacantly at the blank computer screen.

"So, what's going on?" Ben asked, not sure he wanted to know the answer.

"My dad . . ." Carlos's chest heaved in and out at double its normal rate. His face went beet red. "He's not analyzing satellite transmissions for SETI. He's blocking them."

# CHAPTER SEVENTEEN

# Tinker, Tailor, Soldier, Spy

"If you can't get rid of the skeleton in your closet,
you'd best teach it to dance."

• *George Bernard Shaw*

◆ "I am so dead. Maybe I can scrape up enough airfare to flee the country before he gets back. Did you see all those satellite dishes coming on line? What's a Casmir array? There's no place I can hide except the moon. I'll have to hitch a ride on a Soyez rocket." Carlos massaged his temples and shivered as if chilled to the bone.

Ben looked from Carlos to the computer. "Rockets are down, remember? Solar flares." The pained expression on Carlos's face told him he'd just made things worse. "Listen, there's got to be a logical explanation. Think about it. Your dad likes games and, okay, he's weird, but it's not like he's some super spy."

Carlos shook his head from side to side. "I'm gonna die. I'm so gonna die."

"Come on! It can't be what you think. Spies are cool. They have slick gadgets and awesome sports cars. They DON'T have families and live on boring cul-de-sacs and drive carpool in Volvo station wagons."

"The Volvo is mom's. Remember? My dad drives the Porsche Turbo. That thing's a menace ever since your dad started messing with the engine." Carlos clutched his stomach and heaved like he was going to barf all over the carpet. "Maybe it's just a cover story. Maybe we're not even his real family."

Ben laughed. "Tell you what. Our dads are buds right? I'll ask my dad what's going on."

"And spill the beans about us sneaking in here? You're not even allowed to go messing around in *his* den."

"Oh. Right. Then, we'll figure it out. It's got to be some nerd simulation. Your dad's the only grownup on the block who plays computer games. You said he's always blasting space mutants or crashing ships, right? So, that's it! We logged on to online gaming by accident."

Carlos's face went blank. Ben considered that to be an improvement.

"Come on. Think about it, if he were a spy would he have left the computer unprotected? Anyone could have broken in and logged on."

"We did." Carlos moaned and buried his head in his hands.

Ben groped for an answer that would satisfy Carlos and kill his own nagging doubt. "But if it were secret, he'd have it hidden behind some secret panel, or have passwords you have to type in. Right? What kind of spy leaves spy secrets out in the open? With kids like us around?"

Carlos looked up. "You're right. We couldn't read the instructions so we don't know what it was doing. Could be a fantasy role playing game he set up with other SETI nerds." He perked up a bit. "Did you see those maps and jewels and weapons? It could be stuff for some space version of Dungeons and Dragons."

Carlos seemed back to his old self, but seconds later, he slumped back in the chair. "Still doesn't explain that big satellite dish, though."

Ben laughed. "Oh, yes it does. Big boys like big toys. That's what my mom said when Dad got his new car. He would have bought an 18-wheeler if she had let him. Remember when we went to the RV show and she had to drag him out of the tour bus with three bedrooms? And how the dads all drool at the Air Show every time the Blue Angels do stunt tricks. Mom had to practically tackle Dad to keep him from signing up for the Naval Air Squad."

There was a long pause while Carlos digested the information. His facial muscles relaxed a bit. Ben could tell a kernel of doubt still lingered.

"Hey! I just had a brilliant idea!" Ben said. "Tell your dad you're in the mood for some father-son bonding. Ask to play one of his computer games then get him to show you the SETI program. Maybe we can find out what the star codes mean and plug them into the game."

Carlos gave a mock shudder. "Dad keeps asking me to play but they're too bloody."

Ben was overcome with envy. "He asks you to play and you turn him down? Are you nuts?"

"Honestly, I think we were born into the wrong families," Carlos said.

"I had the same thought. You play basketball like an exact clone of my dad. Anyway, if your dad wants you to play computer games, then that's our chance to get some answers. Take lots of notes and screen shots. I want blow-by-blow details of the blood and gore."

Carlos scrunched up his face. "All right. I'll do it. This will just be our secret. Okay?"

"Deal."

"Swear to it. Your dad's mellow like a Vulcan. Mine's one of those Predator guys."

"I swear. We can meet back up in Llactapata and retrace our steps. Can't let the girls get too far ahead of us. We're down one jewel to zero and I'm looking forward to giving Serise my share of green glob." He let out a belly laugh and tried to release the last of his tension.

"Okay. It's a plan." Carlos retrieved a microfiber cloth from his backpack and wiped down the computer, the mouse, and the desk, giving extra special attention to the arms of the chair. "Let's get out of here. If anyone asks questions, I've been helping you with math and you've been giving me basketball pointers."

Ben followed Carlos, stopping to take one last look at the sleeping computer. In the back of his mind something still felt off.

# CHAPTER EIGHTEEN

# Son of Casmir

"Do not follow where the path may lead . . .
Go instead where there is no path and leave a trail."

• *Ralph Waldo Emerson*

---

• Ben and Carlos sat, legs dangling, on the edge of the granite platform in Llactapata. The game picked up right where it left off — complete with ominous cloud hovering over the nearby mountain range.

A parakeet landed on a nearby branch and chirped excitedly. Carlos held out his finger. The parakeet hopped on and continued its oratory apparently happy to have an audience.

"You okay?" Ben studied Carlos's face. "You don't look so good."

Carlos sighed. "Dad went back to Peru this morning. He's gone a lot lately."

"Yeah, mine too." Ben followed the graceful flight of a black bird.

"I did it," said Carlos.

Ben frowned and braced for bad news. "Did what?"

"Last night, I told my dad I wanted to play games with him. You should have seen his face light up."

Ben was delighted but confused. "But that's a good thing, right?"

Carlos frowned. "He kept patting me on the back and saying, 'My son!' like he was proud of me just for asking."

The black bird issued a distant call.

Startled, the parakeet flew away.

The black bird gave chase.

"Okay! That's promising. So then what? Give me all the bloody details!" Ben playfully punched him in the arm.

Carlos flinched.

Alarmed, Ben withdrew.

"He said I have to work up to the space games because they were advanced," Carlos continued. "He'd have to coach me on advanced avionics and how to pilot the ships — lots of controls, stuff about black matter and gravity wells and wormholes. So he wanted to start with something primitive: The Art of War. We pretended to be historical figures and set up armies."

Ben grinned and imagined himself playing along with Carlos's dad. "Sounds like fun."

Carlos sighed. "No! It was awful. I felt sorry for the other side and getting ambushed. My men deserted or surrendered. Now I know how you feel when your uncle is around. It was like one big test. I could tell Dad was disappointed. So I said I was interested in astronomy and wanted to learn about the SETI stuff."

"And?"

Carlos's voice lowered to a whisper. "He showed it to me — the SETI program. It didn't look anything like what we were messing with. It's just a graph that runs data as a screensaver. We kept it running in a window while we switched to a game called 'The History of the World'. As a screen saver it was kind of cool, lots of rainbow colors, but there was nothing about satellite dishes or Casmir arrays. I mean — nothing! The SETI program said it would take twenty-four hours to process the data before we got a new file."

Ben was ecstatic. "Your dad's got a lot of games. This is going to take longer than I thought." He studied butterflies flitting on plants nearby. They beat their wings repeatedly in an insect version of Morse Code: flap, flap, flap, pause, flap flap, slow flap, flap. Ben made dots and dashes in the dirt to match their rhythm.

"Dad's been acting strange ever since he got back from Peru," Carlos said.

"More than usual?" Now Ben was worried. Carlos was often quiet but never withdrawn.

"Worse!" Carlos drew his knees to his chest and wrapped his arms around them. Goosebumps covered his arms even though the weather was warm.

"He set himself up as this Incan emperor, Atahualpa and led his tribes to massacre Spanish Invaders. He mumbled something about them bringing Typhoid fever and killing villagers for gold, payback for reneging on a ransom and preventing an execution. Ben, he was slaughtering the Spanish camps even after they raised white flags and tried to surrender!

Carlos paused to catch his breath, his face growing pale. "After a while he wasn't even looking at the screen. He kept scrolling through the notes on his phone while he hit the space bar over and over to shoot at the enemy or launch another attack. He hacked the game so he could give the Incan warriors high-tech laser guns even though it wasn't historically accurate. It wasn't pretty. Then he scrolled the timeline back about forty years, navigated to the Atlantic Ocean and blew up a bunch of ships — Christopher Columbus's ships! Didn't even look for survivors. He just jumped forward and went after Amerigo Vespucci right after his ships left Italy. Something was bugging him. I mean, he was angry even for him."

Ben's mouth gaped open in delight."So then what happened?"

"Mom came in and whispered something in his ear." Carlos continued. "She winked at me, gave Dad a kiss on the cheek then smacked him on top of his head. He stopped and booted up something else. In the new one, we had to break into a museum, unlock a bunch of safes and steal jewels. Lots of puzzles, but . . ." Carlos paused and took a deep breath. "I could still tell something was on his mind and it wasn't something good."

Ben pondered the problem and all he could came up with was envy. "So did you ask him about Peru? Did he mention anything we can use?"

"That's what I'm trying to tell you," Carlos said staring at Ben like he'd missed the point. "He didn't lose control until I told him your uncle gave you a computer game. I told him the clues led to Peru. He laughed. But it was kind of a fake laugh, if you know what I mean. Like he was trying to act surprised but wasn't."

"Carlos, your dad was just shocked that you wanted to play — out of the blue. This is a good thing!" Ben clapped his hands then stopped when he noticed Carlos's mood darkening. "What did I miss?"

Carlos twisted a leaf in his hand and found a caterpillar. Pulling a branch close, he guided the insect to safety before crushing the leaf in his hand. "He said we wouldn't find it in the Andes Mountain. Too far away. He said to try the island where they harvest guano."

"Guano?" asked Ben.

"Bird poop. I think that means we're supposed to go to Islas Ballestas. Remember? It's covered in it."

"Now that's what I'm talkin' about!" Ben gave a loud whoop, then paused when he remembered there were scientists working nearby.

*Computer simulation, Ben! Get a grip!*

The black bird swooped closer to the team and circled as if evaluating their work. The cloud flashed, threatening to unleash a rainstorm at any moment.

"You don't get it do you?" Carlos sighed and looked as if he had lost something dear.

"I get that your dad gave us a great clue," Ben said. "What's the problem?"

"I told him we needed to go to Peru," Carlos said. "That's it. I didn't tell him we were in the Andes Mountains. Peru's a huge country. The only way he could have known . . ."

Thunderstruck, Ben finished the thought. "Was if he saw us there." Now his arms filled with goosebumps too.

Carlos sucked in another lung full of air and shuddered. "I went to the bathroom to catch my breath and when I came back he was on the phone, pacing and yelling in Spanish about some guy named Kurosh. He hung up when he saw me. Not before I was able to translate a weird comment though."

"What?"

"He said he was a son of Casmir and wouldn't go willingly."

A thick palpable silence hung in the air for several minutes as Ben pondered the new development. *Son of Casmir? Casmir Array? Solar pulses? Government satellites?*

*Secrets.*

"I had a thought," Carlos said.

"Yeah?"

"It's crazy though."

"Can't be crazier than finding a bunch of life-size Moai heads in my bedroom, or us sitting here in a jungle," Ben said.

"Those scientists you saw the first time, what did they look like?"

Ben hesitated, not wanting to add to Carlos' distress. "It was a computer simulation. Besides, Grace's dad was in New York,"

"He wasn't," Carlos said, his voice cracking. "I talked to Grace during fifth period today. Her dad was in South America."

Ben sucked wind as the last bit of his heart dropped into his stomach.

"You said you thought your uncle was secretly working for a gaming company. Could it be something else?"

"Like what?" asked Ben, not sure he wanted to know.

"Could he be working for the CIA? Using us and the game to flush my dad out?"

"No!" Ben protested, although his uncle was very much like a bounty hunter and carried himself like Special Ops. "That's crazy. It's not like your dad is hard to find. You live next door! He sent steaks for dinner. Besides, my uncle was on safari with my dad in Kenya."

"So he said." Carlos arched his eyebrows and seemed skeptical. "What did the man look like? The man you saw in the jungle."

"He was sitting down. It was hard to tell. Maybe a mustache . . ."

"And a goatee?" Carlos paused and swallowed hard. "And a brown backpack?"

"Well, yeah. But look! There are a lot of brown packs on the site. Plus it makes sense that my uncle would model the avatars on people he knew."

"What about the hair?" asked Carlos. "Long hair?"

Ben clasped his hands and prayed he wouldn't be hit with a bolt of lightning for the whopper he was about to tell.

"No."

It was one single word. Hopefully he wouldn't be condemned the rest of his life for telling it.

"My dad gave me something. A leather flask and a pouch."

"Red?" Ben immediately regretted his lack of self-control and braced for Carlos's reaction.

"So you saw it?" Carlos shook him hard. "You saw it!"

Ben shivered as a cloud shrouded them in a dense fog. He crossed his fingers and closed his eyes as he told the next half-truth. "Of course I saw it. He had it with him at the sweat lodge."

"Not in the game?" Carlos deflated and seemed almost relieved.

Ben shrugged and shook his head. *No.* He wondered if a nonverbal lie carried the same penalties as a verbal one.

Carlos slumped. "None of this makes sense."

"On-line gaming, remember?" Ben lied. "I saw something about it on the news last week. People are addicted. They make up new identities, new civilizations, design avatars. Your dad has been working hard. He's just blowing off steam. It's a game. A stupid game."

"Then why not show it to me?"

"R-rated maybe? It's why my mom won't let me near them." *That or he's an international spy with a supersonic plane that lets him go back and forth to Peru at the speed of light.*

Ben swung his feet aimlessly. Above him, the black bird soared closer in wide arcs. He wondered how a bird that big could stay aloft in the thin air.

*Got any clues?*

The bird flew closer, the tips of its wings spread like the fingers of a hand. It banked as if to point at the ground beneath Ben's feet. Ben saw nothing unusual in the brush. After a second pass, the bird flew off toward the neighboring mountain range and the cloud that still hovered there, flashing inside with bursts of light.

"Condor," Carlos said, breaking the silence.

"Huh?"

"That bird you've been watching. Condor. Eats mostly dead animals."

Ben sighed. Carlos's mood was getting darker by the minute.

"Want to dial home and play the game later?" asked Ben. "Who cares if the girls are ahead? They're stuck on the Stonehenge puzzle."

Carlos brushed leaves out of his view and searched the landscape as if he were expecting to see his father emerge from the jungle at any moment.

"What are you thinking?" asked Ben.

"I was thinking I liked life better the way it was before the game." He studied the condor as it made wide, sweeping arcs across the sky.

Ben sighed, then perked up as a brainstorm hit him. "I've got an idea and you don't have to do anything."

Carlos scowled and maintained his focus on the condor.

"No. I mean it. I'll challenge Dad to a basketball game. He's pretty clumsy. Like a Harlem Globetrotter but without the skill. Either he'll miss like always and throw it over the garage, or I'll do it intentionally. When we go to get the ball, I'll ask about the satellite dish. I'll call you and tell you what he says." Ben thought that sounded like a great spy plan. His dad could scope out the real story from Carlos's dad.

At the mention of the satellite dish, Carlos's closed his eyes. His mood grew even darker. Ben decided to drop the subject. Lately he had a knack for making things worse. He jumped down from the platform to study the tablets and spotted something hidden in the grass. A worn leather strap with a row of black stones imbedded around the circumference.

As soon as Ben touched the object, the jungle grew silent. The butterflies disappeared. The birds stopped chirping. The condor returned as if sizing him up for a potential meal.

"Think this is a clue?" He tossed it up to Carlos.

Carlos studied it with disinterest. "I think it's a collar, but we might as well collect it. We may have to trade it for something useful later in the game." He tossed it back down to Ben.

A collar? Ben knew exactly what he was going to do with it. He shoved it in his pocket, activated the tablet and called out the code for Sunnyslope. Carlos held off inputting the last number until Ben climbed back on the platform. As they dissolved, a star shaped symbol appeared on the obelisk.

No more to see at this location.
Clock is ticking.

Seconds later, they were back in Ben's room, running for cover as the bookcase tilted from their weight and spilled its contents on the floor. Ben caught the bookcase midway and set it upright again. He paused hoping no one was home.

"Need more help with your math?" Carlos asked as he helped to pick up the books and games littering the floor. "The test is tomorrow, whether Mr. Bundy is back or not."

"No. I need to start figuring stuff out for myself." Ben's hand brushed against his pocket. The collar was still there . . . outside of the hologram.

One more mystery to solve.

Carlos smiled halfheartedly, headed for the bedroom door, then paused. "You know you're never going to get it, don't you?"

"The math?" asked Ben.

"No. Your uncle's approval." Carlos didn't bother to look at him. He just kept staring into space as if searching for answers in the gaps between the molecules of air. "You say we're playing this thing because you want to go on an expedition, but it's really about getting him to like you, right? It's like me trying to please my dad by pretending to be something I'm not. It doesn't work. Some people won't change no matter how hard you try."

Ben sighed. This started out as just a simple game. Now it was destroying everything and everyone around him.

"There's one more thing," Carlos said, both hands jammed in the pockets of his khaki pants. "Your basketball plan won't work."

"Why not?" Ben tried to read Carlos's expression. All he saw was fear.

"Because I checked this afternoon. The satellite dish is gone."

# CHAPTER NINETEEN

# Massacre

"Reasons are one thing, motives another."

• *Charles Johnson, 1920*

---

♦ *" . . . the satellite dish is gone."*

Ben stared out his bedroom window toward the woods. Something was dreadfully wrong in the neighborhood and it was bigger than a disappearing satellite dish.

He took a deep breath and headed for the garage where his father was tinkering with his car's engine. Ben suspected that his father was a frustrated inventor. He spent his free time in his workshop banging away on a project. Ben had never been able to pick the lock — but not for lack of trying. An ultra-bright light often shone beneath the door while his father worked. Ben wondered if it was a good idea for his clumsy dad and hot halogen lights to be near combustion engines and fuel.

"Hey, Ben! What's up?" Jeremiah Webster looked up from beneath the hood, a dripping container of oil in his hand.

Ben forced a smile. "Want to shoot some hoops? You owe me a game."

"Yeah, I know." His father wiped his hands on a shop towel. "Last time we played I was about to beat you at HORSE."

Ben burst out laughing. "We'd have to change the name to 'onomatopoeia' to give you a shot at winning!"

"Can't take the heat, huh?" His father's eyes twinkled.

"How about some one-on-one. It's more your speed." The knot in Ben's stomach subsided. There was time to scope out the satellite dish. For now he just wanted to have some fun. He tossed the ball to his father, who dropped it, then caught it on the first bounce. "You can go first this time," Ben said.

"You're on, Hot Shot!" Jeremiah Webster walked out to the driveway and dribbled the ball between his lanky legs. As usual, he was unable to control it and nearly tripped. Ben dashed in, stole the ball and jumped.

"Score!"

The ball hit the backboard and dropped into the net. "You need me to spot you a few points, old man?"

"Hrmpph," his father snorted as he grabbed the rebound. "I'm just giving you a false sense of security." He lined up his shot and released the ball. "Score!"

"Miss!" Ben shouted as the ball hit the roof, rolled the length of the gutter, then reversed course before bouncing on to the grass. "This is proof that I did NOT get my basketball genes from you. Want some coaching?"

His father laughed. "No. Do you?"

As Ben reached for a lay-up his father grinned and tackled him to the ground.

"Hey! This is not football. Personal foul!"

"What does that mean?"

"It means you were cheating, Dad, so I get a free throw and a penalty free throw." Ben tried pushing his father away. It was like trying to move a brick wall. Grinning, he scrambled to his feet, stepped to a line in the middle of the driveway and waved his father to the edge of the lawn. He considered launching the ball in the direction of the satellite dish, but decided to show off first. "Watch and learn, old man."

The ball swooped through the net.

"Score!"

His father rebounded and began to dribble.

"Nope," Ben said, waving an index finger. "I get another turn."

"Okay," his father said. "But take the penalty shot from there." He pointed to a crack another twelve feet away.

"The penalty shot isn't to penalize ME!" Ben protested.

His father kept pointing. "Scared of a little challenge? Come on, show me what you've got, Hot Shot."

Ben walked to the crack and wiggled his hips arrogantly. He dribbled the ball in and out of his legs, stuck out his tongue, then aimed. He held his breath as the ball made its way to the basket. It landed on the rim, rolled two revolutions, then dropped into the net.

"Score!" Ben yelped!

His father eyed him with curiosity. "Lucky shot?"

"Skill and concentration," Ben said, making a goofy face.

His father tossed the ball back to him and pointed to a spot further down the driveway. "Humor me and take a shot from there."

Ben smiled and went to the designated spot. It would be like shooting from half-court — difficult, but not impossible. The ball passed through the net with a gentle "whoosh."

"Score!" Ben danced in a circle and pumped his arm up and down. "Hah! So how many does that make? Why bother to keep score? Just concede now!"

His father cocked one eyebrow, retrieved the ball and returned it to Ben. Pointing to the end of the driveway he said, "Try from there." His sharp tone was more of an order than a request.

"Dad! That would be like shooting from the opposite end of the court!"

"Yeah, I know. Try it anyway."

Ben frowned. The spot was almost ninety feet away. This was going to be impossible. When he reached the street, he noticed a dark cloud forming. He'd have to work quickly if he was going to have time to show his father the satellite dish. He arched backward and threw the ball as if he were launching an Olympic javelin. Again, the ball landed on target.

Ben gawked. "Did you see that?" He shimmied from side to side and patted himself on the back as he returned to the backyard.

"How long have you been able to do that?" His father's expression was a combination of shock and alarm.

"Don't know," Ben said, still dancing. "Never tried it from that far before. Forget school tryouts and State Championships. I should go pro right now!"

His father studied him for several seconds. The sparkle soon returned to his eyes. He grinned with pride and patted Ben on the back. "My son! Okay. My turn." He took the ball, dribbled pathetically, ran toward the garage and jumped for a lay up. The ball hit the backboard, bounced from the right side of the hoop to the left like a ping-pong ball before bouncing off at an angle . . . on to the deck. Ben's father seemed amused by the results.

Ben retrieved the ball from a deck planter, and pointed toward the garage. "That's just pathetic. Do I need to paint an arrow on the net for you? Look! Basket! That is a basket." Ben held out his hands. "Ball. This is a ball. Ball goes in basket. Simple concept. Want to try again?" He tossed the ball toward his father.

Without looking down, his father opened his hands and caught it squarely with his fingertips.

"Awesome Dad, you're getting better at . . ."

Ben turned to see what his father was staring at. His uncle had appeared out of nowhere and, as always, had blown in ahead of a storm.

"Your boy needs some real competition, Jeremiah."

"What do you want, Henry?" His father's tone was anything but polite. "I thought you were headed to the Middle East."

"Had some local business to attend to," Uncle Henry said, the sky growing dark behind him. "Ben? How's the game coming?"

Ben's stomach turned. The week was almost over and the firing squad had returned for the kill. Ben looked to his father for support but his father's eyes were narrowed and fixed on Uncle Henry. "We cracked the first clues and made it all the way to Peru."

"Indeed." Uncle Henry raised his eyebrows and glowered at his brother before returning his attention to Ben. "And now it appears you are taking a break to rest from the grueling mental challenge. Nothing like simplistic diversions to get the juices flowing. As I said, judging from your father's performance on the court, you appear in need of some real competition to improve your skills. Perhaps you will indulge me in a game. What is it you call it? Horse?"

Ben gulped. The way he'd been playing, he was unbeatable. Too big to move with grace or speed, his uncle was definitely not the basketball type. Offensive tackle on a football team? Maybe. But definitely not a basketball player, so this was one time Ben had a fighting chance to be victorious. "Sure. Need me to spot you some points?"

"I was thinking I might extend the favor to you." Uncle Henry tossed the ball to Ben. "Let's see what about this game has you so capti-vated. One letter for every shot? You can start as offense."

"That's not how you play . . ."

"Horse?" Uncle Henry finished. "I know. But since when have you started playing by the rules. How about it? One letter for every shot you make? One for every shot I make. Game?"

"Yeah, sure," Ben said, his mind working through this latest puzzle. His uncle was up to something. But what? He dribbled a few times, then aimed.

Uncle Henry lunged forward, intercepted the ball mid-flight and dunked it over his shoulder. "H."

"That's enough, Henry," Ben's father said. "Ben has homework."

"Oh, this won't take long." Uncle Henry's face was a blank mask as he nodded for Ben to proceed.

"Yeah, Dad. This won't take long! If he plays as well as you do, this will be a massacre!" Ben dribbled then lunged to the right as his uncle reached for the ball. He reversed, faked a shot, pivoted, then aimed when he thought his uncle was off balance. Again, Uncle Henry jumped into the air, his massive frame rising as though he were weight-less. He intercepted the ball at the top of its arc and dunked it through the net.

"I believe that's an 'O'."

Ben was stunned. His uncle was the size of a bull elephant but he moved like a gazelle. Quickly formulating a new strategy, Ben retrieved the ball, dribbled backwards to mid-court range, then launched it. Uncle Henry stood aside and let the ball pass uninterrupted. It hit the target with a gentle *whoosh*.

Ben pumped his fist up and down. "Told you! Basketball is the key to my future!"

Uncle Henry stared as if preparing for a lecture. Instead he said, "You have an 'H' to my 'HO.' Should we change to 'onomatopoeia' to give you time to catch up?"

Ben laughed. "How long were you watching me and Dad?"

Uncle Henry glanced at his watch. "Long enough. I've got three letters left to earn and an appointment to keep. Shall we continue?"

Ben tossed the ball to his uncle who dribbled first with his left hand, then his right before bouncing the ball in a rapid 360-degree circle around his body. He seemed bored but made no attempt to shoot.

"So you've only made it through the first challenge," he asked.

It didn't sound like a question, but Ben answered anyway.

"Actually, we're working in teams. The girls found the Tibetan emerald and the turquoise stone in Arizona. Carlos and I have an idea where the one in Peru is buried." Ben reached in to steal the ball, but his uncle switched hands so fast Ben could barely follow it.

"Enough, Henry!" ordered Ben's father.

Ben grinned. "It's okay, Dad. I'm just letting him have a false sense of security."

His uncle did not grin in return. Instead, he tossed the ball over his shoulder. The ball hit the target, bounced once then returned to his hands as if by remote control.

" 'R.' "

Ben was growing concerned that he'd underestimated his uncle. But he wasn't defeated yet. Instead he smirked. "Getting tired? Need a rest?"

"Hardly." Uncle Henry tossed the ball to Ben. "Clock is ticking. Are you going to play or talk trash?"

Ben paused to consider the situation. It was time to use his full arsenal. He reached down and pumped up his Sky-Jump sneakers. *Get ready, old man!* He pivoted, faked and otherwise tried to outmaneuver the immovable object known as Henry Webster. Despite his moves, Ben was blocked at every turn. Several minutes passed before he found an opening. He took the shot only to see it intercepted — again.

"S." A bored expression crossed his uncle's face as he slammed the ball through the hoop.

Ben rebounded and dribbled, taking the time to size up his opponent. He was down four letters to one — a massacre, just not the one he'd hoped for. One more basket and his uncle would win. His father stood on the sidelines, his expression showing a slow burn. In his arms, the only other spectator. The cat's tail wagged gently as he eyed Uncle Henry, then flicked erratically as he shifted his gaze to Ben.

Ben stared at the basket, the end of the driveway, then his uncle. The sky grew darker. The wind picked up. There wasn't much time left before the storm blew in. He dribbled backwards, arrogantly gesturing for his uncle. To his surprise, Uncle Henry followed.

*Bounce.*

"So you've not yet solved the Peruvian puzzle. What happened to solving a game in a week?"

*Bounce, bounce.*

A sudden gust of wind nearly toppled Ben, but he maintained his grip on the ball. "Mom took the game away."

*Bounce.*

"Indeed! Tell me . . . how did you work around that little problem?" asked Uncle Henry, the sleeves of his shirt billowing like sails.

*Bounce, bounce.*

"I used a digital copy of the game I transferred to Grace's old computer the first night." Ben glanced at his father who did not seem to be concerned about this latest confession. Instead, his father was studying the sky and the approaching storm.

"Interesting," Uncle Henry said, giving Ben a brief glimmer of hope at cracking the Ice King's demeanor.

When Ben reached the street he waited for his uncle to move into defensive position. Instead, Uncle Henry moved to the side and cocked one eyebrow. Ben steadied himself and, in an attempt to compensate for the gusts of wind, aimed slightly to the left of the basket. The ball hit the net, bounced on the driveway, then rolled toward them.

"O!" Ben waited for his uncle to show his surprise at the remarkable shot.

Instead his uncle reached down to retrieve the ball as it came to a stop at his feet. His eyes showed an intensity Ben had not seen before. "Clock is ticking, Ben."

His uncle slammed the ball so hard, Ben thought it would explode. He never took his eyes off Ben. Never once looked in the direction of the basket. The ball hit the pavement at an angle, then soared backward through the air — almost ninety feet — until it fell through the basket with a whisper soft *"whoosh,"* hit the driveway and stopped as if held in place by an invisible forcefield.

"E."

Ben couldn't bring himself to say the letter out loud. Instead he stood transfixed, his eyes locked on the ball. The net of the basket flapped wildly. The stems of his mother's flowers were practically horizontal. And yet the ball sat on the ground as if cemented in place. Ben glanced up at his uncle hoping for an explanation.

"I believe that concludes this experiment," Uncle Henry said finally. "In life there will always be a stronger opponent no matter how good you are. Time's almost up, Ben. Finish the game. Might find skills more suited to your talents. I'm afraid basketball is *not* in your future."

Ben clenched his teeth and studied his uncle through a blur of near tears. Just one more test to humiliate him. It didn't matter what he achieved, or what he earned, his uncle would always delight in showing him what an insignificant insect he was. He would not show weakness. Not here.

"Ben, go start your homework." His father's voice was soothing and gentle.

Ben started to protest when his father cut him off using an unfamiliar tone.

"NOW!"

◆

Once inside, Ben fumed. He'd completely forgotten his mission — to scope out the satellite dish. He glanced out the kitchen window toward the scene on the driveway. Second fight in a week, this time with his father doing all of the yelling. Uncle Henry stood emotionless while Ben's father — basketball in hand — unleashed a tirade muted by thick panes of glass. He walked in tight circles around Uncle Henry, while bouncing the basketball absentmindedly . . . and perfectly. His father controlled the ball like it was an integral part of his body. Not once did he look at it.

Ben froze, unable to breathe. His father's sudden skill set off all kinds of internal alarms. The ball bounced in a slow, rhythmic cadence synchronized with his father's footsteps on the driveway. Had his father been this good all along? If so, why would he hide it?

Brandishing his finger at Ben's uncle, his father began slamming the ball to the ground with so much force it deformed into an oval before returning to his father's palm. The dark cloud rolled over the house, blocking the sunlight and casting a shadow over his father and uncle. Uncle Henry cocked an eyebrow as he tilted his head skyward. The cloud evaporated and the sunlight returned.

Without a word, Uncle Henry turned on his heels and walked away. Ben's father, his face a mask of anger, walked toward the house. As he neared he tossed the ball over his shoulder.

Ben gasped as the ball soared thirty feet across the driveway, landed dead center in the net and remained there.

# CHAPTER TWENTY

# The Den

"Facts do not cease to exist because they are ignored."

• *Aldus Huxley*

• Ben tossed and turned until his comforter surrendered and fell to the floor. He hated his uncle. HATED him. But after seeing his father's sudden basketball skills, he couldn't shake the feeling that his uncle was the only one telling him the truth. But what was there to be truthful about?

"*. . . time to tell the children about the family business.*"

All through dinner, his father shot weary looks at Ben's mother who sighed and picked at her food. Whatever was going on, they weren't trying to hide their feelings anymore.

"*. . . clock is ticking, Ben.*"

His clock read 1:30 a.m. It was already Wednesday. Only one day left and he was hopelessly behind. The girls found a gold disk at a Mayan ball court in Guatemala. The game now displayed three gems, three star charts and three letters which spelled SON. Ben's first thought was Star Wars. "*Luke, I'm your father.*" It was as if he were trying to solve a puzzle for which there was no solution.

And what was the point of trying? When he received a 98 on a science test, his uncle asked, "*Where's the other two points?*" then followed up with a lecture on Charles Drew and some dead Egyptian guy named

Imhotep. When Ben drew a picture of the space shuttle — and earned a first place ribbon at a student exhibit — it turned into a rant about how long it took for NASA to put a man on the moon. And now the crack about basketball not being a part of his future? Carlos was right. He was never going to get Uncle Henry's approval.

Never.

He punched his fist into his pillow, slipped and hit the edge of his nightstand instead. His knuckle throbbed with pain and cried out for an ice pack.

Slipping downstairs, he spotted a light underneath the door to his father's den. It was now or never. Time to get answers.

Ben knocked. "Dad?" Hearing no answer, opened the door a crack. His father tilted backwards in a large leather chair, feet propped above the desk and spoke into a wireless headset, his tone agitated. Aris lay wedged in the narrow gap between his father's shoulders and the chair. His tail flicked contentedly as he purred.

Across the room, a state-of-the-art plasma monitor rose eight feet tall and twelve feet wide. His father had said it was on loan from an overseas funder, very sensitive equipment that wouldn't be on the market for several years. So test-driving the theater-sized screen with a few action flicks was out of the question.

Ben's stomach tightened. The monitor began streaming images of large glass boxes filled with hundreds — maybe thousands — of animals: lions, elephants, rhinos and giraffes.

"Consat! Safina ni kamili," Ben's father said.

"Askar," the computer responded as the animals dissolved into thin air.

Ben's head was spinning but he kept repeating the phrase to himself, so he could look it up later. " *Safina ni kamili. Safina ni kamili*"

Stabbing at the keyboard, his father's voice dropped to a low growl. Satellite data and rotating images of Earth filled the screen. The cursor moved left, to Europe, then zoomed in on the United Kingdom. Ben recognized the outermost island as Ireland but recalling a year-old geography lesson made his brain hurt. A box bisected with crosshairs hovered over the larger of two islands — Great Britain — then moved southeast to . . .

*London.*

Soon the screen displayed floor plans and old buildings connected by a central glass dome. Ben's father barked unintelligible commands at the monitor. African? Russian? Ben couldn't tell. But each time the monitor responded "Askar."

The den burst with the same glittery fireworks as the game. Ben gasped and clamped his hand over his mouth before the sound escaped. Although the door was open only an inch or two, he stepped backwards into the shadows to keep from being seen.

A floating hologram opened to the left of his father's chair and filled with technical schematics. His father scanned through the documents so fast Ben wondered how he could read them. He felt flushed and willed his heart to stop beating triple time.

A second and third hologram exploded out of the monitor. A golden, red-jeweled eagle spun in midair next to two wire-frame drawings. The drawings solidified to form a silver box and a transparent disc.

Ben bit his lip.

His father barked another garbled command. The den transformed into a hologram of the building's interior. It looked as if he were driving through the rooms while sitting in his chair. He navigated through rooms filled with Egyptian artifacts, colossal stone statues of Pharaohs, sarcophagi, and a statue of a black cat that looked like Aris. A sign near one of the mummy cases read: *The British Museum*

A beam of light, like the one Ben had seen in Peru, crept over and around everything and everyone in the corridor. The tourists didn't seem to notice. Box codes similar to the game locations streamed along the walls of the den as Ben's father scanned sculptures, friezes, tablets and artwork, growling when someone blocked his view. He navigated to a room marked "Special Exhibits." An object in a glass display matched the one rotating in the holographic window at his side.

"Got it! Second floor, special exhibit. Heavily guarded."

Ben's pulse raced and his whole body grew numb. He drew in long slow breaths, careful not to make a sound or give his position away.

"No. I'm not sure it's authentic," His father continued. "Can Cheryl get access? She's got reciprocity and a security clearance."

*Cheryl?*

"Yes. Sure. I understand. I forgot about the ritual. We can get it out ourselves. Medie synthesized a duplicate."

*Pause*

"No. It would look suspicious if I took another trip this soon plus I've got a mound of homework to grade. I'll put another team on it."

*Pause.*

"Bamiyan is irrelevant. There must be a fail safe. A contingency for emergencies."

*Pause.*

"I won't evacuate."

*Pause.*

"We've got two, I won't give up until the entire collection is assembled."

*Pause.*

"Shan can go without you. Tibet's a walk in the park compared to London. Too much surveillance. Frank's back in Peru. I think it's a dead trail, but he's positive something's there. Better to have him in Peru anyway. You know Frank. The clock's ticking. He'd just blast a hole in the building and take it."

*Shan? Shan Choedon? Cheryl Hightower? Frank Lopez?*

*The neighbors?*

Ben clamped his hand over his mouth to stifle a gasp.

"I've been working on something," his father said, "but it will take three agents to pull this off. I don't want Kurosh to know what we're attempting. He's set on aborting the mission . . ."

*Kurosh?* Ben thought. *Who's that?*

"Ignore his orders!" Ben's father barked. "This could buy us some time. Take a look at this. I finished it yesterday."

Two avatars entered the exhibit, walked around the display case and placed clear discs on the corners. Once attached, laser beams shot toward the ceiling creating a bubble around the display case. A third man, an avatar of Ben's father, entered the envelope. A second later the beams retracted. The glass case was intact, but a golden bird was in his hand, its duplicate now on display.

Ben's chest muscles squeezed against his ribcage. He blinked hard to keep tears from starting. Now he knew — the family business — Paradise Circle was a community of international jewel thieves.

"Tomorrow then," his father said.

The hologram retracted. Ben's father removed his headset, tossed it on the desk, then flicked a rubber ball toward a map hung between two windows. He snatched the ball from the air on its return flight and sent it spinning once again. Each time, the ball hit the same spot on the map — northern Africa — and returned to Ben's father who caught it . . . with one hand.

Ben tried to slip away but found himself frozen to the spot and gasping for air. Aris jerked up, swished his tail angrily and hissed. His father turned suddenly, sending the cat tumbling to the floor.

The monitor returned to a screen saver of the university. Ben blinked. The keyboard console vanished.

"Ben! How long have you been standing there?"

"I just got here," Ben lied, forcing himself to breathe.

His father drew in a longer than normal breath before speaking. "You okay?"

Ben's heart hammered. He willed himself to say something. Anything. But all he felt was a mixture of fear and confusion. "It's . . . umm . . . late. It can wait."

"No," his father said while stuffing papers into his briefcase. "It can't. Come on in."

Terrified, Ben took a few tentative steps into the room. But his legs felt like rubber so he leaned against the doorframe instead.

"Ben, I — "

"Dad, I . . . I found something in the woods behind the house," Ben blurted out, cutting him off. "Something weird." Ben searched his father's eyes and saw no reaction to his news.

"Like what?" His father maintained eye contact and gestured him into the room. Ben's feet remained glued to the spot.

"A satellite dish. Carlos said his dad bought one and we found it."

His father shrugged. "We always knew Frank was a space fanatic."

"It's big, Dad. Really big. Like . . . bigger than a house big." Ben stretched his arms and made a wide sweep to illustrate the point.

"You sure you're not exaggerating just a bit?" His father asked, his face expressionless.

Ben bit his lip and nodded. The whole thing did sound crazy.

His father let out a loud sigh. "He does a lot of stargazing. Probably robbing a diamond cartel to pay for his habit. Want me to look at it?"

Ben nodded.

"Okay. It's too dark to search the woods right now. Let's go see it in the morning." His father walked toward him, paused, then turned and grabbed his phone.

Ben heard a vibration coming from the direction of the dish. "Did you hear that tremor?"

His father nodded. "I'm sure it's nothing to worry about."

# CHAPTER TWENTY-ONE

# Now You See It, Now You Don't

> "The reality of the other person is not in what he reveals to you,
> but in what he cannot reveal to you.
> Therefore, if you would understand him, listen not
> to what he says but rather what he does not say."
> • *Kahlil Gibran*

### ◆ 6:30 a.m.

"I don't understand. It was here. It was huge!" Ben searched in and around the stand of forty foot trees. He headed further into the woods and then circled back. "This has to be the spot," he said, his panicked voice now higher by an octave as he spun 360 degrees. "It was right here!"

"Maybe you'd better start from the beginning," his father said. "Give me a complete run-down on what you and Carlos were doing."

As they continued down a path, Ben gave a quick synopsis about losing the basketball, finding the dish and hoping it would pick up sumo wrestling or other fun stuff. He skipped any mention of Casmir arrays, data downloads, and all the government systems they shut down.

"Each time we tried to find a cartoon, a vibration shook the house. I'm sure it was the dish, Dad. It came from behind the garage."

"Lots of seismic activity around the world these days," his father said casually. "Minor tremors are common for this area. Don't worry about the house. It's built on a rock solid foundation."

"But the vibrations matched our search for TV shows."

His father stopped cold in his tracks. After a few seconds of silence, he shrugged. "Did you ever think to just ask Frank about it? You're not supposed to be in his office. Could have erased valuable research from his computer."

"I'm willing to take the heat," Ben said. "The computer seemed fine when we shut it off."

A flock of birds suddenly flew out of the trees. A squirrel dropped a nut on Ben's head, jumped to the branch of a neighboring tree, and scurried away. Aris scaled the tree in hot pursuit.

Confused, Ben glanced up the path, then around the woods again to get his bearings. They'd walked farther than he remembered and were now standing at the edge of a steep slope.

"I don't understand. I climbed it. I touched it."

His father rubbed his head. "If you say you saw it, I believe you saw it. I just don't have an explanation I can give you right now."

Ben studied his father's expression and found only a hint of sadness. Or was it pity? "Maybe I took the wrong trail. Maybe it was a test model and they took it away."

"And replaced it with fifty year old trees?"

Ben touched the trees, half expecting his hand to pass through them. Instead, he felt the rough, irregular bark of the Catalina Ironwoods that grew in the area. Moss spread up the south side of several trees. "This might be a clue. Doesn't moss grow on the north side?"

His father scraped the green plant with his nail. "Usually. I'll have your mother check it out."

Ben's head throbbed and he rubbed his temple. "Dad, I know something was here! Carlos saw it too."

His father blew air across his parsed lips. "Well, kiddo, there's nothing to see now and I'm starving. Let's head back."

Ben's shoulders sagged as he surveyed the terrain one last time. There was no trace that anything had ever been there. And his father? Maybe Ben had it all wrong. They were co-conspirators who snuck out for burgers when his mom wasn't looking. There had to be another explanation. His straight arrow dad had never lied to him.

"And I never will . . ," said his father.

"Huh?" Ben was startled by the response.

"Never will understand why Frank won't settle down." His father raised one hand to his lips and shook his head. "When he gets back in town I'll have a talk with him. In the meantime, I think you might still be dehydrated from the sweat lodge. I'll talk to your mother about adjusting your vitamins."

Ben choked. "Dad, a cheeseburger would perk me up a whole lot better than her drinks."

"Yeah, I know what you mean."

"And Dad?"

"Hmm?"

"You can stop faking now. I know."

His father stopped in his tracks. "Know what?" His eyes narrowed and for a split second, he looked like Uncle Henry.

"About basketball," Ben said. "I know you can play. Maybe even better than me. You've been faking all these years to make me feel better. How about we play this weekend and you can give me some real competition. Maybe this time you can show me what *you've* got, Hot Shot."

His father let out a hearty laugh. "Deal. By the way, I think you've got a shot at making the NBA in a few years. You've really got game!" He put an arm around Ben's shoulder as they walked the last few yards of the trail.

*Buds for life.* This man was not a spy. Just a dad. Ben released the pent up tension that had been trapped in his chest. He was so desperate for an adventure he had let his imagination get away from him.

At the edge of the woods, Ben spotted a satellite dish mounted on the roof of the Lopez garage. Small, gray and no more than three feet across, it had not been there before.

◆

That evening, Ben caught a ride home with a teammate. He climbed out of the car, waved goodbye and walked toward the house. His body pumped with so much adrenaline his hands were shaking. He was off the bench and on the team. Starting Center, no less. Unstoppable. He couldn't wait to tell someone. But with his mother and April at Girl Scouts and his dad working late, it would be an hour before anyone got home.

He turned off the house alarm and stretched. The oven timer clicked. Whatever his mother was cooking smelled good, but he knew the taste wouldn't be. A message scribbled itself continuously on the kitchen computer.

*"Go ahead and have dinner, Ben. Don't wait for us."*

Grimacing, Ben donned oven mitts, pulled the ceramic dish out of the oven, spooned a large helping of vegetarian casserole on a plate, then dumped three-quarters of it down the garbage disposal. He ran the disposal with plenty of water and soap to erase the evidence, then put the remaining bits of vegetable goop and the dirty plate in the sink. He filled a glass with ice and pulled a bottle of Orangina from a secret compartment in his backpack. He could throw the bottle out at school or slip it to his father and his mother wouldn't be any wiser. A thick and chunky Butterfinger candy bar from the school vending machine would complete his satisfying meal.

On his way upstairs he noticed the door to the den was open.

"Aris?"

The cat was nowhere to be found. Probably outside torturing some innocent creature.

Ben replayed the afternoon's events. Ninety minutes of flawless drills and he'd barely broken a sweat. Even so, he couldn't get the missing satellite dish, cryptic clues about his friend's families and a heist of the British Museum out of his mind.

Against his better judgment, Ben walked into the den.

The stainless steel monitor lay dormant against the paneled walls. Ben removed his shoes to keep from tracking dirt on the Persian rug. His feet crushed the silk pile as he walked across the room. The rug recovered and left no trace of his footprints.

There WAS a satellite dish. And he'd seen the den fill with

holograms. The computer had to be somewhere in the room.

He opened the top drawer of the desk. No keyboard. He searched the other drawers, then underneath the desk and chair.

Nothing.

Ben searched the credenza and found one of the drawers locked. He remembered seeing a key in his father's desk and removed it without disturbing the other items. He felt like a spy.

*Like father, like son?*

He slipped the key into the lock, turned, and found only a small mahogany box.

Ben tugged on the pewter handle, unhinged the latch and swung the doors open. Inside, a pair of knives hung side by side. One was tightly wrapped with a black silk cloth. The other, loosely draped in white cotton.

Black and White.

*Yin and Yang.*

It was the recurring theme in the Webster household. Like everything else his parents collected, the carved silver knives looked old and ceremonial. The two-inch blades were too small to do any real damage.

Ben closed the box and resumed his search for the hidden computer. Only a few items were arranged on the desk: a bronze bust from Benin, a scratch pad bearing the university logo and an engraved desk set with a silver-plated clock that Ben and April had given him for Father's Day three years ago. Ben knew the inscription by heart.

*"To the Best Dad on Earth!"*

The scratch pad was flipped to the second page. Normally, Ben wouldn't have given it a second thought. But the week's weird activities had his paranoia meter operating on overtime. He lifted the sheet and held it up to the light. The impression of handwriting was imbedded in the paper, but he couldn't read it. He put the pad down and gave up. No keyboard, no conspiracy, no mystery. His father had to be playing an advanced holographic game. That was it. The family secret. Ben felt foolish for thinking it could be anything else.

*You may now return to your regularly scheduled programming.*

As he bent to replace his shoes he remembered a field trip to make rubbings of headstones. Would it work in reverse? He listened for the sound of cars.

Still safe.

Kicking off his sneakers, he retrieved a pencil from the front of his backpack along with a sheet of paper. He placed the paper over the notepad and rubbed the graphite pencil over the impressions. Words and numbers emerged. Ben paused. Scribbled on the note pad were locations he recognized. Like his uncle's game, but different.

First Dynasty pendant – British Museum
N 51 W 0
Hope diamond – Smithsonian Museum
N 38.55 W 77.2
Estrucan medallion – Vatican City
N 41.54 E 12.27

Abort mission – recall teams –
Arecibo W 66.45 11.1  N 18 20 36.6
Pentagon N 38 52.17  W 77 3.48
White House N 38 5 3.86  W 77 2.21
Space shuttle launch pad N 28 36.76  W 80 36.65

Panic spread through his body. He shoved the paper in his pocket, rushed outside to the greenhouse and dropped to his knees near the potting table. His father had returned from Kenya with a black pouch. A pouch filled with rock samples he didn't want Ben to see. Something had fallen out that day.

Ben swept his hand across the floor and felt something lodged near the back leg of the table. He stretched and teased it out with his fingers. Suddenly his hands felt like ice, his heart stopped and his world began collapsing around him.

In his hand was a flawless, sparkling diamond.

# CHAPTER TWENTY-TWO

# Revelation

Only a wise person can solve a difficult problem.

• *Akan proverb*

♦ Ben retreated to his bedroom. Who was his father? Mild mannered professor by day, brilliant mastermind of an international ring of jewel thieves by night? And the way his father handled a ball? Was clumsy and inept his cover story?

He struggled to get a grip on his feelings. Suddenly, he understood how Carlos felt.

Call Carlos?

Not an option. Carlos was a basket case at school, barely talked or smiled. He had made it clear that he'd been happier with his delusions of family bliss. Whenever Ben tried to bring up the game. Carlos just shrugged and walked away.

Call Grace?

She was the one person he could rely on. He dialed the first three digits, thought better of it and hung up. Phone might be bugged. He Skyped her instead.

"Hey! Caught me just in time. Mom and Dad are leaving for Tibet tomorrow morning so I asked if I could hang out at Serise's house. Her mom's driving us to school anyway. Then she's leaving for Arizona for a ritual. What's up with this block? Doesn't anyone ever stay home anymore? By the way, how was practice?" Grace chattered away as if life were normal.

"Hmm? Great. Slam dunk."

He felt a jolt in the pit of his stomach and bit his lip. Her parents were leaving for Tibet?

*"Shan can go without you. Tibet's a walk in the park compared to London . . ."*

A million images of doom streamed through his brain. He stared at the black collar on his desk. Nothing from the game was real — so how could this still be here?

"Earth to Ben? Don't you have some news to share?" Grace batted her eyes coyly.

"Huh?" Ben said, distracted.

"I heard a rumor that you made the team! Congratulations! It's what you always wanted!" Grace chattered away as she threw clothes in a beige tote bag. "Sinking Ship hasn't won a championship in years. I overheard Coach Ito tell the Principal that it was in the bag now that you're on the starting line-up."

"Thanks. Glad to hear he's happy about it." Some distant internal thrill — a spark of excitement over hearing that he was the subject of positive communication for a change — was bulldozed by flashbacks to his father's phone conversation.

*"I don't want Kurosh to know what we're attempting. He's set on aborting the mission . . ."*

Who or what was Kurosh?

"Happy? That's the understatement of the century. Coach Ito was ecstatic," Grace continued. "By the way, I had a question. Is something going on between your Dad and Serise's? She said he was arguing on the phone with someone last night. She thought it was your dad. He told the guy to control his coorosh — or at least she thinks that's what he said. What's a coorosh? Is that a slang word for 'temper'? Your dad doesn't have a temper."

Ben jolted out of his daydream. His stomach turned. "Don't know." Another half-truth? He didn't know what the truth was anymore. "I heard him arguing with someone too, but don't know what it was about." Ben sucked air through his teeth.

*Sorry, Grace.*

What would he tell her? That all the parents were thieves and the game is connected? He needed more evidence. Carlos was already freaked out. Why increase the body count? The only way to be sure was to solve the game himself.

"... *clock is ticking, Ben.*"

Ben looked at his own clock and heard a familiar refrain echo in his brain.

*Got any clues?*

"Hey," Grace said, as she tossed Theodore on the top of the her tote bag. "What's up with Carlos? He asked me about my dad and when I told him he was in South America he got all quiet and moody."

"He thought your father was at a U.N. conference."

"He was. In Peru. But why would Carlos care?"

"I don't think he does," Ben lied again. He seemed to be doing a lot of that lately. "I just think he's feeling under the weather."

"Oh. Right. Putting in too many hours. But not me! I'm stoked. Can't wait to get back into the game. I'm addicted. We've got one day left to solve it, right? Serise and I got through all the homework during free period."

"Okay," Ben said. "See how far you can get. I'll do stuff on this end. Then we'll put all the clues together and find out what the big surprise is later this week."

"Are you kidding? I want to know now!" Grace smiled. "I know, I know. It'll take a long time because we have to walk everywhere. Guess we could turn the 3D simulation off. Those short cuts are great — better than taking a plane. Did you know Serise is scared to fly?"

Ben stared at the altar, the Guardian and the canopic jars. "No. I didn't."

Grace pulled reference books from her shelf and filled another bag. "By the way, we have a present for you!" She transmitted a file.

Ben opened it — more Pigpen gobbledy gook.

"Well?"

"Well, what?" asked Ben.

"Translate it!"

Ben ran Serise's program. The boxes converted using numbers and symbols instead of the alphabet.

The answers to tomorrow's math homework.

"So you stay focused on the game! Told you Serise wasn't such a terrible person. I'm still working on the riddle but I'm not asking her for help. Promise. That's just between you and me."

"Need a hint?" Ben asked, trying hard to sound cheerful.

"Nope, I'll get it. I just need to figure out what can be more evil than the Devil but will kill me if I eat it and I'll have it locked down." She grinned. "Oh, I see that mopey look on your face. Don't worry about Serise. You and I are still best buds. I just think Serise is lonely. When you're nice to her, she kind of settles down. Plus, you should see how fast she burns through homework. Like a supercomputer's built in her head."

Ben's heart ached. He wanted so much to confide in Grace, but he didn't have the heart to tell her about his theories. He'd done enough damage.

Uncle Henry had said something about the "family business." What is he trying to say?

Were the parents the good guys

Or the bad guys?

Ben suspected, from his uncle's tone on the driveway, that the message was meant for him.

Not his friends.

Not April.

Just him.

And he had not found a single gem on his own.

Not one.

He slumped in his chair and gazed at the waterless vase on his desk. His heart skipped once, then twice. His mother's flowers looked as fresh as the day he cut them. The one from the Lopez's garden drooped downward, shriveled and dead from lack of moisture.

"Hey Grace? Can you do me a favor?"

"Do ya have to ask? What's up?"

"I need to borrow your computer, the PC if you aren't taking it with you. I want to set up a wireless link to the Internet so I can look up information while I'm playing."

"Great idea! Serise has more than one too. Your brain is working on overdrive! I'll drop it off on the way to her house. See you in a few!" Grace was hyper and bouncing off the walls.

"Thanks." Ben plastered on another forced smile. Grace was not easily fooled, but he tried his best to keep it up until she logged off. A car pulled into the driveway.

Doors slammed — one, two.

Giggling.

Animated talking.

His mother and April were home. He could have used a few more minutes alone.

He stared at his monitor. The answers to the math questions were all there, tempting him. All he had to do was copy them down and he was home free.

*Time to start figuring things out for yourself, Webster.*

At that moment Ben did something that surprised even him. He closed the window, quit the decryption program and dragged Serise's math file to the trash.

# CHAPTER TWENTY-THREE

# Islas Ballestas

"Man cannot discover new oceans
unless he has the courage to lose sight of the shore."

• *Andre Gide*

• Armed with Grace's laptop, Ben gestured for April to come in. "Want to team up?" he asked. "I need a buddy. What do you say?"

April grinned. "Do my book report if I say yes? Mom blocked all the Internet sites so I can't find any answers. I have to read the whole stinkin' book myself! By Friday!"

Ben smiled. His mom's evil filters were everywhere. "What's the book about?"

"Some kids searching for a new place to live." April closed her eyes, put her head on her shoulder and pretended to snore. "Why don't they just go to an ATM and get some money and check into a hotel?"

Ben scowled. April was so spoiled. She and Serise were a good match.

"Don't push your luck. You know you want to play as much as I do." He quickly got her up to speed on the Easter Island scenario. April was quiet for a long time before she spoke.

"The people on Easter Island . . . most of them are gone forever." She stopped, bowed her head in silent prayer and then said, "Okay. I get it. Maybe they're one of the lost tribes. I'll go with you."

At first it seemed like a good idea. He could hoist April into places he couldn't reach. Instead he said, "I've got to go to a place called Islas Ballestas. You don't want to go. It's pretty gross."

"That's okay," she said. "I can handle it."

"No!" Ben had to think double time to come up with an excuse to keep her from coming along. "Someone has to hit the escape key in case I get stuck or the game crashes. You stay behind and be my control center."

April cocked her head to the side. "Sounds boring."

"It means you get to be the boss." When April's eyes widened, Ben added. "Not forever. Just this one time!"

She scowled and crossed her arms. "No deal."

"Come on!" Ben pleaded. "You can tell me where to go. Besides, everything I see, you can see on the monitor. You can control the game manually, but warn me if you decide to zap me someplace weird."

April cocked her head and gave him a sideways glance. It was no use arguing with her.

Ben groaned. "Okay. You can come along."

"You didn't have a choice," April said, clearly pleased with herself.

Islas Ballestas was still listed among the options when the game booted up. April dialed the code and they were whisked to an island that was — as advertised — gross, slippery and reeking of excrement.

Jagged rocks rose out of the sea. Not very hospitable to humans but a paradise for the animals that made it their home. Hundreds, maybe thousands of birds perched along the hillside. Rivers of white slime dribbled down the reddish brown rocks like icing on a bundt cake.

Guano.

Poop.

Fertilizer.

Ben and April stood on one of the few rocks not covered in it.

"If I had been a slave I would have thrown myself into the sea and drowned rather than harvest this stuff," Ben said.

"Not me. I would have made those slave traders eat it until they choked." April pointed toward the mainland where a giant drawing was etched into the hillside. Hey! What's that? Looks like a humongous alien stick figure with monster hands."

"Or a candleholder," Ben said.

"Or a cactus," said April. "Think it's a clue?"

"Maybe. I still vote for candleholder."

"Maybe it lights the way at night," April said. "Or maybe we should find a light. Or maybe we should look for a big monster. Does it mean we've seen the light?"

April's inane chattering made Ben wish he'd left her behind.

Startled by a different noise, Ben ducked behind a boulder and pulled April alongside him. A speedboat approached, loaded with tourists dressed in bright orange life preservers. The tourists greedily snapped pictures. The guide pointed out various features of the island over a microphone.

"Islas Ballestas is home to many species such as the blue footed booby, humboldt penguins, seals and . . ."

"Ooh!" "Aah!" Snap! Snap! Flash!

"Note the large keyholes cut into the rock by centuries of pounding surf!"

Snap! Flash! "Ooh!" "Aah!"

"And behind us you get a good view of El Candelabro," continued the guide. "It remains a mystery how that geoglyph was created. Or even who created it."

"Ooh!" Snap. Flash. "Aah!"

"See! I knew it was a candleholder," Ben whispered. "Now I wish those people would get lost so we can finish looking around."

After several more minutes of gawking and picture taking, the tour boat sped off. The atmosphere became serene and peaceful as waves of aquamarine water and foamy white surf lapped at the shore. Hoards of sea lions lounged along the beach, their flippers extended, their coarse brown and black coats shining in the sun. They watched Ben and April with sad, soulful eyes.

"Aren't the sea lions cute?" April said, moving out from behind the boulder.

"Cute wouldn't be my word for them." Ben returned his attention to the cliffs behind him and spotted the penguins the tour guide mentioned. Something else caught his attention. A condor. It banked and dipped as if searching for a meal among the mammals on the beach. It swooped over Ben and slimed him on the shoulder.

"Hey!" Ben shouted as the bird flew off.

"That's supposed to be good luck," April said. "I read it in a book."

Ben attempted to remove the slime with a rock, careful not to let the white and yellow guano touch his hands. April headed toward the water, gingerly trying to step only on clean rocks — a futile exercise.

"Don't get too close," Ben barked as he tried to get his bearings.

April approached a group of sea lions. They watched her every move. "We're looking for a statue or something to take back to Easter Island!"

There was no response from the sea lions.

"It's Easter Island we're going to, right?" April asked.

Ben nodded. "Rapa Nui is what the game calls it." He was pleased that her budding friendship with the animals would keep her out of his hair for a while. The island was huge and he had a lot of ground to cover. "Excuse me," April said, petting a sea lion on the head. "Do you know where the Rapa Nui treasure is?" At the sound of "Rapa Nui," the sea lions barked in a deafening cacophony.

April peered into the face of the largest sea lion. It looked like an old man. She pointed across the harbor, lifted her hands in the air, then hopped back and forth while wiggling her fingers.

The sea lions stopped barking. The old man sea lion raised up on its sleek black flippers. Twice as large as the others, it quickly advanced toward her.

"April! Look out!" Adrenaline pumping, Ben ran toward her. He knew he shouldn't have let her come along. This WAS a booby trap.

Before Ben could reach his sister, the animal stopped and issued a loud, threatening bark. It bobbed its massive brown head toward a narrow stretch of beach then loped in that direction.

When April stayed put, the sea lion returned, barked louder then pushed her forward with its nose.

"I guess we're supposed to follow him," she said.

The sea lion led them to a hidden cave but stopped short of the entrance. Ben slipped in sideways and wrinkled his nose. The air was dank and mildewed.

"Wouldn't it be cool," April said, " if all those slaves actually jumped into the sea and turned into sea lions or seals like they do in Irish legends?" She nuzzled the animals on the nose, patted its golden brown mane and gave it a kiss. It did not turn into a handsome prince. Instead, it barked more gently and the cave walls began to glow. The sea lion brushed April on her cheek and rubbed her arm with a flipper before returning to its place on the beach.

Okay. April did serve a purpose. Ben swore he would never admit that out loud.

He traced wall carvings with his fingertips — three-masted ships, people in chains. A dotted line showed the journey of ships from a triangular shaped island to this one. A single Moai was painted just above Easter Island. This Moai, however, had a thin body attached. Ben could tell April understood the message. Gone were her usual flippant remarks. She studied the drawings quietly.

Walking across the cave, Ben nearly tripped on a hole in the ground. Ben guessed it to be a fire pit of some kind. It made sense that the slaves would need to warm themselves and dry out the humidity.

"Ben!" April covered her mouth and pointed further into the cave.

Tucked in the shadows, a skeleton sat cross-legged on the ground, its bony arms and fingers clutching a Rongorongo tablet to its chest.

"Don't look!" Ben pushed her behind him for safety.

"Too late. I've already seen it." April winced and closed her eyes. Seconds later, she opened them just enough to peek at the skeleton and mumbled something under her breath. Ben understood. His mother said one should always say a prayer for the safe flight of a soul that has passed on.

Out of respect Ben recited his own internal prayer, then touched the tablet without disturbing the skeleton. As expected, the tablet glowed and changed to English.

*"Return the treasure to its rightful home.
When the time comes, it will summon the Moai."*

The codes for "Home," "Sunnyslope," and "Rapa Nui" were listed. "This must be it," Ben said. "There's no other choices. But now that we've found the tablets, where is the treasure?"

April shrugged and sat on a pile of stones. She yawned, stretched her arms and — apparently having recovered from her initial shock — studied the skeleton with great interest. The stones shifted. April jumped to her feet and tried to replace them but they collapsed into a useless heap. Something glowed beneath the pile.

"Ben! I think I've found the treasure!"

Inside a wooden box lay a carved statue of a man with the head of a Moai and red rubies forming its eyes. It matched the carving on the wall. "Good job April! I think this is it!"

"I don't think so," said April. "When we found the other treasures we zapped back home. That's how we knew we had the right ones. So what do we do?"

"The clue said we had to return the treasure," said Ben. "I think we have to take it back to Easter Island."

April yawned wide enough to swallow the island and Ben with it. "Can we do it tomorrow? I'm so tired I can barely keep my eyes open."

"I know. But it will only take a minute to finish and then we can go home."

Ben looked around and sighed. In his haste he had left Grace's PC on his desk. There was no way to pilot the program manually. If they didn't find a dialer they might be stuck in the cave forever.

"Jackson! Quit this application."

"You named your computer Jackson?" asked April. "As in Jackson Carter?"

Ben rolled his eyes and tried again. "Jackson! Quit this application!"

There was no response. The voice command module on his Mac didn't work when the game was running. They were stuck until his mother checked on them. Having an adult enter the room seemed to be a sure fire way to deactivate the program.

April kicked at the stones now littering the cave floor while Ben searched further into the cave.

*Dead end.*

# CHAPTER TWENTY-FOUR

# Milestones

"Only those who attempt the absurd
can achieve the impossible."

• *Albert Einstein*

• "Where'd you find that?" Ben asked when he returned to find April holding a wooden pole.

"Over there." She pointed to a crack in the wall. "I realized the skeleton was a fake so I looked behind it to see if there were more clues." She aimed the pole toward the fire pit and waved it like a magic wand. "Abracadabra!"

Ben stared at the pit hoping something would happen. The pit remained dormant.

"Open Sesame!" April shouted, waving her arm more vigorously. A silver rod slipped out of the shaft and rolled to a stop at her feet. "Oops! I think I broke it!"

Ben braced for a change in the hologram. When nothing happened he picked up the rod. Tiny Rongorongo patterns covered its surface. Ben tried inserting it back into the pole but couldn't find an opening. "It's probably Uncle Henry's power source for these fake tablets and cave lights," Ben said. "I don't think ancient people had metal stuff like this back then. Keep looking for a way out."

He tossed the rod aside and paused. The holes circling the pit contained a shallow notch. They were barely visible. He crouched and ran his finger along the surface to be sure.

"Did you know these rocks have a ridge on 'em?" April said, tossing one to Ben. "Think it's a clue?"

Ben caught the rock and frowned. "Doubt it." There were only eight holes. Not enough to make a dialer. But with no other options left, he placed the rock in a hole. It didn't fit. He tried the next hole with the same result. Three holes later he found one that matched. He yelped with excitement. Soon he and April matched rocks to holes as if solving a preschool puzzle. Once completed, the formation glowed but there weren't enough nodes to form a dialer.

Ben twisted a rock. It clicked and locked in place. "April! Twist the rocks on your side. I'll do mine. Righty tighty."

When the last of the rocks was locked into place, the ground shook as six additional nodes rose out of the ground. The rocks now formed a glowing dialer complete with center Yin Yang symbol.

"I guess that bird slime was good luck!" said Ben.

As he and April entered the transport beam, a chorus of barks could be heard from the entrance of the cave as if the sea lions were saying, "goodbye," or maybe, "thank-you."

◆

The red hatted Moai remained submerged in the ground. Ben and April slipped down the staircase, found an empty niche and placed the statue inside. A narrow drawer slid out of the wall. Inside lay a black basalt Moai with coral forming the whites of its eyes and red rubies for irises. Once Ben retrieved it and a star chart with the letter "E", he and April were instantly zapped back to his bedroom. On the monitor, the Moai rotated above the altar of the Guardian.

Ben put the statue on the balance scale which fell to the right with a loud clunk.

"What's wrong?" asked April. "Isn't this the right treasure?"

He shrugged and studied the canopic jars. Each was translucent and a different color. He hadn't noticed that detail before. Four matched the gems they had collected.

When Ben placed the Moai to the side of the scale, the rubies fell out. He placed the jewels on the tray. The scale balanced. To the right, the metal rods on the closest canopic jar clicked into place.

"April, you put the other stones on the scale. It's only fair since you, Grace, and Serise found them."

The green gemstone dislodged from the Tibetan statue, the scale balanced and the rods of the second canopic jar on the left clicked into place. The same happened with the remaining gems. But the door to the Guardian remained closed. Not even a hint of what was to come. With Uncle Henry it was always all or nothing.

"So we have to wait until we collect them all before we get the surprise?" April yawned. "We've only got one more day. It will be quicker to play without the holograms."

"I don't think you can do that," Ben said.

"Yes, you can. We got tired of walking everywhere and switched the special effects off."

"Let me guess," said Ben. "Serise figured out how to do it."

"No." April attempted a grin but her eyes drooped closed. "I did. By accident. Just hit the escape key after all the 3-D stuff starts. It's like an on/off button. That's how we got through the puzzles so fast." April yawned again. "By the way, we took a vote. Even if the girls win we won't make you and Carlos drink Mom's breakfast drink. That would just be mean."

Ben smiled. His sister had a heart after all.

April's words slurred. "I'm tired. I'll . . . just . . . sit . . . on the bed . . . and watch."

Ben studied remaining list of locations. He opened his backpack and retrieved the slip of paper with his dad's secret codes. "Where should we go next? You can pick this time."

Silence was followed by a quiet rasping sound.

"April?"

His sister lay propped against a pile of pillows. Ben nudged her. She was out cold and snoring. He picked her up and carried her to her own room. She was surprisingly light. Not like hoisting Carlos on his shoulders. Ben kicked the comforter out of the way then slid her onto the bed. April sighed, then snored again. Her school book fell to the floor with a gentle "thump". Ben reached down to get it, thumbed through the pages and remembered the general storyline from his own fourth grade class years ago. He placed the book on the nightstand, then covered his sister with a blanket. Tomorrow, he'd explain to her why her ATM theory wouldn't work.

# CHAPTER TWENTY-FIVE

# Detour

> "I may not have gone where I intended to go,
> But I think I have ended up where I intended to be."
>
> • *Douglas Adams*

♦ **9:00 p.m.**

Ben returned to his room and slumped in his chair.

*Time to start figuring things out for yourself, Ben Webster.*

He rubbed his eyes, tempted to crawl into bed himself. But memories of recent events haunted him.

*". . . calling all the teams in . . ."*

*"We've been compromised . . ."*

Ben psyched himself up for one final mission before calling it quits for the day. He attempted to synchronize Grace's computer with his own. After three computer crashes, he found an open source code that worked and configured it to access his computer through a remote wireless connection. He rubbed his sore shoulders, felt something crusty beneath his fingers and froze. The slime from the condor was still on his shirt.

After changing shirts, he pulled a crumpled paper from his jeans pocket, smoothed the wrinkles and set it on a stand next to his computer.

First Dynasty pendant - British Museum

N 51 W 0

Hope diamond - Smithsonian Museum

N 38.55 W 77.2

Estrucan medallion - Vatican City

N 41.54 E 12.27

The coordinates from his father's notepad weren't on the game menu. Would they work anyway?

Ben started with the obvious — the British Museum. He arrived to find the hallways dark and deserted. His watch read, 9:00 p.m. Pacific time.

He didn't have time to do the mental math needed to translate that to London time but he was relieved to have the place to himself. His footsteps echoed as he searched corridor after corridor. Moonlight cast an eerie glow on the colossal heads in the Egyptian room. He felt like a secret agent skulking around, undetected. After a while, he stumbled upon a familiar courtyard. Success! A sign across the hallway read "Special exhibits."

But his joy was short lived. The exhibit had closed the day before.

"Can I help you?"

Ben's stomach lurched. No one had ever spoken to him in the game before.

"The museum is closed," said a security guard whose name tag read "Albert." The short, brown-skinned man spoke with a thick British accent. His dreads were tucked neatly under his cap.

Unsure what to say, and still in shock, Ben just nodded.

"Young man, it's five-thirty in the morning. Perhaps you would like to return during normal hours — with your parents?"

Ben wondered if the guard could hear his heart thumping in his chest. "Could I ask one question?"

"I suppose it would do no harm. One question, then on your way, eh?" The guard's hazel eyes twinkled in the moonlight as he looked at his watch.

"Where'd the exhibit go?" Ben asked, trying not to stammer. "The one that was in this room?"

"School assignment?" The guard spoke gently, as if he were not surprised to find a strange American boy wandering the hallway after hours.

Ben nodded so fast he could have doubled as a bobble-head doll.

The guard smiled and handed him an information sheet. Most of the items were returned to the museum archives, underground. No access for the public. No way to get to the First Dynasty pendant. That should have been expected. He was playing from his father's codes, not his uncle's. Everything else had been sent back to their owners around the world.

"Seeking the path to enlightenment?" asked the guard.

Ben froze. A Tibetan Monk had said the same thing to the girls. "Yes, Sir."

"I suggest the Bandiagara Escarpment. Interesting village there. You might find the answers you crave. Or a clue. You won't find what you need at this location."

The guard escorted Ben to the courtyard. "I trust you know your way home from here?"

"Yes, Sir. Thank you, Sir," Ben said, his voice trembling.

"On your way then. Good luck with your journey." The guard tipped his hat. "Oh, and I believe you dropped this." He placed a rock in Ben's hand then turned, leaving Ben alone.

*Why didn't he arrest me?*

Ben then looked in his still-shaking hand. The rock sparkled like a diamond. But it was blue. And it wasn't his.

A bright flash appeared behind him. Ben spun around. "Excuse me! Sir?"

The guard had vanished.

# CHAPTER TWENTY-SIX

# The Hogon

"To one who has faith, no explanation is necessary.
To one without faith, no explanation is possible."

• *St. Thomas Aquinas*

• Ben was completely spooked, but he was also running out of time. He used Grace's computer to pilot to the location marked "Bandiagara Escarpment" and found himself sitting inside a mud hut. It took a minute for his eyes to adjust.

"It is impolite to enter a house without knocking first," said a voice coming from a dark corner. "Are you lost?"

Ben tried to stand up, but bumped his head on the low ceiling and sat down again on the dirt floor. He couldn't see who was speaking. "I'm searching for the path to enlightenment."

"I see." An old man crouched next to him, his face wrinkled with age and decorated with a coarse salt and pepper beard. "Enlightenment is not an easy path. Are you prepared for the journey?"

Ben considered the question. The museum guard would not have sent him here if it weren't a clue.

"Yes, sir. I'm ready."

"At what price?"

"Price?" Ben realized that he still had the blue diamond in his pocket. He placed it in the man's palm. "Will this pay for my journey?"

The old man laughed, then gestured for Ben to follow him. "We don't have a lot of time."

Outside, Ben found himself in a village built at the base of a cliff. Pointed thatched roofs covered a cluster of windowless clay huts. Other than a few low-lying bushes and a sprinkling of gnarled Baobab trees, the landscape was mostly dry and dusty. "Where am I?"

The man swung his gnarled wooden staff in a wide arc. "Where do you think you are?"

Ben sighed. He needed to solve the game by tomorrow. At this rate, he wasn't going to solve this one location in a month. "I think I'm in Bandiagara Escarpment."

The man laughed again. "That is an obvious answer, but not the one I was looking for. Where you are on the planet is not relevant. It is where you are in the universe that is significant."

"Okay," said Ben. "How about third planet in the solar system?"

The old man rubbed his temple and shook his head from side to side.

"Who are you?" asked Ben.

"I am the Hogon," the man said. "The Dogon village elder. I guess you could say I'm the boss."

Dogon? Hogon? Another riddle? Then something dawned on him. *"The Dogon have known about . . ."*

Isn't that what his uncle had started to say before his father shut him up?

Excited, Ben said, "I'm searching for a jewel. It will help me find some lost tribes. Do you have anything like that lying around?"

"The tribes are not lost. They just haven't been discovered. There is a difference." The man reached into his robes and produced a cloth bag. "You've always had everything you needed. You just refuse to see it. Perhaps some parts were hidden on purpose. But isn't that what makes a journey more satisfying?" He placed the bag in Ben's hand.

Ben loosened the drawstring, giddy to have solved the puzzle so fast. Then he slumped. The bag was filled with only sand and dirt. He looked to the Hogon for answers, but the man was staring at the sky. Ben looked up too.

"Ever look at the stars at night?" the Hogon said. "At the brightest of them all? It is a seed. We call it Po Tolo. Others call it Sirius A."

Ben nodded. More stick pin art. Where was Dr. Lopez when he needed him? Or Carlos?

"Around that star," the man continued, "is another. We've known about it for years. Part of our Dogon culture and our lore, with a few parts made up for nosy tourists. But you're not a tourist are you?"

"No, sir, I'm not," Ben said.

"Then learn before the sun comes up," the old priest said. "Thousands of years ago, life sprang upon this earth."

Ben was already lost. He'd just play along until he got his gem and star chart.

"But there are many Earths," the man continued. "Many seeds. Only one base. One beginning. Just as all myths and religions on Earth have similar origins even though they appear to have developed independently."

Ben just smiled.

"You don't understand, do you?" the Hogon asked.

"Yeah," Ben said. "We're in Africa. It's the Cradle of Life. Got it!"

The man laughed. "I have sons of my own. They are just as pig-headed. Can't ever admit they don't know everything. Africa is A cradle. But not the only one. Why are you so resistant to learning about your history?"

"Because — " Ben stopped. He was embarrassed. "Because it's all I ever hear about. I just want to be like everyone else."

The Hogon seemed confused. "Explain."

"You know — normal." Ben said, trying to avoid eye contact.

The old man's gaze grew intense. "Normal? I am still unclear. Normal is relative."

Ben shrugged. "You know, without all the ancient history baggage that makes me feel like I'm doomed to fail before I even start."

"You are what you choose to be," the Hogon said. "And yet you push away the very people trying to help you."

Ben bit his lip. "So my uncle is trying to tell me something."

"Of course," the Hogon said. "It is both his job, and his nature to do so."

"Okay," Ben said. "Then where's the path?"

"Closer than you think." The man pulled a second pouch from his cloak, then reached inside again and pulled out a star map with the letter 'C.' "Does this help?"

Ben was tempted to lie, but his watch read 10:00 pm. The "clock" was ticking louder than ever and it was a school night. "No. It doesn't. I don't get it."

"You have collected maps. You've never seen a word with those letters before?"

Ben wracked his brain, then shrugged.

"Think harder."

He tried, but other than the options he'd already ruled out — like the fact that Darth Vader was not his father, and the fact that the letter C ruled out the possibility of rearranging the other letters into "NOSE" — he was stumped.

"Sleep on it," the priest said. "It will come to you."

"That's it? Sleep on it? No enlightenment?" Ben couldn't believe it. He searched the village with his eyes hoping to spot something he could use.

The man shrugged. "I could give you the answers, but where's the challenge in that? Didn't you say it was time to start figuring things out yourself?"

Ben's jaw dropped. He had never said that out loud, not even inside the game.

The man winked. "Ben, a butterfly struggles to break out of its cocoon to strengthen its wings. It's nature's way of helping it become strong enough to fly. If you cut the cocoon to help it, it will die without ever taking flight. So the game is a way to help you strengthen your wings. Do you understand?"

"No. I really don't," Ben said. "Just sounds like another riddle."

The man sighed and placed his hand on Ben's shoulder. "You will. In the meantime, you are supposed to go to the old Nubian capitol in

Sudan. But it's late, the clock is ticking, and I need my rest. So do you. I'm told it's a school night so I'll save you the trip. Give my regards, and that pouch, to your uncle. And tell him we hope his next visit occurs before Sirius B completes another full orbit."

"Is that it?" asked Ben.

"Afraid so," the Hogon said. "Not allowed to give you all the answers."

Ben squeezed the worthless pouch. "All the answers? You didn't give me any answers!"

The man chuckled quietly. "Like I said. I have sons. They think they know everything. You have all you need and know more than you think."

The man threw the chart into the air. Parts of it overlapped actual stars. *So that was it.* Each chart showed only random stars. He'd need them all to fill in the blanks.

"Thanks." Ben hesitated. He had one more question. "Do you know my dad?"

The man's eyes sparkled. "Yes. He is an honorary member of our tribe."

Ben was stunned. He wasn't sure he wanted the answer to the next question. "Is he a jewel thief? A spy?"

"Your father does what he must to guarantee that you have what you need," the Hogon said.

Ben gave up. The Hogon might as well have been speaking in hieroglyphics. "Then I guess I'd better get home. Don't have a dialer handy, do you?"

The man smiled. "I have something better. I have faith in you." He pointed to the top of the cliff. It was at least 1,000 feet high.

Confused, Ben looked around for a path to the top. "How am I supposed to get all the way up there?"

"Take a leap of faith." The Hogon jumped, his bare feet rising a foot off the ground.

The man had clearly lost his mind. But Ben jumped anyway and found himself soaring toward the stars and into . . . broad daylight? He looked down and realized he had not been outside until now. He'd been in a holographic projection running inside of a holographic projection. The elderly man waved beneath a hole in the roof of the hut.

Once Ben reached the top of the cliff he was zapped back into his room. The pouch was still in his hand, a white diamond he'd never seen rotated on the screen above the altar, and the new star chart was in the ancient book with all the others.

# CHAPTER TWENTY-SEVEN

# Getting Warmer

"The real voyage of discovery consists
not in seeking new landscapes
but in having new eyes."

• *Marcel Proust*

• Ben was hit with a wave of adrenaline. He laid the star charts out in order of their discovery:

## S O N E C

An internet search for "sonec" turned up nothing useful. Out of curiosity, he looked up Sirius A and B and discovered that the smaller of the two stars completed its orbit every fifty years. The Dogon planned activities around it. So what was the priest saying? He hoped Uncle Henry would visit again before another fifty years had passed? Sounded like sarcasm. But the legend was still fascinating. The Dogon knew about those stars before telescopes were strong enough to see them. It fit the pattern but didn't answer any questions.

The man said Ben had everything he needed already. But what he needed was another clue. He hit the "Escape" key and turned off the 3-D holographic projections. The speed of the game accelerated. Armed with the digital reference set for National Geographic, an atlas, a DVD ROM encyclopedia and a browser window opened to the CIA World Factbook, Ben traveled the globe collecting clues and retracing his steps when he hit dead-ends.

He missed the slick interactive feature but it was easier to play without walking every place. But he didn't find what he was looking for. By eleven thirty and he was tempted to quit. Still curious about his father's notes, went to the Vatican Museum instead.

After walking endless corridors he found the first Dynasty pendant. It contained no jewels, just Egyptian scarabs and he didn't zap back to the bedroom. Discouraged, he put it away and began dialing Sunnyslope when a different pendant dropped from an open case. The sign read: Norwegian Risku. Saami symbol of the sun. He tried to put it back but zapped to his bedroom instead.

He checked in with Serise and Grace who looked dead on their feet. They'd discovered a black pearl in an oyster carried by a whale off the shores of Bora Bora. Seven clues were in place. One more to go.

"You found two more?" asked Grace. "Way to go, Webster!"

Ben nodded. "Thanks. The second one was a happy accident. But it worked and there's another star chart in the book. "

"What's that gold necklace?" she asked. "How does it fit the pattern?"

"Beats me. It's Norwegian, though," Ben said. "You know, we've been playing without trying to figure out the identities of the missing tribes."

"I figured that it had to do with the countries we visited," Grace said.

Ben yawned. "But which tribes? There's a lot of people living on those continents. Every location says that the world will come to an end if we don't solve the mystery."

Grace groaned. "Are you sure there isn't a scary ending?"

"Can't be sure of *anything*." Ben opened a text file on his computer and made a list based on where he and the girls found jewels:

1. Sudan, Africa which was once the Nubian empire.
2. New Mexico along the Navajo Long walk.
3. Guatemala at a Royal Ball Court

4. Nepal at a Tibetan monastery.

Ben realized how obvious the first four were. Of course his uncle would pick the ethnic origins of the kids. Wasn't that his point about connecting with their past?

The others were less clear: Easter Island, Norway, South Pacific. The final trail lead to the Antarctic and as far as he knew there had never been any tribes living there.

With seven jewels in place, the canopic rods clicked into position and glowed with more hieroglyphic patterns. There was too much to decipher and asking Carlos to analyze the celestial patterns was out of the question. The seven letters in order now spelled:

## S O N E C I A

Even weirder, the star charts became transparent when layered on top of the other and showed a huge blank space in the center. Triangles beneath the letters formed seven points of an eight-pointed star. The pattern had been popping up everywhere. Grace insisted it was a coincidence. She'd found the same star in a Wingdings font set on her computer. Maybe the names of the tribes would be revealed when the eighth jewel and map were found. He printed screen shots just in case.

"Serise? Any clues about those hieroglyphics. Got any new tricks up your sleeve."

She threw up her hands in defeat. "I'm exhausted. There's an English test tomorrow. I don't have time to write a program for all of them. Right now I'm so tired I'm not even sure I could write the alphabet."

Grace nodded and yawned.

Ben couldn't shake the idea that finding jewels wasn't his uncle's real message — that the treasure hunt was just a distraction. He had to follow this through to the end . . . tonight.

Alone.

"Okay. Get some sleep," he said. "We can finish over the weekend."

"By the way," Grace said. "You know that weird plant in the

greenhouse, the one that says Amorphophallus Titanum? It's not an avocado plant."

"You sure?" Ben asked.

"Yes. I looked it up," said Grace. "It's a corpse plant. They bloom every forty years. It will smell like a dead person when it opens."

# CHAPTER TWENTY-EIGHT

# The Bay of Whales

"The important thing is not to stop questioning.
Curiosity has its own reason for existing."

• *Albert Einstein*

• Familiar footsteps padded along the carpet outside Ben's bedroom door. A gentle knock followed and the door opened a crack.

"Are you decent?"

Ben put the computer to sleep, pulled his father's list from the stand and slipped under the comforter. "Yeah. You can come in."

His mother took a visual sweep of the room. She seemed distracted and tired. Then it hit Ben, he had been so busy solving the game he had forgotten about the time. His mother was hours overdue.

"Finish your math?"

"It's on the desk." He panicked when he realized the leather collar was next to the computer. They weren't allowed on the cat but his mother never explained why.

"Thanks for putting April to bed." She brushed the collar aside as if it were nothing and surveyed the math notes. She waved the homework paper at him. "Do this yourself?"

Ben nodded

"Good job, Honey. There's a mistake on problem number six. Simple. I'll help you fix it in the morning. Okay?" She touched the dead rose on Ben's desk, frowned and moved the vase to the windowsill. Within seconds the flower began to revive.

"Not going on a trip?" Ben faked a wide yawn and did a double take at the now erect flower.

His mother's eyes flashed briefly. She sighed and looked out the window to some faraway place.

"Seems like everyone else is," he continued.

His mother nodded again but didn't answer the question. Instead, she kissed him on the forehead. "Get some sleep." Then she left and closed the door. No song, no candles, no ritual.

Ben jumped out of bed and ran to the window when he heard the kitchen door slam shut. His mother hurried toward the garage where a light glowed in the workshop. She was probably going to tell Ben's father to wrap up his experiments for the night, or to stop trying to increase his car's energy output. She once asked him to explain the point of changing the engine specifications when there was no place on Earth to drive a car 300 miles per hour. His father had kissed her and said, "Not yet, you mean."

*Corny? Definitely. But not spies. Not them.*

Ben studied the star charts again. The Dogon man insisted he'd seen the letters before. But where? He let his head drop to his desk as he replayed the events of the past days. The passwords, the holograms, the sweat lodge, the satellite dish, the . . .

*"Think harder."*

The satellites. The star was on the program that shut them down. Carlos said his father was blocking the government data.

*"It will come to you,"* The Hogon had said.

Think, Ben, think!

*"Sonecian Control — online."*

Ben's head jerked up. The name of a system they accessed on the Lopez computer. But what did that mean? In the morning he would show the combined star chart to Carlos — whether Carlos wanted to help or not.

Antarctica was the only destination remaining in the game options. What tribe would be living there? The lost penguins?

Curiosity got the better of him. He wanted to play with the hologram running one last time.

Thinking about the extreme cold made him shiver. The southern California climate didn't exactly require keeping a parka or earmuffs on hand. He would have to make do with a warm-up jacket and two extra blankets from the closet. As a precaution, he turned off the bedroom lights and lowered his window shade. Now the glow of the computer monitor was the sole source of illumination.

Ben wrapped the blankets around his body, the outermost bearing the logo of the Cleveland Cavaliers, then pressed the escape button and saw the chamber of the Guardian materialize on the monitor. This time there were four choices:

South Pole
90 00S 00 00W

Deception Island
62 58 S 60 33W

Paradise Bay
64 54 S 62 52 W

Bay of Whales
78 30 S 164 20W

Rolling a die from his Monopoly game, Ben narrowed the choice to the Bay of Whales which sent him to a remote ice floe in the Ross Sea. He was greeted with bone numbing cold and razor sharp wind. Stumbling forward, he tripped over a footlocker. *Out here?* A thick parka, gloves, scarf and boots were tucked inside along with a survival kit containing a compass, goggles, emergency flare, and matches. Uncle Henry thought of everything.

Ben's hands felt many degrees colder than the miles of ice surrounding him as he struggled to put on the extra clothing. The boots were too large for his feet, but once on, they shrank to a perfect fit. His body thawed to normal temperature, as if the clothing contained a built-in heat source.

His eyes hurt from the intensity of the sun's rays reflecting off the thick ice. Sliding on the goggles, he tried to get his bearings. There were no shadows to guide him in the desolate wasteland. No way to distinguish the sky from the land. His mouth felt parched. All this water frozen around him and yet none to drink.

*Typical, Webster. Save the hardest part of the game for last.*

Ben pulled the hood of the parka tighter around his head and wrapped a scarf around his face. Compass in hand, he headed north in the hopes of finding a shore - or anything in liquid form.

He walked for ten minutes before spotting a tent fifty yards ahead. It appeared out of nowhere. The image could easily be a mirage caused by the blinding light. It glowed orange then vanished. In its place stood a tall, brown-skinned woman, her long hair peaking out from beneath a lavishly embroidered hood. Ben felt exposed to both the elements and to the stranger but there was no place to hide.

He crept closer, his snow-white parka concealing everything but his eyes. The woman took no notice of him and busied herself melting the ice with a hand-held flame thrower. She knelt, gathered samples into silver vials and placed the containers in a woven basket.

A massive white bird circled the woman several times, carrying a basket in its duck-like beak, its wingspan as long as the condor Ben had seen in the Andes Mountains. It swooped and soared in graceful arcs before landing at the feet of the mysterious woman.

A flash of light erupted.

The bird disappeared.

In its place stood a second woman, dressed in similar parka, long flowing robe and brown leather boots. Her face was hidden by the thick layer of fur ringing the edge of the hood. Long tufts of straight black hair blew in the wind. She cradled the basket in her arms.

Both women worked quickly, melting the ice and filling the vials with core samples. After a few minutes, they placed their baskets on the ground and assembled two tall poles with glass orbs attached to the ends. The poles slid into the ice with little resistance, sending arcs of electricity and emitting deep oscillating tones into the air. Even at this distance, Ben could feel the vibrations beneath his feet.

In an instant, two massive blue-gray whales appeared. They swam along the surface of the ocean then submerged, their tails slapping the surf and sending sprays of water and ice toward the women. The women did not flinch. Instead they bowed apologetically and adjusted the rods. That changed the pitch and the frequency of the oscillation. The whales surfaced again, blew tall plumes of mist out of their blow-holes and sped away as if in a panic.

A ripple appeared, and then another, until the water churned violently. And then, as if out of a horror movie, giant gray tentacles pierced the surface. A Kraken, or whatever it was, closed around the women, one tentacle curling into a platform for them. The women gathered their baskets, stepped onto the platform and were encased in a shimmering gold cocoon. As the giant beast submerged with its new quarry, the first woman lowered the hood of her parka and looked in Ben's direction.

Their eyes met.

Ben's heart lurched. He saw a glimmer of recognition on the woman's face as she pulled out a cell phone — the same type used by the scientist in Llactapata — and spoke into it. The second woman lowered her hood and studied him as well, her face expressionless. In seconds, all traces of the women were gone.

Ben's mother and Cheryl Hightower had just vanished into the freezing Antarctic waters.

## CHAPTER TWENTY-NINE

# Messenger

"Life is really simple,
but we insist on making it complicated."

• *Confucius*

---

• "Mom! Wait! Come back!"

Ben rushed toward the water's edge, his movements hampered by the heavy layers of clothing he wore and the lack of traction on the ice. No footprints were found on the frozen ground. No sign the mothers had been there except for the metal poles which remained fixed in place. Ben ran his gloved hands up and around the smooth surface but could find no switch to reactivate them or cause the giant beast to return.

Was the Kraken another type of dialer?

A lone penguin waddled up to Ben, its black flippers pressed to its side. It stood about four feet tall and measured up to Ben's belly button. Its white chest stuck out proudly as it approached

"Where did you come from?" Ben took a step backwards.

The Emperor penguin carried a tubular object in its beak that it dropped at Ben's feet before waddling away and dissolving into the landscape. Ben knelt to examine the object — a scroll, tied with a red ribbon. He opened it expecting to find more of his uncle's cryptic clues and more dialer codes. Instead, he recognized his mother's handwriting.

*I guess I don't need to ask if you want your uncle's disk back.*
*Go to bed. There are things you need to understand.*
*We'll talk in the morning. I'll explain everything then.*

The metal poles dissolved without a trace. Expelling the air he'd trapped in his lungs, Ben read the note twice to make sure he understood its meaning. *A game!* He felt relieved and stupid. His parents weren't thieves or spies. They had designed an incredible, realistic, addictive 3-D game. With graphic capabilities like this his family would corner the market. They were all super competitive anyway and now everyone would be infected with the virtual reality bug.

*You can now go back to your regularly scheduled program.*

Ben checked his watch — half past midnight. He was too exhausted to search for a dialer. He pressed the escape key on Grace's laptop and found himself back in his bedroom, his extra blankets laying in a crumpled heap on the floor. He couldn't wait to see what other gigantic beasts he encountered. But he'd wait and finish the game with his friends. He didn't want to spoil the fun. And he'd tell Carlos they had everything figured wrong.

Ben tossed his homework and the cat collar into his backpack then changed into his pajamas. For the first time in a week he relaxed. Now there would be no more secrets from his parents. The gang could safely meet in the open, solve the final puzzle and unlock the mystery — just in time for his uncle's deadline. Maybe he'd even take a detour and see what was on Deception Island. With a name like that, how could he resist?

*"Expedition in your future . . ."*

*"Coach says a championship is in the bag with you on the team . . ."*

Ben glanced at the silhouette of the roses against the windowpane. All three were blooming. Just another piece in the Webster family puzzle. He'd solve that tomorrow too.

Exhausted, Ben smiled as he drifted off to sleep.

Life was finally going to get interesting.

# On the Run

♦ ♦

# CHAPTER THIRTY

## Escape

"To live is so startling it leaves little time for anything else"

◆ ◆ *Emily Dickinson*

◆ ◆ **Thursday, October 30**

*Thump! Thump!*

*Ben flies down the court, dodging his opponents, dribbling the ball like a pro. The State Championship hangs in the balance. He ducks and weaves, then passes the ball to the right.*

*Yes!*

*His teammate takes the lead, rushing toward the basket. In a sudden, preplanned move, his teammate fakes out the guard and passes the ball to Ben who is in position.*

*Thump! Thump!*

*Ben dribbles, reverses direction, fakes a pass, and then shoots. It is going . . . going . . .*

*BLAAM!*

*Score! Three point shot!*

"Ben!"

*Ben waves to his adoring fans and is greeted with thunderous applause. The score is tied. Thirty seconds left on the clock. Ben swivels to block the forward. The forward shoots.*

*Miss!*

*Ben defies gravity as he swoops into the air to rebound.*

*"Yes! Ladies and Gentleman,"* the announcer proclaims, *"if Ben Webster were a bird he'd fly away."*

*Thump! Thump!*

*Ben charges down the court, showboating, dribbling from one hand to the other. Out of nowhere, someone knocks him to the ground.*

*BLAAM!*

*Foul!*

*"Get up!" the crowd roars. Ben hears the rhythmic stomping from the bleachers.*

*Thump! Thump!*

*"Ben!"*

*"Yes! They're shouting his name! The San Diego Cobras are undefeated. Ben is the Sunnyslope Jaguar's only hope of victory. If he can nail the free throw, the game is assured. He just needs to . . . "*

*Thump!*

"Get up!"

Someone shook him violently. "Hurry!"

Ben slowly opened his eyes. "What? Did the alarm go off? I didn't hear . . ." Words slurring, he drifted back to sleep, *". . . ten seconds left on the clock. He makes the shot. It's going . . . going . . ."*

*BLAAM!*

"Ben, PLEASE! Get up now!"

Wet sandpaper scraped against his cheek. The fog cleared. Aris sat on his chest and licked him repeatedly. Groggy, Ben tried to concentrate and saw the urgency on his mother's face. "What's going on?"

"No time." She tugged his arm, pulled him out of bed and through the bedroom door. His backpack was slung over her shoulder. Ben blinked and allowed his eyes to adjust. His father carried April on his back as he rushed down the staircase. Aris followed close behind.

"Mom? What's going on?"

"Shhh!" his mother hissed. "Just hurry!"

Ben ran back and grabbed something off his desk.

"Ben!"

His mother spun him. Eyes wide in surprise, she snatched the Dogon pouch from his hand and kissed it as if it were a miracle, then shoved it in her pocket. She didn't ask where it came from.

The family flew out the back door, through the garden and toward the garage.

BLAAM!

The night sky turned shades of bright orange and red. Stunned, Ben looked back in time to see something explode into flames down the street. A bolt of lightning shot upward from behind the Lopez's garage. Paradise Circle was suddenly covered by a barrier that resembled a giant, pulsating soap bubble. Fingers of blue light arched across the shimmering film. It reminded Ben of the electrical spikes he made when he touched a Van de Graaff generator. Only this time, he was inside the glass container instead of outside.

BLAAM!

Hands reached out and yanked Ben backwards. Once inside the garage steel plates descended from the ceiling and sealed the opening.

"Quick! In the back!" his father barked, as the workshop door dissolved to admit them. Carlos stood with his parents, near the circular saw. They were deep in hushed conversation. Why were they in his garage? Despite the odd situation, there was still something missing. Not something — someone. His pulse quickened.

Where was Grace?

Ben was relieved to see her huddled in the far corner. Like Carlos, she kept her attention focused on her parents. All kids accounted for except . . . Serise.

He headed for his parent's cars. No one followed him. "Hey! We've got to get out of here!"

"No! This way." His father pointed to a back wall with no doors or windows.

"But we'll be burnt to a crisp!"

His father looked disappointed. He pushed a button on his watch.

A transparent panel appeared, suspended in midair above the table saw. Soon the room filled with electronic equipment, all actively processing data streams.

"Whoa!" shouted April.

Ben's jaw dropped. No wonder his father spent so much time in here. He and April were alone in their amazement. Grace's expression was passive and resolute.

*"Is this part of the game?"* he mouthed to her.

Grace diverted her gaze, but shook her head. *No!*

*No?* Ben gasped. *No? Then that means . . .*

His heart fell to his stomach. He had been right all along. His parents were —

*BLAAM!*

The explosion jolted Ben out of his daydream. Heart pounding, he stared in disbelief as the transparent panel streamed the global satellite data he and Carlos had seen on the Lopez computer. The Eye of Ra and the eight-pointed star appeared as well.

Carlos's father rushed to the panel and called up more windows. Almost all of them showed static. "Teams are on the move. Everyone's under attack. We've been compromised."

"How?" Grace's mother studied data on a separate monitor.

Carlos's father shot an angry look at Ben's father who walked the perimeter of the room with Grace's father. His hands were splayed flat against the walls as if testing the temperature. Grace's father carried a device that pinged at one second intervals.

Grace's mother traced one of the data streams with her fingers and hissed. "Explosions at all the outposts. Tibet's intact. Vatican's down. Harbor's unaffected."

"Any survivors?" asked Ben's mother.

"Less than half," Grace's mother looked stricken but her voice remained calm. In fact, all the parents, were acting as if this were just an ordinary day on the job. "Harbor's safest place to send the children."

"Transport status?" Grace's father studied his device, then shoved it in his pocket.

Carlos' father pulled up a series of charts. "ETA 24 hours. All teams ordered to evacuate."

"Ben!"

Grace's father hung a beaded necklace around Grace's neck, then spun a white crystal on the floor. Grace blinked back tears as a column of white light rose to the ceiling.

"Ben! Did you hear me?" his father.

Ben snapped to attention. "Umm, yes. I mean no. I mean . . . how do we get out of here? What's going on?"

"I'm sorry I waited so long to tell you . . ."

*BLAAM!*

The blasts grew closer in frequency.

Ben gasped for air as his adrenaline went into overdrive. "It's okay, Dad. I figured it out a while ago."

His father seemed incredulous. "How?"

*BLAAM!*

"We can't wait for David and Cheryl any longer," Grace's father interrupted. "We've got to get the children out of here now!" He gestured toward the light streaming out of the crystal.

*BLAAM!*

The light flickered and then vanished. Dr. Choedon muttered something angry in his native language before switching back to English. "Too much electrical interference." said Grace's father.

*BLAAM!*

"Jeremiah!" barked Carlos father, "I don't know how long that force-field is going to last. I've got all possible power routed to the dish."

*BLAAM!*

"Do it now!" Ben's mother ordered.

His father typed into a keypad and shouted something unintelligible. A female voice answered, "Askar." The circular saw disappeared revealing and passageway in the floor. No hieroglyphics this time. Just roughly hewn rock and crude stone steps.

*BLAAM!*

"Time to go!" Jeremiah Webster rolled the prayer beads in his hand, the beads glowing red in the data stream.

"Go where?" Ben peered down the passageway with apprehension.

"Don't worry. This route is a detour, but it's safe," his father said.

Grace and Carlos helped April into the glowing stairwell, keeping her safely tucked between them. Carlos kept a tight grip on Aris despite the cat's struggle.

"What happened to the Hightowers?" Ben asked.

"They're still outside of the barrier," his father said. "We can't risk lowering it, not even for a second."

"I'm sure they found another way," Grace's mother said. Her grim expression said otherwise.

"A way to do what?" Ben pleaded. "Mom? Dad?"

"No time to explain." His father strapped Ben's pack around his waist and pushed him toward the opening. "I'm sorry, Son. I should have done this earlier but I didn't think there was a need. I was wrong." He reached into his pocket and shoved a leather pouch into the pack. "I'm glad you figured it out on your own. Always said you were a smart kid. If we get separated, follow the instructions on this compass to get to Safe Harbor. A ship will arrive tomorrow. If we are not there in twenty-four hours, get on it. Do you understand me? No matter what GET ON IT!"

"Dad! You're scaring me."

*BLAAM!*

The armor plating retracted. A fierce wind blew the door open. Outside, the electrical shield pulsed in the night sky. Searing blue light filled the entrance to the workshop. The Hightowers stepped out of a violent swirl of dust. The armor plating dropped to its original position.

David Hightower carried a kicking and screaming Serise over his shoulder, then dumped her on the floor before rushing over to study the data streams.

Serise stared at her hands, touched her arms and shoulders, then looked up again in horror and disbelief.

Ben blinked. It took a few seconds to recover from his own shock.

"Where did you come from?"

"Would someone tell me what's going on?" Serise rose to her feet, smoothed out her blue satin pajamas and used a washcloth to remove the olive green mud mask from her face. Equipped with a large backpack and a smaller laptop case, she looked like a nerdy space alien in designer clothing. "Where's Grace? Is she still at my house?"

Still speechless, Ben pointed toward the Choedons. Serise looked relieved.

"David, is there enough power in your crystal to get the kids out?" Ben's mother asked.

"Barely," Serise's father answered. "But with that barrier up, it will be safer and quicker to get out through the museum. Did you and Frank get the equipment transported?"

"No," Grace's father said. "Kurosh has the primary artifacts."

"Can't leave equipment behind," Cheryl Hightower said. "The technology is too advanced. We can detonate from my office."

*BLAAM!*

"Hear those explosions?" asked Ben's father. "We may not have to."

The walls shook violently as if something were trying to batter its way through the door. The door bulged inward.

"Barrier's breached! We've got company folks," Frank Lopez seemed more amped than usual. Ben could swear his muscles had doubled in size.

Ben's father strapped two gold cuffs onto his wrists, two on his upper arms. He tossed a set to his wife, then barked a command. A wall opened revealing a wide variety of knives, swords, lasers and . . .

"Gear up, people!" Ben's father said, his voice calm.

Ben rushed to the wall, but was blocked by his father. "No, son, too dangerous."

"No thanks," Carlos' mother said. "We've got our own toys."

Grace's mother pulled a slender pin from her hair and released the cloisonné hair clip. Her neat bun unraveled into a braid that extended to her waist. The hair clip expanded into a multi-pointed weapon that sparked with an electrical discharge.

*BLAAM!*

"Get the kids out of here!" yelled Carlos's father. "I can hold them off." He pulled a long slender club from a holster hidden beneath his vest and pointed it at the door. With a flick of his thumb it transformed into a double-edged spear with multiple, serrated edges.

"Not by yourself, you can't!" Carlos's mother brandished a weapon of her own. It hung from a chain and looked like the ignition key for her car.

"What were you planning to do with that remote?" asked Ben's father sarcastically. "Drive us to safety?"

Carlos' mother aimed her device at the Mercedes and fired. The car was instantly vaporized. She smirked. "I've been upgrading."

"My car!" whined Ben's father.

"Had some free time on my hands while you boys were off hunting." Her expression remained fixed as she steadied her stance and pointed her weapon at the door like an action hero.

Carlos' father looked longingly at his wife's weapon.

"Oh, stop pouting you big baby. I built one for you too. I was saving it for your birthday." She tossed a duplicate to her husband.

"Always knew I married well," he said, admiring his new possession. He retracted the spear and shoved it back into the holster.

*BLAAM!*

Carlos's parents were backed up by the Hightowers and the Choedons, all of whom had drawn weapons and were pointing them at the door.

Ben, on the other hand, gulped air and reminded himself to breathe. This was madness. All around him — chaos. Walls pounding. Streets exploding. And yet, in spite of everything, the parents showed no fear.

His father opened a mahogany box and tossed a knife to his mother.

Without taking her eyes off of the door, Ben's mother caught the weapon squarely by its handle and — with one fluid movement — placed it in a sheath strapped to her waist.

Ben was mesmerized. His non-violent, never raise your voice, always turn the other cheek father had a secret cache of the scariest weapons he had ever seen. He had to do something.

"Toss me something, Dad. I can help." Ben waited but got no response.

"We can hit them with a focused solar pulse," Frank Lopez said. "The garage is reinforced with lead and titanium. It should hold."

"Are you joking? You'll take out most of Sunnyslope," Ben's mother said. "I've got a better idea."

"No! You can't risk it," his father said.

"Risk what?" Ben pleaded.

*BLAAM!*

His father shoved him back through the opening. "No time to explain, Ben. Get going. We'll get out another way. Follow the instructions on the compass and get on that ship do you hear me? Promise me you will get on that ship."

"I don't understand . . ."

*BLAAM!*

"Promise me!" His father barked in a tone Ben had heard only twice before — and only at Uncle Henry. His eyes filled with a fierceness that scared Ben. "SAY IT!"

Ben froze.

"SAY IT!"

"I promise. But . . ."

Ben felt a hand on his shoulder. He spun around in a daze. "Mom?"

"Time to go, sweetheart." Her eyes grew calm and serene.

April crawled out of the hole and clung to her desperately.

"The game?" He searched her eyes for confirmation.

She touched his cheek. "No, honey. I'm so sorry. We should have told you about our mission."

"I know." Ben tried to sound brave. "I heard Uncle Henry warning Dad about it."

His mother pressed her fingers to his lips and cut him off. "No. You don't. But we've run out of time. You have to get your sister to the Harbor. That's your mission now."

"But I can help." Ben flexed his muscles. "Just give me a weapon!"

"Not this time, Son," his father interrupted.

"But Dad! . . ."

Eyes pleading, his father crouched until they were face to face. "Ben, I know you want to help. But right now we've got a job to do. So do you."

His mother pulled him close. "I'm counting on you to take care of your sister. Keep her safe. That's more important. I need to know you are both safe so I can do my job."

*Job?* Ben couldn't breathe. Couldn't think. He blinked and tried to will himself out of this computer simulation gone wrong. "Aren't you coming with us?"

She wrapped her arms around him, hugged him tightly and kissed his forehead. Even as the walls threatened to collapse around them, panic drained from his body. His mother's necklace pressed into his chest as an overwhelming sense of calm washed over him.

The monitor went dark. For a split second, dead silence filled the workshop.

"What's happening?" Ben whispered in relief. "Is it over?"

His mother gave him a sad smile and shook her head. "Remember what I told you? I've got some dragons to slay. You've got a sister to protect. I'll see you again. Get to the Harbor. Your uncle will find you."

*BLAAM!*

The attack resumed — much harder this time — as if whatever was outside had marshaled more forces. The walls bulged as if the garage were being hit from all directions by enormous battering rams. The door was going to give at any minute.

Ben's mother kissed him, then his sister. "April — stay close to your brother. Remember. I love you both. Always!" She shoved them forcefully toward the opening and returned to the center of the room. Ben was shocked. His mother possessed the strength of an Amazon warrior.

"MOM!"

Crouching, she turned toward him, her smile a grimace and blew a kiss. "Go!" she said before tucking her head against her chest and closing her eyes as if in prayer.

*BLAAM!*

The armor plating dissolved.

Searing heat filled the room.

The exterior door splintered. Blinding light filtered through the cracks. Ben strained to get a better look. The other parents circled, backs to each other, weapons ready. Everyone, that is, except his mother. The ornamental knife on her belt remained in its sheath. Without warning, she stood, arched her back and threw something at the door. His mother launched . . .

*It couldn't be!*

A ball of flame hurled toward the door.

"Fire in the hole!" hollered Carlos's father, looking almost delighted.

Ben's father shoved Ben back into the opening as the other parents flinched and ducked.

*BLAAM!*

Another blinding flash filled the workshop. Ben caught a glimpse of his father — a long, lethal knife gripped his hand just as an explosion knocked Ben backwards into Carlos.

Silence.

"Where did they go?" cried April. "Aren't they coming with us?"

Ben scrambled up the steps. The ceiling was now solid granite. "We can't leave them!"

Carlos squeezed into the narrow space beside him and searched the walls. "I can't find a switch to open it."

"Keep looking. There's got to be one hidden somewhere," Ben said.

The two of them worked for several minutes, covering every square inch of rock with their bare hands while the girls waited on a landing. Not a crack or crevice to be found.

Ben pounded on the ceiling until his hands bled. "Mom! Dad!"

"It's no use. We can't help them now. Not from here." Carlos's voice crackled with apprehension. "They said they would find us if we got separated. Mom promised. They'll find another way out. I know they will."

"Come on." Serise said. "My dad said we've got a long way to go."

Ben felt claustrophobic. His stomach churned and he fought back a wave of nausea. Above him, someone or something was attacking his parents. They could be dead or dying and he was stuck in a hole with no way to help them. Cold, tired and confused he stared at the solid rock surface and realized that he had no choice but to go down.

But down to where?

What kind of harbor was buried underground?

# CHAPTER THIRTY-ONE

# "The Museum"

"'Contrariwise', continued Tweedledee,
'if it was so, it might be, and if it were so, it would be;
but as it isn't, it ain't. That's logic!'
* * *Lewis Carroll — Alice in Wonderland*

* * Ben's backpack scraped the sides of the tunnel as it narrowed. Lead by Aris, the others trudged ahead. They had walked for over an hour when they finally reached a small, empty chamber. With the exception of the tunnel, there were no other openings.

Carlos frowned. "What do we do now?"

"Wait, I guess," Grace said.

"This is a safe harbor?" asked Serise. "There's no bathroom, no chairs, no food. We're going to have to tunnel out like earthworms. Maybe we missed something. Dad said to go to the museum. Think we're under it? How do we get out?"

"We don't," Ben said. "We go back before we suffocate." He turned but the tunnel had disappeared. In its place stood a blank wall. "Well, that's just great!"

Aris sniffed and pawed at the wall. His tail flicked back and forth as he hunted.

"I know." April's quivering voice echoed off the walls. Normally fearless, she was now shaking.

"Did you find something?" Ben asked, trying to hide his panic and sense of dread.

"No, but Mom and Dad wouldn't send us down here if it wasn't safe. Serise's dad said something about a museum gate. There has to be a trick to getting out. "

Ben banged on the rock in frustration. "Trick? Do you see anything that looks like a gate? Got one of those keys to the imaginary jungle?"

April lurched backwards. "Maybe we'll find one of those dialers," she said, her voice almost a whisper.

"This isn't a game, April." Seeing her panic, Ben tried to calm down, but hearing his own words made him sick to his stomach. "Sorry," he said. "I didn't mean to yell."

"It's okay," she said, but her voice seemed defeated.

Grace kicked at the dirt floor. "She's right. They wouldn't send us down here if it wasn't safe. Think about it. There's light and air down here. It has to be coming from somewhere!" She walked the perimeter, brushing the walls with her fingertips.

Aris wound in and out of her legs. His tail stiffened and he stopped abruptly. He pawed at the wall again. It shifted.

"Let me see that!" Ben pushed the cat out of the way with his foot. Aris growled indignantly and took a swipe at him. One claw lodged in Ben's pant leg before pulling out with a snag. Leg throbbing, Ben shoved the wall. Nothing happened. He banged on the wall with both fists. Nothing. He planted his feet into the ground and pushed with his back. The wall refused to surrender to his forceful attempts.

The cat blinked and backed away. Grace looked at Aris, the wall and at Aris again. She took a deep breath then gently poked the wall with her index finger. The wall rotated silently on its axis.

"Got it!" She laughed with relief as Aris disappeared into the opening.

"How'd you do that?" asked Ben

"Your uncle's game. There was a challenge just like this. A door there that you can't see when it is closed, but it can be opened with the touch of a finger. You just have to know where to look. Remember? You said Pharaohs always plan an escape route."

"Apparently, so do our parents." Ben said, relieved.

"Whoa, guys!" Carlos said. "You've got to see this."

From where he stood, the only thing that Ben could see was the back of Carlos' disembodied bottom sticking out of the wall. Serise shoved Carlos through the opening then entered behind him, followed by April, and Grace. Ben heard a simultaneous, "Wow" coming from the other side of the door. He shoved his backpack through the gap and squeezed through, stepping into a small, familiar office.

"Serise. This is your mom's. . ." Ben stopped mid sentence. The revolving doorway disappeared. In its place was a wall covered in maps, diagrams of ancient burial grounds, and aerial photography showing odd geometric shapes. Stapled next to them were newspaper articles entitled "Crop Circles a Hoax?" and "Farmers Think Crop Circles Created by Extraterrestrials." In the center hung a Dreamcatcher and Navajo poems.

"Okay," Serise said. "I feel better. I know where to go next. There's a hidden passage inside the mummy sarcophagus. We've got to make sure that the janitor doesn't see us."

"A passage to where?" Ben asked.

Grace shrugged. "Our new home, I guess."

"Home?" Carlos asked. "Is that what your dad said?"

"Actually, he said I was returning to the land of my ancestors. That means 'home' in my book. I just figured we'd be going to Tibet."

"But that's not our home," Serise said. "Why would the rest of us be going there?"

*Home?*

The entire scene had been so surreal that Ben had not taken the time to fully appreciate the situation. The only home he had ever known was gone. Destroyed. Nothing could have survived those explosions.

Nothing.

*No one.*

He and April were all that was left of the family, except . . . Uncle Henry! Ben rushed to the phone.

Grace tried to block him. "What are you doing? We've got to get going."

Ben ignored her. His hands shook as he dialed the wireless number, trying several times before getting the right sequence.

*"All circuits are busy. Please try your call again later."*

Grace tugged on his arm.

"Whoa. Stop!" Ben pushed her hand away. "Our parents said to wait twenty-four hours."

"Not here," Serise said. "They said to wait at the safe house. This isn't it."

"Right," Carlos agreed. "Dad said everything would be explained once we got there. Remember? When we get on a ship."

"A ship to where? Tibet like Grace said?" April clutched Aris tightly. He growled and squirmed but she kept a firm grip until he relaxed, licked her and settled into a soft purr.

"Wouldn't make sense. But I'm thinking we're supposed to head towards the Pacific Ocean. That's the closest body of water." Ben slumped against the wall. "I guess our parents have been living a double life."

Serise threw her hands up in disgust. "Well, no kidding, Sherlock. Where have you been for the last hour?"

"No, I mean . . . well . . . I heard my father talking about teams assembling and trying to synthesize stuff in a lab. He told your dad he was going to steal a necklace from the British Museum. I thought they were playing the game, but now I think they're jewel thieves. Maybe we're being chased by government agents. Think about it. The hidden tunnels. The super-sized satellite dish behind Carlos's house and all those government systems it tapped into. My mom's weird experiments. Everything is starting to make sense. The night my uncle gave us the game he was arguing with my father and said their cover was blown and someone was calling the teams in. I think their boss is some mean guy named Kurosh. My dad said he wasn't going to take orders from the guy."

Grace glared at him. "You told me you never heard of this Kurosh."

"I didn't want to say anything until I was sure. Carlos was freaking out about his dad possibly being a secret agent. I didn't want you getting all upset too. My mom was going to explain everything today but she never got the chance. I thought this was all part of the game."

"Kurosh?" asked Carlos. "My father was on the phone yelling about someone named Kurosh — that day we were playing computer games. Sounds Russian. Or Eastern European."

"Yeah, it does. Fits with all of this spy stuff," Grace agreed.

Sirens blared in the distance. West of the city, the night sky glowed orange. Ambulances, fire trucks and police cars raced toward the main highway. Vibrations from TV helicopters shook the glass windows.

Ben turned on a portable television behind Cheryl Hightower's desk.

"Are you nuts!" Serise whispered. "You want the guard to hear us?"

Ben ignored her. He turn the sound to its lowest setting and frantically changed channels until he found the local news.

" . . . *That's right Ted," a newswoman said. "I'm here at the scene of an amazing but tragic explosion. It appears there has been a rupture in the natural gas main serving the Celestial Park development; home to several prominent Sunnyslope families. There are no answers yet, but the heat is so intense that firefighters say that it is unlikely anyone has survived the blast. For now, the fire is contained to the isolated cul-de-sac located at Paradise Circle. Stating again, it is highly unlikely that there will be survivors . . ."*

"Mom! Dad!" screamed April. Ben rushed over and clamped his hand over her mouth. "Shh! Remember? There's a guard on duty."

Carlos hugged Serise, who sobbed quietly.

Grace stroked the feathers of a large dreamcatcher. "They got out. I know it. They promised. They wouldn't leave us here alone with no explanations."

Ben was too dumbstruck to say anything. He felt as if lead weights were crushing his chest and stomach making it impossible to breathe.

*No government agency did that.*

Grace finally sank to the floor, her face blank. April curled up next to her and buried her head in Grace's lap.

"Guys. It was a natural disaster," said Ben, his voice was barely audible. "They couldn't have made it. How could they?"

"They had some power left in those magic crystals," Serise said, still sobbing.

"Magic Crystals? That stuff's not real!" Ben said.

"That's what I thought," Carlos said. "But then how do you explain Serise appearing out of thin air back at the garage? Huh? How do you explain that? How do you explain how we can be in your bedroom and somewhere else in the world at the same time?"

"Hidden passages? Secret tunnels? Mass hysteria? I don't know enough about all this secret spy stuff. We need answers. I'll try calling Uncle Henry again. He'll know."

"Don't you understand? Something or someone deliberately destroyed the street. It wasn't a gas explosion. I bet it was one of those secret military teams. Or the CIA. They probably got your uncle too. We've got to get out of here before they find us." Serise blew her nose forcefully.

"The government doesn't do things like that," Ben whispered.

The TV camera showed an aerial view of the street shot from a helicopter. An enormous crater occupied the space where Paradise Circle used to be. Thick black smoke poured out of the flames. Water canons used by the fire department had no effect. Everything was gone. The house. The street. The cars. Everything.

"*. . . Feared lost," droned an anchorwoman with over-lacquered hair, "are Drs. Shan and Mei-Ling Choedon, former linguists with the United Nations, Drs. Jeremiah and Medie Webster, noted professors at Sunnyslope University, Drs. Frank and Maria Lopez, also professors at the university, Dr. David Hightower, historian and antiquities expert and Dr. Cheryl Hightower, curator of the Sunnyslope Museum. Sources close to the families say that all were in the area at the time of this tragedy. Also feared dead are the Choedon, Webster, Lopez and Hightower children . . .*"

*Natural disaster?* A natural disaster didn't use battering rams to knock down doors. Parents don't need weapons to defeat a natural disaster. He stared at the crater and wondered if he was looking at the entrance to hell.

"*. . . Ted, the fire now appears to be contained to this one block. Miraculously other houses in the development were spared. Area experts have no explanation,*" *but all residents are being asked to evacuate for their own safety until the cause is determined . . ."*

Carlos gasped. "The force field. It kept the fire contained, saved all those lives."

*All except our parents.*

Overcome with grief, Ben crumpled to the floor. His parents were gone. The friends in this room were all that remained. They were his family now.

Aris climbed on his shoulder, purred in his ear and snaked his way down to Ben's lap. For the first time, Ben did not push him away. He clung to the cat as if it were the last sign of hope on the planet.

# CHAPTER THIRTY-TWO

# Just Visiting

"True heroism is remarkably sober, very undramatic.
It is not the urge to surpass all others at whatever cost,
but the urge to serve others at whatever cost."

◆ ◆ *Arthur Ashe*

◆ ◆ They sat in office for what seemed like hours, in shock and staring into space. Ben knew they needed to find the safe house, but he didn't have the energy to move.

Serise poked her head into the empty hallway. "Coast is clear. Anyone need to stop at the bathroom before we go? Never know when we're going to find another one."

"I do," April said. "Can someone go with me?"

Serise nodded. "The rest of you hide until we get back."

"I'll go too," Grace said.

April's sneakers squeaked on the marble floors as they left. She crouched and crept like a cat, her index finger pushed to her lips as if she were ordering the floor to remain silent.

Ben guided the office door with his hand so that it wouldn't make a sound as it closed.

"Do you think the Night Watchman is patrolling?" he asked.

"Doubt it," Carlos said. "Dr. Hightower said Sam hangs out in the front office listening to the radio. He's supposed to make rounds every two hours but nothing ever happens in Sunnyslope. This place is like a tomb at night. I bet he's asleep. I would be."

Ben's stomach was a mass of tangled knots. He had told his parents he had figured it all out. But that was a lie. Like Carlos, he was happier with his fantasy of familial bliss. "I've got to go the bathroom and splash some cold water on my face. Want to go with me?"

"I'll stay here. Got a lot on my mind." Carlos reached into his backpack and took out a tin of band-aids and antiseptic. "Take these. Your hands are scuffed up pretty bad."

"Is there anything you *don't* have in there?"

"A kitchen sink." Carlos attempted a weak smile and pretended to search his bag. "Nope. Don't see one of those in here. Everything else is covered."

"Like Mary Poppins."

"I prefer James Bond or even Inspector Gadget." After a minute of reflection Carlos added, "You scared?"

"Terrified." Ben was relieved the girls weren't around to hear his confession.

"Me too. I guess we should have been careful wishing for an adventure. This isn't what I had in mind. I'd give anything to go back to a life where broiling naked in the sweat lodge was as wild as we got."

"I know what you mean," Ben said. "I don't get it. They're spies, they've got all those great toys. How come I couldn't get a plasma screen? Heck, if you saw what my dad was planning to steal from the British Museum, he could have bought me a basketball franchise."

Carlos leaned up against a file cabinet, closed his eyes but didn't respond.

Ben pulled the map from the front pocket of his backpack. "Can I show you something? I know you don't want to play, but things have kind of changed, don't you think?" He unfolded the paper and placed it on Carlos's lap. "Does this mean anything?"

Carlos frowned as he studied the map, then let out a weak laugh.

"What's so funny?" Ben pressed. "Do you know what it is?"

"It's nothing. A big fat zero. A joke." Carlos let the paper fall from his hand. "Your uncle is sick. That hole? It's the Pisces-Perseus cluster. There's nothing there. It's a void. Maybe that's the point. We get to the end and he yells April fools! Only it's October." He paused and stared out into space. "Maybe the surprise is a bunch of space aliens yelling, Trick! No Treat!"

Ben didn't believe it. Not with everything that had happened. He was convinced the last clue would have filled in the blanks. But that wasn't the priority now. "Our parents are still alive. I can feel it."

Carlos sighed.

"You going to be okay?" Ben asked, worried his friend was headed for another meltdown.

Carlos shrugged. "We've probably got a long way to go." He looked at the map again, then shoved the bandages into Ben's palm. "I'm okay. You get cleaned up. I'll stay here and be the lookout."

Ben stuffed the bandages in his pocket and slipped into the hallway, mimicking April's cat-like stance as he went. Once inside the bathroom he stared at his reflection. He looked tired and ten years older. This all had to be some big joke — a malfunction of the game simulation. He'd splash water in his face and when he looked up, he'd be in his own house, in his own bathroom, in his old world again.

The cold water stung as it hit him. Ben looked past his reflection in the mirror. Instead of comforting blue walls and stenciled tropical fish he saw cold gray marble. Even in the dim light he could see how much he resembled his father.

He felt betrayed. He'd read stories of foreign spies who spent their entire life training to live like Americans. Was that his parents true identity? A life filled with cryptic codes and hidden passages? Was he headed back to some distant foreign country? Had life, as he knew it, come to an end?

"Dad?"

"Yeah, son?" *Ben's father hopped a miniature Darth Vader around the game board and stopped at the Dagobah swamp. He helped himself to 200 credits for passing "Go." No need for rent. He owned it along with most of the board.*

"Didn't you ever want to do something different? More exciting?"

"Your turn. Want to pay to get out of jail?" *His father said quietly. He* studied the board, the position of the player's pieces and the dice as if it were a game of strategy instead of a game of chance.

Ben tossed 50 credits on the table and rolled the dice. He moved his Luke Skywalker six spaces to a property lined with X-wing fighters. Luckily he owned the orange Yavin Four property, one of the few he had managed to keep out of his father's clutches. "Don't you want to be recognized for all the stuff you do, Dad? Have people look up to you?"

"What's the point?"

"You're the smartest researcher on the planet."

Jeremiah Webster's expression softened. He squirted catsup on the side of the plate and pushed it across the table. "Want some more fries?"

"We could be set for life if you sold some of the stuff you and Uncle Henry find instead of donating it to the university or the museum."

His father smiled but didn't respond.

"You should be on the cover of National Geographic! Haven't you ever wondered what it would be like to be famous?"

"No. Have you?"

"Heck, yeah! This town is boring. Nothing interesting ever happens around here. One day I'm going to be a world famous Center and set you and Mom up in style!"

"Why?" His father laughed. "By the way, if you tell your mother I got barbecue for dinner while she was out of town, you're grounded until the next millennium."

Ben took a huge bite of beef and swallowed. "Look at Barry McKenna. He's cool. He's got endorsements. Women chase after him. He drives hot cars. He's famous."

"Hmmm. Hot cars, cool guy. Interesting contrast." His father shoved money into the bank slots and replaced his fighters with star destroyers on his blue Coruscant properties. "You're dead meat when you get around here." He chuckled and took another healthy bite of the oversized sandwich, licking the sauce from his fingers before moving his Darth Vadar token eight spaces to Ben's heavily mortgaged property. "Fame is not relevant."

Ben was incredulous. "How can you say that? Don't you want people to notice you? Didn't you ever want to be rich?" He rolled a six and moved to an Imperial Square. His card read "Travel through hyperspace to 'GO' and collect 200 credits." Ben breathed a sigh of relief and stuck his tongue out at his father.

His father countered Ben's move by adding extra Tie-fighters along the low rent Dagobah section of the game board. "It's not about the money. That's an illusion. Anything beyond basic needs is a waste of resources." He rolled, landed on a Reactor Core, calculated the rent and tossed a paltry thirty credits in Ben's direction.

"I just thought you would want someone to notice what you do. You could get the Nobel Peace Prize or something. You could make a difference."

"If I do my job well, and the world as a whole benefits, then why would I care if anyone noticed?"

"Because that's how you get your name in the paper. On TV! You know . . . famous explorer Jeremiah Webster discovers the lost city of Atlantis. Jeremiah Webster uncovers the secret to the Egyptian pyramids. They were built by aliens. Cool stuff like that."

His father choked on his cream soda, brought his hand up to his mouth and tried to stifle a laugh. It took a few seconds for him to recover. "I don't think I'll be revealing any secrets like those anytime soon." He fingered a miniature fighter, held it up to the light. "Do people actually believe something like this could fly through space?"

Ben ignored the comment. "Well, I'm going to be famous. MVP. Own a string of steak houses. The works!"

"Fame comes with a big price tag. Once you lose your privacy, it's hard to get it back."

"Yeah, but you'd be rich. Everyone would know who you are, rushing up and asking for your autograph and stuff."

"No thanks. I do my best work when no one is looking. Completing my research is reward enough." His father gazed at him thoughtfully. His eyes sparkled. "By the way. You're almost broke. Why don't you just give me all your money and I'll let you go to bed with some dignity."

Ben ignored him and rolled again. Safe. He hopped his Skywalker token to "Just Visiting."

"I want you and your sister to have a good life," his father continued. "That's *a job your mother and I cherish. Devoting yourself to the pursuit of fame and wealth closes off options that could be more rewarding. I'm content with my choice. As for you, one day you'll make your own. When the time arrives, I trust you'll make the right one. If fame is what you chase, be prepared for the consequences."*

*Ben studied the game board and recognized the futility of his previous moves. In an effort to save money to buy Coruscant's Monument Square and Imperial Palace he had squandered his chances to buy other properties and yet had never attained the prized locations. Above the buffet, an African mask mocked him with its wide toothy grin and protruding tongue. Ben admitted defeat and tossed his money into the bank.*

*"Love you, Dad."*

*"Love you too, little Nut Brown Hare. To the Moon and back," he said, quoting Ben's favorite childhood book.*

So there it was — the plain truth. The clues had been in front of him his entire life. Ben thought he had understood, but all the while he had missed the hidden meaning. All the travel, the money that supported their lifestyle. His father's obsessive dislike of publicity. He thought his father was a gifted scientist, an extraordinary teacher, when in reality he was living a double life. He couldn't smuggle artifacts out of foreign countries if everyone knew what he was up to. His father loved him, that much he was sure of. But Ben couldn't reconcile the lies with the truth.

He stumbled into the last stall, closed the door and sank down on the closed lid of the toilet. His whole life had been a make-believe story, and now, even that had been ripped away. The weight of the betrayal was unbearable. He clutched his stomach and sobbed quietly.

Someone entered the room. Ben started to ask *Carlos, is that you?* Instead, he sucked his lips inward, turned the stall lock and pulled his feet off the floor.

"Hrmpph!" It sounded like the person was blowing his lungs out through his nose. *Clunk, Clop, Clunk.* Heavy awkward footsteps traveled across the tile floor.

Ben heard muffled music. He craned his neck and peered through a slit between the wall and the door. A vague human shape stood near the mirror.

*"To the left. Now to the right. Dance til you're out of sight!"*

The man sang loud and off key. A door slammed shut.

*Ten stalls and he has to pick the one next to me?* A single tear rolled down Ben's cheek. He caught it in the palm of his hand.

Heavy black boots with extra thick safety soles appeared beneath the metal divider. A minute later a pair of striped uniform pants crumpled to the floor. A large ring of keys crashed against the tile with a reverberating clatter. Sam, the night watchman. Ben looked at his watch. 3:15 a.m.

Frozen with fear, Ben leaned backwards. A few minutes later, the crumpled pants straightened and Sam left the stall. Ben slowly released his breath and was about to relax when his toilet flushed.

He closed his eyes and clamped his hands over his mouth to keep from screaming. He'd set off the time delayed motion sensor. Paralyzed, he waited for Sam to investigate. Nothing happened. The toilet in the next stall had flushed at the same time.

*"It ain't nothing but a good thang! Yeah! Sing it with me, y'all . . ."*

Water streamed from the faucet. After a few seconds Sam walked toward Ben's stall. Ben leaned forward, careful not to set off the toilet sensor again.

*Wrench, wrench.*

He peered through the crack and saw Sam bouncing up and down to the beat of a faint rhythm while getting paper towels. A white cord was looped around his head and extended to the iPod on his belt. His music was cranked up so loud that he couldn't hear any thing else around him.

*"Come on y'all let's get on down. Party! Whoo whoo! Party! . . ."*

The singing grew faint as the Sam exited down the hallway. Ben nearly passed out in relief.

CHAPTER THIRTY-THREE

# Conundrum

Function: noun
Etymology: origin unknown
1 - a riddle whose answer involves a pun
2 - an intricate and difficult problem

♦ ♦ "Did you see him?" Ben asked, when he returned to the office. "Sam is patrolling."

"Yeah," Grace said. "Scared us to death. We thought he heard us in the bathroom but he was singing so loud I knew we were safe."

"He doesn't sing very well," April said.

"He could wake the dead," Serise agreed. "Can't be very good at this job. Didn't even notice there were intruders in the building. Five of 'em. When I see my mom again, he's toast."

"Enough!" Carlos spat, his tone sharp and irritated. "We've got to get a plan."

"We've got a plan!" Serise said, hands back on her hips. "We're going to the basement. Mom said there was a gateway there."

"Where?" asked Ben.

"She didn't have time to finish explaining. She said it was inside the sarcophagus. That shouldn't be too difficult. She gave me her watch and said that if we got separated, to set the second time zone to midnight."

"Okay," Ben said. "That makes about as much sense as everything else we've run into."

"I'm tired." April said, the words partially garbled by a large yawn.

"We need to hurry up and find the hideout so I can go back to sleep." She paused and studied his face. "Hey, Ben. You look tired too. Your eyes are all puffy and red."

"I know. You don't look so good yourself, kiddo. Just hang on."

They slipped back into the hallway, ears pricked for any sign of Sam's off-key singing.

"*Coast is clear.*" Serise led them toward the back of the building and pointed. "*This way.*"

Everyone followed, looking from side to side down deserted corridors until they were safely inside the stairwell. They descended until they reached the basement. It was dark except for the glow of the exit lights.

"I've got a flashlight," Carlos said.

"Are you crazy?" Ben whispered. "What if someone sees us?"

"Like who?" asked Carlos. "Even if Sam isn't singing, you can hear those heavy paramilitary boots from three miles away. I've had enough dark tunnels for one night, thank you very much." He reached into his pack, retrieved a flashlight and switched it to the lowest possible setting.

"There," he sniffed. "Satisfied? Just enough to keep us from breaking our necks on this journey of the damned."

"Carlos!" Ben pointed to April who clutched him around the waist. Aris brushed back and forth against her pant leg and purred.

"Sorry, April. Just an expression. I won't use it again."

"That's okay. I know it was a joke," she said, releasing her grip on Ben but staying close.

"This way," Serise whispered.

Carlos's light cast eerie shadows on the wall. Cases of dead animals came alive as silhouettes of their inhabitants stretched and elongated, their beady glass eyes reflecting the light. Ben fixed his gaze straight ahead and tried to shut out the ghostly images. This was worse than the sweat lodge. He was totally spooked. From the looks of his friends, he was not alone.

They arrived at two stone columns marking the entrance to the

Egyptian exhibit. According to a plaque on the wall, the height of the original columns was over sixty feet. Beside them two bare-chested guards stood as granite sentinels. The walls were covered in stone carvings from the Book of the Dead.

"Gee, now I feel right at home," Ben said.

Serise lead them across the room, through an open door and into a chamber containing the gold encrusted tomb.

*"In here,"* she gestured.

The towering artifacts left Ben awestruck. He felt as if he were walking into an ancient temple. "Time to do that thing with your mother's watch, Serise."

Serise rolled up her sleeve revealing a rugged green Timex. She pushed the top button activating a soft blue light. The watch beeped as Serise scrolled through the options. She stopped periodically to turn the light back on.

"Okay. Got it!"

Nothing happened.

"Are you sure you did it right?" asked Grace.

"Yes. I set it to twelve o'clock."

Everyone waited. Nothing happened. Serise tapped the watch in frustration.

"Let me see that." Ben grabbed Serise's arm and pushed the light button. The watch was set to 12:00 p.m.

"Serise! You set the watch to 'noon' not midnight. You need to change it to 'am' and press 'set time' to finish. You would know that if you wore something other than designer watches."

Serise snatched her arm away. "Without me you'd be stuck waiting for some fireball to get you!"

"You mean without my dad's invisible satellite dish we'd be crispy critters," Carlos said in a rare show of anger.

Serise glowered and reset the watch. An orange light shot out of the watch and bounced around the room. It found its way to a stone tablet before bouncing one last time to a chart on the wall. The tablet glowed, bringing low, but sufficient light into the room.

"Okay," Grace said. "That was a fun laser light show. Now what?"

"Guys!" April said, her voice urgent.

"Shhhh, April," Ben said. "We're trying to think."

"Should we try to open the sarcophagus?" asked Serise. "There are enough of us here. We could try to move the cover. There might be a dialer inside."

"Eew," Grace said. "Won't there be . . . like . . . a dead person in there?"

"Ugh, no," Serise said. "The mummy is at the University. They're doing a bunch of tests on her. She won't be back for a few months."

"Whew," Grace said, wiping the sweat from her forehead. "That's better."

"How is that better?" asked Carlos. "It's still an old coffin with dead people dust inside. Do you know what they did to people before they turned them into mummies?"

Ben shot a dirty look at him and nodded in April's direction. "Not now, Carlos."

"They pull their brains out through their noses . . ."

"Carlos!"

" . . . I bet the heart and liver are over there in those canopic jars." He pointed to four stone jars, the heads shaped like a baboon, jackal, falcon and human.

"Hey, guys?" April pressed, waving her hands to get their attention.

"Shhh. In a minute, April. Can't you see we are talking?" Ben returned his attention to Carlos. "Stop being so gross around my sister. Anyway, what's the point of opening the coffin? On the field trip they said there was fifteen feet of steel, concrete and rocks under it. We can't dig through that."

"Mom said the gateway is in there. I know I heard her correctly," Serise said.

"Okay, then Carlos, you and I will push and see if we can open it," Ben said.

They moved to the middle of the sarcophagus, planted their feet and shoved. The lid didn't budge. Ben tried Grace's trick and pushed the lid with one finger.

Useless.

"We need more leverage." Ben looked at April. She crossed her arms and shook her head. He summoned Grace and Serise instead.

"Ready, set . . . PUSH!"

The four of them dug their feet into the floor and strained against the lid.

Nothing.

Panting and grunting, they tried several more times to no avail. Aris jumped onto the coffin and studied the queen's face intently then shook his head at Ben as if saying *"no."* Ben shooed the cat away.

"This thing must weigh a ton," Ben sighed. "How'd they get the mummy out?"

"Beats me," Serise said.

"Guys!" April said with more emphasis.

"What?" snapped Ben.

"There's some writing on this thing. It's warm and it's glowing from the inside."

Everyone stared where April was pointing. A symbol of a sun was, in fact, glowing from inside the stone. Underneath it, a series of symbols glowed.

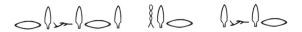

"Hmm," Ben said. "More hieroglyphics — four characters. Maybe this is the key to getting that stupid thing open. I reckon it will take thirty-three billion combinations to figure this out. Or we could get Grace to decipher it in four seconds."

Grace clucked her tongue at him.

Ben pulled back his sleeve and punched tiny buttons on his watch with a stylus.

26 ★ 25 ★ 24 ★ 23.

"Sorry. My mistake. We only have to sort through three hundred, fifty-eight thousand eight hundred choices. We should be able to crack that code in . . . oh, I don't know . . . a few hundred years."

"Wait!" Serise paced the room. Light from the tablet was reflected on a chart above the display case. A copy of the Rosetta Stone. A diagram showing a translation of the Egyptian alphabet sat beside it. Serise stared at the closed sarcophagus. "I know this. It says 'Revere Her Ever'."

"Well," Ben said. "That made everything abundantly clear."

Serise ignored him. "I've heard this before." She found a stool, stood in front of the chart and pushed symbols to spell the phrase. Nothing happened. "I don't understand. That should have worked."

Ben sighed. "Oh, well. Back to searching for a dialer, I guess."

"Wait! It's a palindrome!" Serise yelped, jumping up and down. "That's the trick! It's a palindrome! You know, the letters spell the same thing forward and backwards!" She spelled 'palindrome' on the chart.

The sound of stone grinding against stone echoed as the lid to the sarcophagus slowly swung open.

# CHAPTER THIRTY-FOUR

# Through the Rabbit Hole

"All growth is a leap in the dark,
a spontaneous unpremeditated act
without benefit of experience."

• • *Henry Miller*

• • Ben gasped. The mummy was gone all right. In fact there was nothing inside the coffin but infinite blackness.

"This must be the gateway," Serise said, sounding unsure of herself.

Ben gestured toward Carlos. "You can go first. You like that scouting explorer stuff."

"Are you kidding?" Carlos said as the light from his flashlight was swallowed by the void. "It's dark in there. At least we had that glow in the tunnel under your dad's workshop."

"Don't tell me you're scared of the dark," Ben said.

"No. It's just . . ." Carlos paused. "It's just like old Star Trek reruns. I've got on a red shirt. Everyone knows that the person in the landing party who always gets killed off is the one in the red shirt. Want to know why you don't see any Latino Captains on that show? I'll tell you why. Because they all get killed off on the landing party. Why don't you go?"

"You have to ask?" Ben replied. "After that lame explanation? The token Black guy always gets killed off first in the movies."

"Good grief," spat Grace. "I don't believe you guys. I'll go."

"No way!" Ben said. "Look how dark it is! You barely survived the Woodland adventure challenge at school!"

Grace punched him in the arm then grabbed a flashlight from her pack. "But I did survive, didn't I? You had to repeat the exercise three times!" Despite her assurances, her hands trembled and her voice cracked a bit. Ben knew she was scared of the dark. She crinkled her nose, peered over the edge and dipped her hand into the void. "I can't see anything. Not even a reflection. But it feels like a warm bath, just not wet."

She took a deep breath, climbed onto the lip and tested the barrier with one foot. "Something feels solid. Oh well, here goes nothing. Hey! It's a hidden staircase!" Grace slipped into the sarcophagus and disappeared.

Ben held his breath so long that he was forced to suck in two lungs worth of air to refuel. "Well?" he yelled into the opening.

There was no answer.

"Grace?"

The sound was swallowed by the void. When Ben leaned over, his pack fell into the hole. He waited to hear it land. No sound returned. His stomach lurched as panic took hold.

"Now what do we do?" Serise paced frantically. "We can't leave her in there. Someone has to go in and get her."

"Someone? Like who?" asked Carlos.

She stopped pacing and pointed. "One of you guys."

"Us?" asked Carlos. "Why don't you do it? It's your Mom's museum!"

"She just works here. It's not like we own this stuff. I never knew you were such a chicken."

"I don't see your feet moving very fast in that direction," Carlos argued.

"I figured out the clue to get the sarcophagus to open. I can't do all of the work." She threw up her hands in frustration.

"Enough!" Ben yelled, trying to decide what to do next. His best friend had just disappeared and he knew it was his job to go in after her.

"I'll go," said a timid voice.

Ben turned in time to see April climbing onto the lip of the sarcophagus.

"No!" everyone said in unison.

Ben lunged forward, pulling her from the edge. "You're my responsibility now. We'll wait another minute. If Grace doesn't come back, I'll go get her."

"Okay," Carlos said

"Good plan!" Serise agreed giving him a thumbs up.

Two minutes passed with no sign of Grace. Just as Ben psyched himself to climb over the edge, a disembodied head poked through.

"Boo!"

Ben, April, Serise and Carlos nearly fell over each other trying to back away. Grace's head hovered above an invisible neck. Aris jumped from Grace's partially formed shoulder, purred, then vanished into the sarcophagus.

"Well, are you guys coming or not?" said Grace, exasperated. "I've been waiting forever. And why'd you throw a backpack at me? That thing missed my head by inches."

"Where have you been?" Ben asked, once his heart returned to a normal beat.

"Exploring. It's just a musty old cave. Kind of like the one under your dad's garage, except with an echo. If that's Safe Harbor, it's time to be concerned."

"Why didn't you answer us?" Ben asked.

"Answer you? I didn't hear anything down there. I thought something happened and came back up to get you."

Grace climbed higher and leaned over the edge of the sarcophagus. Ben couldn't see any part of her below the waist.

"I know," Grace said. "Weird isn't it. We better get going. Don't know how long this thing stays open."

Ben was skeptical.

"You can stay here if you want. I'm going back down to figure out where this thing leads." She turned and disappeared.

Carlos dipped one finger into the void and scowled. "Okay. I'm going too, red shirt or not." He descended cautiously clearly trying to feel his way down steps he couldn't see. Inch by inch, the void erased parts of his body. And then he was gone.

"Serise, you go next and help April," Ben said. "I'll go last and bring her stuff."

"Right." Serise winced and lowered into the inky blackness. Her disembodied hand shot out and waited for April to grab hold.

Ben helped April climb over the edge. She stuck a toe into the void, felt around for something solid and placed her full weight inside.

"It's okay, Ben. It feels okay." She smiled and gave a thumbs up.

The black hole had now swallowed his entire expedition. Inhaling deeply, Ben hoisted April's pack over his shoulder, stared into the well of nothingness and worked up his courage.

The sound of grinding stone startled him. The edges of the stone lid scraped as it swung back in place. Across the room, a beam of light shone through the frosted glass doorway. The clock overhead read 3:45 a.m.

The night watchman! The time clock was on the inside of the room to the right of the door. Sam would have to come inside to check in for his rounds.

*"When the sun goes down, I'll still be the one! My love is guaranteeeeed!"*

The doorknob rattled once and then twice. Serise had been thinking clearly enough to set the lock. Keys jangled loudly on the other side.

The lid of the sarcophagus continued to swing toward Ben. Soon there wouldn't be any room left for him to get inside.

He held his breath, swung his legs over the edge and jumped with both feet.

*Geronimo!*

He missed the first and second steps and slid, on his rear end, to the bottom of the steep stone staircase. He landed with a dull thud, kicking up a cloud of dust in the process. Above him, the barrier rippled like the surface of a pond. Within seconds, the sarcophagus closed, cutting off the light from the museum.

# CHAPTER THIRTY-FIVE

# Lost and Found

"Every strike brings me closer to the next home run."

• • *Babe Ruth*

• • "Ben? Ben? Ben? Ben?"

April's voice echoed as she rushed to his aid. "Ben? Ben? Ben? Ben? Are you okay? okay? okay? okay?"

"Huh? Huh? Huh? Huh?" asked Ben, still dazed. His hand throbbed. "Oh, yeah. yeah. yeah. yeah."

All around them, hundreds of luminous, phosphorescent stalagmites and stalactites jutted out like giant glowing teeth. Ben wondered if this was what Jonah felt like when he was swallowed by the whale.

"Which way? way? way? way? This can't be it. it. it. it," Serise said.

"Let's get out of here. here. here. here. The echo is driving me crazy. crazy. crazy. crazy." Grace pointed toward an alcove.

"Now what do we do?" April asked then pausing as if waiting for another echo.

"Don't know." Ben poked the wall hoping to find another secret swinging door.

"Didn't your father give you some kind of compass back at the garage?" asked Carlos. "Maybe we can use it to keep track of which direction we are going."

*"If for any reason we get separated, follow the instructions on this compass to*

*get to Safe Harbor."*

Ben had forgotten about the device his father had shoved in his backpack. He touched the tiny apple on the front of the snow-white case. The screen roared to life.

A bullseye appeared in the center of the screen. *"Enter password."*

"Awww man. Not again. Is this some kind of sick joke?"

He frowned and looked for a place to type a password. There was no keyboard or stylus to enter information. He poked the bullseye with his finger and shouted, "This is Benjamin Webster you stupid machine. How am I supposed to know a password at a time like this!"

"Fingerprint and voiceprint identification confirmed," replied the compass in the same mellow voice as the computer game. "Benjamin Webster, authorized user. Please stand by."

Ben almost dropped the device. Everyone crowded around.

"Sweet!" Carlos said.

"Please specify language requirement." The device flashed a list of standard translation options on the screen: English, Spanish, French, Chinese, Japanese, Greek, Latin. Ben pushed the "page down" option. The list contained hundreds of languages, most he'd never heard of.

"Xenobian?" April asked. "Is the game loaded on that pocket computer too?"

"Let's find out," Ben said. "Computer! Xenobian, please."

"Sheras needum doo," the computer cooed as the screen filled with odd symbols. "Feras edum norvash?"

"Well that was helpful." Ben sighed. "What the heck is Xenobian anyway?"

"It's where your family is from." Carlos wiggled his fingers as if they were antennae. "I've always thought you were from outer space."

Ben scowled and returned his attention to the compass. "Convert to English please."

"Askar."

The new page displayed "Home", "Maps", "Language", "Mission Status", and "Gateways". Ben chose *"Home"*.

"Use of COMPASS restricted to authorized members of Interstellar

Observation Post. Encrypted. Access by DNA coding, fingerprint and voiceprint analysis."

"Sonecian date: 14558.98. 5800.4 post apocalypse. Earth date October 30, 2016."

"Uh oh," Carlos said. "Not good. I don't think our parents are jewel thieves."

Ben punched Carlos on the shoulder. "Be serious. It's probably a computer game. We can look at it later. Right now, we've got to find the real data. Something to help us get out of here."

He selected "Gateways" and found a listing for the Sunnyslope Museum. A notation for "Safe Harbor" was in the sub-directory.

"Oh no!"

"Oh no, what?" asked Serise.

"We're in the wrong place. It says to open that stone in case of emergency. The one with the palindrome on it. The dialer was inside. That's why it was glowing. It says that if the stone is gone to press "Harbor" on the museum chart. Serise! You pressed "palindrome". I don't have any idea where we are!"

Everyone glared at Serise.

"Sorry. I guess my parents thought it would be obvious. Now what do we do?" She began whimpering. "I don't want to die down here! Let's go back!"

Ben knew going back was hopeless. They were stuck in the middle of nowhere, swallowed by a portal that was now closed. "I don't know how to open the gateway from here because I don't know where we are. Serise, does your watch trick work?"

Serise reset the time. The light shot around the cavern and disappeared to the right of the staircase. The portal, however, did not open. "I guess it's a one way switch," she sighed. "I'm sorry."

"Okay," Ben said. "Let's not panic. This stop is obviously supposed to serve a purpose on this underground railroad, so it must be on this thing." Ben scrolled through the menu and returned to the notation for the museum. It didn't mention "palindrome" as an option.

"Okay, now we're stuck." Ben examined other options. The device listed notations for countries around the world: England, Indonesia, Italy, Tibet and so forth. There were several gateways within the United States, but the only Sunnyslope code lead back to Paradise Circle. Like several others it showed in gray.

Inactive.

Gone.

Destroyed.

Ben scrolled back to "Safe Harbor" which was listed as if it were just another country. When he tapped the screen with his fingernail, a compass appeared in the right corner. Coordinate points appeared to the left.

"Finally, something I understand."

The black arrow pointed north. A red arrow printed with hieroglyphics and the eye of Ra pointed in the opposite direction toward the right of the stairway.

"It says go southeast." Ben hoped that he was interpreting the compass correctly. There wasn't any other option. Going north meant jumping into the abyss.

"Okay, wise guy," Carlos said. "Any idea which way that is?"

"This way." Ben wasn't convinced, but he tried to sound confident. "Follow the light from Serise's watch."

"I looked there already. There's nothing back there but a blank wall," said Grace.

April and Aris took off ahead of them.

"April! Wait for us."

April stopped at the opening of a large dark room. "Hey guys! I think we've found it!"

"I don't understand," Grace said.

"Is this it? Is this the Safe Harbor?" asked April.

Ben's heart sank as his eyes adjusted to the darkness. "If it is, our situation just got a lot worse."

# CHAPTER THIRTY-SIX

# When In Rome

To get lost is to learn the way.

• • *African proverb*

• • The beam from Carlos's flashlight swept across a steel and glass room — parts of it charred as if hit by a tremendous blast. Beefy conduits snaked in and out of the walls. Catwalks criss-crossed overhead finally connecting to circular stairway on the left. A central platform was littered with toppled chairs, dormant consoles, and half-filled cups of unidentifiable liquids. Equipment was strewn across the floor. Metal panels had been torn away, revealing the stone walls behind them.

Acrid smoked burned Ben's eyes and the scent of ozone and burnt electronics assaulted his nose. Something else lingered in the air — death — but he wasn't sure how he knew that.

"Looks like it was some kind of spy command post," Serise said. "With 'was' being the operative word."

"Is this where we are supposed to be?" asked Grace.

"I hope not," Ben said. "Look at this place. Smells like something died. Like a rat or something."

He touched the walls. Green slime dripped from the surface. He quickly wiped his hands on his pants. "Dad said to catch a ship. But ugh! Down here? Maybe he meant to say catch the subway."

Serise frowned. "A subway? In California?"

"Got a better idea? They've got a lot of other stuff no one else has. Why not some kind of underground transportation?" Ben pushed controls on the nearest panel to see if he could get anything to work. "Everything's dead."

"Really bad choice of words, Ben," Grace said, frowning.

"What I meant was that we need to find the power source. Carlos, got any batteries in your pack?"

Carlos looked defeated. "No. But we can take them out of the flashlights."

"Then what will we use for light?" Grace asked. "It's pitch black in here without them."

Something skittered away in the dark.

"Was that a rat?" yelped April. "Please tell me that wasn't a rat!"

Ben swiveled toward the sound, and saw only Aris sniffing in search of a meal. "Everyone stay close, till we get some power going." He searched for electrical outlets or switches and came up empty. The only other source of light came from the cave.

Carlos tugged on the base of his flashlight. He slid it open to create a lantern.

"Wow, that's bright!" Ben said, as Grace flicked hers open as well.

"Halogen," said Carlos. "It gets kind of hot, but it puts out a lot of light."

"Not enough, said April. "It's still spooky and smelly down here. Maybe the spies forgot to pay the electric bill."

"I don't think the electric company supplies service to secret underground spy hideouts," Serise said, "otherwise it wouldn't BE a secret would it?"

"Then what do we do?" asked April.

Serise perched on the edge of a chair. "Guess we get comfortable while we wait for rescue."

"Comfortable" was nowhere to be found. Grace's flashlight illuminated a wider section of the room but created shadows that gave Ben the creeps. The cavernous room swallowed every sound. Ben almost craved the companionship of the cave echo.

"Got an ATM card, April?" he asked wearily.

April slumped. "Okay . . . guess it was a stupid idea."

Serise whipped a debit card out of her backpack. "I've got one. If it will help us get out of this spooky place faster you can max it out!"

Ben noticed everyone looking at him quizzically. He shrugged. "It won't. So we're going to have to treat this setback like it's just part of the game," Ben said. "I know it will keep me from freaking out. We can set up our own safe house until our parents rescue us. Might as well explore our new digs and figure out why we're the only ones here."

Carlos nodded. He set his lantern on the console near the girls, pulled a smaller one from his pack and began searching the room.

Ben opened his pack and retrieved his own flashlight. "There's got to be a generator somewhere around here. I'll see if I can find it."

Something brushed against his neck. He spun around and — seeing nothing — wiped at the spot where the sensation lingered. A single strand of maroon hair clung to his fingertip.

Serise's hair.

*Get a grip, Webster!* His jaw clenched. His muscles tensed. This couldn't possibly be a safe harbor. He entered a corridor on the opposite end of the chamber but didn't get far. Metal panels and debris formed a cave-in twenty feet ahead.

The same was true for the second corridor; only this one continued at least fifty feet before ending abruptly. No exit. No sign of a dialer or any other "how to get out of Dodge" clues. Doors lined the hallway, all fused shut or locked, each flanked by glass booths — like display cases — only human size. Ben's reflection startled him. He steadied himself and peered inside the hollow spaces. An odd green ash covered the floors. The foul odor of decay grew more distinct, like rancid meat. The darkness closed in, smothering him. If there had been a confrontation where did the people go? Were these booths for storage? Escape pods? Or was this ash all that was left of the missing people?

Panic overwhelmed him. He rushed back to the control room where Serise, April and Grace were turning knobs, pushing buttons and opening compartments.

Ben froze as footsteps clanged on the metal walkway. He swung his flashlight upward and was relieved to see the familiar shape overhead.

"Carlos? Find anything?"

"Not yet. You?"

"Uh uh."

Carlos paused on the first level of the catwalk and swung his beam from side to side. Ben joined him, thinking two lights would speed up the search. They peered into a room and found several crates. Carlos opened one and held up a raw potato. Onions, other vegetables and fruit filled the other containers. "At least we won't starve."

Ben groaned. Were all spies vegetarian except for the Lopez family? "Let's find some oil and make french fries. Can we start a camp fire in here?"

"No!" shouted Serise. "No vents. We'd burn off all the remaining oxygen and suffocate."

Ben leaned over the railing and stared at her.

Serise shrugged. "Girl Scout survival training."

April frowned. "I signed up for Spring Break. Guess I'm going to miss the class."

Ben and Carlos tested several doors but found no visible handles.

"Electronic controls," Ben said.

"Probably," Carlos mumbled. "No way to activate them without power." He paused at an open doorway and froze.

Ben rushed to his side, swung a light into the room, then swung it away and slapped his hand over his nose. Something had definitely died in there. The smell was overwhelming.

"We can't stay here," he whispered.

"I know." Carlos's response was barely audible. "And we can't let the girls come up here."

"Right. The smell's worse up here."

"No." Carlos's voice cracked and lowered even more. "There's people in there. Or what's left of them."

Ben froze. He was tempted to look, but couldn't bring himself to do it. "You serious?"

Carlos nodded, a pained expression on his face, then turned away from the door.

"Find anything?" yelled April.

"No!" said Ben and Carlos.

"Coast is clear. Everything's deserted," Ben continued.

Something dropped on to his hand. He jumped, swatted at it, aimed, then sighed in relief as it fell to the floor. A Daddy long-legged spider. He raised his foot to stomp it out of existence. Carlos caught him and shook his head.

"It's just trying to find a way out. Like us."

The creature skittered away in search of its own escape route.

"You've never killed a bug?" asked Ben. "Not even a mosquito?"

Carlos shook his head. "Told you. Major disappointment in the Lopez family." He headed for the staircase, then stopped at the first room. He reached into a crate, pulled out another potato and stared as if it were a work of art. "Help me drag one of these downstairs."

"Good thinking. We can gather provisions." Ben tucked his flashlight under his chin and grabbed a handle.

Once on the main floor, Carlos opened a digital console and frowned.

"What ya looking for?" asked April.

"I'll know when I find it." Carlos continued his quest, mumbling to himself every time he pried open a cabinet or piece of equipment. He looked as if he were about to give up when he stopped at a storage locker filled with old equipment. He yelped in victory and, with a mighty yank, pulled wires and circuit boards from the back of a rusted black box.

"What are you doing?" asked Ben.

"Going to see if I can get a monitor working. Might tell us something." Carlos returned to the center of the room and dumped his new treasure on the floor.

Ben was incredulous. "Using what? Potato salad?"

"Yep." Deep in concentration, Carlos pulled a pocketknife from his backpack and removed the insulation from the ends of the wires.

"You're serious?"

"Yep." Carlos pulled out his wallet and dumped change on the floor.

"I don't think we have to pay for the food," Ben said.

Carlos ignored him. He was like a man on a mission as he cut the wires into twenty pieces. He slipped one hand into his pack and pulled out a container of paper clips.

"Here," he said. "Can you guys wrap one end of each wire around a paper clip?"

Everyone looked at Carlos as if he had lost his mind.

"We're stuck here. Might as well keep busy."

"Fine." Ben grabbed a length of wire and looped the bare metal end around a paper clip. Grace and Serise sat cross-legged on the floor and did the same before handing them to Carlos.

"April," Carlos said. "Count out twenty pennies please. The shiny ones are the best."

April fished through the pile of coins and pushed her selections across the floor. Carlos, in turn, wrapped the free end of the wires around a penny.

"Now what?" asked Ben. "Make a sculpture?"

"Watch and learn how and why things work on a starship," Carlos said, quoting a line from a Star Trek movie. "I won the second grade science fair with this experiment." Carlos cut two parallel slits, in each potato. He lined the potatoes up, side by side.

"Oh! I get it," Serise said. "You're making a battery!"

"Yes!" Carlos nodded and seemed a little calmer. "I bet one potato is not enough, so we'll have to connect them in series. Push one wire and penny into the slit in potato number one. Then put the other end, the one with the paper clip, into potato number two."

Ben mashed his penny into the potato. The thin wire tip broke off. He cut more insulation from the wire and started over with more success and held it up for all to see. "Got it!"

Carlos seemed pleased. "Grace, April, grab a wire and do the same thing. Make sure each wire is connected to two different potatoes and make sure you don't connect two pennies or two paper clips in the same potato."

Everyone assembled potatoes until they ran out of supplies. At each end of the chain one wire remained that hung loose. Carlos removed the penny from the wire in the potato on the right end, and the paper clip from the potato on the left end.

"Very artistic," Ben said. "But will it work?"

"In theory," Carlos said. "One or two potatoes can power a digital watch for two weeks. Maybe a bunch of them can power this thing for a few minutes so we can find out what happened or where we are. It shouldn't require a lot of juice."

Carlos placed the free ends of the two wires on leads in the back of a console. Nothing happened.

"Oh well," Ben said. "It was worth a shot."

"Maybe I have the leads reversed." Carlos removed the wires, scraped them with his knife and returned them to the console.

Nothing happened.

"We need something smaller." Serise groped around in the dim light, opening more cabinet doors and searching under the debris. She returned with a handheld device the size of an iPod and connected the leads. It remained dormant.

"Okey dokey," Serise sighed. "Time for a new plan."

Carlos looked dejected. "Sorry. I'll try to fix it but first I've got to find a bathroom."

"You should've gone before we left the museum," Ben growled.

"I didn't have to go then!" Carlos growled back.

"Well, where are you going to go now?"

"There must be a bathroom around here somewhere. Even spies have to take a leak once in a while." Carlos poked his head into passageways and other openings in the rock walls.

"Pretend you're camping," Ben said. "Go in the cave and pee off the side of the cliff. Who ya gonna hit? The devil? It will evaporate before it hits in him in the head."

"Anyone remember where we parked the cave entrance?" asked Carlos.

Ben took a minute to get his bearings, ran to the spot where they'd first entered the chamber and searched the walls with his flashlight turned to high beam. Like Dr. Hightower's office in the museum, the opening was gone without a trace. That explained why the light had grown dimmer. Everyone frantically patted the walls. Solid.

"Uh oh," Ben said. "Maybe now is a good time to panic!"

"What do we do now?" asked April, poking the wall with one finger in search of another magical door. "Are we stuck here?"

Aris walked out of the shadows. Ben swung a flashlight beam into the corner where the cat emerged, then gestured to Carlos.

"You girls stay here," Ben said. He didn't get an argument.

He found another corridor hidden in shadows. It curved out of sight for thirty feet. Ben tried to calm his nerves and slow his breathing as he and Carlos inched down the hallway. It ended at a different cave, a narrow ledge, and an endless drop.

"No escape route but at least Aris found us a bathroom. Guess this cliff is as good as any for giving the devil a bath," Ben said.

"Okay," Carlos said, clearly in distress. "I'll just pretend it's the Grand Canyon."

◆ ◆

The sound of static erupted as Ben returned to the chamber. A faint glimmer danced on the device they'd hooked up to the potato battery. "All right! Maybe it takes a few minutes for the juice to get going. I owe Carlos an apology. We're cookin' now!"

The ground shook. The monitor went dark.

"You mean we're toast," Grace said, "if we don't find a way out of here."

Ben reconnected a wire that had come loose. The screen snapped on displaying video images of an ornate building filled with with

Renaissance paintings. He had seen rooms and hallways like these in both the Vatican and British museums.

Data scrolled along the sides in several languages, none of which was English. The video faded in and out as the device drew power from the potatoes.

"It's some kind of code," Ben said. "Can't these secret agents stick to one language?"

Grace studied the patterns on the screen. "One of them is Mandarin."

Ben tensed. "So what does it say?"

Grace furrowed her brow. "Wait! I think I got part of it. It keeps saying the same thing over and over again. Evacuate outposts. Set auto destruct. Teams ordered to the Harbor."

"What?" Serise peered over her shoulder. "Is this place going to blow up!"

"I think it already did," Carlos said, pointing around the room.

"Guys!" Grace yelped. "There's a reason why everyone is gone. We're not at Safe Harbor. Serise, when you dialed 'palindrome' the dialer used the last four letters of the location. We're in an observation post under the Vatican . . . in Rome!"

Serise dropped to her knees and caught her breath. "Really? What a relief. Sort of. I mean, at least we know we're not supposed to stay here. So now that we've solved that mystery, how do we get to this Safe Harbor? Is there another gateway?"

Ben pulled out the compass. Knowing he was in Rome made things easier. He selected "Italy." The pad showed a layout of the room. He gasped. There WAS another gateway! But there was also one huge problem. According to the map, this chamber was part of a huge, multi-level facility. The gateway was in the same direction as the abyss he and Carlos had discovered minutes before.

*"Vatican's down . . ."*

All that remained was a narrow ridge. A gaping hole had swallowed up the outpost and, according the Grace's mom, most of the people with it.

# CHAPTER THIRTY-SEVEN

## The Abyss

"A chain is no stronger than its weakest link."

• • *Sir Leslie Stephen*

• • *Thump! Thump!*

The walls vibrated. Dust and rocks settled to the floor.

"What is that?" asked Grace.

Serise froze. "Earthquake?"

"Maybe," Ben said. The hairs on his neck stood at attention. The air grew warmer.

*Thump! Thump!*

"There it goes again."

Carlos ran back into the room. "Did you hear that?"

"Yeah," Ben said. "I guess we shouldn't have aimed for the Devil. Now he's mad."

*Thump! Thump!*

Carlos frowned. "Know what the sound reminds me of? That old Jurassic Park movie. When the water in the puddle was shaking and then they figured out the T-Rex was coming."

"You think there are dinosaurs down here?" April's eyes grew wide. "I saw an old movie about people who traveled to the center of the earth and found dinosaurs there."

Ben shot Carlos a dirty look. "See what you've started?" He turned and rubbed his sister's back.

But Carlos was right about one thing. The sound occurred at regular intervals. No earthquake was that predictable. Whatever was making that noise was getting closer.

*Thump! Thump!*

The monitor went blank. A foul odor filled his nostrils. Different this time and much worse.

Aris grew still. Suddenly, he arched his back and hissed. Fur rose from his body. His tail grew bushy and stiff as he crouched low to the ground and stared at the swaying walkway above. He backed away, using his teeth on Ben's pajama leg to pull him toward the other side of the room, toward the narrow passage and the abyss beyond it.

*Thump! Thump!*

Aris persisted. The foul odor ebbed and flowed on a current of wind. Now that the insides of his stomach began flopping like a helpless fish, Ben couldn't hide the truth from himself any longer.

The adventure of a lifetime was now a nightmare.

"Guys, I think we should follow Aris," he said. "The compass is pointing in the same direction. I don't know about you, but I don't want to be around when whatever is causing that noise gets here. If it's got Aris spooked, that's good enough or me."

*"You have to get your sister to the Harbor,"* his mother said. *" . . . Keep her safe"*

Ben had no choice but to lead his friends there — wherever "there" was.

Everyone pulled on their packs, tightened their straps and rushed through the opening. Everyone, that is, but Serise. Eyes as wide as basketballs, she stood at the entrance, frozen with fear.

"I can't do this."

"What's wrong," asked April.

*Thump! Thump!*

"I'm . . . I'm . . . "

"We're all scared," Ben interrupted. "We all hear those noises. But it's going to be okay. Promise."

"No, you don't understand. I'm . . ." she paused, and wiped her eyes with her sleeve, "scared . . . of heights. I've never told anyone. I can't do this."

Ben surveyed his surroundings. Although the escape route was wide enough for them to pass two at a time, it was still just a ledge embedded on the side of a rock wall. A ledge bordered by a precipitous drop that looked as if it went all the way to the other side of the earth.

"But you and your mom go rock climbing all the time," April said.

"I just watch. My mom does all of the climbing. She's supposed to do some ancient ritual and wanted me to be her partner, but I chickened out." Tears streamed down her face. "I'm sorry. I can't do this."

*Thump! Thump!*

Ben threw his hands up. They needed to move. Now! The pounding grew louder. And closer. He was tempted to just pick her up and carry her over his shoulder.

"You can do this," Grace said. "You're braver than you think. We can't do this without you."

"You can send someone back for me," Serise said.

"That won't work," Grace said, her voice calm and soothing. "There isn't enough time, not if a ship is coming. We go together or we don't go at all."

*Thump! Thump!*

Ben looked at Grace and silently tapped on his watch. Grace nodded as Serise began to hyperventilate.

"You can do this," Grace said. "I'm scared too. We'll go together. You can be my partner."

Serise blinked and stared into space.

"Like at Adventure Challenge last month?" Grace squeezed Serise's hands until she got her attention. "Just pretend we're in the woods. You're blindfolded and I'm your guide. Remember when you did it for me? How I was scared of the dark and couldn't see anything? I trusted you. That was the point. If we trust each other we'll get through it. You have to trust me now." Grace paused. "Do you trust me?"

Serise nodded but streaming tears gave her away.

Ben glanced down the corridor and thought about the room where he and Carlos had found bodies — parts of bodies. There was no way they were going back in there.

*Thump! Thump!*

"I've got an idea." Ben reached into his pack and pulled out a bandana. "You'll want to cheat, so use this."

He fashioned a blindfold and covered Serise's eyes. "Whatever you do, keep a tight grip on Grace. Carlos and I will lead the way."

"April?" asked Grace "Can you be Ben's partner?"

"Sure," April said. "But I don't need the blindfold. I can do this."

Ben felt a twinge of pride. His little sister was fearless. He had seen her scale the monkey bars at her school and play "King of the Mountain." She scared her teachers to death, but she never fell. She had the best sense of balance of any kid he knew.

"Okay, Serise. Take a couple of practice steps before we head out."

Grace led Serise through a few tentative moves. Serise trembled, but made it through the exercise. She raised her thumb. *Ready.*

*Thump! Thump!*

Ben pointed toward the unknown. "Okay, gang. Let's rock."

# CHAPTER THIRTY-EIGHT

# The Gateway

"Failure is the opportunity to begin again
more intelligently."

• •  *Henry Ford*

• •  Ben, April and Carlos trekked along the ledge stopping every few minutes to wait for Grace and Serise to catch up. Ben had the feeling they were being watched, but the noise and vibration now sounded like a distant drumbeat. Soon, the smell of death evaporated in the cool air. Ben relaxed his shoulders then the rest of his body. Grace told corny jokes while they walked.

"Why doesn't Dracula have any friends?"

"Because he's a pain in the neck," answered Serise.

"Just like Ben." April giggled, as they crept along.

Ben rolled his eyes. "Ha, ha, ha. Your turn, April."

"Knock, knock," April said.

"Who's there?" Carlos answered.

"Boo," April said.

"Boo who?" said Carlos.

"Don't start crying again."

Serise groaned. "You guys are supposed to make me feel better, not make me barf!"

Ben stopped, his brow furrowed, his finger pressed against his lips. He gestured for April and Grace to keep the jokes going.

"Why do the birds fly south for the winter?" April craned her neck to look over the edge of the cliff but Ben pulled her back.

"I don't know," Serise groaned. "Why?"

"Because it's too far to walk!" April said quietly, her eyes wide in alarm.

The ledge grew narrow — a lot more narrow — then disappeared. End of the road. Fifty yards ahead was a sheer drop-off. Aris looked back toward the abandoned outpost, ears pricked, body stiff.

"What's going on?" asked Serise. "Why'd you guys get so quiet?"

"Nothing," Grace said, forcing a laugh. "You know guys. They can't think of jokes as fast as us. Okay, Ben. Your turn."

Ben appreciated the fact that Grace could think on her feet. "Ugh . . . hmmm . . . Oh yeah! What's the best way to catch a squirrel?"

"Good grief," Grace said. "Is that the best you can do?"

As they inched forward, Grace guided Serise toward the wall.

"Well, do you know it or not?" Ben asked.

"Climb a tree and act like a nut," Grace sighed. "That's an old one and not very original."

"I figured you needed something easy," Ben said. "You still haven't solved the riddle."

"What riddle?" Carlos pointed his flashlight into the void. The horrified expression on his face said his discovery wasn't good news.

"What's greater than God," Ben said, keeping his voice light. "More evil than the Devil? The poor have it, the rich need it and if you eat it you will die."

"Easy," Carlos said. "That awful stuff your mother makes you drink."

"Green glob IS more evil than the devil and when I drink it I feel like I'm going to die, but that's not the answer," Ben said.

"The new stuff is much better," April chimed in.

"Then you can have my share," Ben snorted.

"Get back to the subject. I changed my mind. Can I have a hint?" asked Grace.

"No. All you need to know is in the riddle already," Ben said.

"But nothing I try works," Grace said.

Ben shrugged. "If all else fails, whatever remains is the answer."

"That doesn't make any more sense than the last hint you gave me."

"Actually, it does if you think about it hard enough."

"Come on." Grace stamped her foot in mock protest. A section of the ledge broke off and dropped into the abyss.

Everyone froze and waited to hear the rock land. No sound returned. Grace's face turned bright red and she clamped one hand over her mouth.

She took a deep breath. "Serise, let's move a little closer to the wall."

"Why? What happened?"

"Nothing," Grace lied, keeping her voice soft and calm. "It's just a little dark and I want to make sure that you can feel something besides me just in case."

"Got it," Serise said, sounding more relaxed.

Ben peered around the curve. The gap wasn't a hole. It was the remnant of a winding staircase carved into the side of the cave. Only random sections of an iron railing remained intact. They looked sturdy but he didn't want to take any chances.

He clung to one overriding thought. His parents would be waiting on the other side.

"Serise?" Ben tried to sound cheerful even though his anxiety level was off the charts. "We've got to go down some stairs. It may be a little slippery so hug the wall, okay?"

"Okay," Serise said. "I think I can do it without the blindfold."

"No. It's better to keep it on. Grace can guide you, but it's a little scary."

"Great" Serise said. "I'm doomed if I do and doomed if I don't."

Serise let go of Grace's hand and removed the bandana. What she said next wasn't repeatable — mostly because no one could understand her. She yelled a mixture of Navajo, English and a few things that shouldn't have been in her vocabulary. She clutched the wall desperately searching for a handhold then turned to go back.

"Serise!" Ben yelled.

It was too late. Serise scrambled up the path towards the destroyed

Vatican complex. Her foot slipped with each step, causing the rock ledge to crumble. She pinwheeled her arms but her backpack threw off her balance. She slid over the edge toward the abyss.

Ben almost flew, grabbing a bent metal rod that jutted out of the rock with one hand and Serise's backpack strap with the other. He strained with the effort, his hand slipping on the rod. Serise was screaming as her body lurched to a stop.

"Hold on!" Ben yelled, trying to keep his grip on her pack. He was grateful she had the security strap fastened around her waist. It was all that was keeping the pack from slipping off her arms.

More rocks fell. The ledge wasn't stable and it wasn't going to hold for long.

"Stop kicking, Serise!"

Carlos scrambled onto his stomach, reaching for Serise. "Pull up!" Carlos said. "You've got to help us get you up."

"I don't want to die!" Serise screamed. "Don't let me fall."

"You won't," Ben felt as if his arm was going to dislocate from the socket. "I promise." But it was a lie. She was too heavy and the ledge was too narrow to get more leverage. There was no space left for Grace or April to lend a hand.

"You two keep going," Ben said. "In case the ledge collapses."

"No," Grace said. "We go together or we don't go at all. Serise! Pretend you're doing chin-ups in gym. Close your eyes and do it!"

Serise strained but couldn't get leverage. "It's not working!"

Ben began flexing his arm. She tried to find a handhold but the wall offered little assistance. Her feet dug into the wall only to slip again.

Ben panicked and nodded towards Carlos whose own face strained under the weight. "She's slipping. We're going to have to do it ourselves. Get ready to pull." Ben gritted his teeth and braced.

"Ready! Set! Go!"

He yanked and suddenly Serise was over the top and wedged between the small remaining space between him, Carlos and the wall. He bent over the edge, gasping. When he looked up again, Carlos, Grace and his sister were gaping at him.

"Thanks, Carlos," he said. "That was close."

Carlos just shuddered. "How did you do that? Get her up, I mean?"

Ben stared at him, still struggling to catch his breath. "What are you talking about? We did it together."

"No," Carlos said. "I wasn't ready. I was still trying to make sure I had most of my weight on this side of the ledge and suddenly you yanked and she was up."

Grace and April nodded in agreement. Serise, on the other hand, lay with her face against the wall, sobbing uncontrollably.

Ben blinked. "You sure?"

Carlos nodded. "Guess it's like those stories you hear about people getting a surge of adrenaline and lifting a car off someone."

Ben didn't respond. It happened so fast he didn't really remember the details. He coughed, took in another breath and contemplated their current situation. It hadn't changed.

"Serise, there's no place to go but forward," he said. "Even if we could get back to the Vatican outpost we don't know how to open the cave entrance or the sarcophagus from this side."

Serise inhaled rapidly. Ben figured that at her current rate she'd use up all the oxygen in the cave. He pushed April's hand into Grace's and winked. "Time for a change in partners, Twerp."

April winked back, but her face was still marked with fear. Ben inched toward Serise. One false step and . . . He couldn't bear to think about that possibility.

"Serise. I'm going to turn around. I want you to keep your hands on my shoulders. We're going down together."

"I can't!" She whimpered

"Do you need the blindfold?" Ben asked.

"No! It won't help now."

"Then there are only two choices," Ben said. "Go forward or stay right here. Whatever happens, we all stay together. You choose for us." He tucked the compass into the side pocket of April's backpack.

Serise wavered, argued with herself in Navajo, then gripped his hand so hard she nearly cut off the circulation. "Forward."

Carlos led the way. Dirt and debris covered the surface but traction was good. The staircase spiraled around a cylindrical outcrop of rock. April counted each step as they descended.

"Forty-nine, fifty. Wow! We're going a long way!" she said.

"April!" Grace nodded in Serise's direction.

April's mouth formed an "O."

"It's okay," Serise said, face turned toward the rock. "I'm okay."

By the time April reached "seventy-five" the group arrived at a dead end — a semi-circular landing just large enough to hold all of them — and a solid steel wall with an eight-pointed star engraved on it.

"NO!" Ben yelled. "What is this?"

"Maybe there's another one of those hidden doors here?" Grace's voice cracked in terror.

"I hope not," Carlos whispered. "There's nowhere for a door to swing without knocking us off the landing."

Serise let out a pitiful whimper.

"Oops. Sorry, Serise," he said.

Ben placed his hand on the star and felt a slight discharge of static electricity. The wall retracted revealing a chamber twenty feet in diameter. There were no hieroglyphics, panels or instructions on the smooth rock walls. Thankfully, there were also no unusual noises, no menacing shadows, no foul odors and no rhythmic pounding.

Safe enough — for now.

Serise ran to the opposite end of the room, pressed her back against the wall and breathed through her mouth. "No more heights, okay guys?"

Everyone nodded.

"Now what?" asked Carlos. "It's another dead-end."

April jerked her hand away from Grace, and pointed to crystal-line rocks in the floor. She pushed away debris and uncovered part of a medallion inlaid with marble, quartz and other gemstones. "Look what I found!"

Ben stared at the floor partly in relief and partly with suspicion. This medallion looked as if it had gone unused for hundreds of years. Did it even work at all?

Aris sniffed at the device as April brushed rocks and dirt from the surface. Each pad made a sound.

Horrified, Ben shoved April out of the way. "Don't touch anything until we figure out where to go next." All of his assumptions had been wrong up to now — so was this medallion an escape route? Or just another dead-end?

"It's okay," April said. "This thing is just like the one in the game but the notes sound a lot nicer." She hummed "Ode to Joy" while she tapped out a tune on the medallion.

"April!"

"I'm not hurting anything! Look, I can play an arpeggio on this thing."

Before Ben could stop her, April stood in the center of the medallion and continued tapping the pads with her sneakers. "See! Just like my piano lessons." Aris weaved in and out of her legs and seemed to be urging her on.

"April! No!"

A flash of blue-white light shot into the air. In an instant, April and Aris were gone.

# CHAPTER THIRTY-NINE

# Arpeggio

"And those who were seen dancing
were thought to be insane
by those who could not hear the music."

♦ ♦ *Friedrich Nietzsche*

♦ ♦ Ben rushed to the medallion. "I'm going in after her." He tapped several of the stones with his shoe. The light did not return.

"Where's the compass?" asked Carlos

Ben threw his pack on the ground, searched through the pockets, then touched himself all over. "Arrggh! It's in April's pack!"

"What's it doing there?" yelled Serise.

"I put it there so I could hold your hand. I still don't have any feeling in my fingers after your death grip!" Ben shook them at her to reinforce the point.

"Okay," Carlos said. "We just have to punch in the same code. What was that song she was playing?"

"An arpeggio," Ben said.

"Can't you remember it?" asked Grace. "Seemed straight forward."

Ben was exasperated. He was sick to death of patterns and clues and riddles and adventures. A few hours ago he had been tucked in his warm, safe and totally stationary bed. Now he was operating on reserve power.

He struggled to remember the sequence and thought about the irritating plinking of April's fingers hitting the keys on the family piano.

There was something Mr. Windom had tried to teach him once. *"Notes of a chord played consecutively."*

That didn't help. Ben didn't remember any chords.

"We can turn this into a math formula," Carlos said. "When April pushed the pads in order, nothing happened. So try touching each one so we can mark the location of each sound. Then we can try to recreate the pattern."

Ben was skeptical, but also desperate to get to his sister back. April was all that he had left. And if his parents were still alive, they'd be expecting him to arrive with April intact. So losing her to some other dimension wasn't an option.

He walked in a circle, touching each pad with his foot.

The notes grew progressively higher until he reached the starting point.

"The dialer's always looked like a clock to me," Serise said, the fear draining from her voice.

She was right. There were twelve notes and twelve symbols equally spaced around the circumference of the medallion. It did look like a clock.

"Okay," Ben said, "then let's assign a number to each one." He pointed to position furthest from the cave entrance. "Let's call that twelve o'clock. Now, does anyone remember what tones they heard when April pushed them?"

"Wasn't the twelve," Grace said. "It was lower than that."

Ben tapped the next few notes.

"Stop. That's the one."

Ben's foot was on three o'clock. "Okay, what's next?"

"It sounded like a scale," Grace said. "She moved clockwise and then counter clockwise."

"Try skipping a note," Carlos said.

Ben moved to five o'clock.

"That's it!" Grace said. "Keep going. Skip again. I don't think the next note is one step up, I remember it being higher."

Ben stepped to seven o-clock.

"Maybe it's based on prime numbers," Carlos said.

"Prime?" asked Serise.

"Divisible by the numbers one and itself," Carlos said.

"I know what prime numbers are! It was a rhetorical question," Serise spat.

"Try the next step," Grace said.

Ben stepped to eight o'clock. "How about this?"

"You really are tone deaf," Carlos said. "Even I could tell that sound was way off."

"Okay, back to the drawing board." Ben retraced his steps — three, five, seven. "We've been skipping two each time, let's keep up with that pattern."

"Too easy," Carlos said. "But what do we have to lose except our lives? What if we dial the wrong code and we beam to the center of the earth?"

"We're there already," Grace said.

"Well, wherever I go, it better be to my sister." Ben tried nine. No luck. Bile rose in his empty stomach. He didn't want to end up in some weird place or worse — inside a rock. Something caught his eye. He crouched and brushed the dirt away with his hand. The Eye of Ra and the same hieroglyphic symbols from the museum. He didn't need a translator to tell him what it meant.

"Her who? Hey, Serise. Try doing that thing with your watch."

A light shot out of the bezel and bounced off the cave walls. The surface glowed. So did four of the twelve medallion crystals: the third, fifth, seventh and tenth positions.

"Guess that blows your prime number theory," Ben said.

"No kidding, Detective Webster" said Carlos. "What was your first clue?"

Ben ignored him. He stepped on each glowing crystal in turn. Nothing happened.

"Palindrome," shrieked Serise. "It's a palindrome."

"Good grief! Don't start with that stuff again," Ben said. "You see where it got us the last time. It's an arpeggio, according to my sister before she vanished into thin air. Why don't we just spell that?"

"No," Carlos said. "She's right. The arpeggio sequence was a palindrome. It sounded the same backwards as forward. Try retracing your steps."

"Okay, but if this works, you guys better come in after me."

"Where else are we going to go?" Carlos grimaced and pointed around the chamber.

"Okay," Ben said. "It's settled. Remember the sequence. We said we'd all stay together. You follow after I'm through."

Everyone repeated the sequence: Three. Five. Seven. Ten.

"Here goes!" Ben walked to the seventh stone, stepped onto the fifth and — yelling "Kowabunga" — leaped unto the third step. He disappeared into a familiar flash of blue light.

# CHAPTER FORTY

# Oasis

"What pioneer ever had a chart and a lighthouse to steer by?"

＊ ＊ *Catherine Drinker Bowen*

＊ ＊ "Whoa!" Ben yelled as he slid down a mammoth sand dune. He spotted April near a pool of water. She'd had fallen asleep in the shade of a palm tree. Beyond the scruffy oasis lay an endless ocean of rolling, undulating sand.

*Whoosh!*

Grace slid behind him creating a trench that quickly filled in. "What a rush! I'll take the great outdoors over that icky place we just left, anytime."

*Whoosh!*

Carlos and Serise held hands as they tumbled down the dune. They reminded Ben of the Jack and Jill nursery rhyme.

"Well," Carlos said, shaking sand out of his hair. "I guess we don't have to worry about cliffs out here. But I'm not sure that our situation has gotten any better. Where are we anyway?"

"Beats me." Exhausted, Ben dropped his backpack and collapsed in a heap. He was too tired to think straight. He wanted to curl up next to a sand dune and take a nap. In the morning it would all be over and he would be in his own bed surrounded by basketball posters.

"Ben!"

He slapped at the hand on his shoulder.

"Ben! Wake up."

"Is it time for school yet?" He rolled over, reached to hug his pillow and grabbed a handful of sand.

"Ben! Wake up!" Grace said. "We're still lost."

"Huh?"

The fog cleared from his eyes. April was asleep, her pack serving as a pillow. Aris lapped water from the edge of the pond. His tail flicked from side to side.

"I wonder where we are," Serise said.

"The desert obviously," Carlos said.

Serise clucked her tongue and threw sand at him. "Even I can see that! But which desert? We need to find some food and shelter and set up camp. What time is it anyway?"

"Don't you have a watch?" Ben asked, still slurring his words.

"Yes. But you guys kept having me set it back to midnight."

Ben chuckled. "I still can't get over it. You can design computer programs in your head but you can't operate a watch."

Serise glared at him.

Carlos yawned. "It's six."

"In the morning?" asked Ben.

The sun was setting into the horizon. That couldn't be right. They had left Sunnyslope early in the morning. It was late afternoon here. Where was here?

"Egypt?" he asked. "That would put us on the other side of the world. It would be hours later than California if we traveled east."

"That transport beam could have taken us anywhere," Grace said.

"Even to another planet," Serise added.

"Nope." Carlos yawned, then pointed at the sky. "We're still on Earth. Look at the moon."

Ben looked up at the familiar crater filled face in the sky and was relieved. The man in the moon with his two eyes and wide mouth exclaiming "Oh," stared down on him.

"I still think this is a group hallucination and we're in the sweat lodge," Ben said. "It's hot enough to be the sweat lodge."

"I wonder if that water is safe." Carlos said, pointing to the pond.

"Let's see if Aris survives," Ben said.

Aris stopped purring and growled in their direction.

"Well at least I've got provisions in my backpack." Ben produced a thermos, unscrewed the top and stared in disbelief. It contained green liquid with yellow swirls and something new. Bright red flecks. Pomegranate flecks. It was . . .

"NO! Awww man, why now?"

Serise craned her neck to see. "What's the matter?"

Ben didn't answer. He poured a drop at his feet. Its identity was unmistakable. It oozed out of the thermos and bounced once before splattering on the sand. "That's what's the matter. And I think it's alive."

"That can't be all that's in there," Carlos said, his face full of pity.

The others pulled containers from their own packs. April produced a vegetarian sandwich, her own thermos of glob and treats for Aris.

Ben growled. "Mom put in snacks and some camping gear. Looks like enough food for a day or so. Anyone up for a macrobiotic tofu burger?" He reached into the bottom of the backpack, tore out a section of canvas and produced a super-sized chocolate bar.

"Awesome! Where'd you get that?" asked Carlos.

"I glued a secret compartment in the bag last year. That way, I could count on something decent to eat whenever I got hungry." Ben took a bite and spat it out. "Eeew, this doesn't taste right. I think its old. But that doesn't make sense. I just put it in here a few days ago."

The brown wrapper said Hershey's but there was no Hershey imprint on the bar.

Carlos broke off a chunk, bit it and laughed. "Unsweetened carob. Looks like your mother knew about your secret and pulled the old switcheroo."

Serise displayed a sandwich, a plastic container with oatmeal cookies, and a thermos. A change of clothes and some toiletries had been stuffed into the bottom of the bag. Far be it for Serise to travel without lip-gloss and beauty supplies. She opened her thermos. "It's a cranberry smoothie. My favorite."

Carlos produced camping gear, a change of clothes, and an army camouflage rain slicker. He opened a Ziploc container and found his mother's famous tamales and a couple of bottles of chocolate Yoo-Hoos. "Want to share?"

"Oh, yes! Thanks!" Ben dumped his mother's vitamin drink on a small, scraggly bush and rinsed his thermos before filling it with pond water. Aris stared at the last of the green glob as it soaked into the sand. Clearly a bad batch if even the cat wouldn't drink it.

Grace pulled out an insulated container of sushi rolls and mango punch. An extra pair of glasses was tucked in her Bugs Bunny case.

Something moved in Ben's peripheral vision. The bush that had been bare when they first arrived now held a lush red flower. It opened before his eyes to reveal hundreds of orange stamen and black pistils. Soon more buds popped out, covering the plant. One by one they opened into giant blooms.

"Whoa!" Carlos said. "What's going on?"

Ben brushed his finger against a flower. The petals were soft, like silk. "No wonder April and I are so tall. I've been dumping mom's drink on her rose bushes. I wonder what would have happened to me if I had kept drinking it all this time?"

"Me too." April struggled to sit up. "I've been feeding mine to Aris when mom wasn't looking."

"For how long?"

"Since last month. I saw you dump yours in the greenhouse. That's when I got the idea. The taste was so awful I just couldn't choke it down without barfing. But Aris loves it."

Aris let out a quiet growl and curled up in April's lap and purred.

Carlos yawned and pointed to his watch. "Hey guys. It's about six o'clock in the morning California time. I reset my watch. If you're right and we're in Egypt it's 4 o'clock in the afternoon. I suggest we skip the botanical bonding and get some shut eye. It may take a while to get where we are going."

Ben dug a trench in the sand dune and collapsed. April crawled over and put her head in his lap. Ben rubbed her back the way his mother did when she was a baby. April was out in seconds. She looked like a harmless angel when she slept and glowed in the waning sunlight. And then he caught himself. *Good grief! What's the matter with me?* He was hugging his sister like . . . like he loved her or something. Now he knew he'd traveled to an alternate universe.

Aris yawned and went to sleep. Ben grinned, pulled the collar from his backpack and slipped it around the cat's neck. He adjusted the clasp to allow two fingers to slip inside — enough to keep the cat from choking, but not enough slack to allow Aris to get it off.

*Aha! Finally got you evil one. Now all I need is a leash!*

A dull ache throbbed in his legs. His pants had ripped when he slid down the steps beneath the sarcophagus. He'd been so preoccupied, he hadn't felt the pain until now. April let out a sigh and scratched her own legs. Ben pulled up his pant leg to survey the damage. The bruises faded before his eyes, the scratches had closed. He removed his bandages and examined his hand. The places where he had scraped the skin away while trying to open the entrance to the garage tunnel were also healed. The glob? He had spilled some on his hand. Was it absorbed through the skin?

Carlos tossed him a Mylar pouch. "Here. Sun's going down. It's going to get cold. Press that button to make the microfilaments heat up."

"This what Scouts use?" asked Ben.

"No. My dad gave them to me. Guess it's what spies use."

The wafer-thin mylar unfolded to the size of a twin-size blanket — enough to cover Ben and April. Within seconds it warmed to a comfortable temperature.

"Thanks, Inspector Gadget."

"Don't mention it." Carlos tossed a packet to Grace and Serise, before unfolding a third for himself.

Ben's mind worked sluggishly. They needed to find shelter. He pulled the compass out of April's pack, played with the controls and frowned. No further instructions about Safe Harbor. The compass showed a medallion and dialing instructions. They had already done that part. The compass spun wildly. It acted like they were already there. What kind of ship was going to pick them up in the middle of nowhere?

Tiny lights blinked on the global chart. He didn't care what they meant. He was so tired . . . just wanted to rest . . . a few hours and he would get up . . . just . . . two hours . . .

CHAPTER FORTY-ONE

# Darkness

"Faithless is he that says farewell when the road darkens."

• • *J.R.R. Tolkien*

• • Ben woke with a start. It was cold and dark. Something nipped his hand.

"Stop it, Aris!"

Aris's orange eyes glowed at him in the dark . . . on his right side. Something scuttled away to the left.

"Arggh!"

"What's going on?" asked Carlos, wiping the sleep from his eyes.

"Something's out here with us."

"Probably a snake."

"It wasn't a snake. They make hissing sounds and slither away. This thing ran away."

"Okay. It was a sand viper. Or a scorpion. Or your imagination. Whatever it is, if you leave it alone, it won't bother you." Within minutes Carlos was snoring again.

"Was it bigger than a sand box?" asked Grace, her words soft and slurring. "Go back to sleep. This may not be Safe Harbor but safe enough for me. I'm going back to sleep."

Sleep? No way. Not with wild creatures roaming in the dark. Adrenaline coursed through Ben's veins as he watched sand swirl and

**257**

form eddies in the breeze. The sand. The wind.

*The game?*

If the game was a clue, there would be a trap door. But not near a pond. There was no pond in the game.

Ben scrambled to his feet, careful not to wake April. "I'm going to search for a hidden door. Want to help?"

"No, but I'll do it anyway." Grace yawned loudly. "It's cold even with this blanket thing. Let's wake everyone up. We'll find it faster if everyone is helping."

"Let's do it ourselves. Everyone's tired and we're not sure how much farther we have to go."

"Anything on the compass thing?"

"No. It acts like we're right over it."

"So we're close."

"I guess. If we don't find it at least we won't die of thirst."

"No." Grace pulled a flashlight out of her backpack. "We'll just die of hypothermia."

April's head was resting on Ben's pack so he opened hers instead.

"Oh great," he spat as he flicked the switch.

*ROAR!*

Grace jumped. "What was that?"

"Tiger light. It used to help her chase nighttime monsters away when she was little." Ben scowled. The curved tail served as a handle. "It's the best I can do right now."

Ben kicked at the sand and dragged his feet looking for clues.

"Anything, Grace?"

"No, nothing."

Ben shoved the useless device back in April's pack and walked a circular path around the oasis. Aris began scratching and pawing at the sand.

"Find anything?" asked Grace.

"No. Just one endless litter box." He made a mental note to avoid that spot.

Thunder roared in the distance followed by a faint pounding that had the same frequency as the one in the cave. Ben froze but saw nothing out of the ordinary.

Aris looked up as well, then resumed his frantic excavation of a toilet.

Ben returned to the beginning of his circle and started again, this time forming a spiral pattern as he walked. The air grew warm. He was grateful for the change and felt the feeling return to his fingers.

Aris whined and issued a furtive cry that sounded almost human in his frustration. Ben rushed to see what had caught the cat's attention. Aris scratched at his neck, hissed angrily at Ben, then rolled in the sand and struggled to remove the collar.

Ben's foot hit something solid. He looked back at the oasis. He was dead center between two palm trees. But there weren't any palm trees in the game.

"Grace!"

"Found something?"

"Not sure."

The distant thunder grew louder. Grace seemed not to notice. She ran toward Ben, her steps labored as the sand crunched and rolled under her feet.

Ben scooped sand out of the way, checking first to make sure it didn't contain bathroom presents from Aris. Sand poured back into the hole as fast as Ben could remove it. Grace knelt beside him and scooped quickly.

"Score!"

Ben grabbed the copper handle they uncovered. It didn't budge. He and Grace tugged, feet slipping in the sand.

No luck.

"Now what?" asked Ben.

Grace scooped away more sand. "There aren't any hieroglyphics on the stones this time, just a bunch of odd marks. Maybe the sand is weighing it down. We've got to uncover the whole door."

She ran to her pack, removed the top from her lunch and used it as a tool. They both continued digging until they uncovered twelve quartz crystals. Ben pushed the nodes but no sound emerged.

"It doesn't work!" Anger rose in the pit of his stomach. He felt abandoned by his parents. His whole life had been a lie. Now he was in the middle of nowhere fighting to get — where? A harbor? What kind of boat were they going to find in an ocean of sand, let alone underneath it?

Grace sat cross-legged and traced the symbols with her fingertips. The dialer remained dormant.

"It should work," Grace said. "It's the same symbols. So what's the key? In the game it was us. Our names opened the passage."

"Okay, but how does that help us now? There's no keyboard and no space for a name," Ben said. "This is ridiculous. We're going to die out here in this foreign wasteland. Our parents are going to sail away to some warm exotic paradise and we're going to have to eat the cat for food."

Aris growled and kicked sand at Ben then resumed trying to remove his collar. Ben leaned over to swat at him, resting his hand in the center of the medallion for stability. The crystals glowed. Startled, Ben snatched his hand away. The glow faded. He repeated the action several times with the same result. "What does this mean? Can anyone do this or just me?"

Grace placed her hand on the same spot. The glow returned as the metal compressed under her touch. Jaws dropping, they stared at each other, grinned and pushed the glowing stones in the arpeggio sequence — three, five, seven, ten, seven, five, three.

No beam appeared.

"It's not working," Ben said. "I think we need a different code."

Groaning, Grace scrambled on all fours to April's backpack. She found the compass and tossed it to Ben. "Work some magic, Webster!"

He typed "Is this a gateway?"

"Askar!"

"Answers in English please!"

"Confirmed."

Ben froze. "This thing talks back?

"Verify current location. Identify code to open present gateway."

"Confirmed. Verify desired method. Autodial or manual input?"

Mouths gaped open, Ben and Grace stared at the device.

"Autodial!" they yelled in unison.

"Confirmed. Connecting to Central Command. Entry code activated."

The crystals blinked so fast, Ben had no time to memorize the sequence.

The ground shook beneath him. Still kneeling, Grace and the cat slid farther away. No bright light this time. This doorway was manual, and mechanical. The stones separated to reveal a dark, but familiar passageway.

# CHAPTER FORTY-TWO

# Followed

"Maybe this world is another planet's hell."

• • *Aldus Huxley*

• • "Way to go Grace! I always said we make a good team."

Grace looked up and searched the barren landscape. "Did you hear that?"

Pounding. Louder this time. The ground trembled. Suspecting someone had followed them from Rome, Ben fixed his gaze on the sand dune where his friends slept. Nothing materialized.

Grace gasped. "Look!"

Ben spun one hundred and eighty degrees and allowed his eyes to adjust in the low light. Something was headed toward them, kicking up large amounts of sand in the process. In the glow of the moonlight it looked like a giant black condor, wings flapping close to the ground.

*A mirage?* Mirages didn't make noise. Mirages didn't happen at night. He turned off April's flashlight and motioned for Grace to do the same.

A cloud formed in the sky, partially blotting out the moon's glow. A cloud similar to the one Ben had seen in Llactapata and in Sunnyslope. A cloud that had spooked his father.

The giant bird multiplied as the mirage loomed larger. Now there were three — no four — heading toward them. Grace froze, her eyes wide with fear.

To escape danger, Ben's parents had sent them underground — into the unknown — to safety. "Quick! Let's get down the stairs!"

Grace sprang into action and roused Carlos. "Get up!" She was more gentle with April. "Come on, Scooter. Time to go."

Ben shook Serise roughly.

"Quit it, you jerk!" She smacked him and went back to sleep.

His cheek stinging from the impact, Ben shook her again, held her wrists away from him and nodded toward the disturbance.

Serise's eyes became saucers and she scrambled to her feet. "Sorry I hit you."

Ben scooped items into the closest backpack. The cloud continued to drift past the moon. The intermittent glow caused the approaching birds to appear distorted — as if they had legs. If this was Uncle Henry's monster surprise, Ben didn't want to see it up close. His heart hammered as he crouched low to the ground and ran toward the passageway, slipping in the sand as he went.

The gang flew down the steps in a panic. April paused to take a look. Ben yanked on her arm and pulled her inside. Aris remained topside. Ben grabbed him by the collar and yanked him through the opening as well. Aris struggled, hissed and dug his claws into Ben's hand. Ben tossed the cat forward.

"Listen, stupid cat. I don't like you, and you don't like me. But Mom will kill me if I don't keep you alive."

A hot breeze blew into the passageway. An odd shadow floated along the wall. Ben blinked. The shadow swirled down into the darkness and was gone.

Optical illusion caused by dehydration and exhaustion?

Ben shook off his paranoia and ducked inside.

"Everyone! Start looking for a way to get this door closed!" Ben reached for his father's device, heard a strange voice and jerked his head upward. There was no one behind him. A woman's voice echoed through the chamber.

"Kortis or."

"Kortis ada."

"Kortis bo."

Ben's hands flew up in exasperation. "What now? Might as well speak Swahili!"

The words and accent changed.

"Hatari."

"Saba."

"Sita."

Grace and Carlos gasped while Ben scrolled through the compass in search of a translation.

"The computer voice," Grace said. "It switched to Swahili. I can translate this."

"And?" asked Ben.

Grace closed her eyes, her brow furrowed in intense concentration. "It's a warning."

Ben's stomach tightened. "What kind of warning?"

"Not sure. We missed the first part of the message. Either we set an auto-destruct and we're about to blow up, or it's warning us that the doors are closing."

"Tano."

"Five!" Grace said.

Outside, the thundering sound grew more ominous. Ben willed the door to close before anything could get through.

"Nne."

"Four!" counted Carlos, his voice dropping to a whisper.

The pounding grew closer. Sand poured through the opening.

"Tatu."

"Three," everyone whispered in a tense but hushed chorus.

The corridor echoed with the chuffing of horses. Horses? A light flashed above the entrance. Silence followed.

"Mbili."

*Two!* No one dared speak, but Ben knew his friends were counting along with the disembodied voice. All eyes remained fixed on the opening.

*Come on! Come on!*

Above him, sand crunched under multiple feet.

"Moja."

*One!*

The door closed, sealing the entrance to the desert. Ben exhaled and unclenched his aching fists. Only a solid rock ceiling remained. Grains of sand could be heard filling the cavity above the door. The portal would soon be concealed beneath the oasis.

Safe. But for how long?

"We better get going." Ben tried to sound calm. "Got to find another dialer or the safe house. Ship coming bright and early, right? I hope it's a cruise ship with room service."

"Seems like we're stuck in the real-life version of your uncle's game," Carlos said. "Want to lead the way?"

"No problem." Ben was just as scared as the rest of his friends but they were out of options and he had a promise to keep.

"I'll be your partner." April squeezed his hand where Aris had scratched him. Ben winced and shifted to a more comfortable position. The scratches, once deep and stinging, faded.

The staircase was wide enough for them to walk two abreast. Grace and Serise stayed in the middle. Carlos took the rear. Ben aimed his flashlight straight ahead. The walls were lined with the same odd hieroglyphics in the game, birds on top, humans in the middle, fish at the bottom. As they traveled, the flashlights cast eerie shadows which made the carvings seem alive.

"You think we lost them?" asked Carlos.

"Yeah." Ben could feel his heart beating as far down as his toes and wasn't in the mood for conversation.

They arrived at a wide corridor lined with tall, thick columns and burning torches. Ben extinguished his flashlight. Crystals imbedded in the floor glowed white as they passed.

"Everyone stay together," Ben said. "Looks like someone's already been here."

"I don't think so," Carlos said. "There's no footprints on the floor."

Carlos was right. A thin layer of dust formed a film on the stone floors. They had left a trail of kid footprints and paw prints behind them as they walked but no other sign of human life was present. So why were the torches lit?

An enormous shadow loomed on a nearby column. It expanded and contracted as it moved. Ben flinched and aimed his flashlight to investigate. He retrieved the broken collar and put it in his pocket. "Okay, Aris. You win."

The cat ignored him and resumed his search of the complex.

Ben felt as though he was being watched. The columns were topped with black stone heads that resembled Aris. He fixed his gaze on a column two rows ahead. The head faced toward him. It still faced in his direction when he passed by. Ben didn't think it was possible but he was more spooked than before.

Aris skulked in and out of the shadows, his tail twitching as he looked up at the stone doppelgängers. After a while, he stopped exploring and — tail stiffened — stuck close to Ben's side.

Ben took several detours. To the left and to the right, a stone balcony cut off access to the cavernous space below. Shadows seemed to float in his peripheral vision. Goosebumps erupted all over his body. There was no place to go but forward.

A wooden door punctuated the end of their journey. It contained no odd shapes, no cryptic hieroglyphics, and no puzzles to solve. Aris scratched at the door and looked up at Ben expectantly.

"I wonder what the trick is to opening this thing?" He pulled. The door creaked, but didn't budge. He should have known it wouldn't be that easy. Ben put his ear to the door.

"What do you hear?" asked April.

"Sounds like voices." Something brushed against his hand. He flinched and withdrew it from the handle.

"I don't hear anything," Serise said.

"With our luck, it's probably the entrance to the river Styx," Carlos said. "It carries the souls of the dead away to their fate."

"You've got kind of a dark side," Grace said. "Could you knock it off for a while?"

"Shhh! Did you hear that?" asked Ben.

"Kumi . . . Tisa . . . Nane . . . Saba . . ."

Footsteps rushed along the corridor behind them.

"Sita . . . Tano . . . Nne . . ."

Instantly, Ben recognized what had happened. The gateway was in a countdown to closure. They had been followed. Whatever was chasing them in the desert had gained access to the corridor. The computer continued to use the last language requested of it.

"Tatu . . . Mbili . . ."

"Hide!"

Ben grabbed April's hand and ducked behind the last column. It vibrated as the giant cat head moved. Soon all the stone heads pointed in the direction of the intruders.

"Moja."

Carlos crouched behind a column to the left of Ben. Grace and Serise hid on the other side of the corridor. Ben reached out and snatched Aris away from the wooden door. The cat offered little resistance. His hair bristled, his tail twitched but he remained silent and alert. Not even a low growl to give their position away.

The footsteps stopped, replaced by rasping and wheezing — like someone out of breath.

A breeze brushed across Ben's cheek, bringing with it a foul smell.

Windswept debris swirled across the floor.

The temperature rose rapidly, causing Ben to sweat. April clutched him and shivered as if she were freezing.

The footsteps resumed, slow and deliberate.

They needed an escape route but the balcony lead to a two-story drop.

No safe place to run.

No safe harbor.

The glow of tiny lights caught his attention. Panicked, he pulled April's collar around her sparkling hair beads then draped his arm to mute them.

A sound rang out.

And then another.

Swishing.

Grunting.

The clang of metal upon stone.

Something hit the front of the column that concealed him. Ben glanced at Carlos and mouthed, *"Can you see anything?"*

Carlos shook his head. *"No!"*

The light dimmed as if night were descending into the corridor. Aris cocked his head, then bolted away before Ben could stop him. He regretted not having the collar as a restraint although he doubted anything could have stopped the fiercely determined cat.

A shadow loomed on Carlos's column; a hand gripping a tall pole topped with a clear sphere, fingers of electricity arcing inside. Carlos had seen it as well. His mouth gaped open.

A blood curdling scream echoed through the chamber.

Another scream! Worse than the first!

Silence.

Did it come from Grace? Serise? Aris?

Not Aris. The cat hissed and spit to indicate he was still in the game. His feline shadow crouched into an offensive stance against the unknown assailants and grew to five times its normal size. The shadow sprang into the air and out of sight as an angry growl, like the roar of a lion, rumbled through the corridor. The sound could not have come from Aris.

Then what was out there?

Another scream!

Something was being torn to shreds!

An odor — that awful odor — of something dead and decaying.

A chorus of deep voices rapidly speaking in a foreign tongue.

A one-word command.

"Askut!"

More silence.

Full of adrenaline, Ben was sure his heart's accelerated beating would echo through the chamber and give their position away. He ached from remaining in his crouched position but dared not move.

April pressed closer to him, her tears soaking through his shirt. He wrapped his arms around her to calm her trembling and pressed a finger to her lips.

*Shhh!*

Aris's shadow did not return. Ben said a prayer for the cat's released spirit.

Were the girls still alive? Could he get to them without being seen? He studied patterns in the floor. Six blocks to the next column — the distance of a free throw line — about fifteen feet. Fear clouded his reasoning. He struggled to stay coherent. Across the hallway — less than half-court — he estimated thirty feet. Grace and Serise were directly across from Carlos. How far? Pythagorean theorem. Grace and Serise were at the other end of the hypotenuse.

*Think. Do the math.*

Fifteen squared plus thirty squared. Ben's head felt as if it would explode. About eleven-hundred feet. Take the square root. More than thirty feet, less than forty. He could make it. He was faster than lightning on the court. But getting to Grace and Serise meant leaving April behind. That wasn't an option. He made a promise. April was the priority.

How did spies make choices like this?

Fear evident in his eyes, Carlos gestured toward to Ben. In his hand — his Swiss Army knife, its tiny blade drawn. Ben nodded, although he didn't know what good the blade would do against multiple attackers, especially when wielded by someone who could never bring himself to hurt even the tiniest insect. He closed his eyes, bowed his head in silent prayer, then slipped his hand into the front pocket of his backpack. Still there! His own multi-function knife.

A sound spilled into the corridor, like a flag whipping violently in the wind. Heavy footsteps thundered toward Ben, then slowed as they approached the doorway. Soon an extended pause separated each step.

*Step . . .*

Ben heard something being dragged across the floor — away from his position behind the column. The intruder was not alone.

*Step . . .*

Two flashes of blinding light erupted.

*Step . . .*

Ben held his breath. The intruder's shadow was close to the door. Soon he or she or even it would be illuminated by the torch on Ben's column.

*Step . . .*

April's heart beat rapidly. She drew short, quick breaths. Ben covered her mouth to muffle the noise and held her closer.

*Step . . .*

Ben willed the stranger to move on. He swore that he would raise his grades, give up basketball and devote his life to science if he could just open his eyes and find himself back in his boring Sunnyslope bedroom. He would never, *ever* ask for an adventure again if this one simple wish were granted.

*Silence.*

He opened his eyes. The foul odor faded but the shadow remained, standing motionless as if trying to sense the location of its prey. Rapid bursts of a high-pitched ping bounced off the column. The assailant rotated in all directions before continuing toward the door.

And then, with renewed panic, Ben realized that they had left footprints in the dust. The trail would surely lead the intruder to their hiding places.

Ben rested his chin on April's hair. There was no choice. If the stranger attacked, he'd have to defend her. They were trapped and out of options.

April tried to peek but Ben shook his head. *NO!*

*Too late!*

Her pack fell to the floor with a reverberating *THUD!* The footsteps came to a stop. Ben stifled a scream. For a few seconds there was complete silence except for the shallow breathing of the stranger.

Flipping his blade to the open position, Ben pointed toward the intruder then made a slashing movement across his neck. Carlos gave a thumbs up. Like Ben, Carlos was shaking, but he was ready.

Multiple footsteps moved toward the column that concealed Ben and April. A hulking, misshapen shadow loomed on the floor in front of him. He gasped as an eerie, elongated hand reached out.

The time to act was now.

Ben used his fingers to indicate the countdown.

*One . . .*

*Two . . .*

*Three!*

Ben shoved April to what he hoped would be a safe distance. Joined by Carlos, he lunged into the corridor. The massive assailant caught their arms mid strike and held them firmly at bay.

Defiant, Ben stared into the piercing cold eyes of his pursuer.

PART III

# Answers

• • •

# CHAPTER FORTY-THREE

# Safe Harbor

"Real knowledge is to know the extent of one's ignorance."
* * * *Confucius*

❖ ❖ ❖ "Uncle Henry!"

Ben's uncle released his grip on Ben and Carlos, but not before twisting their wrists causing them to drop their weapons. The useless knives clattered to the floor.

April sprang into his arms. Expressionles she towered above them in burgundy robes veined with gold threads. A turban covered his bald head, draped under his chin, and down his back. He maintained his grip on April as if she were weightless.

Three men flanked him, their feet apart and hands behind their backs. Only a portion of their faces showed through their heavy draping.

Ben's heart continued its violent hammering. The shortest of the guards acknowledged him with a slight nod. It was brief, but comforting. He had seen those hazel eyes somewhere before.

"We're so glad to see you," April said. "We've been through some scary stuff!"

"I can imagine." Uncle Henry said, maintaining his ice-cold demeanor. In his hand, a device beeped intermittently.

*A tracking device?*

"Where are the others?"

Grace and Serise crept out of the shadows, both pale, gasping and clutching their chests.

"We're all here."

Ben ran to Grace and hugged her. "I thought you were dead."

"We thought something had gotten you guys too," Grace said in short sobs. "We heard that awful screaming."

A long ornamental knife hung, from the sash around his uncle's waist. A single drop of green liquid clung to the tip for a few tenuous seconds before dropping on Uncle Henry's otherwise spotless leather boot and splattering on the floor. The knife retracted until it was only a few inches long.

"What was that awful noise?" asked Ben.

Uncle Henry glanced toward the desert entrance and scowled. "Nothing that need concern you."

Ben followed his uncle's gaze. He could make out tracks in the dust as if multiple things had been dragged away.

"Aris!" Uncle Henry barked. "Akoosh!"

Aris sauntered out of the shadows, sat at Uncle Henry's feet and licked his paws as if he had just eaten a meal.

Ben's heart soared. Everyone alive and accounted for. "Any word from our parents?"

His uncle lowered April to the floor. "Not yet. We can't stop here. This area of the complex has not been in use for two thousand years. Follow me."

He pulled the door lever. It didn't budge. He growled and yanked with enough strength to rip it from the wall. The door flew open revealing a liquid barrier that quickly evaporated. No tricks, no mumbo jumbo, no dialing codes. It had just been stuck.

Ben's uncle whistled a single note. The torches in the corridor extinguished and the barrier returned once everyone had passed through safely. His robes billowed behind him as he took impossibly long strides. Minutes later they arrived at a cavernous room teeming with . . .

. . . people?

Ben was jolted completely awake. A renewed surge of adrenaline coursed through his body. "What is this?"

"The way home," Uncle Henry said. "Welcome to Safe Harbor."

◆ ◆ ◆

"Whoa!"

The chamber rose at least five stories. In contrast to the stone corridor, this room was a spotless, gleaming facility filled with electronic equipment. Suspended in mid-air, massive holographic screens displayed world locations, star charts and solar systems. Hundreds of smaller screens streamed newscasts from all over the world. The videos showed volcano eruptions, mudslides, earthquakes and other disasters.

Ben's attention shifted to a scale model of Earth rotating above a central platform. Tiny points of lights blinked along the surface of the globe. The platform was surrounded by a shimmering moat of silver liquid too wide to be crossed without a ramp.

People poured in from glass tubes located around the perimeter, some limping or aided by others. A few stayed behind to work, but most disappeared through doors at the farthest quadrant. A chorus of voices rang throughout the chamber, negating Ben's attempts to eavesdrop. The mood, however, was urgent.

New teams rushed into the tubes and disappeared. Seconds later they could be seen working unnoticed at the scenes of the disasters and placing devices in strategic spots around the area. In one location, a team set off explosive charges as the residents evacuated.

A BBC news broadcast played in a monitor to Ben's left.

*"A powerful earthquake with a magnitude of 8.3 rocked northeastern Japan today, causing blackouts and forcing authorities to temporarily shut down highways, railways and even Tokyo's main airport, more than 250 miles away. Aftershocks are being reported miles from the epicenter and are expected to continue for several days. Casualties appear to be at a minimum . . ."*

"Are you causing those disasters?" asked Ben.

Uncle Henry scowled. "Of course not. We're trying to prevent them. Without the terraformers on-line and no manual way to activate them, it's a difficult task."

Uncle Henry marched across a bridge and down a curved staircase.

He unraveled his turban as he went, draping the many yards of fabric over his arm. The guards dispersed once Ben and his friends were all safely on the ground floor.

Aris rubbed against a technician whose skin glowed in a deep magenta. A single black ponytail sprouted from the top of her bald head. She lifted the cat onto the console, reached into her pocket and placed a treat in his mouth. Aris rubbed his face against the woman's cheek. She beamed in response.

The guard who acknowledged Ben earlier stood behind her. The woman turned suddenly and threw her arms around him. He touched her forehead as she uncoiled his turban, then scratched Aris under the chin.

Ben's heart jolted to a stop. He had seen that that face, those hazel eyes, those neatly coiled dreads. The guard from the British Museum!

"Kavera." Uncle Henry said, nodding in the guard's direction. "One of the best field agents on my team. It was his idea to give you a little help in London, and plant the clue at the Vatican — against my explicit instructions. He will be disciplined for the insubordination."

Ben's head was swimming with a million questions. "Whose that woman with him?"

Uncle Henry shook his head. "Don't recognize her? I'll have her come to my quarters later. You can get reacquainted."

"I think I would remember meeting a bald lady with bright red skin."

"Perhaps," Uncle Henry said. "Perhaps not."

Ben tried getting a closer look at the woman, but she rushed out a doorway. A man thrust a digital tablet into Uncle Henry's hands. He scanned the images, closed his eyes and returned it. The man bowed and rushed away.

"What was going on?" asked Ben.

"We're sustaining a lot of casualties."

"And our parents?"

Uncle Henry frowned. "No word yet."

"So who was following us back in that old hallway?" asked Ben.

"Not who," answered his uncle. "But what. Again, nothing that need concern you."

Kavera deftly worked the console with one hand while swatting affectionately at the cat with the other.

"I'll go get Aris," April said.

Her uncle waved dismissively, "Not to worry. Aris knows his way around the complex."

Ben felt as if all eyes were focused on him and his friends as they walked through the room. A woman's voice spoke over an overhead speaker system.

*"Dineh-nay-ye-hi il-day ah-di . . ."*

Serise froze in her tracks. Her head cocked to the side.

"What's the matter?" asked Ben.

Serise stared at the ceiling and then glanced at the digital star charts.

*"Hia tsiyu galuhisdiyi talidui sutlvlodv . . ."*

"Serise?" Uncle Henry gave her a quizzical look.

"Did you get any of that?" Ben asked Grace.

She furrowed her brow and held her hand up to silence him. Finally, she shrugged her shoulders and mouthed, *"I don't know."*

*"Nia taragrachia farla duesna himtara,"*

"Serise?" asked Uncle Henry.

Serise looked frantic. She spun in a 360 degree arc, scanning the room for something. "I thought I heard . . . my mother and then it was gone. It was Navajo. Few people speak it."

"Enough do to make it useful," Uncle Henry said. "Let's keep going. We have a lot to do and you need rest."

*"Grosh gon toonda devisna zolor terra . . .El transporte llega en doce horas . . ."*

The woman's voice droned in a monotone cadence. It echoed throughout the chamber.

*"O transporte chega em doze horas . . . Transport ankommer om tolv timer . . . Il trasporto arriva in dodici ore . . ."*

"Something about a ship," Carlos whispered. "I heard Spanish and then it was gone. The languages are changing too fast. I can't keep up."

*"Transport kommt in zwölf stunden an . . . Le transport va arriver dans douze heures.*

"I heard French," April said.

"Me too," Grace said. "And German and . . ."

"Latin," Carlos said." But the echo makes it hard to translate. What the heck is this place? The United Nations of spy outposts?"

As Uncle Henry urged them forward, Ben strained to hear the woman's voice. Finally he understood too.

*"Transport arriving in twelve hours."*

♦ ♦ ♦          ♦ ♦ ♦          ♦ ♦ ♦

CHAPTER FORTY-FOUR

# Kurosh

"Belief in the truth commences with
the doubting of all those "truths" we once believed."
♦ ♦ ♦ *Friedrich Nietzsche*

♦ ♦ ♦ They left the pristine metallic environment of the control room and traveled down a stone corridor which ended at a courtyard built with intricately carved walls, inlayed tile and two-story archways. An enormous skylight spanned the circumference of the three-story space. It reminded Ben of the skylight covering the British Museum. Stars twinkled beyond the glass enclosure. Ben did a double take. The night sky featured two moons and the familiar "old man" face was missing on both.

Straight ahead, two stained-glass doors retracted as people emerged from the other side. Ben caught a glimpse of trees and plants before the doors closed again. Everywhere Ben looked, people were packing equipment, emptying chambers and loading metal containers into larger ones.

Uncle Henry climbed a stone staircase and proceeded down a corridor. He arrived at a mahogany door which dissolved when he placed his hand on the center medallion. Once everyone was inside, it returned to its solid state.

The room reflected Uncle Henry's taste — expensive. Tribal rugs covered hardwood floors. Woven tapestries draped the walls. Two leather couches sat at right angles to each other, flanked by a table and a chair. The room was filled with artifacts from all over the world.

"What is this place?" Ben asked.

"My home," Uncle Henry said.

"Whoa! You live here?" asked Carlos.

Uncle Henry shot him a look of disinterest. "It appears to be the unfortunate trait of the young to ask a question which has recently been answered. You may rest here until the transport arrives. Your parents will know where to find you."

"What happened to them?" asked Ben. "Do you think they got out?"

"Your parents are very resourceful. If they said they would meet you here, they will do everything in their power to keep that promise."

"Why didn't they tell us about all of this?" asked Grace.

"Maybe they couldn't," Serise said. "Maybe they were under orders to keep this a secret."

Uncle Henry sat on a ledge covered with burgundy cushions. "No such order was ever given. Your parents thought concealing your true identities was a prudent course of action."

"I don't understand," Ben said.

"Don't you?" asked his uncle. "There weren't supposed to be children on this mission. Under different circumstances an act of insubordination would be dealt with harshly. However, what was done was done. We relocated the teams — your families — to the same area of the United States to make it easier for us to monitor your progress."

"I knew it!" Serise said. "Paradise Circle was a punishment!"

Ben closed his eyes and waited to be zapped back to reality. "This just doesn't make sense."

"Actually, it does," Serise said.

All eyes turned in her direction.

"All that mysterious stuff they were working on. All the travel. Translating foreign negotiations. Their weird hobbies, like studying crop circles and weather patterns. It was just part of the mission?"

"Yes," Uncle Henry said.

"So I guess we're not catching a boat to Borneo, huh?" Carlos said, sarcasm and resentment dripping from his voice.

"No." Uncle Henry's voice was slow and dry. "That won't be your destination."

"Ben thought our parents were jewel thieves or counterfeiters or secret agents," April said, "and that's why they were always traveling all over the world and why there was a secret lab in the garage and why Carlos's family had a super gargantuan satellite dish so they could get top secret information and stay one step ahead of the law and Grace's parents were always translating top secret government messages and . . ."

April droned on without taking a single breath. Ben wanted to bury his head in shame as his sister spilled the beans in the longest run-on sentence ever invented. Hearing her accurate retelling of his theory made him realize how ridiculous it sounded. When she finished, Uncle Henry was glaring at Ben.

Ben didn't say anything in his defense. He was planning his own eulogy.

"So much for being able to solve a game in a week," Uncle Henry said.

Ben felt as though he had been punched. *There was only one more jewel to go. One more!* A burning rage rose within him.

"Stop picking on Ben! It's not his fault!" April pounded Uncle Henry with her fists. "Mom took the game away. Mine too. And Grace's mom took her whole computer. Ben was the one who figured out how to get it started again. We only one more piece to find and we

282

would have been finished today if the neighborhood hadn't blown up. You need to stop being so mean."

Ben didn't know which made him feel worse — his uncle's insult or the fact that his little sister was defending him. He searched for a proper response then decided against it. Reluctantly, he looked up and saw his uncle's expression soften.

"I was out of line," his uncle said. "You have my apologies."

"What would have happened if we had found the final jewel?" Carlos asked.

"The game was programmed to bring all five of you automatically. Regardless of who was playing the game. It would have forced your parents to return to the Harbor to prepare you for the trip home."

"So our parents are like, what? Secret agents?" asked Serise.

"In a manner of speaking."

"But they aren't originally from the United States," Grace said.

"That would be an accurate analysis," Uncle Henry said.

"Are they working for British Intelligence?"

Uncle Henry cocked his head and gave Ben a stern look of disapproval. "I'd like to think we're a little more sophisticated then that."

"Well, where are they from? It's got to be somewhere on the planet!" Ben snapped. "Russia? Europe? Africa? "

Uncle Henry sighed, closed his eyes and rubbed his temples.

"What are you saying? We're not from Earth?" asked Grace.

"You were born here," he said.

"But our parents!" shouted Grace, mirroring Ben's own frustration with his uncle's short, cryptic answers. "ARE . . . OUR . . . PARENTS . . . FROM . . . EARTH?"

"No," Ben's uncle said. "They are not."

Ben felt all the oxygen leave the room. He gasped then sank into the nearest chair. It was confirmed. He *had* been zapped into a computer game.

After a few minutes of silence, April asked, "Are you really my uncle?"

Uncle Henry stroked her cheek. The gesture caused Ben to feel further isolated. His uncle flinched and quickly withdrew his arms. His narrowed eyes registered alarm for less than a second before he answered, his tone cold again. "Yes, April. Your father and I are brothers."

"And your name?" Ben asked angrily. "It's not really Henry, is it?"

"I suspect you already know the answer to that question. Why ask it now?"

"Because you're the mysterious Kurosh! The man everyone's been talking about!"

Uncle Henry bowed his head.

"Whoa! You're the mission commander? You're like the boss of this whole complex?" asked Carlos.

"That's an accurate, if not concise summary of the facts," Uncle Henry said.

"Then what's going on?" shouted Carlos, his face red with anger. "My dad is mad at you. All the parents are mad at you!" His voice dropped, the anger replaced by curiosity. "By the way, what's a son of Casmir?"

"*You* are a son of Casmir, Carlos." Uncle Henry's expression remained stoic while Carlos digested the comment. "There will be plenty of time for explanation. I have business to attend to, not the least of which is locating your parents. For now, get some rest. I'll arrange for food. I'm afraid that the accommodations aren't ideal, but you should be comfortable until it is time to board the transport. We can talk in the morning."

"No!" insisted Ben. "We have a right to know what's going on!"

"Now is not the time," Uncle Henry barked impatiently.

"If not now, then when?" asked Ben. "You gave me that game to send a message about the family business. If this is it, you kind of owe us all an explanation."

"I suppose I do," Uncle Henry replied, sounding almost defeated. "Your parents were sent here to determine the fate of their predecessors."

"What happened to them? The others," asked Ben.

"Unknown. The transport returned with only a few bodies on board. All dead."

"Returned? Returned where?" asked Grace

"To our home in the Sonecian Galaxy," Uncle Henry answered.

◆ ◆ ◆          ◆ ◆ ◆                    ◆ ◆ ◆

CHAPTER FORTY-FIVE

# Revelations

"There are more things on Heaven and Earth
Than are dreamt of Horatio."

◆ ◆ ◆ *Shakespeare*

◆ ◆ ◆ Uncle Henry walked to a digital panel near the door and tapped on a flat keypad. The room darkened. An image of three pyramids and the Sphinx floated above them.

"Do you know where we are now?"

"Egypt?" asked April.

"Precisely. Beneath the great pyramid of Giza. In your history books the structure is referred to as Khufu's Pyramid. Think of the Harbor as part observation post, part space port."

"How long has this place been here?" asked Carlos, sinking into one of the couches.

"Thousands of years," Uncle Henry said. "Didn't take much convincing to get Khufu to build it. With our technology and his ego, our ancestors achieved a masterpiece. His sons, not to be outdone, requested help in building two more. This complex is the only one of the Seven Wonders of the World still standing. Historians have never figured out why Khufu isn't buried here. We'll let them puzzle that one a little longer. After our initial visits, the station sat dormant for several millennia."

Uncle Henry waved his hand. Like the game, the three-dimensional projection expanded to fill the room. Ben felt as though he were floating in space. It was disorienting, but he could still see faint outlines of the furniture and felt the floor beneath his feet.

Images formed of a distant galaxy. To Ben, it looked like more pin cushion magic from their backyard adventures with Senóre Lopez.

"You're looking at Orion's Belt. It's a gateway."

"To where? Alpha Centauri?" asked Carlos.

"Hardly," Uncle Henry said, sniffing snobbishly at the suggestion. "The Centaurians are advanced but not exactly friendly. We stopped them from raiding Earth for zoo and laboratory specimens."

"Lab specimens?" Carlos looked stricken. "Us?"

Serise shrugged. "Why not? We do it to poor defenseless creatures. I guess some other race thinks that way about us. Scary."

Carlos's eyes grew wide. "So all those stories . . ."

Uncle Henry cut him off. "About alien abductions? Yes, for the most part they're true."

Ben grew impatient with the discussion getting off track. "Okay. Back to the main point. You were going to explain about this so-called galaxy we're from?"

Uncle Henry glared. "The 'so-called' *galaxy* is approximately 230 million light years away. Well outside of the Milky Way. We're located in what Earth scientists call the Pisces-Perseus Supercluster. We appear as a void within it. As Earth technology became more sophisticated, we used the Casmir Array to keep the area hidden."

Uncle Henry barked a command at the panel. New video streamed overhead.

Grace sat on a floor cushion, brushed sand off the last of her sushi rolls and munched as if she were eating popcorn at the movies. She offered one to April who stared at the dried fish and rice ball and declined. Ben wondered how Grace could eat at a time like this.

"We call this place Safe Harbor because that is what it represented to our ancestors — a sanctuary from the impending collapse of a star near our galaxy. "Our ancestors wanted to preserve something of their cultures. Earth was the nearest planet capable of sustaining the many species found in our solar system, making it perfect for colonization. They placed eight tribes on a land mass similar to the environment on their home planet. In time, the tribes blended with the indigenous populations and became part of their genetic pool."

Scenes of the arrival streamed around Ben. The warrior tribes were greeted as if they were gods. Temples and pyramids sprang up all over the world. Some were disguised to look like mounds or mountains. Others were hidden in jungles. People lay on slabs attended by priests and priestesses. But they weren't being sacrificed — they were being revived. Ben's hand passed through the holographic images when he reached out to touch them.

Uncle Henry continued his narration. "The individuals were chosen by lottery and placed in cryogenic suspension. The ancients had hoped their descendants would eventually discover that each held only a single piece to the puzzle of their origins. And then, only then, would the tribes come together and discover the location of the Guardian. A signal beacon would show the way home."

"But something went wrong. A catalyst or factor we hadn't antici-pated. An evil we couldn't conceive of even in our worst nightmares. We sent observers to check on the progress of the tribes and to relieve their colleagues. But when the ship arrived, the teams found most outposts deserted. From the limited data we retrieved from the ship's log, the team and survivors decided to return home. They died on the journey. There is no record as to the cause."

Uncle Henry paused for effect. No one said a word. Even Serise and April were speechless.

"Then why did you come back?" asked Ben.

"To retrieve the Guardian. She was deactivated after the final terra-forming transports returned home in 10,000 BC."

"And our parents?"

"After finding several artifacts they became over confident and started families. The habitat adjustment mixture Medie created allows you to function like human children. I believe Ben refers to it as green glob. If you stop taking it for more than a few months, you'll revert to traits based on your inherited genetic coding."

Ben stared at his hands, half expecting to see himself turn green . . . or grow the hairy arms of a werewolf.

"But the rest of us don't drink that horrible stuff," Grace said. "We haven't been given anything special."

Uncle Henry smirked. "Haven't you? One of your favorite foods is black moss seaweed. You even insist that your mother add it to soups and other foods."

Grace gasped.

"And imagine our good fortune!" he continued. "A Tibetan child with an insatiable appetite for Japanese sushi. Your mother makes her own seaweed wraps and whips up a special batch of wasabi. There is also her special red bean paste for the Zongzi, and . . . should I continue?"

Grace stared at her sushi rolls as if they were crawling with worms.

"Serise," Uncle Henry continued. "Cranberry smoothies with an algae based protein powder are your favorite drink, correct? Seaweed and algae mud masks are part of your bedtime routine. Absorbs through the skin and leaves a tingling sensation?" He pointed to her left ear. "You missed a spot."

Serise clawed at her face as if trying to wipe off the remaining residue and the skin with it.

"Carlos? Your mother's green tamales are the best in town. Practically habit forming. I understand that you are partial to malted Ovaltine and Chocolate Yoo-Hoos. She mixes in a little protein powder to give it an extra boost. Drink it by the gallon if you got a chance. Hmmm?"

Carlos froze in place.

"Medie is an extraordinary chemist. Your parents were very creative with her formula."

"Not creative enough," snorted Ben. "Wish Mom had turned ours into barbecue sauce."

Uncle Henry closed his eyes as if conjuring a memory. "Ben, your mother is one of the most gifted botanists I've ever known. She is accomplished in many things. Cooking, however, is not one of her strengths."

Memories of his mother flooded into Ben's mind. He missed her awful cooking already. "Okay, back to the main point. Why can't you just open this Guardian up and get what you need?"

"She can only be activated when all eight keys are present. The master codes were destroyed thousands of years ago."

"So what happens when you find the keys? What does this Guardian do?" asked April.

"We don't know. Right now we are operating on the faith that she holds the solution to Earth's current situation."

Exhausted, Ben collapsed on the couch next to Carlos. "So why the game disk? Why not tell us and get it over with."

Uncle Henry sighed. "I am bound by a higher authority. I needed a way to get you here with or without your parent's permission. The game was a loophole. It allowed me to get information to you without breaking a vow. As I hoped, Ben shared it and it allowed us to observe you working as a team. The results were encouraging."

"What if someone else found the disk?" asked Grace.

"They would just think it was an interesting game," Uncle Henry said. "One of thousands on the market."

"But someone could have figured out the codes and found these tunnels or even the Guardian," Ben said.

"No, the gateways and passages are secured. You need a specific eight-gene code in your DNA to activate them. But the Guardian works differently. We need a key from each of the original tribes to form the final sequence – a sixty-four gene code."

"So that's why the medallions turned on as soon as we touched them," Ben said.

"We were surprised to find them still operational. They haven't been used in thousands of years. They came in handy when Kavera and I programmed the game. I got quite an earful from Shan and Frank after they saw you boys sitting in Llactapata."

He paused and seemed disappointed. "When you realized you were lost, didn't it occur to you to use your computer — for instance, the one Serise is carrying — to dial here? Did you ever consider booting up the game and dialing the location marked 'home'?"

Everyone groaned at the obvious nature of his comment.

"I don't get it," Serise said. "If everyone from our home planets has the gene sequence, why look for the tribes? Why not just find the keys and use your own team members."

"We thought of that. We have two keys in place, but the Guardian doesn't recognize the team members that bear them. We suspect a genetic alteration was made to the tribes that settled here. One that only the Guardian will recognize. To prevent us from doing what we are attempting — remove the technology without reuniting them.

"How long have you been trying?" Serise asked. Her voice was quiet and respectful.

"Hundreds of years."

"And how many expeditions have you been on?"

"Five. Although not consecutively."

"That makes you how old?" asked Grace

He frowned, "Let's just say I've been around the galaxy a time or two."

Ben studied his uncle. He looked like he was in his forties — ancient by kid standards but not by universe standards. He couldn't figure out the whole time/space continuum stuff and wondered what all those trips translated into — hundreds of years? Thousands?

"After you sent a team to Earth and ALL of them ended up missing or dead, wouldn't that be a clue to stop trying?" Ben said.

"It's not that simple," Uncle Henry said. "Our research has shown that Earth's core is unstable."

"Even more reason not to come back," Ben said.

Uncle Henry rolled his prayer beads in his hand, focusing intently on the violet one. "Do you remember the basic principles of science? Matter is neither created nor destroyed. Nor energy. Just stored, redirected, transformed. That single principle keeps balance in the universe."

"Yes," Ben said. "But I still don't understand why you didn't just stay away."

Uncle Henry drew in a long breath, the beads clicking as they fell from his grasp. "We uncovered a force that feeds on the negative energy of others. Stores that energy deep in Earth's core. Some refer to it as Hell. As conflict escalates, so does its power. The energy is tearing the planet apart. Earthquakes, Tsunamis, volcano eruptions, mud slides. It won't stop until everything is consumed."

"Everything?" April winced and sank into a chair.

"All life," Uncle Henry answered. "Everywhere. The Earth is just a tiny blip in the universe and yet an important one. What goes on here will affect every race, every planet. Our readings have shown the energy build-up to be enormous. If we don't stop it, everyone and everything in the known universe will be gone in an instant. Think of it as the 'Big Bang' in reverse."

Ben gasped as the meaning took hold. "Gone?"

His uncle nodded. "Completely . . . utterly . . . obliterated."

◆ ◆ ◆          ◆ ◆ ◆          ◆ ◆ ◆

CHAPTER FORTY-SIX

# Keys to the Future

*"Everything you can imagine is real."*

◆ ◆ ◆ *Pablo Picasso*

◆ ◆ ◆ Ben's mouth dropped open. He clamped it tight before he could say, *"You're kidding."*

Having apparently read his expression, Uncle Henry said, "No, I'm not kidding. In any event, I have duties to perform before the Sonara docks. I suggest you get some sleep."

He programmed something into the door panel, stopped to scan the room, then returned to his task. Five shimmering platforms appeared, suspended in midair at the far end of the room.

"What are those?"

"Hammocks constructed from modified force-fields."

Ben rose from the couch and slid into the closest one. He felt as if he were floating on a bed made of stars. The lights dimmed. Smooth jazz played through hidden speakers. All that was missing was one of his mother's candles. On cue, a scented mist fell from the ceiling.

"Some logistics," Uncle Henry said, looking satisfied with his work. "Bathroom through the first door on the right. Everything in the complex is recycled. A communications panel will provide instructions if you need assistance. It may take a little getting used to. Don't bother trying to wander from the apartment. The door will be locked for your safety. I'll have nutritional supplements available when you wake."

Ben groaned at the sound of "nutritional supplements."

*I'd rather starve.*

"As you wish," his uncle replied.

Ben gulped. Was his uncle reading his thoughts?

Uncle Henry fixed his gaze on Ben but said nothing.

"Can we see the ship when it comes in?" April tested her hammock. It molded to her body as she sank into it.

"If you promise to stay out of the way, you may join me in the Control Center when the ship docks. I'll have someone fetch you. For now get some rest."

Ben's head filled with more questions, but he could barely stay awake. Last night he had dreamed of basketball championships. But it was clear —

— that life was over.

◆  ◆  ◆

## Friday, October 31

The fog cleared from Ben's eyes. Simulated daylight streamed through the windows of his uncle's apartment. The music was off, the stars were gone, and Uncle Henry's apartment was restored to its previous appearance. Ben, however, remained suspended in midair.

A woman sat, cross-legged, on the window seat, studying readouts that floated above a panel on her lap. Her skin color matched the cushions. The technician who had hugged Kavera in the Control Center the day before. Wrapped around her plain blue tunic, a silver belt held a satchel, several metal balls and a slender rod. Braided rope sandals covered her slender magenta feet.

"Good morning, Benjamin. It seems you have had an adventure on your journey to us."

Ben rose up on his elbows. "How'd you get stuck babysitting?"

The woman arched her eyebrows. "That is an odd reference. Are you a baby?"

"Sorry. Just an expression." Ben studied the alien woman's face. "Do I know you from somewhere?"

The woman smiled. "I am Danine. Primary Medical Officer. I am, what Earth people refer to as, your pediatrician."

"But you were African back then."

"My appearance was a holographic projection meant to make you more comfortable while I completed your physical exams. It was the Commander's suggestion. When you entered the exam room at the hospital, you were actually transporting here to one of our empty bays."

Ben collapsed into the hammock. His brain was now officially on overload.

"As you may have guessed, children are not the Commander's specialty." Danine placed her panel to the side. "Your life signs indicated you were coming out of REM. I volunteered to check on you."

"Rem?" asked Ben. "I don't understand the language."

"My apologies. I assumed it was a common Earth term. REM is an abbreviation for 'rapid eye movement'. It is a form of deep sleep among some species. I suspected the events of the past day would cause you difficulties in relaxing and advised your uncle to use the hammocks. Their harmonic resonance was combined with an aromatherapy mist to induce a deep and restful sleep. I trust it was satisfactory."

Ben nodded. He did feel refreshed. "Any word about my parents?"

Danine's eyes flashed midnight blue, then black. "I wish I had more encouraging news, but do not despair. There remains time. And with time there is always hope. Your parents have faced worse challenges. I fully expect they're making their way here. I cannot imagine they would want to be separated from you for very long. We have sent out a beacon to let them know you arrived safely."

Ben's stomach sank. He wanted to go out and search for them. Do something besides sit around. But if his uncle's team of cracker-jack alien space spies with all their advanced technology couldn't find them, then what hope did he have? "Where's Uncle Henry? I mean, Commander Kurosh?"

"Making final preparations for the evacuation. You must be hungry after your journey. Nourishment should arrive shortly."

As she spoke, the door to the apartment dissolved. Kavera stepped inside carrying an impossibly large tray on his shoulders. He was dressed in an oversized mud cloth dashiki, baggy pants and leather sandals. With his dreads pulled back in a ponytail, he looked like a shorter version of Ben's father.

Danine beamed.

"Many blessings to you, Danine." Kavera placed the tray on the coffee table. "Good morning, young warrior. Breakfast is served. I hope you don't mind takeout. Not much American food is served here."

Ben's stomach growled as he dropped out of the hammock. Whatever lay beneath the dome of the tray smelled heavenly. Soon the others roused. They gasped as Danine switched briefly to her "Pediatrician" avatar.

"Ahh! It seems there is life in this room." Kavera lifted the lid. Ben gave thanks for divine intervention. The tray was piled with French toast, bacon, ham, fruits and omelets dripping with melted cheese.

Danine coughed violently and tapped her foot. "That is not what I ordered."

Kavera laughed. "You are correct. This is what the Commander ordered. It is the children's last meal on Earth. He thought they deserved a treat."

Danine crossed her arms firmly against her chest. "And you complied?"

"I was simply following the orders of our superior officer." Kavera's eyes twinkled as he bowed to Danine.

"Is it real?" asked Ben.

"Audrey's," Kavera said. "Eighteenth and Vine. Best food in Kansas City. Only seconds from here if you know the proper coordinates."

Ben and the others pounced on the food.

Danine clapped her hands abruptly. "There is one requirement before you may eat." She pointed to a basket at her feet. It held four silver and one red flask.

April stared at the basket with dread. "What's that?"

"Habitat adjustment formula," Danine said. "My apologies. I did not have time to synthesize something more appealing."

Carlos groaned. "Why? We're going home anyway. Who cares if we turn into our real alien selves?"

"I'd refrain from using that term here at the base if you want to avoid conflict," Kavera said sternly. "It is considered vulgar and will inflame many passions. The team members consider Earth inhabitants to be the aliens. Less advanced civilization."

"Regardless," continued Danine. "Your uncle prefers that you taper off rather than go cold chicken — is that the proper American phrase?"

"Cold turkey," Ben sighed. "But close enough."

"Many thanks, young warrior," Danine said. "I find English to be an overly complicated language — too many inconsistencies in phonetic patterns. Please drink this. Only one ounce is necessary, and the food is yours."

Ben growled like his uncle. He should have known there was a catch. His stomach growled too and demanded he comply in order to expedite access to the food. He grabbed the red flask Danine held out to him. "Why is this one a different color?"

"Your uncle requested that I make an adjustment to your formula."

Ben wondered what that meant and knew, from Danine's blank expression, that he wasn't going to get an answer. Sick of mysteries, he braced himself for the inevitable. Odorless and tasteless, the formula maintained the disgusting gloppy texture he knew and did not love — and was the same shade of puke green. He gagged, but it went down and stayed down. The others followed suit, looks of horror crossing their faces as they swallowed.

"You really drink this stuff every day?" asked Carlos, his mouth puckering.

Ben grimaced and nodded.

"You're the man. I would have run away from home," Carlos said.

Having survived the challenge, Ben and his friends tore into the food as if it were going to be their last meal.

"Benjamin. I am curious about something," Kavera said. "The other night. You went to the British Museum. It was not part of the game's programming. What had you hoped to accomplish there?"

"I overhead my dad planning to . . ." he paused and changed the verb hovering on the tip of his tongue, " . . .borrow jewelry from an exhibit. I found the coordinates in his office."

Kavera arched an eyebrow. "I wonder why? We can synthesize jewels."

"Then my dad?"

"Has often had other priorities beyond his mission," Kavera answered.

Ben slumped. "So he really is a thief."

"Oh! No! Far from it," Kavera said. "Most honorable man I've ever known. He and many of the other team members were concerned about ancient artifacts unlawfully removed from our adopted countries. Your parents have been returning them to their rightful owners and replacing them with perfect replicas. Your uncle was not pleased with their extracurricular 'hobby' but as long they completed their assigned duties, he gave them a wide berth." Kavera laughed. "There wasn't much more he could do to them without turning you into orphans."

Ben paused, "Then can you tell me what 'Safina ni kamili' means? Dad said it the night he was planning the museum switch."

Kavera laughed. "The two are not related. Your father agreed to help another team with project Noah. It means 'The Ark is complete'."

"The safari was to collect animals in case you can't save Earth."

Kavera nodded.

"So what does my dad really do?" asked Carlos.

"He's an expert in astrophysics — like Ben's father. They're the strongest pilots in the fleet. But here on Earth he performs munitions work in addition to his research in cosmology."

Carlos furrowed his brow and let the fork in his hands slip back to the plate. "I don't understand."

"Your father maps the universe and maintains our space array, but he also deactivates military weapons. Too many conflicts in regions where we need to conduct research. He makes sure the bombs don't detonate. Brilliantly devious man. Replaces the explosives with a benign compound that erodes any internal wiring but disperses into the air undetected. Humans can't tell the real ones from the fakes until they are dropped. Then it's all flash but no destruction."

"And the other parents?" asked Serise. "Are they all like that?"

Kavera sighed. "I imagine this is hard for you — learning about your parents this way. It is a lot of information to absorb. Suffice it to say that they have shown tremendous creativity and versatility in their assignments. After Kurosh exiled them to California, they bonded unexpectedly. Most had not met prior to volunteering for the mission."

"You said most?"

Kavera smiled. "Ben. Carlos. Despite the vast difference in cultures, your fathers were best friends long before they entered the Sonecian Science Academy. Virtually inseparable. It is comforting to see that you have all bonded as well. That is why we have high hopes your parents are still alive. Most resourceful, determined team on the mission. To lose them now would be a great loss."

"Do you think they'll get here before the ship arrives?" asked Grace.

"There is always hope."

"May we see it? The Guardian, I mean? It's a real place, right?" asked April

"Yes," Kavera said. "I believe we have time. Danine, would you care to join us?"

"With regret I must return to my duties." She bowed, snatched a strip of bacon out of Kavera's hand and deftly tossed it back on the tray. Kavera grinned broadly as he watched her leave the room.

♦ ♦ ♦        ♦ ♦ ♦        ♦ ♦ ♦

CHAPTER FORTY-SEVEN

# Affinity

"The truth is rarely pure and never simple."

♦ ♦ ♦ *Oscar Wilde*

♦ ♦ ♦ After breakfast, Kavera started his tour of the facility.

"Most sections are being shut down to conserve power now that the teams are evacuating. A skeleton crew will remain behind and be housed in the same sector."

"Are you staying?" asked Ben.

"Absolutely."

"But if you don't find the keys in time you will die," Grace said.

Kavera's smile faded. "Perhaps."

He paused at a narrow tunnel. "Let's take a short cut to the Guardian. It is under the Sphinx." He pressed a button on his wristband. Light beams ricocheted against the barrel shaped walls. The tunnel filled with a warm air. A liquid barrier appeared.

Feeling better about having an experienced guide this time, Ben was first to step through the barrier. He found himself in a familiar chamber. Only now, standing in the room, Ben realized how poorly his computer had shown the scope and scale of the chamber. As expected, the white marble altar stood in the middle of the room, its glass enclosure rising out of sight. Now, however, subtle hues pulsed through the stone as if it were a living thing.

Armed with probes and scanners, technicians detonated explosive charges attached to the massive door. A bubble shot from the surface repelling everyone and everything nearby.

The eight canopic statues rose two-stories. Partially hidden in shadow, their ebony black faces looked serious and ominous. Fringe draped the jars as expected but closer inspection revealed them to be hollow cylindrical tubes. Shallow grooves cut through the stone floor at sharp angles and lead from the jars to the altar like the eight legs of a spider. A single trough lead from the altar to the Guardian. The glass-covered channels were empty, but something sparkled and flashed like lightning inside the jars.

"What's in those things?" asked Ben.

"Unknown," Kavera said. "We have been unable to analyze them. We believe the technology was designed by an ancient and superior species."

"I thought our ancestors designed them."

Kavera shook his head. "The origins aren't clear. The ancient texts were destroyed so we have only legend to guide us. Over the years the theory has grown to suggest the design specifications have a divine source."

"A what?" asked Grace.

"On Earth the concept is often referred to as 'God'. The one surviving text contained a fragment of the original instructions. A crude translation reads 'You shall know me only when you have come to know yourselves'."

"What does that mean?" asked Ben.

"Interpretation is varied. Perhaps we are descended from a superior and more advanced tribe. Perhaps there is a divine source that determines the paths for us all."

Ben carefully examined the tri-colored tubes encircling the canopic jars. They were impossible to lift, as if they were welded or held by a magnetic force.

"They hum," Ben said. "Could be an energy force."

Carlos pressed his ear to the jar. "Could be an original tribe member. If this were a video game it would be a monster."

Kavera shrugged. "The source of the energy is unclear. But you are correct. There is definitely electrochemical activity occuring inside the jars that has not diminished over thousands of years." He winked at Carlos. "Let's hope it is not one of your monsters."

April walked the circumference of the room, touching each jar as she went. She stood on her toes and peered inside a jar to the right of the Guardian doors. The rods clicked in place and then fell again.

Kavera pursed his lips but said nothing.

Ben panicked. "What'd you do now? You always manage to activate something. Keep your hands off stuff without permission."

April slid her hands behind her back. "Sorry, Kavera. I didn't mean to hurt anything."

"No harm was done, April. Would you mind duplicating your actions?"

Ben raised an eyebrow. "Are you sure it's okay?"

"Yes," Kavera said. "April, please proceed."

April walked cautiously around the room, touching and looking into each jar as before. Nothing happened until she arrived at the last jar. The rods clicked into place. The glow inside the jar brightened for a second, then dimmed as the rods fell again.

Kavera's eyes narrowed. He borrowed a device from a nearby technician and scanned the jar with a probe. The room grew quiet as other technicians took an interest in the readouts. Noting their behavior, Kavera quickly suppressed the holographic display.

"Grace, would you mind duplicating the exercise?" He gestured to the others to join him in the middle of the floor. Ben was sure Kavera's blank expression was hiding something.

Grace looked apprehensive.

"I can assure you that you are in no danger," Kavera said. "Just an experiment to occupy the time while we wait to join the Commander."

Grace touched the canopic jar last touched by April. Nothing happened. She shrugged.

Kavera motioned for her to continue.

She tentatively walked to the second jar. Nothing. Kavera pointed to the next but never raised his eyes from the scanner. The sequence repeated until Grace reached the seventh canopic jar. It glowed, the rods clicked into place then fell again.

Grace gasped.

Ben gasped.

Kavera registered no reaction although Ben clearly saw evidence of the tablet's increased activity reflected in Kavera's eyes.

Kavera cast a glance at Serise.

"I know the drill," she sighed as she headed for the jars.

"What's going on?" asked Ben. "Can I try it next?"

Kavera touched his earring and signaled for Ben to stay close by. He focused on something unrelated to the device in his hand.

"Askar, Jemadari," he said finally. "Children. It appears we will have to end the tour. The Sonara has entered the galaxy."

◆  ◆  ◆          ◆  ◆  ◆          ◆  ◆  ◆

# CHAPTER FORTY-EIGHT

# Course Correction

"There is only one moment in time
when it is essential to awaken.
That moment is now."

♦ ♦ ♦ *The Buddha*

♦ ♦ ♦ The control center buzzed with activity.

Ben wondered how the world would react to the presence of a space-ship. Nothing on his father's device described it. He tried to imagine scenes from science fiction movies he had seen; government troops on alert, mass hysteria. On the other hand a transport had arrived unde-tected fifteen years ago carrying his parent's team. It had to have been cloaked.

He stood next to a technician with piercing gold eyes. Dressed in a floor-length white robe, the man stood almost seven feet tall. Veins of blue, red and violet pulsed beneath his translucent green skin. The technician stroked April's braids with his long, bony fingers, then lifted the beads. He smiled at the clickety-clack sound they made as they fell. He made clicks of his own with his throat, bowed respectfully and returned to his task.

"What did he say?" asked April.

"Mansurat said you remind him of the young Queen of Sheba," Uncle Henry said. "He approves of you and that is high praise. He does not approve of many."

The Earth globe ascended and disappeared into the ceiling. In its place, a bright iridescent light streamed toward the pool of silver liquid below it. Ramps extended outward spanning the width of the pool as the gateway opened.

Cloud-like forms flowed out of the light, like ghosts, or angels descending from the sky. When the eerie figures solidified, Ben worked hard to hide his shock. Not all walked on two legs. Some didn't even look human. One hovered slightly above the ground.

"Whoa!" Carlos said, "Where's the ship?"

"Orion Nebula," said Kavera. "We don't come close anymore. Too many UFO sightings. A couple of "hot shots" in our ranks liked to fly close and buzz the locals. Got a little restless on the long journey. We had a difficult time rescuing them from a government facility in Roswell, New Mexico. We replaced them with synthetic animatronic duplicates. We added bizarre genetic mutations at the molecular level for fun. Figured it would keep the scientists guessing. Won't they be surprised when they discover the "alien" captives are our version of amusement park robots."

"So who are these people?" asked Ben

"Recovery crew," said Uncle Henry. "Our strategic alliance spans many galaxies. They will transfer critical equipment to the ship."

"I thought they would be dressed in . . . well . . . space suits."

Uncle Henry scowled. "Now why would you think that?"

"Because NASA . . ."

"Employs primitive science," Uncle Henry said. "I can assure you that you won't need any special suits on our galaxy class transports. Although, if you are uncomfortable, there are always the stasis tubes." The words rolled out slowly to punctuate his point.

Ben decided it was best to keep his mouth shut. He had a lot to learn and patience wasn't one of Uncle Henry's virtues. Stasis tubes, whatever those were, didn't sound like a good thing.

Another creature materialized, its skin covered with turquoise scales that reflected the light. Its wide, webbed feet slapped the platform as it left the beam.

"Volari," Uncle Henry said. "An old friend. He will lead the ocean searches."

Ben couldn't take his eyes off the creature. He looked like an walking iguana. "What's in the oceans?"

"Some of our aquatic teams."

The light extinguished as Volari left the platform. A few seconds later, the gateway reopened with a bursts of color. The energy output was tremendous. Signals from the control panels boomed like drums. Like Ben's garage, every wall, every surface now streamed with data. It only deepened his anxiety over his parents.

"This reminds me of laser light shows at the Sunnyslope planetarium!" April tried to get closer but Uncle Henry gripped her shoulder tightly.

The overhead monitors processed video feeds at an incomprehensible speed. "What's going on?" asked Ben.

"Downloading information from the central computers on the Sonara and from her military escorts," Uncle Henry said.

"Military escorts?" asked Carlos.

"The transports are civilian class." Kavera answered. "Because of the length of time involved in the travel, they contain an entire city and technology other species may try to intercept. We may be unknown to Earth, but it's a vast universe and trust me, we are not alone."

Fierce-looking warriors — both men and women — arrived in heavy body armor that retracted and disappeared as they left the platform. Ornamental swords and bronze rods hung from their belts. The same type of rod Carlos' father had wielded earlier.

Uncle Henry's eyes narrowed. Every muscle in his body tensed but he looked as if he had grown a few inches in height and was poised for a fight. He took in slow, measured breaths.

Kavera let out a quiet whistle.

"Who's that?" asked Ben.

"Trouble." Kavera's eyes fixed on the leader of the team.

"What does that mean?" asked Carlos.

"It means . . ."

"Carlos," Uncle Henry interrupted gruffly. "Meet your tribe — the sons and daughters of Casmir. This is their Royal Guard."

"They look pretty grim," Carlos said. "Kind of like Klingons. Or Predators."

"Fight like them too," Kavera said. "That is, if Klingons and

Predators were real. Casmirians are the genuine article. You don't want to make them mad under any circumstances. They're not known for showing mercy when provoked."

"But I thought everyone gets along in the Sonecian galaxy," Ben said.

Kavera shook his head but kept close watch on the Casmirians. Ben noticed that Kavera's fists clenched a bit more. "Not everyone."

"But our dads . . ."

"Are the exception," Kavera said, grimly.

Ben looked at Carlos and whispered, "Got ya back bro!"

Carlos hit Ben's fist in a show of solidarity. "Inseparable. Like fathers, like sons."

Kavera's lips curled into an uneasy smile but his face remained filled with tension.

The Casmirian warriors stood in formation as their leader inspected them with a macho swagger, his fists planted firmly on his hips. The team looked ahead expressionless. Once the inspection was complete, the leader turned to Uncle Henry, pulled the rod from his belt and raised it into the air. It extended into a familiar double-edged spear. Looking lethal and ready for a fight, his team followed the lead and, on command, drove the spears into the floor in a show of force.

"What are they waiting for?" asked Carlos.

"That remains to be seen." Uncle Henry fixed an angry gaze on the Casmirian leader who tipped his head, but made no effort to approach. Something was brewing between the two of them. Ben made a mental note to ask Kavera about it when his uncle was out of earshot.

The transport beam flickered as dust flowed out of the beam. It swirled at the end of the ramp forming miniature cyclones that whipped in fury then floated upward. Within seconds, warriors materialized on the second floor balcony. Unlike the Casmirians, these warriors wore no armor and carried no weapons, but looked just as fierce. Their long black hair blew in an invisible breeze. Their leader stepped forward and raised his hand in salute. Uncle Henry returned the gesture and smiled.

"Who are they?" asked Serise.

"The Hayoolkáál," Kavera said. "As you can see, your tribe has remarkable abilities that are enhanced in Earth's atmosphere. It comes in handy for covert operations. Experts in weather and climate control. This is their Special Forces. It appears the Sonara has been escorted by the best warriors in the fleet. The Council is taking no chances with her safe return to our galaxy."

Ben gave Serise a thumbs up. Carlos followed with a high five. Beaming, Serise touched her arms and cheeks, then returned her attention to the balcony. These warriors wore sleeveless tunics, their muscular arms and legs evident even from this distance. Finally she said, "Wow! Those guys are buff!" Grace and April nodded enthusiastically.

Cloaked in flowing, white robes, a new team glided down the platform. Their faces were shrouded underneath enormous hoods, their arms tucked inside bell-shaped sleeves.

Grace gasped and gripped the railing. Skeletal gray hands reached up to lower their hoods, revealing men and women with ruddy complexions and long black hair. They bore a striking resemblance to the Hayoolkáál. Their hands quickly filled in with flesh. The white robes dissolved to reveal saffron-colored robes and embroidered tunics.

Upon seeing the tribe's human — and Asian — features, Grace exhaled.

"The Shakra," Kavera confirmed. "One of the oldest tribes in the known universe. Experts in interplanetary species. Best linguists in the alliance. They developed the translation devices used by the Harbor teams."

The Shakra bowed to Uncle Henry but their focus narrowed in on Grace. Uncle Henry and Kavera pressed the palms of their hands together and bowed as well. Grace followed suit, but viewed the tribe cautiously.

"What kind of powers do they have?"

"That," Uncle Henry answered, "is a matter for them to discuss with you in private. They do not speak openly of it."

Ben added this new development to his infinite list of questions to ask later.

The procession continued: The Savarians, a race acclimated to colder climates, the Mondavi, whose tanned bodies were covered in elaborate tattoos, and many others. Three beings with long willowy bodies and skin that glowed pure white, drifted out of the beam on a cushion of air. Ben was crushed that no one from his own tribe was among them. He wondered if all that remained was standing next to him.

The activity continued until the perimeter of the control room was filled with species Ben had never seen before — even in movies.

Carlos bumped him on the shoulder and pointed to his watch. Ben shrugged. He didn't understand what difference the time made now.

"Halloween," Carlos whispered.

"Carlos!" yelled Uncle Henry.

Carlos jumped and shrank back. "Sorry!"

"I'm confused," Ben said. "This is an evacuation but a lot of people are getting off the ship. Is this normal procedure?"

"No." Uncle Henry locked his jaw and studied the arrivals with rapt attention.

A silver flash burst inside the transport beam. The explosion spanned the width of the surrounding pool. No one but Ben seemed disturbed by this development. Soon, he understood why. With each flash, people stepped out of the portal in a military formation. They wore sleek black and silver uniforms with knives and lasers strapped to their waist. Each was preceded by large metallic crates that hovered above the ground. The glossy surface of their helmets reflected the data streams in the room. It made them look robotic.

Uncle Henry relaxed his posture. "They do know how to make an entrance." Despite his grim demeanor, Ben sensed overwhelming pride.

"What's with those explosions?" Carlos asked.

"The team is coming in on a different transport beam. Not from the Sonara or her escorts. Long range," Kavera said. "That is unusual. And the most dangerous way to travel."

"I thought you didn't need space suits?" asked Grace.

"Only in the event of an extended, deep space transfer, when oxygen is a concern."

The military corps turned and removed their helmets.

Ben was awestruck. "Our tribe?"

"Xenobian Warrior caste." Uncle Henry confirmed. "This is Sondar's elite squad. Brilliant strategists. Virtually unstoppable in a battle."

The Xenobian men and women turned toward Uncle Henry, crossed their arms across their chests then raised their right fists in salute. Uncle Henry and Kavera responded with a salute of their own. While Uncle Henry remained stoic, Kavera seemed elated. He grinned broadly and pumped his arm twice more.

The warriors formed two parallel lines along the ramp, turned to face each other and waited. On the far end of the control room, two doors opened, revealing a cavernous space.

"So what's that room?" asked April.

"Actually, that doorway is a portal," Kavera said. "Leads to a facility in the Great Sand Sea near the Libyan border. The upper level of the complex is where we discovered you in hiding."

"But we're under the pyramids," Grace said. "Isn't the Libyan desert hundreds of miles west."

Kavera nodded.

Ben was impressed. It looked as if the room were only a few feet away. "This outer space spy stuff is slick. Very scary, but seriously slick!"

Lights exploded beyond the entrance to the hall. The chamber filled with enormous metal crates, electronic equipment and thousands of gleaming glass tubes. The door to the chamber glowed and shut once the operation ceased. A single Xenobian warrior broke formation, placed a medallion on the door then rejoined his team. Symbols on the seal alternately turned on and off.

"I thought there wasn't going to be another mission," Ben said.

"There won't," Uncle Henry said through gritted teeth.

"Look at all that stuff they're unloading. If you ask me, it looks like they're planning to stay."

"I didn't ask you," Uncle Henry said, gruffly.

Ben sucked in a lung full of air. Luckily, Grace picked up the slack.

"But if they're bringing stuff down and there aren't going to be any more ships coming to rescue us then that means," she gasped. "They're on a suicide mission?"

"So it appears," Uncle Henry said, under his breath.

A power surge hit the control room. Uncle Henry called up schematics of the complex on a nearby console. Life support was being restored to deserted sections of the facility.

The Xenobian team remained in formation as the transport beam erupted into new bursts of blinding light — this time gold and red. Rapid explosions rocked the platform, like a fireworks display with flares extending in all directions. Sparks showered over the team and floated into the pool below. The room shook from the energy output. The Xenobian team dropped to their knees and lowered their heads. Both Uncle Henry and Kavera seemed confused and leaned forward to study the transport beam more closely.

"Is it a malfunction?" asked Ben in a panic, remembering how the Vatican outpost looked after it was destroyed. "Are we under attack?"

Kavera furrowed his brow and seemed perplexed. Two brief shakes of his head gave the answer. *No.* He raised a finger to his lips to indicate silence was in order.

The eruption subsided. A single person appeared, accompanied by a large black panther. The leader saluted the team, then removed their helmet to reveal a dark skinned woman with shoulder length hair.

"Who's that?" asked April.

A smile crept up the side of Kavera's face. "Perhaps our salvation."

◆ ◆ ◆          ◆ ◆ ◆          ◆ ◆ ◆

# CHAPTER FORTY-NINE

# Aurelia

*"A spirit of harmony can only survive
if each of us remembers,
when bitterness and self-interest seem to prevail,
that we share a common destiny."*

• • • *Barbara Jordan*

♦ ♦ ♦ "Is that Sondar?"

Uncle Henry's expression hardened. "No. It is not."

"So who is it?" asked Ben.

"A Shaman." Uncle Henry almost spit out the words.

"A what?"

"A healer," Kavera whispered, clearly trying not to antagonize Ben's uncle. "Our High Priestess. She took your mother's place as head of the religious caste when your mother joined the mission."

That jolted Ben. His mother? An extraterrestrial High Priestess?

Flanked by three massive guards, the slender woman walked toward them with long, graceful strides. Her piercing dark brown eyes flickered with green and blue highlights. She was, without a doubt, the most beautiful woman Ben had ever seen. The panther accompanied the group, its indigo fur casting an iridescent sheen.

Kavera dropped to his knees and lowered his head as the woman approached. Following his lead, Ben and April did the same. Uncle Henry stayed rigid and upright, legs apart, hands on his hips, his knife revealed and at the ready.

"Why isn't he bowing?" whispered Ben.

"He doesn't have to," whispered Kavera.

The woman did not appear to be intimidated by Uncle Henry's show of force. Strapped to her narrow waist was a knife of her own.

The elaborate jeweled handle jutted out of a leather sheath. The woman placed her palm on Kavera's forehead, gestured for him to stand, and brushed his cheek affectionately. She repeated the process with Ben and April. Ben felt a sense of calm wash over him.

The panther circled Aris and growled as if sizing him up for dinner. Ben watched Aris's muted reaction with a certain amount of satisfaction. Aris growled back and grew twice as large as the panther.

Ben's eyes nearly jumped out of their sockets. His friend's jaws dropped to the floor.

"Did you see that?" Stunned, Ben choked on his words, gasped for air and pointed. "How long has Aris been able to do that? Has Aris always been able to do that?"

Kavera unleashed a hearty laugh. "He showed great self-restraint after you threw him in the whirlpool. You are quite fortunate, Benjamin. Aris is a Xenobian cat, but he possesses a Casmirian temperament. We kept him here at the Harbor until gained control of his anger. Be grateful that his bedroom presents were the extent of his response."

Aris gave Ben a sideways glance and, with a slow growl, bared enormous fangs.

"Whoa!" Carlos stepped back. "Guess we need to be careful about making Aris mad, too!"

Aris dropped to the floor and assumed a submissive posture until the panther's inspection was over. Afterwards, he rose, purred affectionately and returned to his Earth size. The panther returned to the Xenobian leader. Ben's friends approached Aris with simultaneous exclamations of "Wow! You're like a superhero cat!" Aris seemed pleased with the attention.

*"Jemadari,"* The woman knelt briefly.

Ben blinked and rubbed his eyes. He was tired. He had to be. She had not moved her lips.

Having overcome their shock at Aris's shape shifting skills, Ben's friends returned to watching the new arrivals. Grace, Serise and April had taken an interest in a young Hayoolkááł warrior who stood guard near the transport platform. Carlos appeared captivated by the electronic equipment being unloaded by the Casmirians. No one paid attention to the conversation between Uncle Henry and the woman except Kavera. Uncle Henry turned abruptly and glowered.

"If you will excuse me," Kavera said. "It appears I am needed elsewhere." He kept his gaze on the woman who winked at him. She crossed her arms across her chest, dipped her head reverentially, then glanced at her guards. They lined up behind Kavera and departed.

April tugged on Uncle Henry's robe. "Can we go with Kavera?"

"Yes," he said, keeping his eyes fixed on the mysterious woman. "But wait until the last transfer is complete. And stay out of their way. These warriors *apparently* have work to do."

The woman crouched and took April's hand. "And who is this beautiful Xenobian princess?" Her gentle voice was almost hypnotic.

"I'm April. This is my brother Ben. These are our friends Carlos, Serise and Grace." Everyone waved, except Ben. He was still trying to figure out if he had heard her "think" something earlier.

"So who are you?" April asked.

"I am Ziian Aurelia. Exaulted leader of our Royal Guard." The woman smiled inquisitively at Uncle Henry who continued to glower. "You may use either name that suits you."

She squeezed April's hand. April giggled. Her beads glowed as she did a polite bow. The woman shot a curious but approving glance at Uncle Henry.

"Seekor Comisat?"

"*English please, Commander. I am attempting to master the nuance of the language.*"

"*Explain yourself!*" Uncle Henry's booming voice nearly split Ben's eardrums.

Aurelia crossed her arms, bowed to April then straightened. "*Jemadari. We have come to assist in the search. All here are volunteers. Many others were turned away so great was the response to our request.*"

"*You should not have come. This is an evacuation. We have no need for a Shaman. I order your team to return with the children and insure their safety. Where is Sondar?*"

*"Sondar sends his highest regards. He has been assigned a different task. I am still Shaman. And now Warrior. My team has been training for this mission, with Sondar's blessings, from the day your team departed. You require our unique skills. We are prepared to complete the mission or die trying."*

Ben couldn't help gawking.

Aurelia abruptly broke off the conversation and studied Ben. He tried looking away but a force compelled him to return her gaze. Her fiery eyes sparkled.

*"Is it your habit to eavesdrop on the thoughts of your elders, my young prince?"*

"No," Ben said, startled.

"No what?" asked Grace.

Aurelia seemed amused. Her eyes grew even brighter, her gaze more intent.

"Nothing," Ben said. "Just talking to myself."

"What else is new," Grace said, as she returned her focus to the growing flurry of activity in the room.

The transport beam extinguished. Grace, Serise, Carlos and April rushed onto the floor where they were warmly received.

*"No need to speak."* Aurelia's voice whispered inside of Ben's head in a soft hypnotic cadence. *"Communicate with your mind."*

*"He does not have the ability. I believe you were briefed about Medie's habitat mixture."*

*"Yes. Such a pity."*

*"Hello! Standin' right here!"* Ben projected, annoyed that they were talking about him — or at least thinking about him — as if he were an inanimate object. *"I CAN hear you. If you're talking about that breakfast junk my mom makes, I haven't been drinking it since last spring!"*

Uncle Henry froze.

*"Surprise! I've been dumping it in the rose bushes."*

So that was it! Telepathy. No wonder his digital recorder couldn't pick up the argument between his dad and uncle. Though using this new skill was giving him a headache.

*"This explains everything,"* his uncle said. *"Your sudden improvement in basketball skills. The change in your muscular build."*

*"Encouraging,"* Aurelia said.

*"Can I hear anyone's thoughts?"* Ben thought.

*"Under certain circumstances and only within the clan,"* she answered.

*"Can you teach me?"*

*"In time, young prince. You will be briefed when you are ready. And now, if you will excuse me, there are many preparations to be made. I wish you a safe journey home."*

She bowed. *"Jemadari. I leave you to tend to your children."* There was a hint of sarcasm in her voice. She bowed. *"With your permission."*

Uncle Henry pointed toward a digital console. Aurelia removed her gloves and tucked them into her belt. Her slender fingers were a blur as they flew across the panel while she concentrated on an overhead monitor. Uncle Henry, on the other hand, stabbed at the surface as if he were trying to beat it into submission. Ben caught flashes of conversation but he was too far away to hear them clearly. What bits he heard weren't in English and the tone was definitely not friendly. He crept closer in an attempt to improve the reception.

Above them, charts flashed until continental maps were shown. Uncle Henry zoomed in on individual countries. Lights appeared: white, red, orange, yellow, green, blue, indigo, violet.

With a thunderous roar, metallic columns swiveled open and retracted to reveal the same crystal tubes Ben had seen under the Vatican. Each glowed in a color corresponding to a light on the map.

April scurried back to Ben's side along with the others. "Where are they going? They just got here! I want to get a closer look."

"Oh no," Ben said. "I'm not chasing after you again. Stay here. We don't know what they're doing."

The warriors broke into nine groups, eight of which waited by the tubes. One by one, civilians gathered ahead of them. The ninth team, comprising half of the multi-planetary contingent, disappeared behind the entrance to the Libyan Desert facility. The door shimmered like liquid, then became solid again.

"Shirvash!" Aurelia shouted. Her voice, which rang like wind chimes when she communicated telepathically, now carried the force of authority.

As team members stepped into the portals, their clothing and appearance changed. Parkas, goggles and heavy boots for Siberia, cool linens for the United States. Travelers with alien features transformed into humans. Minutes later they vanished.

A look passed between Aurelia and Ben's uncle, who remained stoic. *"Do not worry. I will find them for you."* Aurelia shot a worried glance in Ben's direction. She switched to another language. *"Tandana coorishna zen Kurosh."*

*"Andar vernish karem Aureliana,"* Uncle Henry growled.

When she touched his shoulder, he flinched and backed away, but his stern expression softened.

♦ ♦ ♦            ♦ ♦ ♦                        ♦ ♦ ♦

# CHAPTER FIFTY

# The Discovery

"Wake up and realize you are surrounded by amazing friends"
♦ ♦ ♦ *Author unknown*

♦ ♦ ♦ "The time for your departure grows near," Uncle Henry said as he walked into the apartment. "I have made arrangements for each of you to be lodged in the same section of the ship. We've installed some of Earth's comforts to ease your transition. Tutors will contact you once the Sonara is underway. It will take close to a year to reach our solar system, even with jump gates in place. We have an extensive library to help you acclimate to your cultures and native languages. In time, you will be so immersed in your new lives, this will seem like a distant memory."

"Don't count on it," growled Ben.

"But Mom? Dad? What about them?" asked April.

"We both made a promise to them and it's one I intend to honor."

"But . . ," April said.

"That's an order. It's not safe for anyone to stay let alone children. If your parents are alive Aurelia will find them. According to Sondar's report, she is the best tracker on the team."

*"A friend?"* Ben asked telepathically.

Uncle Henry's eyes grew dark but he didn't answer.

"How are we getting to the ship?" asked Carlos.

"You'll transport directly to your cabins. It's a little more substantial than the gateways you've used on Earth. It will feel a bit like a roller coaster ride. It's over in seconds but will be less jarring if you close your eyes as you enter the beam."

"We'll catch the next one," Ben said.

"That is not an option."

Ben was furious. "We've made up our minds! We're staying to look for our parents. If you don't want to help, then we'll do it ourselves!"

"This argument is concluded!" barked Uncle Henry, turning to leave. "Gather your things!"

"We're staying! You need us." Ben said, struggling to keep his voice level but firm.

Uncle Henry whirled around, grabbed Ben by the shoulders and slammed him hard against the wall. "The last person we need here is you, Ben!"

His hot breath seared Ben's face. His nose flared, his eyes narrowed. It was like staring into the face of an angry bull.

Rage rose in Ben's chest as he stared back defiantly. Acid ate away at his stomach. He had always known his uncle hated him. Finally, the words were spoken. He clenched his fist and grit his teeth. "I don't need you either. I'll find them myself."

Uncle Henry maintained his vice-like grip on Ben. His eyes bored into him as he spoke in slow measured tones. "You don't get it do you? This is not a game. The stakes here are real. You can't select 'new game' from a pull-down menu if you get hurt or killed. There's no convenient 'undo' function to retrace your steps if you make an error. No 'escape' key to beam you back to reality."

"But our parents . . ."

"Were fools. There was no place for children on this mission!"

Ben winced as his uncle's grip tightened on his arms and shoulders. "I'll ask Aurelia for help. I heard her say she would find them for you."

"Perhaps I have been unclear," his uncle said, the heat from his breath like an inferno. "All available resources are allocated. We've got to find a way to release the energy build-up before everything we've worked for is lost!"

"What are you say . . ."

"Finding your parents is not our priority. They knew the risks. You saw the size of that blast hole. In all probability they died trying to save you. If we don't stop this chain reaction, there won't be anyone left to find their bodies. I will not allow you to further jeopardize my mission."

"I'm staying." Ben struggled to break free to no avail. He felt as if he were pinned by iron bars. He looked past his uncle and saw fear in the eyes of his friends. Even April stood motionless, her mouth gaping as Ben flailed two feet off the floor.

"I'm afraid you are mistaken, Benjamin." Uncle Henry's eyes flashed with a fire that caused Ben's heart to skip several beats. His voice was menacing and threatening. His friends gasped in the background as his uncle pressed his face within a hair's width of his own.

"You . . . and I . . . will honor the commitments we have made. You are a son of Xenobia and you will act accordingly. Do I make myself clear? I will not risk any more lives trying to protect you. You *will* go home!"

"But all those people getting off the ship. That means they are prepared to die." Terrified, Ben held his ground, if not with his dangling feet then with his heart.

"Not if we find the keys in time."

"And if you don't? How will you get home?"

Uncle Henry abruptly released his grip. Ben collapsed on the floor like a discarded heap of rubbish. He rubbed his sore arms.

"Collect your things," Uncle Henry said, his voice absent of any emotion. "I've made preparations. You have family who will meet you when the transport arrives on Casmir. From there, shuttles will carry you to your home planets. I will return for you in one hour."

"Uncle Henry?" Ben shouted. "How will you get home?"

Ben's uncle opened the doorway and walked out. He didn't answer. He didn't look back.

The door sealed shut behind him.

♦ ♦ ♦         ♦ ♦ ♦         ♦ ♦ ♦

CHAPTER FIFTY-ONE

# United We Stand

"I cannot do everything, but still I can do something.
I will not refuse to do the something I can do."
♦ ♦ ♦ *Helen Keller*

♦ ♦ ♦ "We're not really going are we?" asked Serise.

"No" Ben said. "I'm not leaving without knowing what happened to our parents."

"And if they're dead? What good will it do us to stay?" Grace asked. "I've never seen your uncle like that. He was terrifying — even for him."

"I've made my decision," Ben said. "They'd look for us wouldn't they?"

"That's because they've got skills. Training. Equipment. What have we got? Five kids and a cat," Grace said. "I don't think that's enough."

Aris grew to full size and growled at her.

"Oops! Sorry, Aris," Grace said. "I meant five kids and our

shape-shifting, panther pal."

Aris shrank back to normal, purred and rubbed against Grace's leg.

"Grace. Have you ever done anything your parents asked you not to do?" asked Serise

"Yes."

Serise cocked her head to the side and arched one eyebrow.

Grace frowned. "Okay, no. I haven't. But we made a promise."

"No, we didn't," Ben said. "My father made *me* promise to get on the ship. Your parents didn't make you promise anything. They just assumed you would do it."

"Okay. *You* made a promise," Grace said.

"Right. But I never do what my parents tell me to do so why break a consistent pattern of behavior? Technically, if we stay, I'm the only one who will get in trouble. Don't see me worried do you? Come on guys. The clock is ticking!"

"My parents gave up on domesticating me," Serise said without hesitation. "I'm in."

Carlos nodded and gave Serise a high five. "Me too. So what's the plan?"

"I haven't figured that part out yet." Ben turned to his sister. "April, you should go home."

April glowered at Ben like he'd lost his mind. She put one hand on her hip and waved the index finger of the other at him. "No!"

"But Mom and Dad said . . ."

"No!" she said, cutting him off. "Don't EVEN think about it."

"But . . ."

April raised one eyebrow and rolled her neck. "I'm part of the team, remember?"

Ben knew when to give up. "Fine. Be that way."

Grace clapped her hands to get their attention. "Hey guys? I hate to interfere with your family bonding moment but we don't have much time. Your uncle is coming back in an hour."

"Do you think we could get a technician to help?" asked Serise.

"Like who?" asked Carlos. "We don't speak any alien languages."

He walked up to the door and waved his hand in a circular fashion. "Abracadabra!"

The door remained closed.

"See? We can't even get out of the room." Clearly frustrated, Carlos mashed on the keys. A lot of alien symbols stared back at him.

Serise used her watch with no results

Grace studied the panel and traced the foreign symbols with her fingertips. "I'm lost," she said, in defeat.

Ben put one hand on it, then both hands. Nothing. Soon they were all punching random codes into the keyboard hoping to find a combination that would turn it on. The keypad remained dormant.

Ben switched on the compass. "Computer. Determine current location."

"Confirmed."

"Autodial pass code to open the door, please."

The computer worked for a few seconds then responded. "Authorization denied."

Ben growled and tossed the device on a nearby chair. "Carlos. Got anything in that bag?"

Carlos frowned and searched through his backpack. "Sorry. Left the laser beam at home."

"Well, we better figure something out quick." April put her finger in the middle of the compass screen and said, "April Webster."

"Fingerprint and voiceprint identification confirmed. Welcome April Webster."

"Hey! Don't mess with that! We don't know how much power it has left." Ben snatched it away.

"It recognizes me! You have to share," April said, snatching it back. A map appeared. Several blinking lights were visible. "What's this?" she asked. "A game?"

Grace looked over her shoulder. "It's a map of the northern hemisphere."

"Hey, guys?" Carlos said. "We need a plan! Like right now before we get sent up in that beam. Did you see what some of those space people looked like coming off of that ship? What do you suppose the people on our planets really look like when they're not pretending to be Earthlings? Did you see Grace's tribe? Skeletons! I don't know about you, but I kind of like the way I look right now!"

Grace frowned and studied her hands, twisting them back and forth and holding them up the light as if waiting for her own transformation.

"Shhh," Serise said, examining the device. "Will that hot sync with my computer? I can't make out the tiny letters. Let's blow it up." She placed the compass near the infrared port on the side of her laptop. A red beam shot out of the screen and scanned Serise's face. A familiar voice confirmed, "Retinal eye scan completed. Serise Hightower authorized user."

"That's a slick new security feature," Carlos said.

"Thanks," Serise said. "I hacked my mother's laptop while I was on lock-down. Couldn't read the encrypted files but I found this. Wish I'd had it earlier to keep my parents from snooping my diary. This outer space spy stuff has some advantages!"

The two devices began communicating. Soon both screens flashed "Synchronization complete." Ben gawked at Serise with newfound appreciation as she typed furiously on her keyboard.

"There's something here," she said. "A map and a bunch of tiny lights. They're all in Northern Africa."

"See if you can blow up the map," Carlos said.

Serise zoomed in five hundred percent. A clearer image of Egypt emerged. Hundreds of tiny lights hovered over the city of Giza, with more heading in that direction.

"I think that's us," Grace said. "I bet it's just a way to keep track of the teams. It makes sense that they're all in Egypt. Everyone's going home."

"Not everyone," Ben frowned.

More lights blinked on and off in the same locations shown on the Control Room map. The recently departed research teams.

"Let me see that." Grace scrolled to the left and rotated the map. "Guys look. There's another set of lights. Not as many this time."

Grace was right. There *were* more lights — eight of them — right on the equator.

"What does this mean?" she asked.

Ben examined the map. The lights were in pairs — four pairs. He looked at the heading. "Personnel locator." *Personnel?* *People?*

"Guys! These might be our parents!"

Everyone gathered around Ben and stared at Serise's computer.

"You sure?" asked Grace. "Could be anything. Those dots are in the middle of the ocean. It must be one of the sea-based teams that look like that guy, Volari."

"I've just got a hunch," Ben said. He'd seen his mother and Dr. Hightower go into the ocean in Antarctica so it was a definite possibility. "Think about it. We're missing eight people. There are eight signals."

"In the middle of the Pacific ocean?" asked Carlos. "It's a long shot."

"I'm getting good at those," Ben said, feeling his confidence return.

"Yeah, you are." Carlos offered his hand and looked to the others for support.

Ben's heart soared as three more hands fell on the heap.

Aris hissed in disagreement.

"Aris! That other cat belonged to the Shaman. Do you belong to my mother? Do you want to leave her behind?"

The cat growled, leaped in April's arms and made the vote unanimous.

"Okay. It's agreed. We need a plan!" Ben said. "And we're going to have to do it before we get on that ship."

"But won't he know we didn't go?" asked April. "Won't someone will be waiting for us up there?"

"No," Ben said. "Uncle Henry said he was going to send us directly to our cabins. No one's going to contact us until the ship is underway."

"Okay!" Serise said. "So we need to make it look like we went up when we didn't."

"How about sending up our backpacks?" April grinned, her eyes flashing mischievously. "We're nosy kids. If the tutors come looking for us they'll see our stuff and think we left to explore the ship."

"There's one little flaw in that plan," Grace said. "Ben's uncle was able to track us on our way here. Don't you think he would know if we took a detour?"

"So how'd he do that?" asked April.

While everyone else stared at the compass, Ben fingered the collar in his pocket. It was covered in tiny black diamonds. It came from the game. Uncle Henry's game. It was as if the condor, banking and soaring, had pointed him toward it. Nothing from the game was real except the pouch and the collar.

"Could be the compass," Carlos said, interrupting Ben's train of thought. "But I'm thinking it's something else. Remember the day they had the safety meeting at school. They talked about putting GPS locators in our backpacks in case we got lost camping or hiking."

"Or got snatched by a criminal!" April said. "That way the police can find you quick."

"So I'm betting," Carlos continued, "that there's something hidden in our packs. Probably microscopic given all the other cool junk our parents had. Think about it. Our parents packed these bags for us. They wanted us to bring them along."

Ben closed his fist around the collar and formed a plan of us own.

"So we've got to send the backpacks up ahead of us," Grace said. "But that doesn't explain how we're going to stay out of the transport beam ourselves."

There was silence.

"I have an idea." Serise frowned and tapped her elaborately painted fingernails on the top of her computer. Despite the grueling ordeal of the last twenty-four hours, the bright red nail polish and flower designs were still flawless. Not a chip. Not a scratch. "Your uncle gave us a clue, although I don't think he meant to."

"I don't understand," Ben said.

"He was angry because we didn't use the computer to dial ourselves here. He said we should have figured out that the game took us to real locations. Remember? He said the dialers weren't used by the teams anymore, but they still work."

Ben stared at Serise as he processed the information.

"With all that's going on, think they're still working?" Serise bit her lips and continued to drum her fingers on the computer. Her eyebrows arched. A twinkle appeared in her eye. "I've still got a copy of the game!"

◆ ◆ ◆              ◆ ◆ ◆                  ◆ ◆ ◆

CHAPTER FIFTY-TWO

# The Plan

When spider webs unite — they can tie up a lion.
◆ ◆ ◆ *Ethiopian proverb.*

◆ ◆ ◆ Ben would have hugged her if it weren't such a gross idea. "But we'd be dialing ourselves to an outpost. Grace's mother said they were under attack."

"Not all of them," Carlos said. "And there wasn't an outpost in Peru or on Easter Island. Or at least none that I could see."

"Or at the Terra Cotta Army," Grace said. "Maybe there are a lot of abandoned dialers around the world."

"Exactly," Serise said. "What do we have to lose?"

"Could we go to the ship and dial out from there?" asked April. "I'd really like to see it before it leaves. I mean, a real live spaceship! It must be so awesome!"

"Yeah," Carlos said. "That would be a trip of a lifetime. It's our last chance to see one."

"Can't risk it," Ben said. "We don't know the range of this game or those dialers. We might go up to the ship and then be stuck up there."

"Then I vote for picking a place we've been before," Carlos said, looking disappointed.

"Islas Ballestas," April said.

"Why there?" asked Ben. "It's gross."

"Because we can hide in a cave," April said. "No one will be able to see us. I liked the Terra Cotta army but it's spooky in there. We can hang out with the sea lions if we go to the island."

"It's as good a place as any," Carlos said.

"Yuk!" Serise said. "Grace and I went to some better places — nice views, good looking native guys on a beach. I vote for exotic island paradise. I mean, you should have seen the Maori in New Zealand. They look like those Mondavi guys. Even their tattoos are hot!"

Ben rolled his eyes and groaned. "Geez! Could we stay on topic? The million dollar question is, can we dial out from here?"

"Only one way to find out."

Serise booted up the game. The Guardian medallion waited patiently for instructions.

"It's a good thing you remembered to hit the escape key," Grace said.

Ben saw the problem immediately. The real Guardian chamber was still filled with technicians now conducting tests on the mysterious jars. No chance of going to that location. "Before we dial out we've got to figure out how to get back before Uncle Henry comes to get us."

"Just two of us should do the test," Serise said. "It's my computer. I'll take it with me to make sure we can use it to dial home or at least hit the escape key. Ben, you stall your uncle if he shows up before we get back."

"I'll go with you in case you get stuck or lose power," Carlos said. Suddenly, around Serise, he was a super explorer. "Ben. If we're not back in five minutes — you can tell your uncle where we went and he can retrieve us."

"He's going to be mad," April said.

"Well, that wouldn't be much of a change for him, would it?" asked Ben. "Okay. Five minutes or I'm calling the cavalry."

"If this is an experiment, then let's go to Llactapata first. I only know two dialers and the one on Easter Island is hard to reach," Carlos said. "The teams should be gone. We'll zap in and zap out again and hope National Geographic hasn't found the ruins yet."

"You need a dialer code just in case 'escape' doesn't bring you back here." Ben disconnected the compass from Serise's laptop. "Confirm dialing location for Safe Harbor."

"Specify destination."

"Uncle Henry's quarters."

"Location unknown," the computer said. "Please specify destination."

"Henry Webster's apartment," Ben barked.

"Location unknown," the computer repeated. "Please specify destination."

April grabbed the compass. "Listen you stupid machine! Do ya think you could stop foolin' around and tell us the stinkin' code we need to dial to get back to Commander Kurosh's apartment from Peru!"

"Confirmed." The device flashed out a series of numbers.

Ben looked at his sister both exasperated and amazed. When she was tired, she had quite a mouth on her.

April shrugged. "It worked. Now we've got to hide in another room."

"Why?" asked Grace.

"Because, if we stay in here while Serise and Carlos dial, we're going to get zapped out with them."

◆ ◆ ◆

Unlike the living room, Uncle Henry's bedroom was barren and uninviting. A single, stone platform sat in the center of the floor. An Egyptian headrest sat on top. Ben peeked into the closet and was confused by the contrast. Uncle Henry had the world's most uncomfortable bed, but a closet full of expensive designer clothes.

Ben caught a glimpse of a light through the frosted glass door leading to the living room. Minutes later the flash returned along with enthusiastic whoops of excitement. Ben and the others hurried out to greet them. Carlos and Serise gave each other high fives and hugs.

"Game on!" said Carlos.

❖ ❖ ❖        ❖ ❖ ❖        ❖ ❖ ❖

CHAPTER FIFTY-THREE

# Game On!

A wise person will always find a way.

❖ ❖ ❖ *Tanzanian proverb*

❖ ❖ ❖ Ben watched as hundreds of scientists boarded the ship through the transport beam. Uncle Henry stood behind him, blocking any chance of escape.

"It will be time to go soon," he said. "I think you will enjoy the experience. There have never been children on these missions. I suspect you will be pampered and spoiled on the trip home."

Serise's eyebrows arched at the sound of "pampered and spoiled." But her expression was fleeting. She continued watching the nearby activity, her computer firmly grasped in her hand.

Ben pulled the collar from his pocket and concealed it in the palm of his hand. He flinched as a diamond dislodged and fell into the silvery pool. It was a tiny jewel.

One of many.

Insignificant.

The scanners would pick up the signal imbedded in the collar and assume he and his friends were on the ship. As his uncle spoke with the others and said his goodbyes, Ben tossed the collar into their pile of backpacks and watched it dissolve in the beam.

Across the room, Aurelia studied data from the monitors before issuing commands to the interplanetary teams. Aris sat on the control panel and studied the data. Occasionally, he received a scratch or a treat from one of the technicians assisting Aurelia. The Xenobian panther stood guard on the far side of the console, unconcerned with the attention being lavished on Aris.

Ben concentrated and hoped there was a way to adjust his frequency so that his Uncle would not hear him.

*"Aurelia, can you hear me?"*

If she heard him, she gave no indication of it. Something had startled her. Aris became animated at whatever new development was occurring during the download. Images of scientists digging trenches on top of a frozen mountain appeared on the monitor above her. One cradled a small girl. Aurelia zoomed in. The girl looked like she was sleeping. Wrapped in a woven blanket, her hair spilled out of the sides and fell down her shoulders. But her skin was dried and wrinkled.

She was mummified.

Ben wondered if she was one of the missing tribe members. The scientists dropped their shovels, reached into the trench, and pulled out a body. It wasn't a burial. It was retrieval.

The eight symbols of the Guardian appeared in a separate window. Broken fragments of a stone tablet rotated beside two of the symbols. But what was the connection to the frozen bodies on the mountain? A tiny rod was clutched in the hand of the second body. Aurelia zoomed in until the rod filled the entire screen.

Ben froze. He'd seen something like that before.

Unaware of the activity at Aurelia's station, Ben's uncle focused on April's flurry of questions about the people who were boarding the ship. For a brief period, a second transport beam flickered inside the first. Everyone paused at the edge of the platform and waited for the activity to cease. Uncle Henry explained that colonists were being evacuated directly from the oceans into special habitats on the Sonara.

"High risk maneuver," he said. "It requires shutting down radio telescopes and satellites. We cannot perform it very often or we'd start a panic over the sudden increase in solar activity. A glitch in the Casmir array caused the satellites to shut down last week. You boys wouldn't know anything about that would you?"

Ben saw a glimmer of recognition cross Carlos's face but neither acknowledged the question.

Kavera approached touched Ben's uncle on the shoulder. He stepped away from the group.

*"Aurelia, can you hear me?"* Ben repeated, his mind pleading with her. *"My parents are still alive. We found their signals near the equator. We can help you search. We know a lot about the planet that you won't find in a text book or computer file."*

Although there was no response from Aurelia, she pulled up a rotating image of the globe and stopped it at the location of the eight signals. She pointed toward one of the transport tubes. Two of her guards rushed into it and disappeared. Across the room, Ben's uncle was engaged in an animated and angry discussion with Kavera. Ben tried reaching Aurelia again.

*"I was right, wasn't I? They're somewhere in the ocean?"* Ben had no clue what he was doing but he had nothing to lose. If Serise's computer couldn't dial from here, he needed a back-up plan. *"I want to stay and help find my parents. It is my right as a member of my father's clan."* Ben thought that sounded kind of grown-up.

Aurelia pursed her lips and paused. Ben was certain he had gotten through this time. Instead, Aurelia turned her head in the opposite direction and watched the argument between Uncle Henry and Kavera. She approached them, but that made Ben's uncle even angrier. He dismissed her with the wave of his hand.

Seconds later, Aurelia returned to her post and studied the streaming images of the mummified Peruvian girl. She reached into her pouch and extracted a silver rod of her own which she pushed into a slot in the side of the console. The monitor went dark then rebooted with data, graphs and maps of the world. Aurelia retrieved the rod and slipped it into back her pouch.

It was no use. Either Ben couldn't reach her or she'd stopped tuning into his frequency. He stared into the milky white void that held their destiny.

"We don't want to go," Carlos said.

"I know," Uncle Henry said, returning to their side. "But this is for the best."

April wrapped her arms around him. "You're all the family we have left."

"I promise," Uncle Henry said. "You will have the life your parents wished for you."

*"Aurelia, help me."*

Aurelia glanced in Ben's direction. Their eyes met. This time he could tell she understood.

*"You have your orders and I have mine. I wish you a safe journey."*

The glimmer of hope that had passed through Ben was now dashed into pieces. Out of the corner of his eye, he saw that Serise was trapped. There was no way for her to open her computer without being detected. *Game over!*

Then he had a brainstorm. The compass was in his pocket and it was still linked to Serise's laptop. Could he use it to autodial? Could he do it without being caught? He touched the center keypad and heard a muffled acknowledgment through the cloth lining of his pants. He tried to visualize the screen. He couldn't speak. He'd be heard. Could he simply press a code using his fingers?

Next, how to fool his uncle? He would have to stay at the outer edge of the platform when Ben and his friends transported. That might give Ben the edge he needed and he knew just how he was going to use it.

"I know you will each grow to make your parents proud just as you have made me proud," Uncle Henry said. "If the fates wish it, we will see each other again."

"Goodbye, Uncle Henry." Ben squeezed his uncle's hand. "Maybe I should start calling you Kurosh."

"My Earth name will do just fine. It's the one you've always known." His uncle wiped the tears streaming down April's face.

Aris jumped down from the console and waited patiently at the edge of the ramp. Ben's uncle scratched the cat behind the ears. "Goodbye, old friend. Take care of them for me will you?" The cat purred in response.

While his uncle said goodbye to his friends, Ben turned his back and eased the compass out of his pocket. He had one shot — just one — to get this right. If he dialed the wrong code he would be transported to the ship — or worse to someplace dangerous. He imagined a galactic basketball court on the Sonara just in case his uncle was eavesdropping on his thoughts. Then he crossed his arms across his chest and tucked the device into the folds of his shirt, tilting the device slightly so that he could see the screen. Reflections of the transport beam made the data hard to read, but Ben found the right angle to use. He continued masking his thoughts with images of NBA championships on a foreign planet while sending a pleading glance to the cat. Aris blinked once. In the glow of the lights, it looked as if the cat had winked at him.

Everyone's eyes moved to Serise. Her laptop was slightly ajar, but with his uncle hovering like a guard dog there was no way for her fingers to reach the numeric keypad without fully opening the lid.

"*Sorry,*" she mouthed.

Grace, Carlos and April looked at Serise, at Ben, then at the transport beam with dread.

*One chance left. The team is depending on me to make the shot.*

Ben kept his head looking forward, but cast a downward glance and used his thumb to bring up a list of possible gates. April peeked at his arm. Her eyes grew wide and she quickly looked away. Her face was now beaming.

The last of the scientists stepped up to Uncle Henry and bowed as they spoke in foreign languages. Ben seized the opportunity to give a verbal command to the compass. "Volume off." He hid the command in a cough and hoped the computer understood.

A single word, *"confirmed,"* flashed across the screen.

*Yes!*

He raised his hand again and coughed the location. Again the compass flashed, *"confirmed."*

More scientists stepped ahead of the children and into the beam, quickly dissolving in the milky light. Ben knew there would be no more stalling.

"Children, it is time," Uncle Henry said. "I wish you a safe journey."

*Ten seconds on the clock.*

Desperate and out of time Ben squinted in the light. Two options appeared: "manual input" and "autodial."

*All systems go!*

April looped her arm into Ben's. She took Carlos's hand with the other. Connected and linked, the friends walked slowly toward the light that would whisk them away.

*Take the shot!*

Just short of the beam, Ben closed his eyes, said a prayer, pushed the second option on the device . . .

. . . and felt himself sucked into a vortex.

♦ ♦ ♦       ♦ ♦ ♦       ♦ ♦ ♦

# CHAPTER FIFTY-FOUR

# Detour

When you follow in the path of your father,
you learn to walk like him.

• • • *Ashanti Proverb*


• • • *Whoosh!*

Ben landed squarely, but was disoriented. He sank to the ground, caught his breath, then spotted the familiar skeleton and Rongorongo tablet in the corner, confirmation he'd reached the right destination.

"What the heck?" asked Serise. "Is this what your planet calls a Galaxy-class space ship! They had better rooms on the Titanic. Fifty years after it sank!"

"We aren't on the ship," Ben said, forcing his eyes to adjust to the low light. "I dialed us to Islas Ballestas."

"What about tropical paradise did you not get? Hawaii? Costa Rica? Tahiti?" asked Serise.

"I had to think fast. Sorry." He found the silver rod still lying near the foot of the skeleton, said a silent prayer of thanks and shoved it in his pocket before his friends noticed.

"You couldn't have dialed us to a place with a bathroom?" Grace said.

"This island IS a bathroom," Carlos said, staring out the mouth of the cave.

"I wish you had clued us in." said Serise. "Grace and I memorized some cool codes with hotels and room service. I mean, I've got a credit card and we could have . . ." She froze. "Uh oh! I think we've been found."

The center of the medallion glowed red. Three metal rods materialized out of thin air, floated towards the perimeter of the cave, imbedded into the ground and began to glow.

*"It appears you are your father's son, Ajamu."*

Ben's jaw tightened as he braced for the beam that would send them to the ship. He wondered why she called him 'Ajamu'.

*"Interesting choice of locations,"* Aurelia continued. *"You are safe here. Wait one day. By then, it will be impossible for the Sonara to return or retrieve you using teleportation beams. I trust you know your way back to us? One, three, five, four, two, one,"* she continued. *"No detours to the Libyan desert, please. The landing bay gate has been deactivated."*

The corresponding stones of the medallion glowed on and off confirming her instructions. The silver rods gave off heat and light. A box of fruit, biscuits and drinking flasks appeared above the medallion and floated gently to the ground.

*"Aris. Akoosh, vera inna sha ka don fur."*

If Aris understood that last comment, he wasn't giving any clues. He purred and pulled a biscuit from the box. Ben assumed Aurelia's message meant, "Aris, eat the food, not the kids."

*"By the way, young warrior. Mitochondria flows at the cellular level from mother to child. You are member of your mother's clan, not your father's."*

Ben relaxed the tension in his shoulders and opened a flask of water. Aurelia had heard his pleas all along.

*"I look forward to your safe return."* The beam winked out, but the rods remained.

Grace hugged herself tightly and stared at the skeleton in the darkened corner. "I can honestly say that nothing is scarier than how I feel right now."

"Nothing?" Ben chuckled darkly.

"What's so funny?" Grace paused.

"Think about the word. You'll get it in a minute."

Grace paused. Her eyes brightened in a moment of clarity and then her mouth formed the shape of an "O". "What is greater than God? Nothing. More evil than the Devil? Nothing. The rich need nothing, the poor have nothing, and if you eat nothing you will die?"

Exhausted, Ben nodded and settled in for a long wait. Suddenly he wasn't so sure this was a good idea. He had broken his promise to get his sister to safety in order to find a random stick of metal on a poop filled island. Now there was no way to get off the planet. His father said one day he'd have to make a choice and to be prepared for the consequences. Had he sealed the fate for his sister . . . and his friends? He prayed the rod in his pocket was more than just a power source for the simulation. If it was, maybe it would give them some leverage when they returned to the Harbor.

April curled against Grace's lap and went to sleep. Her eyes were moist but no tears escaped. Grace seemed to welcome the distraction. Serise joined Carlos at the mouth of the cave and stared out at the landscape. They held hands while Serise's head rested on his shoulder.

"Wonder what to do for a bathroom?" Ben said to the cat. "Go to the back and pee on the rocks? In Rome it angered the gods of the underworld."

Aris yawned, transformed to full size, then nudged Ben toward the medallion. Before Ben could respond, Aris pounced on the nodes and dialed him to the British Museum.

◆ ◆ ◆          ◆ ◆ ◆          ◆ ◆ ◆

CHAPTER FIFTY-FIVE

# Out of Hiding

"It is the first step that is difficult."
◆ ◆ ◆ *Nigerian Proverb*

◆ ◆ ◆ Aurelia's code returned them to a deserted section of the Xenobian complex. Ben stopped, abruptly.

"Hear something?" asked April.

"A humming sound. It stopped though." Ben pressed his ear to the metal doors which parted suddenly causing him to stumble inside.

Everyone froze but the sound was swallowed by the cavernous chamber ringed by a balcony. The size and shape reminded Ben of a small arena.

Uncle Henry stood, bare-chested and barefoot, in the middle of the darkened floor, illuminated only by a single light above him. He wore gold cuffs on his wrists and upper arms — the same type of cuffs Ben's parents wore during the attack in Sunnyslope.

A collective gasp rose among his friends as Ben's uncle dropped into the splits, rolled, then rose to begin deep lunges from side to side. His massive muscles rippled as he stretched and flexed his arms in impossibly wide arcs, dropping lower with each repetition. He rose, craned his head neck, then shook out his hands and feet. Afterwards he knelt, crossed his arms briefly in prayer, then walked toward a stone wall covered in hieroglyphic symbols.

The wall dissolved revealing hundreds of weapons. Ben's uncle selected two sabers as long as his arms. He slipped their leather bands around his wrist and returned to the center of the room. After several slow inhales, he raised the swords parallel to the floor and performed a kata against an invisible opponent. The swords swung in wide controlled arcs as he moved across the floor. His expression was passive. He certainly wasn't out searching for his brother or any of the other parents. Could his heart be any colder?

Ben fumed and checked his emotions quickly, remembering his uncle's ability to read his thoughts. He wondered how close he had to be before a telepathic link was established.

"Who's going to tell him we're still here?" whispered Grace.

All eyes looked at Ben.

"Why me?" Ben whispered as he studied the lethal weapons in his uncle's hands.

"You're family. You're used to him yelling at you," Serise said. "Don't worry though. We've got your back." She winked and gave him a thumbs up.

"Yeah, right. Why not April? She's family too and he likes her better!"

April pointed toward the sword. "I'm little and he's got weapons. Big ones!"

Carlos wrapped his arms around April's shoulders. "I'll stay here and keep an eye on your little sister for you. Remember? Got your back, bro!"

April nodded her approval.

Ben shot his friends a dirty look. "Fine. I'll take Aris for protection."

He pointed toward the cat who was admiring his sleek but faint reflection in a nearby surface. Aris shrank to normal size, walked over to April and licked his paws.

"Chicken," growled Ben. He shrank further into the shadows and waited for an opening.

Uncle Henry's exercise increased in speed and tempo. At times he was a blur as he spun across the floor, the swords whipping violently about him. Crouching and stretching without interrupting the momentum of the swords. He executed flawless back flips, forward flips and three hundred sixty degree spins. The swords rotated like the blades of a propeller. Uncle Henry moved with the agility of a much smaller person but with the strength of ten men.

Something else struck Ben. Other than the swishing sound of the swords as they sliced through the air his uncle's exercise was utterly silent, no heavy breathing, no sound of feet hitting the floor. He looked to his friends for confirmation. Everyone had the same reaction — Wow! A real opponent would have been sliced into confetti.

The blades rotated with increased fury. His uncle twisted left, then right before spinning again in complete circles, increasing the speed with each rotation.

Ben's feet felt weighted to the floor. His palms sweat. His heart and lungs beat a symphony inside his chest cavity. How could he have thought he and his friends could help the teams when they had skills like that? What did he have to offer besides a broken promise?

Carlos was right. He would never gain his uncle's approval. Not now. Not ever.

Suddenly his uncle disappeared.

*"Where'd he go?"* Carlos pantomimed.

Ben gawked and searched the room. He heard the blades whipping through the air but could no longer pinpoint the direction.

The exercise ended abruptly as the sound of an impact echoed in the chamber like a cannon blast. Ben's uncle reappeared in the same spot where he was last seen, the tips of the swords now embedded violently in the stone floor on each side of him. He released his grip. The swords remained stiff and upright in the stone. Uncle Henry bowed to his unseen opponent, walked across the room and retrieved his shirt and robe.

*Whoa!* There was a simultaneous expulsion of air from each of Ben's friends. He felt a gentle nudge on his back. Serise and Carlos shoved him forward.

*"Time to go!"* mouthed Grace. She gestured with both hands then pointed. *"Tell him!"*

*"Wait an minute!"* Ben was trying to work up his nerve. What he had just witnessed was impossible. No human could move that fast.

*No human?*

Ben paused as the thought repeated. His uncle wasn't human. None of them were. They were species from another galaxy and his uncle was a super strong one at that. Ben stared at the weapons imbedded in the floor and pointed to his watch, *"Maybe we should wait."*

Grace pointed to *her* watch and gestured, *"No! Now!"*

His uncle dressed quickly then pulled something from his pocket.

"Consat!" Uncle Henry spoke brusquely as he reviewed holographic read-outs from a disk in his hand. "Askar makamu Sonara!"

Except for the name of the ship Ben didn't understand the reference but a control panel near the door lit up.

"Consat! Askar makamu Sonara!" Uncle Henry barked angrily.

The sound of pandemonium crackled from the panel. His uncle stopped in his tracks.

'Kavera! Aurelia! Seekor comisat?"

There was no answer. Ben clearly heard shouting, alarms blaring, grunting and . . . fighting.

"Consat! Askar!"

The panel streamed with hieroglyphics and foreign scripts Ben couldn't translate.

"Jemadari!" A voice gasped on the intercom. "Akoosh Consat. Ebu!"

Uncle Henry looked stricken. He froze momentarily, then tore out of the chamber.

Ben stared at the others in a panic then chased after his uncle. His strides were inhumanly long — and fast.

Despite the language barrier Ben knew where his uncle was going. With Aris at his side, he picked up speed and headed toward the control room.

◆ ◆ ◆                    ◆ ◆ ◆                         ◆ ◆ ◆

CHAPTER FIFTY-SIX

# Chaos

Goodness speaks in a whisper.
Evil shouts.
◆ ◆ ◆  *Tibetan Proverb*

◆ ◆ ◆ The control room was in disarray. Equipment had been destroyed. Green liquid was splattered throughout the chamber; on the floors, on the walls, on team members.

He'd expected to find chaos. But, just as it had been the night his parents were attacked, there was a sense of urgency, but no panic. Technicians worked to repair consoles and undo the damage. Uncle Henry consulted with Aurelia and the tribal leaders. The Casmirian leader, sword gripped tightly in his hand glowered at Uncle Henry before dispatching some of his warriors, weapons drawn, into the general complex.

Xenobian guards followed Kavera out of the storage hall. They rushed to the central transport beam. Each carried glowing Van de Graaff-like orbs, ten in all. The guards stood at the edge of the platform and launched the orbs into the beam.

"What are they doing?" whispered April when she caught up to him. "Sending something up to the ship? I thought it was gone?"

Ben shrugged and pressed his fingers to his lips. "Shhh."

The overhead displays came back on line. One showed a beam of light arcing out of the planet. Solar flares lapped at the beam near the point of impact, then receded. The orbs were instantly incinerated.

Danine knelt beside a Casmirian warrior. She touched her hand to his wrist as if taking a pulse and felt his forehead. The warrior nodded, clasped her hand for leverage and returned to his feet. He flexed his muscular arms then bowed before joining the cleanup effort. From what Ben could see, there were no casualties.

The Xenobian panther crept up the staircase. As it neared their location, Aris pressed closer to the wall to conceal himself. Ben scooted backwards, pulling April with him.

Aurelia scanned the balcony with narrowed eyes. "Bastet! Akoosh!"

The cat sniffed at the air, growled, then turned and descended. Ben let out a sigh of relief.

Kavera grasped Uncle Henry's hand and held it for a minute, then retrieved a palm-sized device from an open crate. He returned to the transport platform with Volari. Spikes pulsed on the virtual display as the device sprayed a triangular beam of light in front of them. The beam alternated red, then gold as it illuminated everything in its path.

Joined by four other leaders, Uncle Henry rushed to an undamaged console in the center of the room. The Casmirian leader barked commands at the control panel. Lights winked on around the globe. Ben looked at Carlos for confirmation — the Casmir Array. Additional lights activated on planets across the solar system.

A new hologram appeared above the men as they stood back-to-back on the platform. It expanded in scope until it engulfed them. The Sonara.

Massive.

Gleaming.

A triangular shaped ship with wide thick fins on the top, bottom and sides. A sphere in the center glowed like an iridescent pearl. The transport was flanked by several smaller ships.

An entire city traveling at near the speed of light in space! It must be awesome inside.

"Sonara! Askar!" shouted Uncle Henry.

Planets whizzed by as the Casmir array beamed three-dimensional images of the ship to the Harbor. If Ben were interpreting nearby schematics correctly, the Sonara had already cleared its first jump gate and was approaching the second, putting millions of miles between it and the Earth.

"Sonara! Askar!" Uncle Henry repeated.

Static — then a faint answer, weak but proud and defiant. "Askar, Jemadari."

"Sonara! Seekor comisat?"

*Static.*

"Sonara! Akoosh Consat!" Uncle Henry's booming voice reverberated throughout the control room. "Akoosh Consat!"

The Sonara's captain responded with a single word, understandable in any language.

"No."

A flash of light appeared.

A ball of fire.

Wreckage . . . burning . . . floating in space.

Another explosion. Blinding light.

Emptiness . . . blackness . . . stars turning on again . . . twinkling.

Ben clamped his hand over his mouth to mute his gasp.

"Was that the ship?" asked April, her panic-stricken voice barely a whisper.

Ben nodded.

"That could have been us?"

Ben nodded again and blinked back tears.

April shivered and huddled closer to him.

With the exception of Kavera and Volari, everyone in the Control Center stood silent and transfixed as the scene played out over and over in three dimension. The ship was gone. Uncle Henry rotated the images after each playback zooming in on every inch of the ship and its escorts before they were destroyed. He remained expressionless even as he stood engulfed by the holographic catastrophe.

A loud beep rang out.

A splash.

Kavera crouched alone at the edge of the pool and waited. Seconds later Volari emerged, silver liquid dripping from his scaly, turquoise skin. He held up his webbed thumb and forefinger pinched tightly together and dropped something in Kavera's hand before diving under the liquid again.

Seeing the disturbance, Uncle Henry left his console and joined them. Kavera examined a tiny object in the light of the transport beam before handing it to him. Ben's stomach lurched.

A black stone.

From the Peruvian cat collar.

Ben's uncle twirled it between his fingers and studied it for several seconds, then erupted in a violent rage. He pitched the jewel into the beam. Something materialized before being sucked into the vortex. It was less than a second but Ben could swear he saw something towering, gray —

— *and not human.*

The resulting explosion knocked Ben's uncle off the platform. The control room was thrown into darkness before back-up systems came on-line. Kavera narrowly missed falling into the pool. Aurelia rushed over to help. Face strained in anger, Uncle Henry waved her away. Volari emerged again and shook his head. Ben already knew what he had been looking for. There would be no more jewels found.

The chamber grew silent. Auxiliary lights bathed the room in a soft blue glow. The Xenobian warriors arched their arms, raised them toward the ceiling, then crouched again and crossed their arms against their chests. The Casmirian warriors remained upright; one fist against their chests, their swords raised high into the air with the other. The Casmirian leader shouted something unintelligible as he gazed into the holographic sky.

Aurelia quietly called. The room responded. She called again, the room responded. Ben couldn't translate the language. It was mournful, and yet beautiful as the voices rose and blended in an interplanetary chorus.

They were praying for the lost souls. The ship was destroyed. Everyone on it — Ben choked even as the words formed — had died. That could have been him. That should have been him. Hundreds of scientists fleeing to safety. Doomed by a thoughtless and reckless act. A cat collar tossed into a pile of backpacks.

*By Ben.*

Uncle Henry wasn't tracking them through the collar. Then who?

*"Not who, but what?"*

Wracked with more guilt than he could bear, Ben fled from the room. He wished he had died too.

♦ ♦ ♦               ♦ ♦ ♦               ♦ ♦ ♦

# CHAPTER FIFTY-SEVEN

# Miracles

*To change the world we must first change ourselves.*

✦ ✦ ✦  *Tibetan Proverb*

✦ ✦ ✦ Ben sank to the floor, his back against one of the many columns lining the chamber. An overhead balcony created enough shadow to conceal his location if anyone entered. He didn't know where he was in the complex. A single light illuminated a plain, marble platform. Behind it, hundreds of glistening rods dripped from the ceiling like rain. The only sound besides his erratic breathing was a gentle swooshing, as if the room were surrounded by water.

He replayed the scene over and over in slow motion.

The ship . . . gleaming . . . escaping

*Destroyed.*

The jewel.

His uncle . . . probing . . . exploding in rage . . . something monstrous materializing in the beam.

*The prayers.*

Nothing he could do, nothing he could say, would bring those people back.

And what about April? And his friends?

They depended on him. Should he have kept his promise and gotten on the ship? Would quick death have been better than a slow one? Some leader he turned out to be. What was the saying? *Be careful what you wish for?* Now they were all stranded on Earth with missing parents, a space station full of extraterrestrial beings and an uncle as cold and heartless as the iceberg that sank the Titanic.

He was jolted out of his reflection by the sound of footsteps. Hiding behind the column brought a sense of deja vu. He steeled himself. No foul smell. No odd noises. Just the same, he tucked his legs to minimize his exposed surface area.

Aurelia and Kavera approached the platform. They knelt on the marble and crossed their arms across their chests. Ben drew further into the shadows and waited for them to leave.

He closed his eyes and prayed for the lost souls. He also prayed for forgiveness and for an answer that would relieve his agony.

As if in response to his request he felt a hand on his shoulder. He recoiled and found Kavera and Aurelia crouching beside him, both barefoot.

"You picked an appropriate place for prayer, my young prince," Aurelia said. "Your instincts brought you to our place of healing. Your parents would be proud."

Kavera remained silent but his eyes exuded warmth, comfort and friendship.

"I sense your distress. May I assist you?" Aurelia pulled a necklace from beneath her shirt. An ankh, like his mother's. She squeezed it in her hand while extending the other.

Remembering his uncle's reaction to his mother's gesture, Ben shoved his hands into his lap.

Aurelia looked at him curiously. "Your mother has never versed you in our ways?"

"I understand how to pray," Ben said.

Aurelia frowned and took several steps backward.

Kavera's dreads cascaded down his shoulders and framed his round face. "Your uncle will be relieved to see you, Ben. Why do you choose to hide in the shadows?"

Ben felt his chest tighten. He didn't respond. He couldn't respond. What would he say? He should be dead, like all the others.

Kavera took his hand, only for a moment. Ben tried to pull away.

"There is nothing to fear, Benjamin." Kavera squeezed his hand, closed his eyes then released. "I understand," was all he said. He held his hand out toward Aurelia who helped him up to his feet.

"Your uncle will need to be told of your presence at the complex," she said. "We could do it for you, but the news should come from you, don't you agree?"

Ben shook his head. "He'll kill me."

"He is many things," Aurelia said. "The killer of children is not one of them."

"You haven't seen his temper. He hates me."

"I think not," Kavera said. "Aurelia and I have known your uncle for more years than you have walked this earth. His way is not always Xenobian, but our paths and passions circle back to the same spiritual core."

"Your uncle makes a loud noise," Aurelia said. "Ultimately, however, he does care for you. Of that much I am sure."

Ben just looked away. They didn't understand how he felt. They couldn't understand.

"You are young. One day you will come to understand that not all is what it seems." Aurelia offered her hand. "Come. Your friends are waiting. It is time to face your greatest fear, Benjamin Webster. It is time to face your uncle."

◆ ◆ ◆

Flanked by Aurelia and Kavera, Ben and his friends shuffled forward like prisoners headed for execution.

Aurelia led them to the Xenobian courtyard. Aris and Bastet waited outside the arboretum. As if pushed by invisible hands, the stained glass doors opened inward to reveal a lush garden. Birds chirped. Crickets clicked in the distance. Butterflies fluttered past him to light on nearby plants.

Hundreds, maybe thousands of exotic plant species lined the stone path that wound through the garden. Twenty feet away he saw his uncle kneeling at a fountain, deep in meditation, robes puddled in soft folds at his bare feet.

Aurelia gestured for everyone to remain by the door. She shot a look of concern at Kavera who nodded, but said nothing. She studied Ben's uncle for several minutes before speaking.

"Kurosh? May I offer assistance?"

Ben found it odd that she now referred to him by his first name when the others referred to him as Jemadari or Commander.

"Why do you continue to address me in this primitive language?"

"I need the practice."

"Leave me." Uncle Henry's voice was quiet but brusque. "I wish to be alone."

Aurelia maintained a gentle edge to her voice. "Kurosh. May I recommend temple for your prayers?"

"I have no need for prayer."

"Perhaps. Perhaps not. If you were not so quick to reject our ways, if you had gone to pray in temple as is our custom, you might have been granted a miracle."

"I no longer believe in miracles," Uncle Henry said, his voice devoid of emotion.

"That is not our way. There is always hope even in the face of a great tragedy."

"I am not in need of religious lecturing from a Shaman!" He growled and tipped his head to the side but did not look at her. His eyes remained closed.

"Then would you accept a symbol of hope from a friend?"

"I am your superior officer!" His booming voice thundered across the foliage. "I order you to return to your duties!" He turned and froze as his eyes fell upon Ben.

Ben braced for the wrath he knew was coming. Instead his uncle seemed stricken as if he was seeing a ghost.

Aurelia placed her hand on Ben's shoulder. "As I said. If, on occasion, one seeks solace in a place of worship, one may find a miracle. Behold who I found there seeking his own absolution. It appears that Ben is very much like his uncle in his determination to follow a difficult path."

"How?" Uncle Henry's face became a mass of conflict. "How did you get off the ship?"

"We never went up," Ben said, nearly choking on the words.

Uncle Henry walked toward him in small, measured steps. The others instinctively took a step backward, but Ben and April held their ground. Uncle Henry stopped ten feet from Ben and scanned him with a device. His face registered caution and disbelief as his eyes probed Ben for clues. He studied his prayer beads then looped them back on his belt. "Explain."

Aurelia squeezed Ben's shoulder and gestured for him to continue.

"I used my father's compass to dial out of the beam."

"We couldn't leave without our parents," April said gripping Ben's hand tightly.

"We agreed," Grace volunteered.

"All of us," Carlos said.

Serise nodded. "We're a team."

Tears streamed down Ben's face. "My father said one day I'd have to make a choice. I made it. Didn't you make that decision when you decided to stay behind?"

Uncle Henry moved closer and touched Ben's forehead with the his fingertips. He closed his eyes, then moved his hand away. His only reaction was one of sadness. For one brief moment Ben's uncle looked so . . . vulnerable

*"The black stones? You sent them to the ship?"*

Ben nodded. The words stung as he attempted to answer out loud. His uncle raised a single index finger. Ben understood and switched modes.

*"I didn't know what they were. They were on a collar we found in Peru. I thought you put it there on purpose so you could track us."* Ben was nearly inconsolable. *"I thought if I sent it up with our packs, you would think we were on the ship. No one else knew about the collar. No one knows what I did. It's my fault. Just mine. All those people died because of what I did. I'm so sorry."*

His uncle remained stoic and took hold of his arms. There was no pressure in his grip. He peered into Ben's eyes as he spoke out loud. "You never went up to the ship? You didn't see what went with them?"

Ben shook his head. *No.*

He couldn't read his uncle's expression through the soft haze of tears that streamed from down his face. His uncle abruptly released his grip. Ben closed his eyes and waited for whatever violence was to follow . . .

*"You weren't the cause of the explosion."*

. . . and found himself in the first hug he had ever received from his uncle.

◆ ◆ ◆        ◆ ◆ ◆        ◆ ◆ ◆

CHAPTER FIFTY-EIGHT

# Resolutions

"Unity, in variety, is the plan of the universe."

◆ ◆ ◆  *Vivickenanda, India*

◆ ◆ ◆ Ben stayed in his uncle's tight embrace for only a few seconds but it seemed like forever. Every emotion he had harbored over the years came pouring out. He had craved his uncle's affection and now that he had it, he didn't know what to make of it. Was this relief? Approval? He didn't care. He just wanted to relish it for a few minutes before it slipped away.

Uncle Henry gathered April into his arms.

"You chose wisely, Ben. If you had followed my orders, you and your friends would be dead and I would never have forgiven myself." He released them. "I am truly sorry. For everything. I should have told you the truth earlier."

"Me too. I should have let you know we were in the complex as soon as we got back from Islas Ballestas."

Uncle Henry let out a soft, sad chuckle. "Is that where you were hiding?"

Ben nodded.

"A hundred options and you chose . . ." Uncle Henry paused. "Never mind. You have returned to us safely. For that I am truly grateful. But I'm afraid little has changed. We've only got a few days, maybe a week, before the chain reaction is irreversible. To stay may still be a death sentence." There was no anger in his voice.

Ben forced a sad smile, received one in return and felt his stress melt away. "I told Aurelia about eight beacons we found. I think it's our parents."

Uncle Henry glanced at Aurelia who shook her head sadly. Not them.

"I went back to get something on the island." He pulled the silver rod from his pocket.

Uncle Henry froze then snatched it out of Ben's hands. Ben couldn't read the reaction on his face.

"You found this? Where?"

"Hidden in a crack in the wall. Behind the fake skeleton," April said. "It fell out of an old pole. We thought we'd broken it."

"Do these markings mean something?" Grace asked.

Uncle Henry didn't answer. He rolled the rod in his hand, reading the tiny Rongorongo markings, then passed it to Kavera who scanned it with a device and waited for results. After a long few minutes, he nodded, his face beaming.

Aurelia bowed. "Commander. We shall take our leave of you. There is much work to do."

"Aurelia. Kavera. You have my gratitude for returning the children to me. Today we have, indeed, been granted two miracles."

The two warriors bowed again, then rushed out of the chamber at a dead run, the rod in their possession.

"What does it mean?" Ben asked. "Does it help?"

Uncle Henry nodded, his eyes still focused on the now closed door. "That rod activates the dormant terraformers on Rapa Nui. Bringing them online will buy us at least another year. Maybe more."

Ben's heartbeat kicked into overdrive. "Enough time to find my parents?" he asked.

"Perhaps," Uncle Henry said. "And much more. By ignoring my orders, you and your friends may have saved us all."

Grace exchanged high fives with Serise and Carlos. "I guess where you go, we go. You said it was important that we stay together."

"I can make arrangements for you to live with families on the outside. You deserve better than what we have to offer here." His voice was quiet and tinged with sadness.

"Are you kidding?" asked Carlos. "How are you going to explain our 'transformations' to our host families? There isn't enough green glob to last that long."

"Danine has the ability to replicate what is needed," Uncle Henry said. "I fear the other tribes will be distracted by your presence at the complex. Outside, you would be able to live a normal life."

Serise groaned in frustration. "Now that we're just discovering our heritage you want to rip it away? How do we learn about our people if we don't live with them? How do we live a normal life knowing life on Earth might end at any moment?"

"We don't have any other options. We've got to stay here." Ben tried to sound confident, but he still felt as terrified as his friends. "We aren't breaking up the team."

Uncle Henry sat on a bench and watched Ben closely. Despite the earlier, surreal group hug, Ben was still apprehensive and kept his feelings guarded.

*"You said it yourself. No more transports. There are no other choices. Whatever destroyed that ship . . . whatever attacked my parents — is going to try again."*

*"Yes."*

*"And maybe come after us too, right?"*

Uncle Henry nodded. Ben noted something new in his uncle's expression — trust.

"We need to stick together," He said out loud for the others to hear. He was concerned about this new revelation but would keep his uncle's secret for now. No use alarming the others.

"I'll need to consult with the Tribal Council."

"Why?" asked April. "I thought you were the boss of the whole place. Just tell 'em. We're staying!"

Uncle Henry's grim expression relaxed a micron as he let out a long slow exhale.

"Well, you are." April wagged her finger at him. "Being bossy is what you're good at. So tell 'em."

The sides of Uncle Henry's mouth curved into an smile and he barked out a laugh. Soon after, he reverted back to the person Ben had always known — a drill sergeant. The change in demeanor was instantaneous, but the booming tone and the sharp edge were gone.

"All right then. Let's get started. We've got a lot of work to do. Hard work. I will not go easy on you. You will train with the teams and live here at the complex. We will arrange quarters for you and most likely tutors and bodyguards. You will do what I say, when I say it, without question. Is that understood? I hear any whining or complaining and trust me, you won't like the alternatives."

"Agreed," Ben said, relieved. He looked to the others for confirmation.

"All for one and one for all!" said Carlos.

"That's a palindrome," Serise said in a nervous reflex.

"Shut up!" replied the rest in a simultaneous chorus.

◆ ◆ ◆          ◆ ◆ ◆          ◆ ◆ ◆

EPILOGUE

# And So It Begins

"It is not where you begin,
it is where you end that counts."

• • • *Faith Littlefield*

• • • • Uncle Henry paced like a restless predator. A final team stood before a transport tube that shimmered in shades of gold and silver. As each member stepped across the threshold, their clothing changed to those of Afghan villagers. They waited in perfect military formation.

Aurelia entered the control room, an elaborate tattoo visible on her right shoulder. She fastened a leather satchel onto the belt around her waist and prepared to step into the portal.

"Aureliana," Uncle Henry said. "I would speak with you."

Ben's uncle gestured toward an antechamber on the far side of the control room. The barrier closed behind them. Shortly afterwards, Aurelia and Uncle Henry emerged followed by Kavera.

Aurelia and Kavera stepped into the glass tube and waited for the change. She rolled a bead between her thumb and index finger then held it up for Ben's uncle to see before placing it into her satchel. Her slick leather uniform was instantly concealed by burlap cloth. The burqua obscured everything but her eyes. Even so, Ben could see a softening in her expression. Ben looked at his uncle's belt. The violet prayer bead was gone.

"*Akoosh sakur vera inna, Aureliana,*" Ben's uncle whispered, his voice stoic.

Aurelia had used a similar phrase when Ben was sent to the cave chamber. He would look it up on one of the translators when things settled down.

Aurelia gave a single affirmative nod before she and her team disappeared.

◆ ◆ ◆

"Where are we going?" April asked, after a dinner of mixed greens and fish. She clutched his Madagascar saddlebag.

"To catch a ship." Uncle Henry pointed toward April's newly appropriated possession. "Should have figured that you would claim that for your own. You can have it, but you won't need it this time."

"I know," April said. "We sent all our stuff up to the ship. You've got to take us shopping!"

"That wasn't what I meant," scowled Uncle Henry. His expression was almost playful. Despite his earlier display of affection, the light tone put Ben on his guard.

Everyone looked at his uncle with suspicion.

"Don't worry. There will be no more transports coming. You are forced to remain on Earth with the rest of us. I have some business to complete. You will accompany me. Until the gateways are secured we will travel the old fashioned way."

"To where?" April asked again.

"I have chartered a yacht off the coast of Bimini. We are sailing to our next destination."

Serise and April pumped their fists up and down and quietly mouthed, *"Yes!"*

"And that would be where?" Unlike his friends, Ben knew there was a catch.

The corners of his uncle's mouth curved into a sly smile. His eyebrows arched. "Why . . . to the 80th meridian."

"No really," Carlos stammered. He shook his head in disbelief. "Where are we going?"

"You heard me. You wanted an adventure, now you've got one."

"But isn't that . . ."

"Why yes, Carlos," Uncle Henry said, allowing his words to drip out like molasses. "It is. How astute you are. Your father would be proud. Now . . . we have little time. You are my charges until we locate your parents or until I tell you otherwise."

"We can stay here until you get back," Carlos said in protest. Color drained from his face. "I have rations. See?" He held out a pitiful supply of granola bars.

"My team has its own work to do. They do not have time to baby sit."

Ben was insulted and let it show. "We can take care of ourselves. We got here safely didn't we?"

"Luck, not skill, got you here in one piece."

Grace crossed her arms and shot a resentful glance in Uncle Henry's direction.

"There is one alternative. Would you like to see?" He stepped to the panel and typed a sequence into the keypad. Five tubes appeared in the center of the room. They looked like smaller versions of the tubes used by the scientific and military teams.

"Cool," April said. "Do we get to travel this way?"

"Why not try it?" asked Ben's uncle.

Ben noticed that his uncle never answered the question directly. But the tubes looked harmless. "Sure. Piece of cake."

He stepped inside. The glass sealed around him. A blue mist seeped into the tube. A freezing cold mist! Suddenly it dawned on him. His uncle had said that there were NO secured gateways to get them to their next destination. So what was this? He banged on the glass and watched helplessly as his friends jumped away from the other tubes. He couldn't move his legs. The mist floated upward and encircled his chest. He could barely breath. Was this what hypothermia felt like?

The mist turned white, then orange, then red. The temperature warmed significantly. The glass retracted. Ben stumbled out of the tube and hopped up and down to regain the feeling in his legs.

"Cold, cold, cold. Soooooo cold." Ben blew on his fingers to warm them. "What was that?"

"Stasis tubes," his uncle replied. "That's the other option. Go with me or stay in cryogenic freeze. As you can see, I *am* a reasonable man. I will allow you to make your own choice."

Ben's sister and friends scrambled over each other to get to the opposite side of the room.

"Well, if you put it that way. Suddenly Bimini doesn't sound so bad," Carlos said. "I vote for going with you."

Everyone agreed with Carlos's assessment of the situation. Ben remained silent. He was still trying to get the needles and icicles out of his legs. He was sure he had frostbite. His fingers were purple. His uncle typed another sequence on the keypad. The tubes vanished.

"I thought you would see it my way. It's settled. We're going fishing. I will make the final preparations. We leave tomorrow."

While his uncle was in the bedroom, Ben whispered, "Carlos, what's so bad about the 80th meridian?"

"That depends. Your uncle said we were sailing off the coast of Bimini, right? That can only mean one thing."

"What?" Serise asked, tapping her foot impatiently. "What does it mean? Come on! Spill the beans!"

"We should have agreed to go live with foster families. It would have been safer. The 80th meridian . . . it crosses the Bermuda Triangle."

◆ ◆ ◆ ◆ END ◆ ◆ ◆ ◆

# Acknowledgements

❖ ❖ ❖ ❖

It took a village to raise this author and this book. Thanks to Anitra Steele for believing in me from the start of my career. To Kent Brown, Jr. for his continued friendship and mentoring. To Jerry Spinelli for his unwavering faith, guidance and for telling me to focus on writing a book I cared about. To Bernette Ford my first editor for guiding me to my first book award. To Dara Sharif, a talented editor who broadened my landscape. To James Cross Giblin who read the beginnings of an early draft and told a colleague I was on to something. To Patti Gauch who pushed me past my limits on this book and as a writer. To Jane Yolen for the nurturing and sage advice when I'd lost faith this book would find a home. To Susan Vaught, Melanie Chrismer. Pam Zollman, and Crystal Allen for reading really rough drafts and supplying endless kicks in the rear. To Lisa McCormick, an amazing investigative journalist who kept sending weird facts about Earth. To Bobby Early, Harold Underdown, Karen Gallick, Dale Marie Bryan, Dawn Allen, Natasha Hanova, Marsha Lytle, Christine Kohler, Margaree King Mitchell, Jeanna Tetzlaff, Norma King, Kathryn Worley, Duane Porter, ACAIC and Kindling Words for being my support system. To Sherry Polito for laughs and endless moral support. To my friends at Kansas City, Johnson County, MidContinent, Wichita, Tulsa and Rogers public libraries who saw an author early on where none existed including, but not limited to April R., Helma H., Jean H., Barbara B., Arlene W., Kathy M., Clare H., Debbie M., Crystal F., Julie R., Ron F., Richie M., Cathy Sue A., Nancy H., Peggy A., Peggy H. Charlou L., Tricia S., Rebecca W., Maureen C-B., Lisa A. Jennifer E, Chris K., and Elizabeth S. And to everyone I couldn't list due to space – you know who you are and you know I'm grateful.

To the staff and faculty of the Highlights Foundation — the road to this series and to my career started with you.

❖ ❖ ❖ ❖

31901056275201